CUBAN TRADER

Voyages on the Hell Ship
By
Roger Asquith

Based on his Adventures at Sea
and Experiences of the
Cuban Revolution

Prestbury Books

Cuban Trader

Prestbury Books

Edited by
Alessandro deGaetano

Copyright © 2012 by Roger Asquith
All Rights Reserved.

Library of Congress Cataloging on Request

THE TIMES

It was 1958. Eisenhower was President. Man had not yet landed on the moon. Martin Luther King was arrested for loitering in Alabama. Parking meters had just been installed in London. The "Iron Curtain" divided Europe into East and West, and many desperate young men in East Germany risked their lives to escape to the West in search of a better life. Fidel Castro had begun his revolution in Cuba, and I was sailing into the middle of it and would have one of the greatest adventures of my life.

R.A.

CHAPTER ONE

A Life on the Ocean Wave!

Calm seas, warm sunshine, sandy beaches, cheap booze and a fat paycheck at the end of each month, sounded too good to be true. After two years as a marine Radio Operator plowing through the freezing gales of the North Atlantic, being tossed about in an old Swedish coal ship, I finally wised up. I was on my way to sunny Cuba and the warm waters of the Caribbean as the Radio Officer on the tank ship *Cuban Trader* which carried molasses from Cuba to the United States.

Mike Bradshaw, the ship's agent for Ludwig Berners Tank Ships, which owned the *Cuban Trader*, had just picked me up at their offices in Philadelphia and was taking me to the ship. He was driving much too fast down the Camden Turnpike making it almost impossible to pay any attention to what he was saying. "So where you from?" he asked.

"I'm from England," I responded nervously, watching his every move through the heavy traffic. "But the last two years, I was the Radio Officer on a Swedish freighter carrying coal from Norfolk, Virginia to Bremen, Germany. It was nothing but freezing gales and twenty foot waves."

"Coal? Jesus! Well I suppose some poor bastard has to do it," he replied, obviously not very impressed. "Norfolk? That's in Virginia, right?"

"Right. I came up on the train to Philadelphia yesterday and stayed in some crummy hotel near Bookbinders Restaurant."

"Yeah! I know the place. There's lotsa crummy hotels around there, but Bookbinders is a great place to eat. They serve the best lobster thermidor in Philly."

"That's nice to know. I just wish I'd had more time to look around and see Independence Hall and the Liberty Bell."

"And all that tourist crap. Didja know Philly is a great place to get laid?" Mike said as he rummaged around on the seat for his cigarettes. "Yeah, there's plenty of ass in Philly, especially near that crappy hotel where you were staying." Mike finally lit his cigarette and puffed away for a few minutes. "There's also plenty of ass in Cuba, Sparks. That's the place to let it all hang out. No fuckin' gales or twenty foot waves in the Caribbean," continued Mike, "just gambling, drinking and fuckin'! Hey! You don't mind me calling you Sparks, do you?"

"Of course not. *Sparks - that's what they called all the Radio Officers. It was slang, and I kind of liked it.* "What's the *Cuban Trader* like? I hear she sails under the Liberian flag."

"All Berners' ships are Liberian registry, but you'll have a great time, Sparks. The refinery where you dock in Cuba is right next to the whorehouse," continued Mike. "So you don't have to go far to get laid."

"That's great," I replied, cringing in my seat as Mike swerved to avoid a big truck moving into the center lane. "How much further is it to the ship?"

"Is that why you signed on, for the cheap booze and hot broads?" Mike salivated at the thought of wild sex in Cuba.

"No, I signed on because the pay's twice what I've been getting, although I hear Liberian ships are the pits. Some of them are hell ships."

"Yeah, man! Out on deck, balls ass-naked getting a sexy suntan; drinking cold rum and cola after fuckin' one of those Cuban whores: that's the life." Obviously Mike had a one track mind and wasn't in the least interested in talking about the *Cuban Trader* which was going to be my new home. Liberian ships didn't have a good reputation but the pay was good and that's what I was after. I wanted to build up a healthy bank balance and then quit the sea life. I had been a Radio Officer on British, Australian and Swedish ships for over ten years. I hoped the *Cuban Trader* would be my last.

"It's the sex, Sparks! That's why all the horny bastards go to Cuba," continued Mike, interrupting my thoughts. "That's why so many of those young Kraut bastards go there. You'll have a lot of them on the ship. Most of them are escapees from East Germany, poor bastards, which reminds me, we gotta stop off at U.S. Immigration to pick one of them up," replied Mike, maneuvering his car into the slow lane. "Then we should be at the ship in about twenty minutes."

Mike's timing was as bad as his driving. It took us twenty minutes just to get to the Immigration Building where Mike introduced me to the Duty Officer as the new Sparks on the *Cuban Trader*. "Hi there," he said, shaking my hand, "Where you from?" I handed him my passport which had been checked and stamped when I signed off the coal ship in Norfolk. "So, the Immigration down there only gave you ten days to join a ship?"

"That's right. I was lucky to find the *Cuban Trader* so fast."

"That's because there's a shortage of Radio Officers," he replied, handing back my passport. "You know International Maritime law; a ship can't sail without one."

"Okay, Sparks, let's go," said Mike, opening the office door to leave.

"What about that German kid, the new steward?" questioned the Duty Officer. "He doesn't speak any English, and he looks like a young school kid to me. You wanna sign for him, Mike?"

"Me? I'm not taking responsibility for the little Kraut bastard."

"Well, somebody has to. How about you, Sparks? You just have to make sure he gets on the ship, that's all."

"If you sign for him, Sparks, you'll be responsible for the little Kraut bastard." snapped Mike.

"But we'll board in a few minutes," I replied. "Okay, I'll sign for him. Poor little bugger, I'll bet he's had a hell of a life so far."

While I was signing the form making me responsible for Mike's *little Kraut bastard,* the Officer went to the back room and fetched him. We all stared at the frightened Aryan youth with straggly blond hair, bronzed complexion, and big blue eyes. He was wearing ragged clothes and hanging on to an old army knapsack stuffed with his precious possessions. "His name is Helmut. Helmut Schickel," announced the Duty Officer. "He's from Berlin."

"How old is he?" I asked.

"He's supposed to be sixteen."

"Sixteen? I doubt that. He's too young to sign on," I said. "He should be in school."

"That's what I say," agreed the Officer, "but they keep sending them over here. They say it's supposed to be a better life on a ship than living with those Commie sons-a-bitches behind the Iron Curtain."

4

I motioned for Helmut to follow me. "We are now going to the ship," I said, pronouncing my words slowly, hoping he'd understand. "Okay?"

Helmut nodded, grabbed his knapsack and followed us out to Mike's car and climbed into the back seat. "Poor little bugger looks scared to death," I whispered to Mike as we drove off. "I wonder when he last ate. He's so damned skinny; he looks like the wind might blow him away. "

"They're all like that," replied Mike, lighting up a cigarette. "You gotta watch 'em Sparks. First chance they get, they're AWOL. Gone. Kaput. That's why Berners keeps bringing more and more of 'em over here."

I glanced at the young boy in the back seat as he anxiously looked out the window. I hoped the food on the ship would soon fatten him up. "We will soon be there, Helmut," I said, wishing I could speak German.

"Yeah, we're nearly there," announced Mike. "Can you smell the hot molasses?"

"Phew! I sure can," I replied, rolling up the window. "It stinks. Is it from the refinery?"

"It's everywhere," sneered Mike. "You'd better get used to it from now on. This is how Berners makes his fortune, bringing this hot stinking crap all the way from Cuba."

"To be distilled into rum. Am I right?" The overpowering stench of the hot molasses had now filled the car. "I hope it's worth it."

"Yeah, it makes good rum," Mike assured me. "Sometimes the Customs guy gives me a bottle. I prefer vodka myself, but the wife likes it, but between you and me, Sparks, she'd drink anything if it's free. You know what I mean?"

Suddenly, we bounced across the railroad tracks into the refinery and saw a sleek tank ship unloading at the dock. Mike waited impatiently while Helmut and I scrambled out of the car, and then went straight across the dockyard to the refinery offices.

Helmut and I stared at the ship slowly moving up and down on the incoming tide. I was very impressed. The sleek modern tanker was relatively new and seemed to sparkle in the morning sun. Having pumped its hot cargo of molasses into the refinery storage tanks, the crew, all smartly dressed in their working uniforms, were hosing off the main deck. Others were amidship touching up the white paintwork and greasing the davits of the gleaming white lifeboats. I was especially pleased to see the very latest Marconi radar mast slowly revolving atop the Captain's house, and the radio antennas, which were going to be my responsibility, looked well maintained. Two uniformed officers on the boat deck were checking out the cleaning up operation.

"Isn't she beautiful, Helmut?" He nodded and smiled for the first time, obviously as impressed with the ship as I was. "In about ten days we'll be in Cuba where there's lots of sun."

Mike suddenly pulled up behind us, rolled down the car window and yelled, "Sorry you guys, that's not the *Cuban Trader*. The fucking thing won't be here for another two days. You gotta check into the Seaman's Hotel. Berners went on like a raving lunatic, but it's not my fault."

"Why is the *Cuban Trader* delayed?" I asked.

"It's them fucking Cubans again. Assholes, the lot of them," replied Mike. "Anyway, the Seaman's Hotel's not too far. They gotta a helluva bar, you know with free potato chips and all that crap. You'll be okay. Let's go and check you in; I gotta get back to the office in Philly."

Ten minutes later, while Mike booked us in the hotel, I struggled with my two suitcases into the lobby, followed by a very puzzled Helmut. Mike and I had tried to explain to him what was going on, but he just shook his head completely bewildered. "He'll soon learn English, and I've booked you guys in here for a couple of days so you'll soon get to know him, Sparks. You know what I mean?" observed Mike, rattling his car keys. "I'll see you guys in two days and take you to the ship."

Helmut and I looked around the hotel lobby. It was sparsely furnished with a few brown leather chairs and a faded green carpet that had seen better days. Leading off from the lobby was the bar that Mike told us had free potato chips, and someone had just sprayed the place with an air freshener that didn't quite cover up the stale smell of tobacco. I looked at Helmut who was looking very dejected. "Don't worry, Helmut, we'll be okay."

"Mike Bradshaw has signed you guys in for two days, room thirty-five," announced the miserable looking desk clerk. "But you gotta sign the register first." He pushed the tattered looking register across the counter, and I dutifully scrawled my name. "The room's paid for and breakfast is at eight. Room thirty-five is on the third floor, the elevator is over there." He pointed across the foyer and glared at Helmut. "It's a double, so you'll have to shack up with him."

Helmut looked at me wondering what was happening. He had just been shuffled in and out of Mike's car, been to the docks, looked at a ship and followed us into a cheap hotel carrying his bedraggled knapsack like an obedient puppy.

"Hi there, Sparks," announced a friendly voice. "I'm Harry. I own this dump." Harry and I shook hands. "I was a Third Mate on one of Berners' ships, until I screwed up my leg, so they paid me off, and I bought this place. Mike just explained about the delay. The Cubans are always at it. So, who's the young kid, he looks half starved?"

"His name is Helmut Schickel. He's signed as a steward and just got here from Germany, but speaks no English. Poor kid, he's wondering what's happening."

"Don't worry, Sparks. My wife, Bella speaks German, she'll be glad to tell him what's going on. Did the Immigration make you responsible for him?"

"They certainly did."

"You can't blame them, Sparks, so many of these young kids jump ship and run away. Somebody has to be responsible while they're ashore," explained Harry. "Your room is a double; I'll put a camp bed in there for the kid. Ah! Here's my wife, Bella."

While Harry's wife talked to Helmut I went up to the room. It was clean and neat with a small window overlooking the river. I had no complaints about the room, and the shower stall in the bathroom looked almost new with a sparkling clean glass door.

Bella did a great job explaining to Helmut what was happening. He looked like a different person when I met him again in the foyer. The Immigration Officer was right: he did look like a young school kid.

"Poor boy. He's had a very rough time in Germany," explained Bella. "He does speak a little English so he'll tell you all about his young brother, Frederic, who was captured by the Russians. He's had an awful life. From what I've heard it's not going to be much of a picnic on the *Cuban Trader.*" Bella looked at Helmut and smiled. "*Sind Sie hungrig? Roger wird euch in Philadelphia zu nehmen und kaufen Sie etwas zu essen.*"

"*Vielen Dank, Herr Schparks.*" Helmut's face broke out into a wide smile.

"*Herr Schparks, du bist mein freund.*"

"I told him you would take him into Philly and buy him something to eat," explained Bella. "Then show him around. It will be a welcome change from Berlin."

"I'd love to, but I've only got a few dollars left," I explained. "I was expecting to go aboard the ship today."

"Here's some money, Sparks," said Harry, pushing a fifty dollar bill into my shirt pocket. "Give the young kid a great time. He deserves it."

"Buy him a nice big steak and show him around Philly," suggested Bella. "He's had a very rough life so far, poor little kid; he should still be in school."

Philadelphia was a welcome change for Helmut. It was like another world. He had just endured two weeks on board an old freighter plowing across the storm-tossed Atlantic to Philadelphia and was not looking forward to working on the *Cuban Trader.*

Wandering around the city, Helmut was in awe of the tall buildings and abundance of food, so very different from the bombed damaged East Berlin. We eventually went into a restaurant, and I ordered dinner. It was a joy to see Helmut's big blue eyes light up when the waiter brought us two sizzling steaks surrounded by French fries and side orders of onion rings. Helmut grinned at me. *"Vielen Dank, Herr Schparks,"* he said, waiting for me to start.

"You'll have to thank Bella and Harry at the hotel. They gave me the money to pay for this; they really like you." I watched my young friend digging into his steak. It was probably the best meal he'd had for months.

"Eat and enjoy," I said. "I doubt if the food on the ship will be this good."

Later we sat on a bench in Independence Square, and I tried to explain how the Americans gained their independence from England. He listened attentively, but was still too nervous to say anything in English; instead he kept smiling at me and thanking me in German.

During the two days we stayed at the hotel waiting for the ship, I got to know Helmut very well. He slowly began speaking English, telling me his parents were both teachers who encouraged him and his brother to listen to the British and American radio stations in West Berlin. I helped him with his pronunciation, while he told me about his sad life in East Germany. After his parents were shot dead during a riot, he and Frederic, his younger brother, were left to fend for themselves. Having no money, they survived on cabbage soup and occasionally some stale bread from the Communist food kitchens and listened to the disillusioned adults complaining about the harsh treatment meted out by Russian troops occupying their city. Most young Germans were planning to escape to the west where there was plenty of work and food. Each day Helmut and Frederic looked through the high barbed-wire fence separating the occupied German capital and wondered how they could get across to start a new life in West Berlin.

"What a dreadful life you've had so far," I said. "The *Cuban Trader* will be a new experience for you. The warm sunshine in Cuba and the blue Caribbean, makes it smooth, not rough like the Atlantic." We were heading back to Camden on the bus, watching the passing scenery like a pair of excited tourists. Already the smell of hot molasses from the refinery was blowing through the windows.

"It's hot molasses," I explained. "It's what we will be bringing back from Cuba."

"Hot molasses?" repeated Helmut. "Why they use hot molasses?"

"They make it into rum. I'll let you try some when we get back to the hotel."

"Vielen dank, Herr Schparks," he said.

"Helmut, try saying it in English. Thank you, Sparks, okay?"

"Zank you, Schparks, okay," repeated Helmut, grinning.

Later in the hotel lounge, Helmut blathered away in German to Bella about his day out in Philadelphia.

"Sounds like you two had a good time, Sparks," announced Harry, joining us in the lounge. "The kid looks a hundred percent different from when he arrived. Look, he's even making Bella laugh." Harry sipped his beer and watched his wife and Helmut yakking away in German.

"She had a rough life in Holland when the Nazis took over, the bastards raping and carrying on. Finally she and her friend stowed away on a Swedish cargo ship to Philly. I'm not kidding you, Sparks; she's looked after me better than any nurse after I had the accident. She's the best thing that ever happened to me."

Helmut slowly became more confident speaking in English, especially lying in bed after supper when he told me about his life in Berlin. It was on his fourteenth birthday when he and his young brother decided to make a dash for freedom. The Russian guards had quit patrolling the fence and were sheltering from the rain in their guard huts when the two desperate young boys decided to crawl under the fence. Unfortunately, one of the guards saw them and shot Helmut in the leg as he made a run for freedom, but Frederic became entangled in the barbed wire. Helmut watched in horror as the guards dragged him back into East Berlin, a picture of misery forever etched on his memory.

"You will help me, Herr Schparks?"

"Yes. I promise I will help you." Of course I would help him. He was all alone, both his parents had been shot and his young brother captured by the Russians. He was now having frightening nightmares and often was too scared to go back to sleep. It was after one such nightmare he crawled into my bed, like a frightened child. He was used to sharing one bed with his brother. We lay thinking our own thoughts. Helmut wondering what would happen to him, and I wishing I hadn't left England. I had been safe and secure there with little to worry about, whereas Helmut was alone in the world, one of thousands of abandoned kids nobody wanted.

Two days later Helmut and I were on the dock staring in horror at the *Cuban Trader*. I had never seen such an ugly ship. Instead of a well-maintained seaworthy vessel, we were looking at an old Liberty ship that should have been scrapped at the end of the war. Two huge black pipes connected the ancient tanker to the storage tanks of the refinery, hissing steam and leaking the stinking black molasses all over the deck. The overpowering stench made us sick, sick enough to desert the ship before we had even set foot on board. It was nothing like the first one we had seen and certainly nothing like the photograph of a sleek passenger ship the agent had shown Helmut in Berlin. As we approached the gangplank we could hear the ominous creaks and groans as the *Cuban Trader* moved up and down on the incoming tide. I had butterflies in my stomach. I felt sick, uncertain what to do. I should have listened to my instinct and gone back to the hotel, taking Helmut with me, but I didn't.

Helmut looked at the stinking old ship and was almost in tears. "Let me go, Herr Schparks," he pleaded, picking up his knapsack.

"Where are you going to go?" I questioned. "You cannot stay in America; you have no money, no legal papers and you can hardly speak English. And don't forget you have signed a legally binding contract with the Maritime Agency in Berlin who paid your fare here." I tried to assure him everything would be okay once we had settled down on board, even though I found that very hard to believe.

"Herr Schparks, at the hotel they say this is a hell ship. It is bad for me. I want to go." Helmut clutched his bedraggled knapsack of old clothes and stared at me, tears now running down his innocent face.

The maritime agent in West Berlin had promised him a life of comparative luxury as soon as he signed the agreement. Obviously the agent had lied, tricking Helmut and hundreds of other desperate young teenagers to sign away two years of their lives into virtual slavery aboard foreign registered ships. The situation seemed hopeless. "Let's do one trip, save our money and leave when we get back to Philadelphia," I suggested.

Helmut looked at me and nodded. "You help me, Herr Schparks?"

"Of course I'll help you. You are my friend."

Reluctantly, Helmut and I struggled up the slippery gangplank which was leaning precariously against the ship and stepped onto the rusty deck. "Herr Schparks," whispered Helmut. "One trip and then we go?"

"Helmut, just one trip, but I promise you everything will be all right." I heard myself say the words, but didn't really believe them, especially when we were almost trampled underfoot by a dozen or so frightened young men marching across the deck.

"LINKS, RECHT, LINKS, RECHT," bellowed a uniformed officer standing on some wooden pallets at the side of the deck. We both watched in horror as a small group of tired looking seamen marched back and forth, their heavy boots clattering on the steel deck, bringing back frightening memories of the recent war.

Helmut turned and looked at me like a frightened deer, his large blue eyes pleading with me to let him run away. Suddenly we were confronted by an officer, a tall, blonde German, cruelly handsome and a good example of the Aryan race. I stared into his cold blue eyes and knew immediately I wouldn't like him. "Good Morning," he said in a heavy guttural accent. "I'm Herr Schmidt, the Second Mate, and you are the new Schparks?"

"Yes, I'm Roger Asquith, and this is — " before I could introduce Helmut, Herr Schmidt had snapped his fingers and a young seaman standing nearby sprang to attention.

"Take the cases to the Schparks' cabin," ordered Schmidt, "and the new steward back aft." Like a well-trained robot, the young seaman grabbed my cases and yelled at Helmut to follow him. For a few seconds my young companion and I exchanged glances before he reluctantly followed the seaman across the deck.

Schmidt and I waited while the group of bedraggled seamen marched passed again. "What's all this?" I asked.

"Discipline, Herr Schparks," he replied, grinning. "Chief Officer Bessler says we must have discipline. The deck crew has to learn to obey. There is a revolution in Cuba; already they are fighting in the streets. We have to be ready."

"But this is insane! If there is a war in Cuba, why are we still going there?"

"It is not our war, Herr Schparks. They not bother us. They are just revolutionary peasants," explained Schmidt. "Come, we go to your cabin on the boat deck, and then you will test all the radio equipment before seeing the Captain. That is orders."

I reluctantly followed Schmidt across the deck to my cabin wishing I had listened to Helmut and run away. "The new Sparks is a fucking ring bandit," yelled a familiar voice from amongst the group of seamen marching back and forth across the rusty deck. "Watch your asses, Lads." It was a voice from the past and one I didn't expect to hear. It was my old enemy, J.J. Anderson, a red-necked Australian seaman screaming at the crew. I spotted him amongst the group of seamen marching across the deck sneering at me. He brought back sad memories of our arguments about his wages on board the *M.V. Parakeet*, an Australian coastal ship we both worked on for seven months.

"Now we go to your cabin," snorted Schmidt, ignoring the ribald accusation and leading the way into the officers' quarters below the bridge. "You share with Third Officer Fordson, the bathroom. He's American. He drink too much rum, and is wanted by the police." I followed Schmidt up a flight of rickety steel steps to my cabin where my suitcases were waiting for me.

"Captain Krause will see you in his office to sign papers after you test the radio equipment and make sure the radar is working. It is important," ordered Schmidt. He then clicked his heels and marched back across the deck.

I was met at my cabin door by a tall, handsome blonde thirty-something officer. "I'm Axel, the Norwegian Radio Officer you are replacing," he said. "You're taking my job, right? Come in and I'll show you around."

I followed Axel into the neat little cabin. It was clean and tidy, the walls were painted white, the woodwork a light oak brown, and some colorful skiing posters were attached to the bulkheads. "All my own work," grinned Axel, proudly. "When I first came on board everything was painted green. It made me sick, so I changed it."

"Well I'm glad. It looks really comfortable now, and the porthole is the cleanest I've ever seen," I replied, admiring the shining brass work. "Whoever did that certainly knew how to use Brasso."

Axel grinned. "That was my friend, Kurt. He was my steward. You'll be getting a new one. Kurt is signing off with me today. We're going back home to Oslo for the ski season," he continued. "Six months on this hell ship is enough." He reached down into a small fridge and took out a bottle of Coca-Cola. "We first have a drink," he said, grinning. "You will need many drinks on here. After we drink, I then show you the Radio Room."

Axel was in the middle of packing his suitcase but took time off to fix me a drink. He poured in a hefty shot of rum into a tall glass, topped it off with some *Coca-Cola* and dropped in a couple of ice cubes. "I really wish you luck," he said, handing me the glass. "How you say in England, bottoms up?"

"Yes, that's one saying," I replied, appreciating his welcoming drink. "Wow! This is strong stuff."

"Yeah, Cuban rum is cheap; American *Coca-Cola* is not so cheap, but the ice was free," explained Axel. "The television set really needs retuning, but it does pick up local stations, even the Cuban ones, although I rarely watch anything. Everything works okay in the Radio Room, even the bloody radar which is a hundred years old. The accounts are all in order. You have to enter the crew's overtime and dole them out money to go ashore in Cuba. The Chief Engineer, Igor Petrovich, is Russian. He and his crew are paid separately from Berners' office."

"That's strange, I mean the engineers being paid separately," I observed.

"Sparks, everything is strange on this ship," replied Axel, grinning. "I've left a list of the best frequencies to use.

The Cubans are always changing them. CLN, Santiago de Cuba, usually answers. You have to call them with an ETA to alert the pilot boat, but I've written it all down and you'll soon get used to it."

"What's happening on deck? I mean the seamen all marching like soldiers?"

"I'm sorry you asked that. The Chief Deck Officer, Herr Bessler, is a military man, ex-Gestapo. He thinks the crew, who are mostly young teenagers from East Germany, should be fighting fit. Did Schmidt tell you about the war in Cuba?"

"Yes, he mentioned it, but he said it's just a bunch of peasants fighting in the hills. Surely they won't bother us."

"It's Fidel Castro's revolution, a civil war. It's not just in the hills. They're fighting everywhere, but as long as you pay for the molasses, and the crew makes no trouble at the whorehouse, there will be no problems."

The sound of marching feet on the steel deck outside interrupted our conversation. "For crissake, we're in port. Why is the crew still working on deck?"

Axel sighed, staring at me with his clear blue eyes. I pictured him skiing down the slopes in Norway with dozens of friends. "Sparks, they can't go ashore in America because they have no passports. The Americans are very fussy. Sometimes a sympathetic Immigration Officer is on duty in Philadelphia, and lets them go to the dock store and buy a few things, but never outside the dock gates."

"What about in Cuba?"

"Cuba? The Cubans practically drag them off the ship, especially the whores. There's no need for a passport there, just green dollars."

"Yeah, everyone's after the almighty dollar." I looked around the cabin. "Is that the bathroom?"

"Yeah, you share it with Richard, the Third Mate. He's an American, a very nice guy, but he drinks too much," whispered Axel. "We don't talk very often. Oh! You must remind the Old Man we need penicillin. There's no more left."

"Penicillin?"

"Yes, at least two cases of penicillin. You are in charge of the medicine chest!"

"I'm in charge of the medicine chest?" I gulped the last of my drink. "Nobody told me. For Pete's sake, I don't know anything about medicine."

"Well, you'd better learn how to give a shot of penicillin. Most of the crew are usually, how you say, poxed up to their ears after we leave Cuba, but after ten thousand units in their ass every morning for a few days, and they're okay. Disposable syringes are best, but you'll soon learn how."

"You mean I have to give jabs?"

"Jabs? You mean injections? Yes, but it's easy. Just practice on a melon first, and it's quite interesting to find out who the sex maniacs are."

"Sex maniacs?"

"Yes, it's what the Old Man calls everybody who visits the whorehouses in Cuba," explained Axel, grinning. "They usually acquire a variety of interesting sexual diseases from blue balls to an infestation of crabs, but don't worry. You have the so-called medicine chest full of ancient potions to cure them."

"There was nothing about this in the contract I signed. I'm the Radio Officer and Purser."

"Yes, that's what they told me, but you're also responsible for keeping the sex maniacs fit for work; you'll be surprised what's in that witch doctor's medicine chest, even some rusty manacles to chain the unfortunate patient down to the bench during an amputation," explained Axel.

"Come on, let's go up to the Radio Room, and I'll show you how I do the books."

Ten minutes later, Axel had showed me around the Radio Room, switched on all the equipment to prove it was working, including the ancient radar set on the bridge. The account books were fairly simple, but giving a shot of penicillin scared me to death.

"Just practice on a melon," suggested Axel. "The syringes are marked and sterile. You'll soon get used to it, especially when the sex maniacs start begging you to cure them."

"Jesus, I never expected this," I groaned.

"You'll be okay, Sparks, but watch out for Herr Bessler. He is an ex-Gestapo officer and the Old Man's executioner. Do not trust him." Axel led the way back to the cabin where one of his suitcases was waiting outside the door. "Now I'm off. I'll leave you all my skiing posters. Me and Kurt are leaving for Oslo tomorrow on the *SS Bergen,* a Norwegian freighter."

"Kurt? He was your steward, right?"

Axel sighed. "Yes, he's a young German from Berlin and kept my cabin clean. He also did my laundry, and we frequently slept together. I couldn't leave him here with all those sex maniacs back aft, you understand?"

"Of course."

"I'm glad you do. Our friend next door, Richard the Third, who shares the bathroom, he's a young American who lifts weights for his muscles, but he and I never talk much. I think he was jealous of Kurt and me sleeping together, but why not? He's very good in bed, and sex is sex, right Sparks?"

"Indeed. Sex is sex." Axel crammed another bottle of rum into the over-flowing suitcase on his bunk and struggled to close it. "Was that the new steward you came on board with?"

"Yes, his name is Helmut. He's only fifteen and from East Berlin."

"I saw him on deck. These young Germans are so beautiful."

"We were at the hotel for a few days waiting for this ship. I showed him around Philly."

"Well, he'll probably be your steward, Sparks. Look after him. He looks like a little angel." Axel finally managed to close his case and dragged it outside onto the deck. He then reached out and shook my hand. "You'll be okay, Sparks. I told you, I'll be the Sparks on the *SS Bergen*. I left the call sign on the transmitter, so call me if you have any questions," offered Axel, "and let me know what you think of Heinz."

"Who's Heinz?"

"The number one sex maniac," replied Axel. "He's the first ashore in Cuba and the last one back on board. He'll be your best customer; he's always got the drip, drip, drip and a huge pair of blue balls. You're going to have fun with him."

I helped Axel with his suitcases down the rickety steel steps. "Thanks, Sparks. Look after that cute steward you brought with you, and lottsa luck with Heinz," he shouted, striding across the deck to the gangplank where Kurt was waiting for him.

As I watched them struggling down the slippery gangplank, my uppermost thought was to follow them. I had not yet signed the ship's log. I had forty American dollars, some loose change and an official entry card from U.S. Immigration allowing me to stay in the United States for another week, enough time to find another ship. I hurried back to the cabin gripped with panic and wanted to grab my cases and leave, but any thoughts of escape were interrupted by the creaking sound of the bathroom door slowly being pushed open. "Welcome aboard, Sparks," said a voice. "Welcome to the *Cuban Trader*, Germany's last remaining warship."

I assumed it was my American neighbor, the Third Mate. He was dressed in a white terry-towel robe, armed with two glasses and a bottle of rum. "Hi! I'm Richard the Third," he said, setting the glasses on the desk. "I'll bet you can't make up your mind whether to stay and face the music or take off like a bat outta hell!" He grinned and winked at me. "I guess it depends who's after you ashore: the cops, a woman or an army of creditors. I suggest you have a drink and think about it."

How did Richard guess I was thinking of jumping ship? He held up the bottle. "This is the best Cuban rum; at least they do something right. Truthfully, I hate the place. I hate this fucking ship, I hate the Dolly sisters, Schmidt and Bessler, and I despise the Old Man. They're all bastards, including Ludwig Berners, the ship's owner and all his ass-kissing cronies."

"So why d'ya stay? You're an American. You can walk off anytime," I replied, watching Richard struggling to open the bottle of rum.

"I'm a wanted man, Sparks. No photograph stuck on the Post Office wall yet, but the cops are after me. It's okay, don't get worried. I'm not an axe murderer or anything like that. They say I'm the father of two bastards. Their mothers are chasing me for money, but how do I know those kids are mine?"

Richard finally popped the cork and poured two generous helpings of rum into glasses. He then knelt down in front of my small refrigerator and grabbed some ice cubes and a bottle of Coca-Cola. "This is your best friend," he mumbled, patting the small refrigerator, "and this is your second best friend," he continued, handing me a glass of rum and Coca-Cola. He then slumped down on my couch, his terry towel robe slipping off, revealing his tanned washboard stomach. "Cheers, Sparks. Welcome aboard. I hope we'll be real friends."

"Thanks," I replied, hoping I would soon get such an enviable sun tan.

"We share the same bathroom. There are two doors, but just one bathroom. All very friendly, get it?"

"Yes, I get it," I replied. "One bathroom between our cabins, and we each have our own entrance."

"Axel and I were really friendly at first until Kurt, his swishy little steward started crawling into his bed every night," sneered Richard, scratching his crotch. "I could hear them in here fucking their heads off."

"What did the Old Man say about that?"

"Krause? He didn't know. Anyway he has Deiter, a sniveling little Kraut steward kissing his ass all the time."

I soon realized that Richard was far from sober. I had only known him for a few minutes and he was already giving me a detailed account of sex life on board the ship. Richard finished his drink in one gulp and refilled his glass with straight rum. "I've been nearly married twice but all the bitches wanted was money," confided Richard. "How about you, Sparks, ever been married?"

"No, not so far."

"Not so far? What kinda answer is that? I don't give a shit if you're straight or gay. Everybody's gay on this ship. Ten days at sea without a woman. For crissake, how long can a guy go without a piece of ass? Everybody fucks each other back aft. I wish I could go back there and get me some, but it's *verboten*. That's the Bosun's little empire, his orgy room; he has 'em all. Anyway officers can't start fucking the crew."

"Apparently Axel did and got away with it," I replied, finishing my drink.

"Yeah, nobody bothered him." Richard stared at me and smiled, he was one of the youngest deck officers I had ever met, probably in his late twenties and could have been on the cover of GQ magazine. He was obviously very tired and was almost falling asleep on the couch. He was handsome, with a shock of blond hair and perfect teeth. I liked him immediately, but couldn't figure him out.

Suddenly he sat up on the couch. "The agent said you're a Limey. I hope that's true. You haven't said much, so I can't tell by your accent."

"Yes, I'm a Limey, I was born in Gloucestershire," I replied. "I'm not wanted by the police and fortunately nobody is chasing me. I just signed on because they pay twice as much on here as they do on British ships."

"Well, I hope you'll stay. You're the only one on here who speaks English, 'ceptin one of the cooks back aft, and a drunken Australian deck hand." The Third looked around the cabin. "Axel fixed this place up real good, didn't he?" Richard tugged on his robe to cover his bare thighs. "If Kurt, his steward wasn't being fucked, he was cleaning and polishing this place. Shit! Maybe I should start fucking my steward then he might clean my cabin real good and make me some ice once in a while."

"Doesn't he do a very good job?"

"Not really, not like Axel's steward," moaned Richard. "He was always cleaning up, even polishing the porthole and he made ice as well."

"And he always slept with Axel?"

"Sleep?" scoffed Richard. "They never got much sleep."

"What about the other officers, Bessler and Schmidt?"

"The Dolly Sisters? They're two sadistic bastards; God knows what they get up to in their cabins. Bessler's got a cute little German faggot; he's always beating up, but the poor little bastard must be masochistic because he never complains."

I suddenly remembered Helmut and wondered how he was. "I came on board with a young steward. He's just escaped from East Berlin. The poor little bugger, he wanted to run away when he saw the ship."

"You should have let him. Let him run as far away as he could. They're nothing but slaves back aft. Ludwig Berners, the owner gets most of the crew from an agent in Berlin. They're mostly young German or Polish teenagers shipped over here like cattle. Poor bastards, they've got no papers and can't even go ashore in the States."

"What's the deal with the Chief Engineer, Igor Petrovich?"

"Berners hired some Russians to keep the engine running; a father and three sons. They never mix with the crew. Never talk to anyone. They got their own living area at the back of the engine room. Some of the crew reckon they've got a couple of women stashed away back there, the lucky bastards. I wish I had one. Watch out for them, Sparks, they're tough as nails."

"Don't worry I will." Richard rambled on about life on board the ship and I began to feel quite edgy. "It all sounds very unsavory to me."

"Unsavory? It's hell-on-wheels. I never go back aft.; the Bosun doesn't want anybody poking their nose into his little harem."

"His harem?"

"For crissake, Sparks! Haven't you been on one of these goddamn hell ships before?"

24

"Never, I've only been on British and Australian registry."

"Well you've got a lot to learn. Right now I'll bet that new steward you brought on board is being screwed by the Bosun; a goddamn German weight-lifter by the name of Kimmel. He screws 'em all. It's his harem back there."

"But what about the Old Man, doesn't he do anything?"

Richard sighed and refilled our empty glasses. "You better leave, Sparks. Take your cases and go back to England. This is a hell ship, a fucking hell ship. There are no rules. The Old Man is a fucking drunk like me. The Dolly Sisters, Bessler and Schmidt are both ex-Gestapo and capable of killing anyone with their bare hands. For crissake, Sparks, wise up. Shit, I don't wanna talk about it anymore." Richard swallowed his drink and attempted to get up from the couch. "I should sober up and go on deck; we're leaving tomorrow at noon, but let's have just one more drink."

"But I've got to see the Old Man and sign the log book," I replied, still thinking seriously of jumping ship. The only thing stopping me was Helmut. I had promised him I'd look after him.

"You gotta see the Old Man? Then you'd better have a double. He's the number one bastard on this goddamn ship."

Richard was correct. The Captain was a real bastard. A wizened, bald-headed old man, short and fat with a bloated red face and squinting little eyes peering over the top of his rimless glasses. He glowered at me as I entered his office. "Are you the new Schparks?" he groaned, hardly moving in his leather office chair as he shoved the tattered logbook across the desk. "Sign here."

"Sir, I have to tell you I was not informed about taking over the medicine chest. On British ships it's usually the chief steward's responsibility." I glared at the old bastard pushing the pen and inkwell across the desk for me to sign the official log book.

"JUST SIGN THE LOG BOOK," he shouted.

"Sir, I know nothing about medicine."

"SIGN THE LOG BOOK!" Captain Krause was now red in the face; his temples pulsing rapidly. "YOU WILL SIGN THE LOG BOOK NOW!"

I still had time to escape. My cases were still packed. My only problem was the ship's agent still had my passport and Helmut was back aft. "Berners pays an extra hundred dollars a month for looking after the medicine chest," moaned the Old Man. "You talk to him tomorrow when he comes on board with the ship's agent, then we sail at noon."

An extra hundred dollars a month, I was very tempted. Krause inched the old log book closer. Reluctantly I gritted my teeth and scratched my name. I stared at the tattered page, a list of everyone on board. Some obviously couldn't read or write and signed with a mark. The one before me was Helmut Schickel, a spidery signature against the title, Officer's Steward. At least the Bosun had allowed him a few minutes to sign-on in the official logbook before seducing him.

I stared at my signature and sighed. I was now officially the Radio Officer and Purser of the *Cuban Trader*. I was also in charge of the medicine chest. "NOW GET OUT," screamed the Old Man. "GET OUT." As I left the cabin and again sniffed the sickening smell of hot molasses I wondered, did I really need the extra money?

It had been a long and very traumatic day. I was not only tired and frustrated, I was also disappointed I had not followed my instincts and turned tail and ran back to Philadelphia. I could have taken Helmut back to the ship's agent and told him about the truth, that the *Cuban Trader* was a hell ship, surely he would have been able to arrange for him to sign on to another ship, but it was too late, we had both signed the official logbook.

I glanced at the notes that Axel had left me, especially the one underlined in red about the urgent need for fresh supplies of penicillin. I certainly didn't want the responsibilities of taking over the medicine chest, but apparently I had no choice.

I finished up the sandwiches that Bella had packed for me at the hotel and tried to wriggle into a comfortable position in my bunk. I couldn't help thinking about Helmut. Was it true what Richard had told me about the Kimmel, the Bosun? I knew Helmut didn't like sleeping alone, but Kimmel sounded like a cruel sex maniac.

~~~

CHAPTER TWO

Ludwig Berners' Lecture

"Two hundred thousand units of penicillin?" roared Captain Krause. "Herr Schparks, we are a ship, not a floating hospital for sex maniacs." His stubby little fingers bore down on the blunt pencil, scratching a thick, black line across my order book.

"But Sir, international regulations are very specific."

"International regulations?" he hollered, "I am the Captain on the ship, it is my regulations you will obey. If one more seaman gets the drip, drip, drip from a Cuban whore, then nobody will go ashore when we get to dock in Cuba. That is an order, Herr Schparks."

"But Captain, it's the only chance they have to relax. The Americans won't let them ashore."

"Because they are sex maniacs; no shore leave for sex maniacs," he yelled. I stared at the short-assed, balding old German, the supposed Captain of the ship, squatting in his leather chair behind his paper littered desk. He was supposed to look out for his crew. He should have been working with the American Immigration trying to get them permission to go ashore, but obviously he didn't care. He glared at me over the top of his rimless glasses like an old owl. "That is all, Herr Schparks," he said, sliding my order book across his desk. "No medicine, no shore leave for sex maniacs. Now go, I am busy."

It was only my second meeting with the Captain and already I hated him. I snatched my order book off his desk and waved it angrily in his face. "If you won't sign this, you can get another Sparks. I've only signed on for one trip and it will be my first and last."

"Go! Quit now. I tell Berners to get me somebody else. I don't want you on my ship, you Schweinhund."

As I strode out of his office for the fresher air outside, we both knew it was impossible to find another Radio Officer at such short notice, furthermore, I had already signed the official agreement at the maritime office. Ludwig Berners, the ship's owner was on his way to see the Captain, and I fully intended to corner him and settle the argument about medical supplies. I had checked the medicine chest, there was no penicillin and the Captain refused to sign my order book for a fresh supply. Axel was right, getting medical supplies, especially penicillin, was going to be a major problem.

It wasn't hard to imagine what would happen if, after ten days at sea, the Captain tried to prevent twenty-five or more horny young seamen from visiting their favorite dockside whorehouse, there would indeed be a bloody mutiny on board and if it happened, I hoped he would be the first to suffer.

Thirty minutes later, Ludwig Berners, the ship's owner arrived with an entourage of assistants and headed straight for the Captain's office on the boat deck. I managed to corner him just as he was entering the Old Man's office. "I'm Roger Asquith, the new Sparks and Purser and I need to talk to you privately."

"Later. Later," he hissed. "Oh, by the way, welcome aboard." I followed him and his group of assistants, all of whom were dressed in blue or gray suits with ties and polished black shoes, quite a contrast to their employer who looked like a bum. We all trooped into the Old Man's office where his steward, Deiter, was waiting with a tray of drinks. "Good Morning, Sir," wheezed the Captain, offering his hand.

Berners grunted and reluctantly shook his hand "Okay let's make this short," he said and then turned to his assistants. "You guys can go over the paperwork while Krause and I have a talk. Make sure you check his fucking figures."

The nervous assistants took Krause's file of paperwork and sat down at the table. Each one nervously accepted a drink from Deiter's tray while I looked around for Mike, the ship's agent. He wasn't there and the bastard still had my passport. Everyone was trying to hide their embarrassment as Berners and the Captain's argument echoed around the office. "If you're too fucking stupid to understand that," screamed Berners, "then get the fuck off my ship."

Krause was already a delicate shade of blue. His hands were fluttering about as he looked around nervously. His reply was inaudible as he moved closer to Berners. I too was nervous. I looked up when Richard the Third, my next door neighbor entered the room and calmly helped himself to a glass of whisky. From the look on Deiter's face, he was not very welcome.

"So, Sparks, what's your first impression of our beloved employer?" questioned Richard sitting beside me and sipping his drink.

"He scares me. If I had my passport I would tell him I'm leaving."

"Ah! He's not so bad. It's Krause who's so fucking incompetent. Little wonder Berners gets mad with him." Richard finished his drink and grabbed another as the steward walked by. "It's Cutty Sark," he whispered, winking at me. "Grab one."

I did. I needed it. It was strong, just what I needed to help me with my upcoming confrontation with Berners. "I'm asking for a fresh supply of medical supplies. The so-called medicine chest is empty."

"And I'm asking him for some new navigation charts. I was told the ship's agent is on his way with some new ones, the ones we're using were probably stolen from Christopher Columbus."

I laughed, appreciating Richard sense of humor. "The agent is also supposed to bring my passport."

"Good Luck. He won't hand that to you until we're about to leave, they don't want you jumping ship," replied Richard. "I've ordered a couple of cases of Coca-Cola, and some good Scotch. Cutty Sark will do. What are you ordering?"

"Ordering?" I didn't know what Richard was talking about.

"You can get liquor out of bond. It's duty free. The agent takes the order to the Customs who deliver it just before we sail. Order some Cutty Sark Scotch and some Beefeater Gin, you're gonna need it."

"I'll give you some money, please order some for me. I also need penicillin from Berners. Axel told me he used it on the crew."

"I told you, Axel was an ass bandit, he couldn't wait to check out everybody's schwanz every morning and give them a shot in the ass." Richard finished his second drink. "Looks like the Old Man and Berners have finished arguing. No blood was shed. Now it's our turn."

Richard managed to catch up with Berners as he reached for a drink from the steward's tray. I didn't hear their conversation but I was surprised to see Berners was laughing, perhaps Richard told him about the Christopher Columbus charts he was using. Now it was my turn.

"Sir," I began. "I have to talk to you about the medicine chest."

"Yeah Sparks. I'll give you another hundred bucks a month. Okay?" replied Berners, opening his briefcase.

"Yes Sir, that's okay. I gave the list of medical supplies we need to one of your assistants, and we must have a fresh supply of penicillin right away."

Berners glared at me for a second. "Penicillin?" he replied. "For crissake, Sparks, I've got a lot more things to worry about than penicillin." I caught the Captain's smirk as if to say *'I told you so'* and was about to offer my ultimatum, but Berners pointed to a chair and told me to sit down.

I soon realized the first order of business was to make sure Berners' glass was never empty. We both sat down at the Captain's desk and immediately Henri Bloom, Berners' chief assistant poured out a hefty swig of whisky and handed it to his boss, he then stood, almost at attention with the full bottle of Cutty Sark for whenever Berners glass needed a refill.

"Count this and sign here," snapped Berners, pushing a wad of dollars and some paperwork toward me. "It's fifty-thousand dollars in bank-sealed wrapping, and it's to pay for the molasses. I've told Krause, and I'm telling you, I want three sober Officers to be there when you pay the fucking Cubans for a full cargo of top grade molasses, and not Richard the Third. I hear he's always fucking drunk." Berners grinned. "For crissake, he wants new navigation charts," he continued, swigging his drink. "He's trying to tell me the charts he's using were stolen from Christopher Columbus. Shit! That fucking Limey asshole never even went to Cuba." Berners drained his glass and grabbed another from Deiter's tray. "Richard the Third is a drunken fucking asshole."

I glared at the wads of notes on the desk. I had never seen bank-sealed packages of money. There were ten packages with $5000 stamped on them. "Am I responsible for all this?"

"You're the Purser. You and Krause work together. He keeps this in his safe to pay off the refinery. Argue with the fucking Cuban bastards, Sparks. Don't pay a dollar more than you need to, and don't forget I'm hoping to get a lot of change outta this. Understand?"

During the whole visit Berners and his assistants treated us like cattle, snooping around the ship, opening doors and peering into cabins. I never knew what they were looking for, but I made sure my cabin door was kept locked.

Apparently, Berners' meetings were routine. He signed papers, handed over enough money for the next cargo of molasses, the crew's spending money ashore and a few hundred dollars for bribing uncooperative Cuban officials. If there was any left over, the Captain was authorized to buy fresh milk or vegetables from various Cuban merchants who came on board.

Berners took a swig of whiskey and banged on the desk to get attention. "Well, I suppose y'all ought to know I got word this morning that the refinery managers and our Cuban agent have all fuckin' quit. I guess everything down there is in a fucking mess, and everyone is shit-scared of some asshole called Fidel Castro who's trying to take over the refinery. Anyways, that ain't no concern of ours as long as he keeps supplying us with molasses. If that asshole Castro has taken over, find out who he's put in charge of the refinery and negotiate a price, and y'all don't pay no more than forty thousand bucks, and that's for the top grade blackstrap like we're used to loading."

"Are you certain the refinery is still operating?" I asked. "And what if this Fidel Castro attacks us?"

Berners seemed shocked that I should have asked such a mundane question. "For crissake, Sparks, he won't attack you guys. You're down there to buy their molasses, which they want to sell, and you're paying with American dollars, which they badly need. Only a fucking asshole would attack you."

It was possible, I thought to myself, *that perhaps Fidel Castro WAS a fucking asshole and joined the ranks of all the other fucking assholes in Ludwig Berners' life.* "You said WE have to negotiate, who specifically do you mean?"

Berners glared at me. "Specifically, Sparks," he sneered, "I mean Captain Krause, First Officer Bessler and you. Y'all be there in the office and sign the papers. I wanna know how every company dollar was spent, y'all understand?" Berners drained his glass and held it out for a refill. "Where is Bessler, the First Officer? Is he still frog marching his fuckin' storm troopers across the deck? Somebody go tell that Kraut asshole, the fuckin' war is over! The Krauts lost."

"You want Herr Bessler?" questioned the Old Man, nervously. "He's back aft with the Chief Engineer; they are checking the steering equipment. Shall I send for him?"

"What's wrong with the goddamn steering equipment?" snapped Berners. "I want y'all to just get the fuck out of here on the next high tide. That's at noon. I'm not paying another thousand bucks to keep y'all tied up to this fucking dock another day. So what's wrong with the steering? Who fucked up?"

The Old Man fumbled for words, trying to explain how the propeller became ensnarled with some steel cable. "Uh, we got caught in some steel cable, Herr Berners."

"Caught in some steel cable? Jesus Christ! Where were you going?"

"It was floating in the river," explained the Old Man, wishing he too could have large glass of his whiskey.

"Floatin' in the river? Steel cable was just floatin' in the river?" yelled Berners, shaking his bald head in disbelief.

"There is many such cables, Herr Berners," explained the Old Man. He glanced at me enjoying every second of his interrogation.

Berners scoffed. "I wanna full report. You, Bloom! Take notes and look into it. If'n there was a loose cable *floatin'* in the river, I'll sue the bastards in charge of keeping it fit for navigation. For crissake, I pay enough in port charges to berth the fucking Queen Elizabeth."

Apart from a few more outbursts from Berners · concerning the so-called waste of his money · the meeting ended abruptly when he glanced at his watch and discovered it was time to leave. "Y'all sail on the next tide," he yelled at the Old Man.

"Yes, Herr Berners. Herr Bessler reports the steering equipment is now okay."

"Then you ain't got no more excuses," hissed Berners, as he stuffed the folders into his briefcase and handed it to Bloom, his senior assistant. He stomped out of the Old Man's cabin.

I was waiting for him outside on the deck and again reminded him about the penicillin.

"For crissake, Sparks, is that all you want is a case of penicillin?" he yelled.

I could have given him a whole list of things we needed but didn't want to push my luck. "Well, I think you should know there will be a mutiny if the Old Man refuses to let the crew go ashore in Cuba."

Berners threw up his hands in exasperation. "Sparks, y'all know I ain't got no control over shore leave down there, that's up to the Old Man, but I'll make sure y'all get a case of penicillin right away. Now, hurry up and get the hell out of here. I don't want you missing the next tide." Berners strode off across the deck followed by his entourage, all-skittering precariously down the steep slippery gangplank to their waiting company cars.

A few minutes later, First Officer Bessler followed me across the deck to my office. "Herr Schparks, you have much angered the Captain," he yelled. "We now log you for disobeying orders." Bessler glared at me with his cold blue eyes; a look of contempt that sent a shiver down my spine. He was a perfect example of Hitler's so-called Master Race and was second in command of the ship. Richard had already confirmed Axel's statement that Bessler had been an officer in the dreaded Gestapo during the war; all of whom were trained to kill defenseless men, women or children with their bare hands.

"All I want is a case of penicillin," I replied. "It's for your crew. You should be just as concerned as I am."

"My crew? They are all sex-maniacs," he snarled, repeating the Old Man's favorite phrase.

"Hell, they're no different from any other young guys. They should all be ashore while we're in port here, not marching back and forth across the deck," I replied. "By God, I'll bet they all hate your guts."

"Ja, but you don't worry, Herr Schparks, I have my spies back aft and they tell me everything," he sneered. "So, Herr Schparks, only one day on board and already you are logged for insubordination." Bessler snapped his little black book shut and strutted back to his office like a well-trained Nazi officer.

"Schparks, it's Deiter, the Old Man's steward who tells Bessler everything that happens back aft," warned Dubinsky, who had overheard my confrontation with Bessler. "Everybody back aft knows Bessler pushed two seamen over the side for threatening to knife the Old Man, and it was Deiter, the little bastard, who told him."

"Bessler pushed two seamen over the side? Are you sure?"

"Yes, Janowski and Slivitz, two Polish deckhands. The Old Man wouldn't pay them their overtime for working on a Sunday. He said he'd send them back to the ghetto if they reported him to Berners. A few days later, it was a big storm off Cape Hatteras. The Old Man ordered Jano and Slivitz to stow some rope up for'ard and then sent Bessler to kick their asses overboard. In two minutes they was gone over the side. Weicecz was the helmsman, he saw everything. Now he's shit scared he'll be next. Sparks, hear me. Don't trust Bessler. Don't get near the rail." Dubinsky kicked out with his foot. "That bastard, he will do that to you."

Richard the Third had also told me the same story with a warning that First Officer Bessler was the Old Man's executioner. Until now, I hadn't believed him.

Thirty minutes later, a taxi drew up to the gangplank and one of Ludwig Berners' smarmy-looking assistants struggled on board with a case of penicillin. I met him at the end of the gangplank. "Here, this is for all you poxed-up bastards," he said, contemptuously shoving a piece of paper at me. "You have to sign for it."

"If you want someone to sign for it, go and see the Old Man," I replied, grabbing the precious box of penicillin. "He's the only poxed-up bastard on this ship that I know of." I left Berners' assistant frantically waving a yellow piece of paper and took the precious case of penicillin to my office.

Helmut was waiting for me outside the office door. He looked sad and very tired. His naturally curly, blond hair had been shaved off and he no longer looked like the young teenager I first met in Philadelphia a few days ago. He smiled. "Herr Schparks," he began. "You can talk to me?"

"Of course, come in." Helmut followed me into the office. "How are you?"

Helmut shrugged his shoulders. "Herr Schparks, I am so sad."

"Sad? What's the matter?" I asked, tearing open the case of penicillin, groaning out loud when I realized there were no disposable syringes. Helmut was obviously nervous. I could see tears welling in his sad, blue eyes. "Helmut, tell me what's wrong." I sat in the chair opposite and gave him my full attention. "Now tell me what's the matter?"

"Herr Schparks, are you my friend?"

"Of course I'm your friend. What is the matter?"

Helmut struggled to think of the proper words. "Herr Schparks, I have to sleep with the Bosun."

"And he fucks you?"

"Ya, he fuck me many times, but afterwards I have to stay with him, I have no bunk."

"No bunk? But every seaman has to have their own bunk."

"No, Herr Schparks. Many seamen sleep in same bunk."

"Why do they sleep together?"

Helmut shrugged his thin shoulders almost scared to go on. "They fuck, but many bunks are kaput. It is bad, Herr Schparks, but Bosun, he do nothing."

"My God, I had no idea it was that bad. It's Bessler's job to look after the crew."

"Herr Bessler, he do nothing. He is cruel man."

Helmut's pathetic story was interrupted by the phone. It was actually Bessler calling from the bridge. "We leave, Herr Schparks, and you are not turning on the radar. It is dead," he yelled, slamming down the phone.

"Helmut, I have to go on duty. Come and see me after dinner, okay?"

"After dinner?" Helmut's face broke into a smile. "Ya, I come and see you after dinner. Thank you, Herr Schparks." He grinned as he left my office. I went to the Radio Room to start my first trip to Cuba.

As soon as the river pilot was on board, the crew prepared the ship to leave; unhooking the telephone to shore, disconnecting the water supply, taking up the gangplank and stowing it on deck. Finally they winched in the cables that secured us to the dock and we were literally free to sail.

Ten minutes later I had switched on the overworked radar on the bridge and we were now underway, moving slowly down the Delaware River to the Atlantic Ocean. It was the 8th of September, 1958, and a new adventure for me on the 9,000 ton hell ship known as the *Cuban Trader* bound for the Los Canos refinery in Santiago de Cuba.

Because the ship had plied between the two ports so many times before, it was now just a boring routine for the crew. Without exception, every one of them had smuggled cartons of Lucky Strikes cigarettes to sell in Cuba. It was a profitable trip for Ludwig Berners, the ship's owner who made an exorbitant profit on the Cuban molasses, and the crew traded a few packs of cigarettes for a cold beer and a hot woman at any of the dockside whorehouses.

It was 9.30 pm when Helmut knocked at my cabin door. I had forgotten that I had told him to see me after dinner. He had obviously cleaned himself up for the visit and he was smiling. "Herr Schparks, it is me," he whispered. "I wait until everybody get drunk back aft."

"Come on in." I marked the page of the book I was reading and sat on my bunk. "What's worrying you, Helmut?" Helmut looked around the cabin, struggling to find the right words. "Why don't you help yourself to a rum and Coca-Cola," I suggested.

Helmut nodded and poured himself a shot of rum, topping it up with some Coca-Cola from the fridge. He sat on the old couch and sipped his drink and then smiled at me like a cheeky little schoolboy. Someone had drastically chopped off his straggly blond curls and given him a crew cut. "Thank you, Herr Schparks."

"Firstly, Helmut, I have made a written report about the state of the bunks back aft, and that many of the crew have to share." Helmut continued smiling at me with his large, blue eyes. "Isn't that one of your complaints?"

"Herr Schparks, you are my friend," he replied in a husky whisper.

"Of course I'm your friend, and I will make sure the bunks are repaired and you will get one of your own. What else is the matter?"

"Herr Schparks, the Bosun, he ..."

"I know. I know," I sighed. "The Bosun is also a cruel man. Does he hurt you?" Helmut nodded. For a moment, I pictured the powerful Kimmel, encircling Helmut with his massive arms and forcing him to submit. I knew that some young seamen idolized Kimmel's power and even enjoyed his rough sexual attention. "But Helmut, it's up to the Old Man and Bessler to deal with that problem, but I will certainly make a report."

Helmut finished his drink and made himself more comfortable on the couch. He looked tired and very sad and was almost asleep, but it was time for me to go on watch from ten until midnight, the last watch of the day. I was also scared Helmut would be discovered in my cabin, definitely not allowed on British ships. "Helmut, I will discuss this with the Old Man tomorrow and then we'll talk some more. Right now you have to go back aft and find an empty bunk, because I have to go on watch." I shook Helmut. He was almost asleep. "I have to go on watch now. We will talk tomorrow."

It took a few seconds before Helmut realized I was asking him to leave. He slowly got off the couch and walked to the cabin door. "Danke, Herr Schparks," he whispered, holding back his tears until he was outside the cabin door. He then turned and looked at me, the tears now streamed down his face as he crept his way back aft. I wanted to reach out and hug him. Never before had I seen such a pathetic teenager, and I was sending him back aft to the hell-hole ruled over by Kimmel the Bosun.

"Why did you kick the poor little bastard out, Sparks?" questioned Richard, as he entered my cabin through the bathroom. "You sent him back aft just in time for the Bosun to fuck him."

"I know, and I'm sorry. I don't know what to do and I'm supposed to be responsible for him. He's so young and vulnerable, just like a school kid," I replied. "I'm late. I gotta go on watch and get the midnight weather forecast from Washington."

"...and check out Cape Hatteras, it's usually shitty weather there," replied Richard. I left him sipping his glass of whiskey and couldn't help wondering if he would have sent Helmut back to the hell hole back aft.

~~~

CHAPTER THREE

Sailing to Santiago de Cuba

The *Cuban Trader* was an old and very expendable Liberty tank ship which had survived the U-boat attacks in the Atlantic. It was eventually sold by the American Government for scrap metal because no country with a respectable maritime tradition would grant the old rust bucket a certificate of sea worthiness. Liberia, a little known country on the East Coast of Africa, wasn't so fussy and provided unscrupulous ship owners with a legal way to operate these deathtraps, with a *flag of convenience*. As soon as the fee was paid to the Liberian Government their red and white striped flag was flown from the ship which was then legally allowed to trade anywhere in the world. Ludwig Berners owned about half a dozen of these death traps including the *Cuban Trader*.

Ludwig was a greedy, uncaring entrepreneur who had no interest in the welfare of the crew. His only concern was in supplying the distillery in Philadelphia with cheap Cuban molasses; consequently all his ships, including the *Cuban Trader* were equipped with the minimum of safety radio equipment; a worn out radar set and scanner, a medium and short-wave transmitter/receiver, and an Auto-Alarm, which rang a bell on the Bridge if any ship within fifty miles sent out an emergency SOS.

As the 'Sparks' I was expected to keep in daily radio contact with the outside world, not an easy task with such ancient equipment.   It was also my responsibility to maintain the overworked radar set on the Bridge; make sure all the phones were in working order; keep up the ship's accounts; figure out the crew's overtime and pay them a portion of their hard-earned wages when they went ashore.

I also reluctantly agreed to look after the "medicine chest" and fully intended to follow Axel's advice and practice on a melon before giving any of the crew a shot of penicillin. Looking over Axel's frequent entries in the medical log book I would soon have to become an expert at jabbing rear ends with the new wonder drug, which apparently was the cure for any rash or pustule erupting on the scrotum, rectum and surrounding areas of the body, whereas any complaints on the inside were hopefully cured with an aspirin or a spoonful of evil tasting castor oil.

The box of surgical instruments looked like a medieval torture chamber full of rusty tweezers, scalpels, tongs and, as Axel had already mentioned, a pair of ancient manacles with faded instructions on how to secure the patient to the operating table when amputating one of his limbs. Only a crazy sadistic maniac would take any of it seriously, unfortunately I soon discovered Captain Krause was a crazy sadistic maniac.

The crew, just like the *Cuban Trader,* were also expendable. We all risked our lives on the floating death trap that should have been scrapped at the end of the war. My excuse for being there was I needed the extra money, but most of the crew had little choice. Like Helmut, most of them escaped from behind the Iron Curtain, arrived in West Berlin and were tricked into signing contracts by the Liberian maritime agents desperate for cheap labor to man their fleet of hell ships, but the young men had little choice and were grateful to be offered a job, and so was Captain Krause. His appalling record of accidents and bad seamanship was well known in all the reputable maritime companies; none of whom wanted him navigating one of their ships, but the *Cuban Trader* was owned by Ludwig Berners, who didn't care about him or his crew as long as they delivered his precious cargo of hot molasses.

"Herr Schparks," yelled Herr Schmidt, calling me on the phone. "The radar is kaput again. You will fix it now." I immediately stopped typing up the weather forecast and scrambled up onto the Bridge. "It is kaput, and we need the radar now."

The radar monitor was hot and had been covered over with the Schmidt's heavy coat. "Sir, the radar has been going continuously since we left dock. It's old and gets overheated; it needs to cool off."

"We need the radar now," insisted Schmidt. "You will make it work."

"Sir, I've just taken down the weather forecast, it's calm seas, a light wind from the West and excellent visibility."

"You will make it work now. NOW," bellowed Schmidt. "Where is the forecast?"

"I was typing it up when you called me, and this monitor is not the place for your coat. The set needs air circulating around it. Otherwise it gets overheated."

Schmidt glared at me with a look of contempt. "I have entered in the ship's log book that the radar set is kaput," he continued. "We are at sea with no radar."

"Yes, in a calm sea, with ten miles visibility in all directions. You don't need the radar," I replied, hanging his heavy duffle coat on the coat rack, "and this is where you keep your coat."

"I will inform the Captain you refuse to repair the radar."

"Go ahead, and I'll tell the Captain where you hang your duffle jacket. Give it a few minutes to cool off. I repeat, the visibility is ten miles in each direction. You don't need the radar."

"Get off the Bridge," yelled Schmidt. "I will enter your conduct into the log book and inform the Captain."

"You do that, and be sure to kiss his royal ass at the same time," I replied, scurrying back to the Radio Room. Weicecz, the helmsman burst out laughing, not a smart thing to do when a sadistic maniac was officer of the watch.

Everyone on board swigged cheap rum during the ten-day trip to Cuba, and cheered when the Captain deliberately went off course, hugging the coastline in order to pick up his favorite American television programs from the various TV stations along the Atlantic coast. The crew welcomed the detour, eagerly huddling around the battered old black and white television set in the crew's dining room, laughing at the crazy antics of Phil Silvers in "Sergeant Bilko" and Lucille Ball in "I Love Lucy." Unfortunately the U.S. Coast Guard, anxious to conceal the secrets of Cape Canaveral, were not too happy with the ancient Liberian tanker chugging close to the shore, and buzzed around in low flying planes. Eventually they boarded the ship demanding to know why it continuously strayed off the approved course. When Captain Krause, a former German U-boat commander, admitted he did it in order to watch television programs, they didn't believe him. It was only at a later stage of the enquiry when he raved about his favorite program, "Heckle and Jeckle" that the Coast Guard officers were convinced Captain Krause was completely insane.

I agreed with them, Captain Krause WAS insane. Whether his insanity was due to the claustrophobic life on board a small German submarine during the war, or the results of watching two black birds flying about in his favorite television program, it was hard to say. But he definitely wasn't competent to take command of a ship.

I first questioned Captain Krause's sanity on the second night at sea. It was just after midnight. I had just finished my watch and was lying on my bunk watching a beam of moonlight moving slowly up and down on my bulkhead with the gentle rolling of the ship. Normally this movement was sufficient to put me to sleep, but suddenly I was aware the moonbeam was moving around my cabin, an indication that the ship was changing its course, but why? Slipping on my robe I went out on deck in time to hear the Captain yelling at the helmsman to change course and avoid a fully laden oil tanker passing dangerously close to our bow. The rules of the sea are relatively simple. Every ship carries a red light on the port bow, and green light on the starboard side. If a ship is approaching in the opposite direction, they must pass each other *green to green* and alter course if necessary.

Apparently Captain Krause didn't follow this international rule of the sea. He always made a 360 degree turn to avoid oncoming vessels. This dangerous and unnecessary maneuver almost resulted in a second collision when we nearly clipped the stern of the slow moving tanker on completion of the circle. The next morning the whole ship's crew were discussing Krause's "crazy circle" and wondering if it was safe to continue working on board the ship.

As Radio Officer and Purser, I was forced to work closely with the old fool. From the very first day he did everything possible to make my life as miserable as he could, entering his complaints in the official log book for Ludwig Berners' attention at the end of the trip. I intended to ignore the idiot and do my job as I was trained, editing the Captain's long-winded telegrams to a bare minimum by using the international five letter code.

Axel never bothered to edit the Captain's messages by using the code and sent the telegrams exactly as the Old Man had written them; consequently Ludwig Berners' office had been swamped with expensive radio messages such as:

> *DUE TO THE INCLEMENT WEATHER AND CIRCUMSTANCES OVER WHICH I HAVE NO CONTROL - WE WILL BE IN SANTIAGO DE CUBA APPROXIMATELY 1700 ON THURSDAY.*
> *SIGNED: CAPTAIN KRAUSE.*

Using the five letter international code, I sent the same message in two words;

> *ETASC 1700T, (ESTIMATED TIME OF ARRIVAL SANTIAGO DE CUBA 1700GMT)*

It said it all in two very inexpensive words. I never mentioned this to Krause, because I knew he would order me not to alter his precious messages. Conversely, the company office congratulated me for saving them money.

Helmut had come to see me in my cabin a few times during the first few days of the trip, telling me what was happening back aft. Richard had been right. Kimmel had raped him many times when he first came on board. When he found out Helmut and I were friends, he ordered the young seaman not to visit my cabin, but Helmut was desperate and hid on the deck until it was safe to creep into my cabin. I always welcomed him, gave him a drink, and he never failed to remind me of my promise to quit after our first trip. I always felt very guilty making him go back aft to sleep, but I had never been on a ship where deck crew were allowed to fraternize with the officers in their cabins. However, after I knew Helmut had no bunk of his own, I occasionally allowed him to fall asleep on my couch. When I returned to my cabin after my watch, I always covered him over with the spare blanket.

The sea was quite rough when we arrived off the coast of Florida. Unfortunately the ship was only half full of sea water to flush out the cargo tanks before we arrived; consequently it was rolling about like a drunken sailor. Despite the many years I had been at sea, I still got sea sick mainly from the overpowering stench of hot molasses which had permeated every part of the ship. On the fourth day, Helmut was also sick, and staggered to my cabin in a pitiful state. It was too rough for him to sleep on the couch, so I made room for him in my bunk which had a wooden slide that could be pulled up to prevent anyone falling out of bed. We huddled as the ship pitched and tossed, appreciating that at least with two of us, we wouldn't roll out of the bunk.

Apart from the constant verbal battles with Captain Krause, my time aboard the *Cuban Trader* would have been very dull had it not been for the English language classes I organized in the crew's dining room. Many of the crew attended, all cleaned up and eager to learn, including my friend, Helmut. They all struggled valiantly through the complexities of the English language, but were more interested in listening to Heinz, a twenty-four year-old German Adonis and the ship's number one stud, recalling his sexploits in the Cuban whorehouse He never failed to make them laugh describing his sexual acrobatics with the Cuban whores who appreciated his stamina.

"Tell them about your sex partners on Australian ships, Sparks," sneered J.J. Anderson, who yelled out when I first came on board. "Remember the time when you and the

Third Mate got caught with your pants down in a pineapple field in Fiji? Tell them about that, Sparks."

I had wondered when Anderson would grab the chance to start heckling me in front of the crew. He was now grinning at me waiting for an explanation. "Yeah, I remember. I was the Sparks on a banana boat in Fiji and got drunk and woke up in huge pineapple patch."

"Yeah, with no pants on, you missed that bit, Sparks," continued Anderson.

I countered with "Remember, in Fiji when you were thrown in jail for being drunk and beating up an old native woman selling oranges and stealing all her money? How old was she, sixty or seventy? And didn't they have to take her to a doctor to get bandaged up? Tell the crew about that, Anderson. Unfortunately, most of the crew know all about Communist bullies and getting beaten up. Do you want me to me to go on, Anderson?" He stared at me for a few seconds and then left.

I had almost forgotten about waking up nearly naked in a pineapple field in Fiji. The Third Mate and I had been drinking some potent concoction in a native bar and got chased and robbed by a bunch of hooligans, and took shelter in a little wooden hut. The next morning we had to walk back to the ship covered with burlap sacks, much to the amusement of everyone on the dock. Obviously Anderson was one of them.

The crew loved browsing through the pile of gossipy movie magazines that Axel had left for me. One of them mentioned Richard Fordson · apparently the rum swigging Richard "the Third", who shared my bathroom. He was the twenty-five year-old son of a wealthy Hollywood film producer, and had been in many of his father's films. The magazine went on to describe him as a six-foot-tall, blue-eyed Adonis with an athletic build. I reluctantly had to agree with the description, and secretly envied him, but Richard always dismissed the gossipy fan magazines as "pure crap" and described himself as a college dropout and a spoiled brat.

Before the so-called July 26th Revolution in 1958, the tiny Caribbean island of Cuba was a dichotomy of very rich and very poor. The wealthy Cuban was either an established land owner, or a corrupt member of the Batista Government, and business between the U.S.A. and Cuba was booming. Most of the large sugar plantations were owned by uncaring foreign corporations who treated the native workers little better than slaves. Thousands of Cubans were unemployed and almost starving to death while wealthy tourists flocked to Havana to wallow in the Mafia-owned gambling casinos and whorehouses, taking up the best rooms in the best hotels, in the best part of town. The scores of marinas dotted along the coast were a popular and inexpensive haven for hundreds of foreign-owned yachts where their owners would drop anchor and bask in the tropical sunshine, gamble, drink cheap rum, and wallow in the numerous sleazy drug-infested whore-houses and night clubs.

Unscrupulous foreign businessmen supported the corrupt Batista regime, bribing officials and exploiting the natives until a festering sore of discontent slowly came to a head. Fidel Castro, a native land-owner was the first to recognize the symptoms, and secretly made plans for a change. One of the first changes he made was to seize all the property belonging to the United Fruit Company in Cuba. He never compensated them for their loss.

While we had been churning slowly southwards, Fidel Castro's revolutionary army had spread out from the Sierra Maestra region to the outskirts of Santiago and was rapidly gaining the support of the peasants who hated the cruel regime of President Batista. We had read in the American newspapers about the peasant uprising in Cuba, but didn't expect to be involved in the revolution. Until Berners' warning about a Castro takeover of the refinery, the revolt was simply a domestic squabble and of little concern to members of the ship's crew.

We were now steaming slowly at about three knots into the sheltered water of Santiago Bay. I had already contacted the harbor radio station requesting a pilot to steer us through the treacherous sandbanks and take us alongside the storage tanks of the Los Canos sugar refinery and had received a confirmation that he was on his way. We were all now waiting for the pilot boat to come alongside so he could jump on board together with the top officials, all eager to collect their bribes and help themselves to drinks from Deiter's tray in the Captain's office. It was the usual routine according to the notes that Axel thoughtfully left for me.

"Are you going ashore, Sparks?" asked Richard the Third Mate, entering my cabin through the interconnecting bathroom door and pouring himself a hefty drink of rum from my liquor cabinet.

"If it's safe, you know what Berners told us."

"He was talking about the refinery being taken over by Castro's mob. Big deal. We can still go ashore and eat." Richard made himself comfortable on my couch.

"Okay, I'm game. I certainly fancy one of Pietro's steaks you have been bragging about since we left," I replied, putting away my notebook.

"I expect the girls will be waiting for us · Maria and Consuela · I told you Axel and I dated them when we were in port."

"Do you think they'll show up?"

"Of course they will. They're crazy about us." Richard had also bragged how he usually had to satisfy both of them because Axel wasn't very keen. "Axel was scared they'd be poxed up to their ears, but they work in the refinery office, so there's no need for them to sell their ass. They'll also know when we'll be docking."

"But what if Castro has taken over the refinery and their office?"

"Fuck him. I won't bother him if he doesn't bother me. Anyway I always take the girls some shampoo and lots of crap from the drugstore, so they'll be waiting for us, you can bet on it," replied Richard, helping himself to some of my ice cubes and topping up his glass from my last bottle of Coca-Cola.

"Go easy with the ice cubes, Richard. There's not many left."

"Quit bitching, Sparks. It's the steward's job to make ice. I now give mine five bucks a month to make ice and do my laundry. What about your guy?"

"You mean Hans? I never see him. He makes up my bunk, and I occasionally get a clean towel, and that's it."

"Well, give him five bucks a month and he'll make ice, do your laundry and keep the cabin spick and span, and for another buck, he'll kiss your ass as well."

We both laughed. "Okay I'll give him five dollars a month; it will be worth it to get a good supply of ice."

"Well, right now there are only two cubes left, so we'll have one each. Shall I fix you a drink, Sparks?"

"Later. We're not alongside yet." Richard sprawled across the couch and took a hefty swig from his glass. "Shouldn't you be back aft right now?" I asked. "Checking up on that mutinous deck crew of yours? We should be alongside very soon."

"And shouldn't you be in the Radio Room sending out an S.O.S. to New York? Goddamn it! There's a civil war going on here in Cuba. Do you see any other ships in the Bay? No you don't. We're the only one stupid enough to go on trading during this revolution. Ludwig Berners, the greedy bastard, doesn't give a shit about us risking our lives in this hell hole."

"Richard, we all know that. Why don't you finish your drink and go on deck. I think I can hear the pilot launch coming alongside. The Old Man will go crazy if you're not out there when he comes on board."

"What do you mean, the Old Man will go crazy? He's already crazy. Crazier than a dingbat and way past the point of no return," replied Richard, finishing his drink before reluctantly going out on deck to greet the Cuban pilot.

Despite Berners' warning, it seemed very calm when the pilot guided us safely alongside the loading dock of the refinery. It was like a scene from a black and white monster movie where a gigantic black octopus had slithered onto the refinery wrapping its tentacles around all the storage tanks, hissing steam and dribbling hot black strap molasses all over the place, the sickly smell of which nearly made me vomit.

The Cuban pilot told us that Fidel Castro was stirring up a lot of trouble in the town, and many Government officials and businessmen had taken their ill-gotten gains and gone to Mexico, but not the refinery boss and his cronies who boarded the ship as usual with the Pilot, and were now drinking and collecting their bribes in the Captain's office. There were even more minor officials on the dock waiting to clamber on board and get what was left of the free goodies.

While the Cuban officials drank the free booze and collected their bribes, Richard and Herr Schmidt supervised the crew and refinery workers sweltering in the afternoon sun connecting two enormous black pipes to the empty tanks of the *Cuban Trader*. After about two hours of yelling and shouting, the pumping began, and the old ship purred like a contented fat black cat lapping up a dish of cream.

When the noisy pumps began to fill the ship's tanks with hot crude molasses, the deck crew hurriedly hosed off the sticky black mess with salty sea water and got ready to go ashore, ignoring the Old Man's orders forbidding them to leave the ship. I had secretly paid them all five American dollars out of their wages to spend ashore, and many were now creeping down the gangplank carrying a paper bag full of goodies to trade in for a night of sensual delight at the dockside whorehouse. Apparently very little money changed hands. Toiletries, such as shampoo, soap and face cream, sent most women into a spasm of wild delights, guaranteed to provide enough passion to satiate the appetite of even the randiest seaman. I was told a few packets of cigarettes were swapped for a bottle of cheap rum, and a carton of Lucky Strikes for a steak at Pietro's, the best restaurant in town.

I sat in the Radio Room writing up my log, listening to the SPLASH, SPLASH, SPLASH as Deiter, the Old Man's steward tossed the empty booze bottles over the side, all except one that rolled across the deck and stopped by the Radio Room door. Seconds later Deiter followed after it. "Have they all gone now?" I asked him. "The Cubans, have they gone?

Deiter glared at me. "Why you ask?" he snapped.

"Because I want to go and see the Captain, that's why."

"The Captain, he no want to see you, Herr Schparks," whined Deiter. "He is too tired."

"Too drunk you mean. I counted the bottles you threw over the side. Twelve or more. That's a lot of booze." Deiter bent down to pick up the empty bottle. "I'll bet the Old Man had more than his share."

"The Captain he is tired. He no want to see any more peoples," drawled Deiter.

"That's fine by me. Just tell him I'm officially switching off the transmitter at sixteen hundred hours," I replied. "Now I'm going off watch."

Deiter snorted and hurried back to the Old Man's cabin trying to avoid three drunken refinery officials staggering across the deck. I looked across at the Old Man's cabin, wondering if there were any more so-called officials in there soaking up the free booze. Deiter watched me with a look of contempt then slammed the cabin door. *What a stupid little Kraut*, I said to myself, *no wonder he was ostracized by the rest of the crew.*

So this was the infamous Los Canos refinery, covered in black molasses and filling the air with a sickening stink that brought vomit to the back of my throat. Little wonder the crew all rushed to the adjacent whorehouse now reverberating to Elvis Presley's latest single and enjoying a few hours of well-earned relaxation away from the ship.

Helmut saw me on deck and approached smiling. "Herr Schparks, zank you for the money." I had handed out five dollars to each of the crew, although most of them had bags of shampoo and soap to exchange for a cold beer and a hot Cuban *puta*.

"Are you going to the whorehouse?" I asked. "I am sure you'll have a good time."

"Ya, I go with Hans," Helmut replied, sheepishly, "but he says we no fuck."

"That's okay. Have some rum and Coca-Cola and dance to Elvis Presley. The whores will give you a good time."

"Are you going to the whorehouse, Herr Schparks?"

"No, I go with Richard the Third. We are meeting two of his friends at Pietro's Restaurant." Helmut was obviously disappointed by my reply. "But next time I go with you."

"Herr Schparks, but we leave in Philly. Yes?"

How could I tell my friend that I was legally obligated to sign on for another trip? "I hope to leave in Philly, but we'll talk later. Here's another five dollars to spend because you have no toiletries to trade in. This will buy lotsa rum and Coca-Cola."

Helmut reluctantly took the five dollar bill, "Zank you, Herr Schparks," he said, slowly walking back to the gangplank where Hans was waiting for him. If Helmut was disappointed, so was I, but I was legally obligated to make three trips. I assuaged my conscience by promising to make Helmut's life more tolerable.

I looked across the dock to the whorehouse now reverberating to the voice of Elvis Presley, perhaps the only American welcome in Cuba. But what else did Santiago de Cuba have to offer? According to Richard, Pietro's served the best food in town and Maria and Consuela were eagerly waiting for us to take them out to dinner.

~~~

CHAPTER FOUR

Caught in the Crossfire

After a hot shower, I changed into some comfortable clothes and lay on my bunk salivating about the steak at Pietro's. Richard had raved about it ever since we left Philadelphia. He said it was one of the few places left in town where one could get a decent meal in clean surroundings and be served by professional waiters who didn't resent anyone with more money than themselves.

I was thinking about Consuela, a friend of Maria's who was Richard's steady date when he was in Cuba. Axel had mentioned the girls in his notes. In his opinion, they were hoping to get pregnant and get a free ride back to the USA. He also warned me that most women Cuba were "poxed up to their ears."

Richard was cleaning up, getting ready to go ashore. He had been on duty all afternoon, hooking up the ship to the refinery storage tanks, helping the sweating seamen cursing and moaning slipping and sliding across the molasses covered steel decks. Everything was hot and sticky, and the nauseating stench of the hot blackstrap molasses turned the ship into a sweltering steam bath from which there was no escape.

Glancing through my porthole, I saw more freshly-showered seamen, slicked up in their best clothes, hurrying down the gangplank waving at the crowd of whores, pimps and traders eagerly waiting to fleece them of their hard-earned money as soon as they set foot on Cuban soil. Not one of them even looked at the notice board posted at the top of the gangplank forbidding anyone to go ashore. Axel had warned me about the various venereal diseases I would be expected to treat, so I already knew the various fringe benefits acquired from cavorting with the dockside *putas.*

I would have been quite content merely to take photographs of the local scenery had not Richard been so determined to get me a date with Consuela. On his first visit to Cuba he had been introduced to Consuela and Maria who worked as secretaries in the refinery office. They not only spoke English, they also knew the exact time we would arrive, and were always ready and waiting for Richard to take them out for dinner. Naturally, Richard appreciated the fact they didn't make a living satisfying the sexual desires of randy seamen, and consequently appreciated their company. Now he hoped I would take care of Consuela.

Having finally scrubbed off most of the embedded black treacle, Richard was drying off in our shared bathroom. "Have the girls contacted you yet?" he asked.

"Yes they did. A young boy delivered a note while you were in the shower, and I gave him my last bottle of Coca-Cola. The girls will be waiting at Pietro's at five o'clock."

"Okay, I'll be ready. This goddamn humidity, I never stop sweating. I sure need another drink. It's a pity to waste these," he replied, entering my cabin, rattling the ice cubes in his empty glass.

While I was fixing us both another rum and Coca-Cola, Richard stood in front of the Sears & Roebuck electric fan that Axel kindly left for me and tried to cool off. "I'll buy one of these fans when I get a chance. Fuck it. This shirt's too loose, and the pants are too tight," he groaned, struggling with his zipper. "Hopefully I'll be stripping all this off very soon. We usually go to a small hotel after dinner. Is that okay?"

"Are you sure these girls are okay? No venereal diseases?" I asked.

"They're not whores. They work in the refinery office," replied Richard, admiring himself in the mirror. "I've never caught anything from Maria. I suppose Axel warned you about them. That faggot."

"I've seen the medical log book for penicillin injections after a visit to Cuba. It's full of names."

"Okay. Okay, don't fuck Consuela if you're scared, I'll take care of her as well." Richard glanced out of the porthole. "Half the crew have already gone to the whorehouse, so you'll have plenty of customers on the way back to Philly. And I think Berners was full of shit about this revolution. It was just a scare tactic."

I handed Richard a tall rum and Coca-Cola while he continued to cool off in front of the fan. "Thanks, Sparks. So, what do you say? Do you want to take Consuela back to the hotel?"

"I don't know. I haven't even met her." I opened the cabin door and groaned as the humid air hit me like a stinking wet blanket. "I sure as hell don't want to come back here right away and I'm taking my camera with me."

Twenty minutes later we were picking our way down the slippery gangplank to a waiting taxi. Stepping foot on Cuban soil for the first time was no thrill, especially if what Berners had said was true. The taxi driver stood patiently beside his old blue and white Chevy. Richard had been with him before, but it was still necessary to negotiate how we were to pay for the trip. Apparently, the Cuban paper money was useless, and he didn't really want American dollars.

"How about these?" asked Richard, holding up three packs of Lucky Strikes. The taxi driver grinned. The deal was made, and we were soon rattling along the deserted streets to Pietro's.

If any decor could be described as Spanish-Victorian, Pietro's was it: faded red plush velvet covered booths and well-worn mahogany tables; ornate brass wall sconces hung with dusty crystals; and from the high ceilings, a dozen or so ancient brass and crystal chandeliers tinkled in the evening breeze whenever anyone entered the restaurant.

Maria and Consuela were waiting for us in the deserted foyer. Maria had squeezed her overripe figure into a silk, turquoise colored dress, while Consuela was dressed in a dark green satin outfit. Like most Latino girls, they had raven black hair, sparkling brown eyes, pearly white teeth, full, salacious lips, and they never stopped talking.

Squealing with delight when we entered the foyer, Maria immediately threw her arms around Richard's neck and showered him with kisses, briefly tearing herself away to twirl around and show off the dress he had bought for her in Philadelphia. "How you like?" she yelled. "It is beautiful, yes?"

"It looks great on you," agreed Richard, a little embarrassed by her enthusiastic welcome. If Maria had known that Richard seduced the salesgirl in the Philadelphia dress shop and spent half the night in her bed, she would have torn the dress to shreds. Seconds later she was all over him again, kissing his grinning face while Consuela and I watched the passionate pair with amusement. When the two lovers finally pulled themselves apart, Richard introduced me to Consuela. We smiled at each other and politely shook hands, much to Richard's amusement.

The restaurant was almost deserted. The comfortable old booths at the back of the room, probably reserved for the affluent businessmen and their dates, were all empty. The maitre d' smiled and escorted us to the best table in the main dining room. I ordered my favorite aperitif, a vodka martini, while Richard selected a bottle of wine. He sniffed the contents of the glass like a connoisseur much to the amusement of his date. The girls had so much to say, but they both spoke at the same time and very little information was gleaned from their incessant chatter. Thankfully, when the steaks arrived, we wasted no more time with small talk and concentrated eating the best meal I'd had since we left Philadelphia.

Having been so preoccupied devouring the steaks and listening to the girls telling us all the news, we hadn't noticed the waiters were unusually nervous. We had heard the distant rattle of machine guns all day, but Richard and I didn't think the clash between Castro's rebels and Batista's troops taking place in the hills was our concern and therefore tried to ignore it. We continued to eat and enjoy our steaks and wanted to order a second bottle of wine, but Maria and Consuela were getting very worried and chatted away nervously in Spanish.

"You promised to speak English," I reminded them. "What are you worried about?"

"The Fidelistas, they're getting closer," replied Consuela. "Can't you hear their machine guns?"

"We'd better leave," suggested Maria. Go back to my place. It is safe, and we have food there."

"Do we have to leave now?" I asked, staring at the better half of my steak. The loud rattle of a machine gun made me jump. Richard was more than willing to leave and looked around for our waiter, but the restaurant was deserted.

Consuela grabbed my arm. "We must go," she shouted. Reluctantly I left the table, and we followed Maria and Richard out into the street. The loud crackle of a machine gun and the splatter of bullets all around us jolted me into reality. Consuela no longer had to drag me. I followed very willingly along the now deserted side streets.

"The bastards are everywhere," shouted Richard. "Maybe we should go back to the ship." A hail of bullets ricocheted around us, bouncing off the hard marble facade of the American Cuban Bank Building nearby. Instinctively, we dodged into the wide doorway, pressing ourselves against the shabby marble wall. Strangely enough I wasn't scared. It wasn't my battle, so why should I be involved? A window shattered above our heads, showering us with glass, making it very obvious I was indeed very much involved.

"They're probably after the money in this bank," yelled Richard. "That's what they want, and we're squatting right in the middle of it. Let's get the hell out of here." How many times had I heard that expression in American films? Now, I was doing just that, literally running for my life along debris strewn pavement with a hail of bullets following close on my heels. The street lights were out, but a few shop windows lit up the empty sidewalks. Maria, who was leading the way, darted into a side street, down some slippery stone steps, and into a dark alley. Blindly we followed her, Consuela cursing and swearing in Spanish trying to avoid stepping on the broken glass that littered the pavement.

The crackle of the machine guns became muffled, and bullets no longer spattered around us. We slowed down to a walk, trying to catch our breath, but Maria still urged us on, grabbing Richard's hand and dragging him along with her. Stopping for a second outside a shattered wine shop,

Richard nonchalantly reached into the window and helped himself to a bottle of wine, miraculously still intact. He held it up gleefully. "Well, this is on the house, that's for sure," he shouted, dusting off the bottle. Maria momentarily smiled at her lover before she again set the pace for us all to follow.

After running and walking for what seemed an hour, we eventually arrived at a marina on the other side of town. The acrid stench of hot molasses was exchanged for that of decaying fish. The huge golden ball of the moon reflected in the dark water between the five or six broken-down wooden jetties jutting out into the marina like gnarled fingers on an old hand.

A dozen or so fishing boats creaked and moaned, bobbing up and down on the incoming tide, but except for the lapping of the water, it was unusually quiet. Why was the place deserted? The rich American yacht owners had wisely sailed back to the Florida Keys when Fidel Castro started his communistic chanting, leaving what they couldn't carry to the poor natives impatiently waiting to take over. With little or no maintenance, the once brightly-painted marina was now looking very dingy and neglected.

Maria's small wooden hut, originally a boathouse built on top of a wooden jetty at the end of the dock, appeared to be the only one that was inhabited. She unlocked the door and switched on a light. A naked bulb lit up the room. Richard and I glanced at each other, both wishing we had been able to go to the hotel. Even our cabins on the ship were more comfortable, but at least we were no longer dodging bullets.

Maria had covered the damp walls of her wooden hut with cheap, brightly colored bed-spreads, now flapping about in the breeze from the broken window. Strings of beaded curtains separating the hut into sections, rattled like castanets, and the floorboards creaked ominously whenever anyone moved. The place was sparsely furnished with two single beds; an old kitchen table and four chairs, and there was an ancient electric hotplate on a top of a cupboard near the kitchen sink. Maria had tried hard to add a little color to the drab interior by filling the room with cheap religious artifacts and plastic framed photographs of her family.

The pleasant sound of a wine cork being drawn out of a bottle relieved the tension. "Well, it's not Chateau Rothschild, but I'm sure it tastes all right," announced Richard, "and the price was right." He was an expert at uncorking bottles, just as he was at emptying them. He sniffed the contents for a few seconds. "It smells like Burgundy."

Maria soon put four glasses on the table, and Richard poured the wine. We all looked at each other and grinned. "To all of us," I said. "I reckon we did very well."

"And we're going to do a lot better," replied Richard, running his hand across Maria's generous buttocks. We clinked our glasses, sipped the warm red wine and were all very grateful to be alive.

Despite being chased half-way across town, the girls had clung tenaciously to the bag of toiletries Richard had given them in the restaurant. They now eagerly delved into the contents of the bags. Shrieking with delight, they were like two kids opening their presents on Christmas morning, sniffing the soap and filling the air with the sticky smell of hair spray.

"You two would go hog wild in a Thrifty Drug Store," observed Richard, watching Maria spray perfume between her breasts and wriggling them coquettishly in his face. Seconds later she squealed with delight when he pulled her to him and nuzzled his face in her bosom.

Consuela was obviously a little embarrassed by her friend's natural exuberance. She filled the table with plates of pink jumbo shrimp, black olives and crusty fresh bread, opened up more wine and refilled our glasses. Maria and Richard managed to disentangle themselves, and we all sat down at the table. "After all that running I'm hungry," admitted Richard, "and not just for food." Maria grinned, feeding him with the huge, tasty pink shrimp. It was obvious she was crazy in love, and seemingly ignored the reality of the situation. "I wonder if Castro's mob has attacked the ship," I asked.

"Then you all stay here," replied Maria. "I should like that."

"Stay in bed all day and screw our heads off," added Richard. "Yes, I'd like that as well. What do you say, Sparks?"

"Yes," I answered nervously, "Anyway, let's not worry about Castro and his mob tonight." Consuela and I smiled at each other as Richard and Maria toyed with each other's knees under the table. We enjoyed our wine and agreed it had been an incredible evening. We were lucky to be alive.

A few minutes later it irked me to see the girls kneeling in front of a small makeshift altar covered with a tawdry display of religious ornaments, lighting candles around a plastic figure of the Virgin Mary, chanting prayers and counting their rosary beads. When they had finished praying, they lifted a loose floorboard and pissed like two desperate racehorses into the sea.

"Well that's one way to go," whispered Richard. "Remind me not to go swimming around here."

As usual, Richard was the first to take off his clothes, not in the least embarrassed to parade around almost naked. He topped off two glasses with wine and followed Maria into her little bedroom. "Goodnight, you two," he said. "Don't do anything we wouldn't do." Consuela and I both laughed as we cleared off the table listening to the lovers wrestling on a very squeaky bed behind the beaded curtain.

It was now midnight, the end of a long and very exciting day. I was glad Consuela didn't expect such an energetic performance from me, especially after I had drunk almost a bottle of wine. We both lay back on the tiny bed listening to Richard and Maria's energetic lovemaking in the adjacent bed. Then, Consuela fell asleep.

Early the next morning, while everyone was sleeping, I dressed and went outside with my camera. The early morning sunlight was tinged with blue, giving a definitive sharpness to the distant hills. It was perfect lighting for color transparencies. I was not the only one up at dawn; the fishing boats had already sailed. There was only one left tied up in the marina.

Two old men on the upper deck glared at me, wondering who I was, then got back to work mending their nets. I walked to the end of the jetty, once the docking place for scores of ocean-going yachts, clicking away with my camera. I tried to visualize the scene when dozens of expensive yachts and their wealthy owners used the marina, providing plenty of much needed employment for the local inhabitants.

The FLORIDA YACHT CLUB, its name still prominent in fading blue and white letters on the huge building at the end of the jetty, dominated the scene, but the dingy paintwork and shattered windows now covered with rotting, brown burlap, soon dispelled any notion that the place was full of wealthy American yachtsman. About a dozen or so poorly-clad, but seemingly well-nourished children, were sitting on the wooden steps playing with small fiddler crabs, prodding them with sticks to make them run. The kids smiled at the sight of my camera, and grinned when I took their picture. They seemed quite contented and no longer had to worry about the yacht club security guards chasing them away.

At the end of the marina a group of fisherman, sorting their early morning catch into huge wicker baskets, scowled at me suspiciously when I took their photograph, but the women cleaning fish on the wooden benches, were delighted. Wrapped in old burlap sacks and wearing brightly colored headscarves, they stuck out their chests, and posed outrageously while degutting the fish. Shouting and laughing, they made more noise than the squawking seagulls swooping and diving all around them for the scraps of fish being tossed into the water. Where was the revolution here? Everything seemed so calm and peaceful. Had we really dodged a hail of machine gun bullets the previous evening?

We were a few miles away from the town, judging by the long walk to Maria's hut. I would have preferred to have shacked up at a small hotel near the restaurant, but Maria thought her place would be safer during the fighting, and obviously she had been right. The fishermen seemed unaffected by the civil war. The thieving rebel soldiers assumed they had nothing worth taking and quickly moved on in search of richer pickings.

Richard was still in bed watching the girls get ready for church when I got back to the hut. While Consuela poured me some coffee, Maria tried to coax Richard to get dressed, but it wasn't easy, especially when he kept dragging her back into bed. Eventually, when Richard realized that Maria was serious about going to church, he gave up teasing her and started to get dressed. Sprouting an early growth of beard, Richard and I splashed our faces in cold water at the sink, then very reluctantly agreed to escort the girls to church.

We all trooped along to the entrance of the Marina in search of a taxi. Maria and Consuela, their heads covered with black scarves and wearing their Sunday best for church, both tried to ignore the jeers of the other women walking alongside us.

"What are they saying?" I asked.

"They just jealous, that's all," replied Maria. "Jealous because I have my handsome Ricardo to make love to me."

"So, let's go back to your place and stay in bed all day," suggested Richard, slipping his arm around Maria's waist.

"We have to go to church first," she replied, grinning. "Look, here is a taxi."

I stared at the beaten up old Chevy parked at the end of the Marina. I'm sure the driver wasn't expecting any passengers; he was trying to find a gas station that still had some to sell. He leaned out of the window and asked how we were going to pay him. Maria and Consuela argued with him when he refused the wad of Cuban pesetas they offered him. "He is crazy," yelled Maria, waving a handful of well-worn notes. Richard took out some American dollars, but the driver wasn't interested.

"He knows you are American," explained Consuela. "He is asking for American cigarettes."

"That's all they want." Richard reluctantly offered him two packs of Lucky Strikes and the deal was made. Ignoring Maria's shower of abuse, the driver grinned and opened the doors for us.

The ride into town was bumpy, but certainly preferable to walking. The center of the town was almost deserted. Many of the shops and offices had shattered windows, and we all glared in horror at the smoldering skeleton of the small hotel where they usually stayed. Obviously there was a war going on, and we were in the middle of it. "Santa Maria," cried Consuela. "Our little hotel, it is no more."

"Jesus Christ, Sparks, we sure were lucky we didn't go there." The damage was much worse than we expected, and it was impossible to drive close to the church. Despite our loud objections, the driver dropped us off near the refinery entrance and took off like a bat out of hell.

"He is crazy," yelled Maria, as the cab sped off, leaving us in a cloud of choking exhaust.

"Let's hope the ship's okay. There doesn't seem to be any damage around here," said Richard, leading the way into the refinery.

Minutes later, we all breathed a sigh of relief when the ugly shape of the *Cuban Trader* came into view. For the first time I was pleased to see the ugly black tanker with its sticky black pipes hissing and gurgling alongside the jetty. Nevertheless, I did wonder if the extra money I was being paid was worth all the inconvenience. Perhaps I'd take a passenger ship next trip, visit all the exotic ports, get paid for attending the ship's dances and eat like a king, but I knew that was not practical. I needed the extra money to send home.

The girls felt guilty going on board the ship without first attending Mass, but like all good Catholics, they knew the Lord would forgive them under the circumstances.

Because Richard had already paid Herr Schmidt, the Second Mate, to take over his watch while he was ashore, he assumed he had nothing to do but eat breakfast and entertain Maria in his cabin.

My duties when we were in dock were relatively simple. I paid the crew their shore money, took care of any minor officials, and I was supposed to pay for the extra food items, such as fresh milk, fruit and vegetables that were bought from the dockside traders. But so far none of them had been on board. It was the first time I was really glad to be on board. The girls followed us back to our cabins, chattering away in Spanish. Apparently they were arguing about who was going to be first to use the shower and try out their all their new toiletries.

"We're still in time for breakfast," announced Richard. "I'm starving. I say we all go and eat." His suggestion was well received and we all trooped across the deck to the Officers' dining salon.

The smell of eggs and bacon, fresh coffee and toast welcomed us as we entered. There were already many Cuban officials in there, gorging themselves like a pack of hungry wolves taking full advantage of the ship's hospitality. "War or no war, these hungry buggers know where to find a free meal," I whispered to Richard.

"Yes, and it's the same old crowd scoffing away as usual," he replied. "I hope they've left something for us, the greedy bastards."

The clickety-click of the girl's high heels on the metal deck made all heads turn in our direction. As senior employees of the refinery, they, too, were allowed to eat in the Officers' dining salon, but nevertheless, they still blushed nervously as we escorted them to our table.

Captain Krause glowered at us when we walked in, which was only to be expected. A few minutes later he strode across to our table, and immediately ordered Richard to find out the temperature of the molasses being pumped on board. "The Second Mate will have that information, Sir," replied Richard. "I've paid him to take over my watch."

"I am ordering YOU to find out the temperature, and it's from YOU I expect an answer," snapped the Old Man, glaring at the two girls. "And these whores are not allowed on my ship. Herr Schparks, you will send them ashore now, that is an order." Without waiting for an answer, Krause turned his back on me and marched off across the salon muttering to himself in German.

"I'll get the son-of-a-bitch for that remark," cried Richard, thumping his fist on the table. "If only the bastard would go ashore."

"Him, go ashore? If he did, you'd have to stand in line. Everybody wants to stick their knife in him."

Steve, the Second Chef, nervously crossed the dining room to our table. "Am I glad to see you," he said, taking off his chef's white hat and running his hand through his fair hair. "We've had nothing but freeloaders in here," he continued, glancing at the girls. "Not you, of course. You're welcome and I'm very pleased to see you're all okay, I mean after all the fighting last night."

"No kidding. They attacked the restaurant and started spraying us with machine gun fire. We all ran across town to Maria's place," explained Richard. "Did they come on board the ship?"

"Not that I know of," replied Steve. "Everyone was in the whorehouse."

"Obviously it's the safest place in town. Soldiers don't attack whorehouses," I replied. "Do you still have any eggs and bacon left? We're all starving."

"Of course, I've got the best Canadian bacon for you lot, and I'll make some fresh coffee."

Thirty minutes later we had finished our much appreciated breakfast. Richard then went to find Schmidt, the Second Mate, and the girls went back to Richard's cabin to enjoy the luxury of a hot shower. My immediate problem was to make sure there was still cash on board to pay for the molasses. As I unlocked the office door, I silently thanked Berners for insisting the money be kept in the office safe, hidden at the back of the supply cupboard.

Ludwig Berners was well aware the Old Man usually got drunk while in port, and was therefore not to be trusted.

I closed and locked the office door behind me, then opened the safe. It was all there, fifty thousand dollars in new bills, neatly stacked in the drawer, but would the rebels accept American money? I had heard rumors that other ships were trading in Swiss gold francs. If that was true, it was going to cause a lot of headaches back in Philadelphia.

After locking up the safe, I went to my cabin. Consuela had finished her shower and, wrapped in my tattered old blue terry-towel robe, she was drying her hair in front of the electric fan, combing her lustrous black tresses back into shape. She was a beautiful woman and deserved a lot better than a wandering sailor who had no intention of getting married.

Fixing me a rum and Coca-Cola, Consuela grinned when she plopped in two ice cubes. "You're so kind to let me use your shower," she said, handing me the drink, "and your soap and shampoo, everything."

"You know you're very welcome." I lay on the bunk appreciating the blast of cool air from my noisy fan.

I already anticipated Consuela's next question. "You will be here again in two weeks, Roger?

"I expect so, if the refinery is still operating." My answer brought a smile to Consuela's face. She had beautiful dusky skin, long silky eyelashes and sparkling, dark eyes that were usually smiling. She was a natural beauty and didn't need all the all makeup she was about to put on.

"Rogera, I not look so good without my makeup," she said, combing out her long black hair into a ponytail and fastening it with a bright blue headband. "Gracias for all the talcum and face cream. It is most welcome. Rogera, close your eyes and rest."

"Rest? I'm gonna have a shower." I left Consuela making herself more beautiful and stepped into the shower. Wallowing in the warm water, I felt sorry for the two girls. We all knew the leisurely trips to and from Cuba were about to end. If the Philadelphia office didn't cancel the deal with the sugar refinery, the Communist revolutionaries would. They hated everything American, even the almighty dollar.

~~~

CHAPTER FIVE

Hostages

Consuela and I were reading some American magazines when Maria came into my cabin through the inter-connecting bathroom. She had a tray of coffee and toast. She looked comfortable wearing Richard's old white terry-towel robe and leather slippers. "Ricardo says we all go to Mass," she announced. "That is okay? You will go with us?"

Consuela and I were surprised by the request, but reluctantly agreed to go with them. It was my guess that Maria had refused Richard's request for another round of sex until she had cleansed her soul. She grinned at us, then returned to Richard's cabin. Within minutes I could hear them both wallowing in the shower together.

We all agreed to leave the girls at the church while Richard and I had a quick tour of the town to access the damage. Afterwards we would all spend the rest of the day relaxing on the ship. I knew this was a compromise between Maria's need to satisfy her religious beliefs, and Richard's need to satisfy his sexual ones.

Herr Schmidt, the Second Officer, had agreed to take over Richard's job of checking the cargo, and watched us enviously as we all skittered down the gangplank to the waiting taxi. Cuban taxi drivers preferred Lucky Strikes cigarettes as payment for the fare so Richard handed the driver three packs in exchange for a ride into town. The streets were littered with debris but the driver finally dropped us off outside a church swarming with women and children, but very few men. After promising to be back in an hour, Richard and I set off to see what had happened the night before.

Our first thought was Pietro's Restaurant, which was only a block away. During the short walk, we passed a lot of bullet scarred buildings, but were horrified to see our favorite restaurant had also been partially destroyed by a fire. The windows were shattered. The once elegant furnishings were charred and covered with debris, and the only signs of life were a few scavengers picking through the remnants of food left in the burned-out kitchen.

"My God, Sparks, I'm so glad we got out of there in a hurry," observed Richard.

"That's the end of the steak dinners, and I never even got to finish mine," I replied, crossing the street to take a photograph of the damage. It certainly made a very distressing picture, but nevertheless represented the truth about the revolution. What was the point of destroying one of the finest restaurants in town just because it had catered to wealthy tourists?

Suddenly the screech of tires close by made me shudder. Four uniformed soldiers, armed with rifles, jumped out of an old army jeep, raced across the street, grabbed my camera and forced me into the back of their truck. A fat, stinking slob, brandishing a pistol, jumped in beside me, squatting on my face. I could hear Richard shouting across the street. Seconds later, he was literally tossed into the back beside me. Because he had resisted arrest, they had clobbered him over the head with a rifle and tied him up like a young bull at a rodeo, roping his wrists to his ankles. We were then pushed into the corner of the truck and covered over with a filthy army blanket. As we rattled along the bumpy streets, Richard continued to yell in agony as the ropes tore into his flesh.

After a long and painful ride, we finally screeched to a halt outside the police headquarters on the edge of town. I was literally dragged from the truck. My arm was forced painfully behind my back, and I was hustled across the deserted street into the courtyard of the building. "What have we done?" I yelled, scared to death they would break my arm.

Laughing and jeering, the soldiers hustled me inside the once magnificent marble-tiled building. I could hear Richard yelling in pain as he was dragged up the steps of the entrance. We were dumped in a corner piled high with sacks of garbage. Our captors gathered around the front desk arguing amongst themselves until an officer appeared. The only difference between him and his men was his bottle-green uniform. It was a little cleaner.

Gleefully, the soldiers pointed to us crouched painfully in the corner. Grinning like a deranged idiot, the officer swaggered across the courtyard to see what his henchman had dragged in. "You were taking photographs for the American papers," he snapped. "You are Yankee spies and will be shot."

'We are not spies," I shouted. "We are officers from the *Cuban Trader*."

"Then why you take photograph, for the Yankee newspapers, yes?"

"Of course not, I was . . ."

"Shut up! I say you are spies," yelled the Officer.

"Undo this fucking rope," groaned Richard. The officer stared at us for a few seconds, and then barked some orders in Spanish before swaggering back across the dusty courtyard to his office. Seconds later, two of his cronies untied our ropes and dragged us to our feet.

Ignoring our demands for an explanation, they pushed and shoved us across the yard toward a row of cells which formed a semi-circle around what once had been a decorative marble pool and fountain. One of the guards dragged open the squeaky iron-barred door of a small cell, pushed us inside and locked the door. He then made double sure we would not escape by wrapping a hefty steel chain around the bars and securing it with a padlock the size of his hand.

"What the hell have we done?" yelled Richard, obviously wasting his breath. The guards ignored our protests and trundled off across the sun scorched courtyard, disappearing into the main building. To them, it appeared a routine chore, like they had just delivered two sacks of flour.

An open sewer ran through the back of the small cell, transporting the filth from the other cells to some distant cesspool. The overpowering stench, and the millions of flies, forced us to stick our noses through the rusty iron bars to breathe the dusty air outside which smelled a bit fresher.

We could see the cells were built in a semi-circle around a group of stumpy palm trees in the center of the yard, so our fellow prisoners had watched our arrival. Many of them rattled the iron bars of their cells, screaming and shouting in Spanish, sticking their hands through the bars and making rude gestures at the departing soldiers.

Our cell was no larger than my cabin. The dirty grey concrete blocks were covered with Spanish worded graffiti scratched onto the bare wall. Apart from two wooden bunks screwed to the floor, the cell was empty, except for the millions of flies buzzing around the slowly moving stream carrying the effluent from the adjacent cells to some distant sewer..

Richard sat down on the bunk and examined his bloody wrists and ankles. "Those bastards," he said. "What the hell did we do, Sparks?"

"Maybe they really think we're spies. They took my camera."

"That means we'll get shot at dawn, right?"

"I doubt it. They'll try to get the Old Man to bail us out. Maybe fine us a couple of hundred bucks."

"A couple of hundred bucks," yelled Richard. "What the hell for?"

"For the Chief of Police, I expect. It's ransom money." I sat on the hard bunk and stared at Richard. The blood from his head wound had now dried onto his left ear. His normally fair hair was matted together with blood and gore and looked like an ill-fitting brown toupee. "We'll just have to wait until they contact the Old Man and get him to pay the ransom."

"Fat chance. That bastard will laugh his head off. We'll be shot at dawn," groaned Richard, painfully trying to lie back on the bunk.

At midday, a small platoon of soldiers entered the courtyard waving their rifles and laughing like drunken idiots. They opened up some cells, dragged out about a dozen screaming prisoners and tied them to the clump of palm trees in the center of the yard. Laughing like drunken idiots, the soldiers ripped off what was left of the prisoner's clothes then beat them with palm fronds until their backs were raw and bleeding.

"Look at them," yelled Richard. "They're beating the poor bastards to death." My stomach churned over and I felt sick. Richard began rattling the cell bars like all the other prisoners, yelling and shouting, but the flogging continued. Two or three of the guards took off their pants, showing off their erect penises, laughing like drunken idiots before sodomizing the younger prisoners.

"Jesus Christ!" screamed Richard. "They're raping the poor bastards." He continued rattling the cell bars and screaming at the guards until he was exhausted.

"Richard, it's no use! The guards are drunk," I yelled. "For crissake stop screaming at them, or you'll be next." I realized then we should have obeyed Berners' orders and stayed on board. What idiots we were going back into town to photograph the damage. I hoped I was right in assuming we were being ransomed, and whoever had captured us was going to see Krause to collect the reward.

Richard still clung to the cell bars watching the slaughter. The soldiers stood back, laughing and swearing as they surveyed the heap of bleeding prisoners. Then one by one they loaded their rifles and took aim at the writhing mass of humanity, the finale of their day's sport.

"GOOD GOD, NO!" screamed Richard, rattling the iron bars. "They're going to shoot them." Suddenly the air exploded with the sound of rifle fire, the helpless prisoners were being used as target practice, their heads, arms and legs were literally ripped apart by the exploding bullets. We stared at each other in horror unable to comprehend what we had both seen.

"Murderers," screamed Richard as he joined the chorus of protests from the adjacent cells. He rattled the rusty iron bars of the cell until his hands bled, then walked like a zombie back to the wooden bunk. "That's not for us," he said, his face drained of all color. "They won't shoot us, will they?"

We lay back on our wooden bunks, staring at the filthy black ceiling until the gut-wrenching scream of a prisoner being tortured in an adjacent cell brought us back to reality. "You bastards," yelled Richard, again joining all the other prisoners rattling their cages and screaming until the hideous screams of the tortured prisoner suddenly stopped. Had the guards beaten him unconscious? Or worse, beaten him to death? Never before had I heard the horrendous sound of anyone being tortured. The blood-curdling screams made me sick to my stomach. I felt physically ill.

Slowly Richard returned to his bunk and lay down staring at the filthy concrete ceiling. I could hear him sobbing quietly. We both shared the same thoughts. *Were we going to be next?* "They're not going to shoot us, Sparks, surely not us."

"Of course not, we're being held for ransom. It's the way those bastards make their money. I wonder if they've sent anyone to see the Old Man yet." I replied, trying to be practical.

"Do you think he'll give a shit? He'll laugh his fucking head off," replied Richard. "They didn't even get our names. They don't know who we are, or care. They're sadists, all of them. It's like a sport, a game of rape and torture. Human target practice, shooting off their hands and legs and laughing when their guts exploded! And did you notice the prisoners were wearing the same uniform as the guards? What the hell's going on? They're shooting their own men!"

"Maybe they were deserters," I replied. "The poor devils don't know which side to be on."

"I hope they were deserters. I sure as hell don't want to wind up like that." Richard continued to stare at the wall. "It was unbelievable. Some of the poor bastards were still alive when the guards cut the rings and watches off their hands and wrists. Jesus, it's just unbelievable doing that to their own soldiers."

We lay back on our bunks and stared vacantly at the ceiling. I could hear Richard as he started sobbing again, asking me for reassurance that we would not have to face the same firing squad.

About an hour after the executions, some peasants entered the yard with a donkey cart, loaded up the carnage and took the bloody mess away. They were followed by two guards trundling a small hand cart containing a huge steaming cauldron. "It's feeding time. They're bringing around some stew, I said."

"They can shove it," groaned Richard.

The prisoners gathered around their cell doors making rude comments as the guards dipped their pots and pans into the steaming cauldron and deliberately placed them on the ground just out of the prisoners' reach. Eventually, the guards stopped outside our cage. One of them was about forty, unshaven, and wearing the filthiest green uniform of them all. He was probably the *chef de cuisine*, judging by the gobs of dried stew clinging to his ragged leather apron.

"*Comidas,*" he said, grinning, showing off his rotting teeth. He filled two metal pans with stew and left them outside the bars. "*Vino? Quisieras compeer algo de vino rojo?*"

"He wants to know if we want to buy some red wine."

"Our last drink before being shot," groaned Richard.

"Yes, Si..." I fumbled in my shirt pocket and held up two dollar bills. The guard shook his head. "*Yo no quiero dinaro Americano, solamente cigarros?*"

"The bastard," yelled Richard. "He knows they took all our cigarettes when they dragged us in. He's probably pissed in it. Tell him to go and fuck himself."

"*Tu me pages cinco paquetes de Lucky Strikes,*" repeated the guard, holding up a jug and pouring a few drops into the stew. "*Vino rojo.*"

I shook my head, and waved the two dollars. "*No cigarros, solamente dinaro Americano.*"

"Vete ala chingada," yelled the guard, angrily kicking over one of the pots of stew as he trundled away. *"Vete ala chingada."* His companion, a much older man, grabbed the jug and came back to the cell. I handed him the two dollars and he gave me the jug of red wine.

"He's probably pissed in it," observed Richard, sniffing the contents. "You can take the first sip."

"With my dinner," I replied, as I fell on my knees and reached through the bars for the fly covered pot of stew.

"Don't bother," mumbled Richard, "they've probably shit in that." The stew smelled rotten and attracted the flies, but the jug of red wine was welcome. Piss or no piss, we passed the jug back and forth, and agreed it tasted like vinegar, but it was all we had to drink. Eventually, we emptied the jug.

Although we were both hungry, we ignored the filthy smelling stew and left it by the door. "So you reckon we're being held until the Old Man bails us out," surmised Richard, handing me the empty jug. "That means until Hell freezes over."

We concluded that, just like hundreds of other foreigners, we were taken prisoner and held for ransom. The taxi driver had no doubt told the soldiers we were good prospects, and our wallets, which they had taken, must have proved it. Hopefully our captors had already contacted the ship demanding a few hundred dollars for our release. It was now up to Captain Krause to pay over the cash. "The son-of-a-bitch won't do it," concluded Richard. "He hates our guts."

"I know he does, but according to International Maritime Law, he's not allowed to sail without a Radio Officer," I replied, confidently.

"Yes, but how about a Third Mate?"

"A Third Mate, I don't know." That was a debatable point. I had sailed on ships with only two deck officers, with the Captain taking over the third watch. But Richard couldn't think of any ship he'd been on that didn't have a Radio Officer. International Maritime Law was very strict about safety at sea, and Radio Officers were compulsory.

"What are you thinking about, Sparks?" sighed Richard, trying to make himself comfortable on the wooden bunk. I'm thinking we'll never get out of here."

"Of course we will. The Old Man will pay up, he has to. Don't think about this place, Richard, think about your home."

"Home. To think, I left home to find some excitement, but not like this. How about you? Why did you leave home?"

"I want to make some money, lots of it."

"Why? What are you going to spend it on?"

"I want to buy a piece of land in Gloucestershire. My parents have a small horse sanctuary."

"A what?"

"It's a kind of horse ranch. It's a place where old and mistreated horses are taken to spend the rest of their lives in comfortable surroundings."

"I thought they were shot and used for dog meat."

"Not if my father can help it. He loves horses, we all do." My thoughts went back to the horses we had rescued back home. They were now all well fed and contented and grazing in the beautiful countryside. "We have about twelve at the moment, and some pit ponies."

"Pit ponies?"

"They're small ponies that were used to haul trucks inside a coal mine. They lived all their lives underground, now they can run around in a huge green field and eat fresh green grass every day and have a warm stable to sleep in," I explained.

"Your folks must be good people," observed Richard, "I mean, looking after the horses like that. I'd like to meet them. If we ever get out of here."

"We'll get out of here, don't worry. And you'll get a very warm welcome from my folks if you came back home with me." I envisaged Richard and I being met at the train station and driven back home in my Dad's ancient Bentley. "Have you ever had much to do with horses?"

"Years ago I had to ride one in a movie my father was making, but I fell off because the saddle was loose, and nearly broke my leg," explained Richard. "So that was it. I made up my mind it was safer to ride on top of a woman. But now, with all these bitches chasing me with their paternity suits, I'm not so sure."

We both lay on the wooden bunks thinking our own thoughts. I was remembering the rolling green countryside surrounding the village of Prestbury where I was born. There was a famous race course there, and my Grandfather owned a racing stable. All my life I had been used to caring for horses.

"Jesus, what a life," concluded Richard. "I can't help thinking about the pit ponies, spending all their lives down a coal mine."

"Not all their life, now they sleep in a warm stable and run around in beautiful green fields."

"Do your folks run this place on their own?"

"They get some financial help from a charity, and help from our neighbors. I also have a young sister she's fifteen and has already won some medals for riding."

"Good for her."

"But we need to buy more land, that's why I came back to sea, to save some money."

"Why, to look after more horses?"

84

"I suppose. It's a good feeling, but how about you? A famous Hollywood playboy."

"That's a joke," sighed Richard. "I'll tell you something, I'd rather be in the shit there than here in Cuba."

"In the shit? Are you running away from something?"

"I told you about the paternity suit. The bitch. She's shacked up with half the guys in Hollywood, but picked me as the father, because she's a two-bit actress and wants to get into movies."

"You may not be the father. What about a blood test? Why don't you have it done?"

Richard sighed. "Yeah, I thought about that, but what if they prove I am the father? Then what? That's not all. My parents are always at each other's throat. My mother spends my father's money like water because she knows he plays around. He bribes me with a new car each year to keep my mouth shut and she gives me a thousand bucks a month to spy on him and tell her what he was doing, and who he was doing it with. It was hell on earth. So I got out. I went to Seattle and worked on a ferry boat. It's beautiful up there. For two years I went back and forth on the ferry until I got my Third Mate's license, but my dick got me into trouble again. Too many girls jumping into my bed. Why can't they just enjoy good sex? Why do they always want to have kids and get married?"

"It's nature. A female seeks a suitable male to father her children and provide a cozy nest for them to live in. Apparently, they thought you were the ideal husband."

"Well, I'm not. I'm too young to settle down and have kids. I don't want to screw the same broad all the time. Marriage is not for me," concluded Richard, trying to get comfortable on the wooden bunk. "You know what, Sparks? That wine was crap, but it's making me sleepy."

"It was like vinegar, but if it makes you sleep, even on these hard bunks, then I wish we had some more." I rested my head on my jacket, and lay back on the bunk.

The jug of sour wine we shared had dulled our senses a little and taken away the sharp edge of reality. Escape, we concluded, was out of the question. It was possible we might die of a fever. The stench from the open sewer was unbearable. Fortunately, after a while the nose gets tired of complaining and shuts down its sense of smell. The flies were a different matter. They never gave up.

"Why do they settle on me instead of that big, juicy piece of crap over there?" queried Richard, staring vacantly at the effluent floating along our indoor cesspool.

"They're resting on you after they've trudged all over it. Anyway, perhaps you smell a little better."

"Sparks, I swear to God, if you weren't here, I'd go berserk. I'd be screaming and raving like those other poor bastards."

"And you know what? If you weren't with me, I wouldn't be in this bloody mess. It was you who wanted to take the girls to the church. God knows why. You already had your farewell fuck. We could have just as easily waved them goodbye from the deck of the ship."

"Asshole."

"Kiss it."

"You know, Sparks, for a goddamn Limey, you know all the American expressions."

"Yeah, unfortunately, I have a very good teacher."

We lay on our wooden bunks and stared up at the filthy ceiling. "Listen, I can hear keys rattling, someone is coming," said Richard, as he got off his bunk. "I think we have a visitor."

We went to the cell door as the guard arrived and wrestled with the lock and chain. The loud screams from someone being dragged across the courtyard made my blood curdle. Seconds later, our cage door was pushed open, and whomever the guard was dragging along behind him was tossed into our cell, and the iron door clanged shut.

"Queremos hablar con el agente!" I shouted at the guard.

"We want to talk to the officer in charge," repeated Richard, rattling the cell door. "You son-of-a-bitch. You bastard. You ugly looking fucking swine." We watched the two guards shuffle across the courtyard laughing and talking, until they disappeared out of sight. "The bastards don't give a shit, Sparks."

Our new cell mate was moaning and groaning on the floor, his hands and feet tied together with a thin rope. His bright green shirt and jeans were all torn and spattered with blood. His feet were bare, covered with blood and dust, and his young face was sweating and contorted with pain.

As soon as we freed him, his eyes blazed like a madman. He started screaming at the top of his lungs, tearing at the bars until his hands were raw and bleeding. The other prisoners joined in and soon the courtyard reverberated in a cacophony of human misery as everyone gave vent to their angry feelings. We knew it was a waste of time.

After five minutes of literally climbing the walls, exhausted and no longer able to speak, the young Cuban collapsed onto the stone floor and passed out. Richard cautiously approached the unconscious form on the floor. "The bastard's still breathing."

"Leave him sleep. It looks as if he's been beaten up and he's only a teenager. I wonder what he's done. Why did they bring him in here when there are so many empty cells?"

~~~

CHAPTER SIX

A New Cellmate

My question was answered in the morning, when our new cellmate finally woke up. He was no more than sixteen, spoke English and could translate for us. His name was Juan. We assumed he was a young pimp who had been dragged off the streets to spy on us. At first, he was nervous, clinging to the cell bars, and staring at us with frightened eyes, answering our questions in one or two words. After a while, when he realized we were off a ship and there was a chance for him to make some money, his attitude toward us rapidly changed. He relaxed and sat next to Richard on the wooden bunk.

"You tell the guards we want to get the hell out of here," said Richard. "Otherwise, I will tell my friend, the President of the United States to send a battalion of troops and use these bastards for ass paper."

"Ugh!" jeered Juan. "They tell you to go fuck yourself." He picked up the pan of stew that we had left the previous evening. I watched him brushing away the flies and cautiously sniffing it. Was he really going to eat it?

"Richard for crissake, let's not confuse this poor guy any more than he already is," I said. "We need his help, okay?"

"Okay. Listen my friend, we want to get out of here," continued Richard, trying to be patient. "How much do we have to bribe these bastards?"

"Cuanto cuesta eso?" I repeated, frowning at Richard.

"The Batistianos make you pay as much as they can get, and if you from a ship, they make you pay more," replied Juan, obviously more relaxed.

"Goddamn it, what is this?" shouted Richard, losing his temper and banging his fist on the bunk. "You mean they have a sliding scale of charges?"

"Richard, take it easy. Yes, Juan, we are from a ship. I am the Radio Officer and he is the Third Mate. We are from the *Cuban Trader* docked at the refinery."

Juan grinned, again sniffing the stew. "Why you not eat this?"

"Because it looks like, and smells like shit," snapped Richard.

"Ah, you Americano, that is not good," sneered Juan, his mouth now full stew. "They no like Americano."

"Tell me. What else is new? Sparks, this asshole is just here for laughs," Richard said, again banging his fist on the bunk, "except I'm not laughing."

I could see Richard was about to explode into one of his famous tempers and tried to keep him calm. "Juan, we want to know what it will cost to get us out of here? *Cuanto dollars?*"

"So you pay in American dollars? They no like American dollars." Juan scraped around the pan with his fingers and licked them clean.

"I have about two thousand American cigarettes," offered Richard.

"Cartons?" questioned Juan, obviously impressed.

"Jesus Christ! I'm not a wholesaler, just ten cartons and that's it."

"And you?" Juan stared at me waiting for an answer.

"I don't smoke. I don't have cigarettes. I have a case of English Beefeater gin and also some Scotch, and about two cases of Coca-Cola."

"You've got two cases of Coca-Cola, Sparks, and you bitched and moaned about me using your last bottle of Coca-Cola?"

"The Chief of Police he will like your English gin, and your Scotch, and he will fine you about a thousand American dollars each. Can you pay that?"

"A thousand bucks, for doing what?" questioned Richard. "Jesus Christ."

I frowned at Richard, trying to calm him down. "Richard, take it easy. We want to get out of here. Okay, Juan, the ship will pay our fine. Tell the Chief of Police to go to the ship's captain."

"He knows what to do. He do this many times. You have cigarette for me?" asked Juan, making himself more comfortable on the wooden bunk.

"No, we have no cigarettes. Those bastards out there took the lot," replied Richard, angrily. "Anyway, how the hell do you know all this shit about fines? You know an awful lot for a pimp."

"A pimp?" snorted Juan, angrily glaring at Richard. "I am no pimp. My sister, she is Chief of Police girl. She sleeps with him," bragged Juan, proudly.

"Bullshit," scoffed Richard, suppressing a laugh. "If your sister shacks up with that bastard, why did they throw you in here? What did she do, give him a dose of clap?"

"You no talk about my sister like that," yelled Juan, thumping the wooden bunk. "My sister, she sleep with Police Capitan many times."

"It only takes once to give him a dose of clap," sneered Richard. "Believe me, I should know."

I scowled at Richard trying to warn him to cool it. "Okay, Juan. Rattle this cage and tell the guards the Captain of the *Cuban Trader* will pay the ransom. He has the money on board, and tell them to hurry before we die of fever."

"What about me?" asked Juan.

"What about you?" replied Richard, angrily.

"What do I get?"

"A fucking kick in the ass," snapped Richard, getting off the bunk.

"Richard, for crissake, calm down. We're in no position to bargain or kick asses. Juan, what do you want?" I asked, wondering how often he did this type of bargaining.

Juan grinned, looking us over, mentally figuring out what we were worth. "Ten cartons of Lucky Strikes."

"Ten cartons just for talking to the guards for us," argued Richard. "I'll give you two."

"Ten cartons," insisted Juan.

"You sniveling little bastard," growled Richard.

"It's a deal," I replied, interrupting another of Richard's outbursts. "Ten cartons as soon as we're back on the ship. Now you talk to the guards, deliver us to the ship, and you can have the cigarettes. Now start rattling this cage and call the guard."

Five hours had elapsed since Juan had gone with the guard to discuss our release terms. During that time, I had managed to get some sleep, but had been awakened at sunset by the noise of rifle shots, and again we witnessed the slaughter of ten more prisoners. Richard, who drank more than his share of the second jug of wine they sold us, slept through all the noise of the executions.

We were both wide awake, however, when Juan was dragged across the courtyard and thrown back into the cell. "Your Capitan, he is a bastardo," yelled Juan. "He no pay to get you out of here. He no pay, he is a bastardo."

Richard and I stared at each other in disbelief. "He can't do that," I said. "It's against International Maritime Law to sail without a Radio Officer on board."

"Sparks, I know that. You know that. It's Krause – he doesn't give a shit," replied Richard, returning to his bunk. "What the hell did the Captain say?"

"He was drunk. He say you sex maniacs, and he sent me off the ship," groaned Juan. "He is a bastardo."

"Did you tell the Captain we were the Sparks and the Third Mate like we told you to?" I asked, wishing I could have written it down.

"I tell him many times, but he drunk," replied Juan. "Now they shoot you. You are American bastards and the guards will shoot you."

"They're not going to shoot us, they want their money, the ransom money," argued Richard, trying to keep his cool. I know he must have felt like me, sick to the stomach with fear.

"Krause is bluffing," I said, thinking aloud. "He's tormenting us. He'll never leave port without his precious radar set switched on, and he needs me to set that up."

Sparks, I know that," sighed Richard, as he stared out across the dusty courtyard. "What in the hell are we going to do?"

"All we can do is wait," I replied, trying not to show how low I was feeling. "The Old Man will have to pay the fine. He daren't show up in Philly without us."

"Sparks, we both know the son-of-a-bitch is insane, he's likely to do anything." Richard paced back and forth across the cell. "You know he hates our guts, he won't pass up this chance to get rid of us."

I lay on the bunk and stared at the ceiling. Never in my life had I felt so scared and helpless, and I didn't need Richard to remind that we were at the mercy of a madman.

Juan curled up in the corner and fell asleep, a small, empty bottle of rum rolled out of his pocket across the stone floor.

A lot more pieces of shit had floated through the open cesspool since we were last visited by the guard. I was very worried about Richard, who seemed mesmerized by the sewer and the stinking effluent floating by. He periodically gave me a detailed account of what was happening in a detached voice that didn't even sound like him. Then he started talking about England. "I'd like to see all those horses you've got Sparks, and all the pit ponies. Do they have names?"

"Yes, my sister has given them all names. Mister Lee is the oldest one. He is a famous racehorse, came second in the Cheltenham Gold Cup. And Anne Louise, she is a beautiful chestnut mare. She was..."

"Look, there's another piece of crap floating by," interrupted Richard. "Look at the flies on it, hundreds of flies."

"Richard, pull yourself together, they've executed ten more prisoners right in front of our eyes, and all you did was count the pieces of shit floating along that open sewer. Are you going crazy?"

"I am crazy Sparks," agreed Richard, now lying quietly on the bunk. "I don't think we're ever going to get out of this place. Look at him, he's crazy too."

We both glanced at Juan the pimp, now curled up like a ball, snoring away in the corner of the cell. We too should have been asleep. It was three o'clock in the morning. The air was cool and the only sound was the gentle ripple of our indoor stream. Even the flies were resting, but peaceful sleep was out of the question.

At seven the next morning, we were aroused by the sound of a tin can banging against our iron barred cell. The guard had brought us some coffee in dirty metal can and some hot water, leaving it as usual almost out of reach outside the bars on the ground. He then ordered Juan to accompany him. Juan's face broke into a smile and he needed no coaxing.

"What's happened?" I asked.

"They tell me I can go," replied Juan, laughing and talking to the guards in Spanish. "And you are an American bastard," he yelled at Richard "Fuck you."

"Juan. Juan, what's happened?" I yelled as he raced across the courtyard and disappeared through the door. The guard grinned and relocked our cage, winding the huge steel chain around the bars to make sure we couldn't get out.

"The little bastard, he could have told us what's going on."

Richard stared at the hot water and steaming can of coffee. "What do you suppose this means, Sparks?" He sniffed the coffee and winced. "I think they have pissed in this."

It was hot, it tasted like coffee, but more important the hot liquid penetrated our sour bellies and made us feel a little more human again. We drank what we could, splashed our faces in the hot water, and appreciated the fact we didn't have a mirror to see what we looked like. Something must have happened, or did they usually give condemned prisoners a chance to wash up before being shot?

A few minutes later, some guards a came along and unlocked the cell. They roughly tied our hands behind our backs, and ordered us to follow them. "Where are we going?" demanded Richard. "What the fuck is happening?"

We were pushed and shoved across the courtyard and into an office. Seated at the desk was a young, clean shaven officer. He grinned at us when Juan came out of an adjoining room looking a lot cleaner than when we first saw him. "It is him," he said, pointing at Richard. "He is a bastardo, an American bastardo."

"My little friend, Juan says you treated him like shit while I have been away," began the Officer. "I have also been treated like shit by you Americans. In Miami they put me in jail, and took turns fuck me, and then they send me back to Cuba."

"I'm sorry to hear that," I said. "I am English. Richard and I are Officers on the *Cuban Trader*."

"You are English?" replied the officer. "Now you work on an American ship. Why?"

"Because they pay more money, I am the Radio Officer, Richard is the Third."

"I know all about the ship at the refinery," interrupted the Officer, standing up. "Your Captain is German. A German bastard. You are all bastards, but you are the worst," he yelled, ordering the guards to take Richard into the next room.

"Now we all fuck you," jeered Juan. "We all fuck you." The guards grinned and shoved Richard into the next room.

"And you will watch them fuck your friend," sneered the Officer. "He is an Americano, they will like fucking him."

I was pushed into the adjoining room where Richard was already naked and lying face down spread eagled on a long sofa. He struggled furiously to no avail as the guards lashed his hands and feet firmly to the arm rests with rope. I turned away, but the guards forced me to watch.

Juan grinned and hurriedly removed his shirt and pants. I hoped I wouldn't be next. Juan had a serious, determined expression on his face and seemed unaware of the onlookers. "Now, I fuck you, Americano," he said, climbing on top of Richard's back. The very sight of the violent sexuality caused me to shudder, not only for Richard, who was now helpless, but also for me, an unwilling participant in the rape of my best friend.

"Goddamn you," Richard shouted writhing in pain as Juan, energetically fucked him.

"I fuck the Americano bastard," yelled Juan, triumphantly. "I fuck the bastardo." I felt sick listening to Richard yelling out in pain until Juan had finished. "Buenos, that was good. I fuck him real good," bragged Juan, sliding off Richard's sweating body and wrapping himself in a filthy towel. "I fuck a Yankee virgin."

Two naked guards strode in from an adjoining room, seemingly appearing out of nowhere. They eagerly stepped forward and took turns shoving their rampant erections into Richard's face. "For you," they yelled. One of them clambered on top of Richard, grinning and laughing like a madman, eager to put on a good performance for his friends. "Americano, I fuck an Americano." His comrades gathered around, shouting encouragement, while masturbating into Richard agonized face. It was a vile disgusting orgy.

"Your friend, he like," the Officer boasted. "See how he moves his ass, he wants more. All my men wait to fuck him."

There was nothing I could do to help Richard, and I prayed to God I wouldn't be next. Unnoticed, I slipped into the adjoining room to get away from the Cuban bastards enjoying the cruel orgy. Three of them had climbed on top of Richard, spread out like a slab of meat on the couch.

"Don't worry, your friend have good time, good fuck. My soldiers, they are big and hard," bragged the Officer. "They like fucking Americanos."

An hour later most of the soldiers had gone off in an army truck, leaving two night guards at their Officer's desk, alone and drinking wine. Richard had cleaned himself up and was dressed. He was surprisingly composed, considering the severity of his rapacious ordeal. He sat with me in the office.

"Sparks, don't ever tell anyone what happened," he groaned, "Never tell anyone." He looked at me as if in a trance. "Where have all those fucking bastards gone?"

"To see Krause," I replied. "We'll soon be out of here."

We sat in silence for what seemed hours. I was lost in thought. I felt ashamed for what had happened to Richard, and couldn't help feeling very sorry for him.

Fifty minutes later two armed guards drove us back to the ship; apparently Krause had agreed to pay the ransom. Helmut and most of the crew lined the deck rail and cheered when Richard and I awkwardly climbed out of the truck. I was surprised my friend was able to walk after the gang-bang.

"Look, they're loaded and ready to sail," observed Richard. "The Old Man waited until the last minute before he bailed us out."

"He hasn't done it yet," I replied, watching our escorting guards heading for Krause's office. He was waiting for them on the boat deck and took them into his cabin while Helmut, Heinz, and Steve were among the rest of the deck crew greeting us like two long lost brothers.

It felt good to be back on board and receive such a welcome from the crew.

Herr Bessler and the Cuban pilot watched impatiently from the boat deck. "We are waiting to leave," yelled Bessler, ordering the Second Officer to prepare the ship for sea. Schmidt dutifully came striding across the deck like a scared rabbit. "Herr Schparks, we are ready to sail," he said. "Herr Bessler has ordered the deck crew to cast off and take up the gangplank as soon as the Cubans have gone ashore."

The Old Man grinned at us from the boat deck, as he watched the Cuban's leaving with the ransom money.

"Sparks, that bastard will never get back to Philly alive. I'm going tie him up and let the crew fuck him to death. He waited until the last minute to bail us out, the bastard," groaned Richard, hobbling across the deck.

I noticed Juan hanging about at the foot of the gangplank waiting for his cigarettes. "You got what you wanted you little bastard, now piss off." I yelled. "I hope your sister gives the Chief of Police galloping dog rot for the rest of his miserable life."

The two Cuban guards grinned at me as they scurried down the gangplank with some cartons of cigarettes. As soon as they had gone, the crew hauled up the gangplank and we were ready to leave. I sighed with relief when I felt the ship's engine shudder into life and immediately Krause ordered the ship to get underway. Obviously the molasses had been paid for in cash, otherwise we would not have been allowed to leave.

While Richard went to work as usual supervising the crew in cleaning up the deck, I went to my office and inwardly groaned when I discovered the office door was unlocked. Inside it looked as if a hurricane had blown through. I could see right away that various items of office equipment were missing. Gone was my portable typewriter, a stapler and the pencil sharpener had been torn off the bulkhead. When I opened the safe it was completely empty. Krause, who had the other key, must have taken at least forty thousand dollars to pay for the molasses, but where was the rest of the money, and where were the receipts? Ludwig Berners had instructed the Captain and me to bargain with the refinery officials for the best price and in no circumstances were we to pay out more than forty thousand dollars. Hopefully Krause had the receipts, but who had ransacked my office, and what had they been looking for?

I watched the Cuban pilot who had safely steered us through the treacherous sandbanks chugging back to shore in the Pilot boat before I went to see the Captain. As usual, he kept me waiting outside his office for a few minutes before inviting me to go in. He was sitting at his desk and just glared at me with contempt. "Herr Schparks, you are lucky to be alive. For you and the Third Mate, ten thousand dollars it cost," he moaned. "Never were you worth it."

"Ten thousand dollars, that's a lie. The ransom demanded was one thousand dollars each, Sir," I argued.

Krause immediately developed his tell-tale nervous twitch. "Are you calling me a liar?" he snapped.

"I'm merely stating that the total ransom money demanded from the Chief of Police for both of us was two thousand dollars. I heard him mention the figure in English." It was my calm, quiet voice that annoyed Krause. As usual, he was hoping to draw me into a loud argument, enabling him to rant and rave in German, and thus have an excuse to order me out of his office and avoid any further discussion. But I was aware of his tactics and remained calm.

"Herr Sparks. You will not argue with me," replied Krause. "I pay the soldiers ten thousand dollars to get you out of jail. We will have no more argument. Now get out of my office."

"Sir, there was fifty thousand dollars in the safe before I went ashore. May I remind you, Ludwig Berners has forbidden you to pay more than forty thousand dollars to the refinery in cash, so where is the rest of the money?"

I enjoyed watching Krause trying to control his temper. His face became red and flushed, and his small piggy eyes narrowed until they were almost hidden by his bloated red cheeks. He twisted around in his chair, and gripped the edge of his desk until his knuckles went white. "Ten thousand dollars for the soldiers, and forty thousand dollars for the molasses. THAT IS FIFTY THOUSAND DOLLARS," screamed Krause. "If I had known what a schwienhund you are, I would have left you in jail." The Old Man's face turned bright red with anger as he waved his finger at the door. "GET OUT OF MY OFFICE."

"All this will have to be sorted out in Philly, when Berners comes on board," I yelled, hurrying out of the office, "especially as you don't have any receipts."

Later that evening I went up on the Bridge and asked Schmidt, the Second Officer, if he had witnessed the payment of cash to the soldiers or the refinery officials, he immediately shook his head, and raised both hands signaling me to back off. "Herr Schparks, I sign nothing but the log book when I am on watch," he replied, nervously. "Captain Krause, he pay the refinery men. I sign nothing. You do not ask me questions about the Captain."

I nodded my head and left him muttering to himself in German. Krause had certainly got him well trained. Even though they were both German, they rarely spoke to one another except on the Bridge to discuss the weather. Herr Schmidt was supposedly writing a book. I often heard his typewriter clacking away at all hours of the night, and wondered what he was writing about.

After my brief talk to Schmidt, I left the Bridge, crossed the deck, and leaned on the deck rail outside the Radio

Room. It was a pleasantly warm and peaceful evening. The bright moonlight reflected on the water like a shimmering highway across the gentle swell of the Caribbean. The only sound on deck was the hissing of the steam pipes inside the tanks keeping the molasses warm.

It was very comforting to be sailing back to America relatively unharmed after the hellish treatment in the jail, but I did wonder about Richard. According to that sadistic Cuban Officer, Richard had enjoyed getting raped. Though, I very much doubted Richard would have the same perspective, if he would speak about it at all. The terrible ordeal had undoubtedly changed him and he seemed in almost a perpetual trance..

I went back to the Radio Room and relaxed in the comfortable old leather chair. I liked the evening watch. There wasn't much to do, and it was usually cool and calm. I turned up the volume on my receiver. Outside on deck we appeared to be the only ship at sea, but listening to the lively radio chatter all around me filling the room, I knew that wasn't so. The air was alive with routine messages back and forth between ship and shore, and it was always comforting to hear the familiar call signs of American coastal stations as far away as New York. To the untrained ear it was a jumble of meaningless squeaky dots and dashes, but to a Sparks, it was an earful of friendly gossip and information. Little wonder everyone on board thought all radio operators were slightly crazy to make any sense out of all that incessant buzz.

I switched on my transmitter and plunged into the noisy melee, calling up the RCA radio station in Miami. When they answered, I transmitted our departure time from Santiago de Cuba to the Head Office in Philadelphia. I wanted to tell them how glad we were to be alive and on our way back, but they wouldn't have been interested.

When Richard finished his watch, he came into my cabin looking very smart in his uniform which the Old Man insisted we wear while on duty. After pouring himself a drink, he took off his jacket, kicked off his shoes and made himself comfortable on my couch. "I heard you blasting away on the radio about an hour ago," began Richard. "You weren't on for very long. What did you tell the office?"

"Nothing much, I just sent the departure time from this hellhole. I'm opening a bottle of Scotch, do you want some?"

"Sure, we have to celebrate. I'm so glad you didn't hand the Scotch over to the guards, and I remember you said you had two cases of Coca-Cola stashed away, but your Scotch will taste much better."

Two glasses, two ice cubes and two generous shots of Glenlivet was the perfect ending to a very exciting day. "I should have told the head office where they can stick their job."

Richard nodded his head in agreement. "Me, too. It's getting a little bit too hairy for me."

"You mean what happened to you in jail?"

"Sparks, do me a favor, never ever mention that again, if I ever meet that little bastard Juan, I'll kill him with my bare hands." Richard sipped his drink and for a few seconds we locked eye contact. "Don't ever mention it again."

I opened my fridge and took out some ice cubes, Richard held out his glass. I plopped in a couple of cubes. "Do you think Berners will keep on trading with these Cuban bastards?"

"Of course they will, because the price is right. Or, rather, the price WAS right. According to Krause he paid forty thousand for this cargo, and ten thousand dollars to get our asses out of jail."

Richard stared at me in disbelief. "He's a lying son-of-a-bitch."

"That's what he says. Anyway he's cleaned out the safe in my office, and there are no receipts." I sipped the Scotch, appreciating the delicate aroma.

"Sparks, it was one thousand bucks each to get us out of that jail. We both heard that bastard Police Chief say so. He said it in English as well. Krause is lying. He IS crazy. Herr Schmidt told me Krause was alone in his office with the refinery officials," confided Richard, sipping his drink and enjoying the breeze from my electric fan. "So what do you reckon, Sparks? Is the bastard on the take?"

"Sure he is. He's taking Berners to the cleaners, but what can we do? He's got us by the balls. He can claim he paid out ten thousand dollars for our release because the Chief of Police sure as hell didn't give him a receipt."

"Isn't he supposed to have two other ship's officers present?" replied Richard, finishing his drink and rattling the ice cubes in is empty glass.

"Those are the rules, but with you and I literally up shit's creek without a paddle, and Castro's mob supposedly breathing down his neck, Krause has the best excuse in the world."

"The bastard, now we know why he didn't bail us out until he was fully loaded and ready to sail," observed Richard, stifling a yawn.

"How about one last shot of Scotch?" Richard grinned and held out his glass.

"I saw the young boy who brings the messages from Maria scrambling up the gangplank, how are the girls?"

"They're Okay. Maria was worried when she heard we were in jail. I only spoke to him for a few minutes then he ran back to tell her we were both okay."

"Does that mean you'll make another trip?"

"Not if I can help it," snapped Richard, finishing his drink. "I think I need to see a proper doctor. That fucking crap you put on my bloody head stings like hell," continued Richard, lying back on the couch to watch television.

My television set, tuned to some station in Key West, was producing a fluttering picture of Lucille Ball in I LOVE LUCY. Finally, we were getting back to civilization. We both stared at the television set thinking our own thoughts for a while. I again topped up our glasses with more Scotch, cursing inwardly when I discovered nearly all the ice had gone. "When do you reckon you'll go back to England?" asked Richard.

"I don't know. I'm trying to save up enough money."

"How much do you need?"

"Thousands of pounds, I'm just saving for the down payment, it's beautiful land."

"I'll bet it is. I'd love to see it sometime and all the horses. I told you the first time I sat on one, I fell off and nearly broke my leg," confessed Richard. "I don't think horses like me, and would probably throw me off at my first try."

"Not if you take it easy. Mister Lee is a faithful old horse. You two would get along great."

"Yeah, I hope so. Speaking of money, I wonder where Krause hid it," Richard mused.

"It must be in his cabin, maybe under his mattress."

"Unless he shoved it up his steward's ass, nobody would want to look up there." We both laughed for the first time in days. The prospect of good weather ahead, and the relaxing effect of the Scotch, soon brought us back to normality, if that were possible.

~~~

CHAPTER SEVEN

Back to Civilization

During the next seven days, Krause and I avoided each other like the plague. I sent out all his routine radio messages, handed him the weather reports, and kept my Radio Room door closed when I saw him wandering around the deck.

Richard and I consumed many bottles of rum and Coca-Cola whilst reliving our death-defying adventures in the hands of Castro's rebels, and discussed what passenger ship we would take next trip. I carefully avoided any mention of the jail gang-rape, but noticed that Richard was much more sympathetic to Helmut's taking refuge in my cabin to escape the aft domain of Kimmel the Bosun.

The crew's English conversation lessons were now very entertaining. We started off with clinical discussions about venereal disease, and ended with each member of the crew recalling the intimate details of his sexual accomplishments.

Heinz, the number one sex maniac and Axel's favorite, was apparently the champion. He was a tall, handsome blond, a typical Aryan male, one Hitler would have chosen to help father his so-called master race, and judging by Heinz's performance in Cuba, he could have accomplished this task single-handed. Yet, despite his incredible good looks, Heinz was extremely modest, making everyone laugh while giving the intimate details of his countless sexual adventures at our twice weekly English classes. His whole life revolved around sex, and he seriously intended to turn professional at the first opportunity. He had already been given numerous gifts by grateful women, and intended to collect a lot more.

I encouraged my friend Helmut to attend the classes. He was very shy and admitted that he was scared of catching a disease from the dockside whores and fully intended to stay celibate until his honeymoon. This response brought howls of laughter from the rest of the group who promised to fix him up with a good, clean woman on the next trip.

Steve, the twenty year-old second cook, was English, he attended the lessons for something to do. Because he had run away from home at an early age, he had very little education and was almost illiterate but too ashamed to admit it. Now he was learning how to understand the menu and the various ingredients. "Jesus, Sparks. They call it fried chicken, boiled chicken, braised chicken and even curried chicken, yet all we do in the kitchen is boil it," confessed Steve. "Now I know why you all moan because it tastes the same."

"Ah! Wait until you start reading some of those French recipes, Steve, they use all the yucky stuff you guys probably throw away."

I encouraged everyone in the class to relate their various adventures. Not only was it good for them to stand up and give vent to their pent-up feelings against their own countrymen who forced them to leave home, it also formed a bond of friendship between themselves and the others who had suffered similar experiences. On the ship they were no longer alone in a very cruel world that, in reality, didn't give a damn about displaced youth from behind the Iron Curtain.

Heinz's lurid description of sex with the famous "Miss Schnapping Pussy" was hilarious. "It is like fucking a vacuum cleaner," he said. "Even my balls went inside her pussy; all the way in. I was scared they would never come out."

Dombrowski also related his sex antics with Miss Schnapping Pussy. "I have zee big balls," he said, proudly. "Now I have zee blue balls."

Everybody laughed, except me because every morning before breakfast I wore the hat of the ship's medicine man, unofficially known as 'The Quack', and faced the rather gruesome sight of at least ten bare-assed seamen waiting for me in the surgery. Each one had contracted a form of venereal disease, including 'blue balls' from the *putas in* the dockside whorehouse.

The infamous drip, drip, drip was the most common. Medically known as gonorrhea, it seemed to be more of a nuisance than a disease. Crabs were a pest, literally and metaphorically speaking and required an overnight application of Gentian Violet, an evil smelling concoction known on board as 'blue glue' which assuredly lived up to its name.

Spotted Balls, Blue Balls and Roses were all very popular and progressively more painful. Being very visible, they were subjected to many homeopathic self-administered potions by the seamen in the hope of avoiding a visit and a verbal bollocking from me, the Quack. Rather than having their name logged in the official Venereal Diseases Log Book, and listen to a lecture about the dangers of unprotected sex, such well known nautical remedies as warm vinegar, Coleman's mustard, Aqua Velva and hot rum-soaked poultices were applied to the affected area but had little effect.

Without a doubt, the most dreaded disease for any young stud was known as 'Shriveled Balls'. This rare phenomenon presented their owner with the alarming spectacle of his genitals reduced to a couple of dried prunes in a wet brown paper bag, and caused much comment and sympathy from his fellow shipmates all of whom wanted to inspect them. Unfortunately, most forms of venereal disease were just an everyday occurrence for some of crew members and considered an occupational hazard that went with the job.

The ship's surgery was a joke. It looked like a mediaeval torture chamber with a box full of rusty instruments. There was also a cabinet of half empty medicine bottles, most of them unlabeled. My real tools of the trade were a pair of large wooden spoons which I had bought for fifty cents in a Cuban vegetable market. They were easily sterilized, never got cold, and were therefore ideal for probing into the nether regions of the male genitalia.

Because it was compulsory to list the name of each seaman receiving treatment in the *'clap book'* and, if possible, to write down the name of the female transmitting the disease, I had to ask each seaman for details of the sexual encounter. "Do you remember HER name, Heinz?" I asked, entering his treatment in the log book while he painfully bent over a chair and spread his thighs.

"Ya, everybody call her Miss Schnapping Pussy, she has the big tits and a schnapping pussy. I never pay her because she likes me," bragged Heinz. "and everybody fucks her."

I inwardly groaned, and gently lifted Heinz's swollen testicles onto my wooden spoon for closer examination. They were turning a delicate shade of blue. "You've got blue balls, Heinz."

"Again, Sir?" he groaned.

"Yes, again, and so will half the crew if they went with Miss Schnapping Pussy." I reached for a disposable hypodermic syringe filled with penicillin, swabbed the left cheek of Heinz's buttock with some surgical spirit, gave him an injection of ten thousand units, then slapped him on the ass.

"Thank you," he said, carefully pulling up his under shorts. "Miss Schnapping pussy is a good fuck, I will tell her not to make you pay, it will be free, Sir." As Heinz left the surgery smiling his usual infectious smile, the thought occurred to me if his brain was as active as his balls, Heinz would be a genius.

The next morning at the short arm inspection, I discovered Heinz was right: half the crew had screwed Miss Schnapping pussy and had the evidence to prove it; balls, balls and more balls, all various shades of blue.

Among the lineup was Steve, the Second Cook. He waited until everyone had gone before entering the surgery. "Did you go with Miss Schnapping pussy as well?" I asked.

"No, Sir, I've just got a dose of crabs."

"Is that all? Do you know what they're called in France? *Papillion d'amour.* Do you know what that means?"

Steve looked nervous, then grinned, showing off his perfect teeth. "Sorry, I don't speak French, but it sounds a lot better than crabs."

"It means butterflies of love. Trust the French to come up with a good name." I handed Steve a large bottle of company recommended crab killer. "Here, read the label, it tells you what to do."

Steve took the bottle, and stared at the gluey looking liquid. "Do I just put it straight on?"

"Can't you read the label?" Steve looked very embarrassed and admitted he still didn't read very well. "It

110

says apply last thing at night and a soak in a hot bath the next morning. If you're still having trouble reading, I'll give you some private lessons."

"I'd like to, but I don't have much time, except after dinner."

"Then come up to the Radio Room after dinner."

Steve's face lit up. "The Radio Room, I've never been up there, but what about the Old Man?"

"Don't worry about him, that place is my domain. I'll see you tonight about eight." It was a very happy young man who jauntily left the surgery carrying a bottle of the dreaded 'blue glue' crab killer. I wondered if the crabs would be gone by the time he learned to read the instructions on the bottle.

At precisely eight that evening, Steve knocked at the Radio Room door. I hardly recognized him he looked so different. I was used to seeing him hot and bothered in an oversized white apron and chef's baggy white hat, sweating and cursing over large steaming pots and pans in the stifling hot galley, doing a job I wouldn't have done for ten times his salary. Now, he looked no more than eighteen with a short blond crew cut, polished smiling face, crisp white T-shirt and freshly laundered jeans. He waited nervously outside the door. "Come in, Steve," I yelled, pointing at the chair next to mine and then continued writing down the weather report.

Grinning from ear to ear, the young chef entered the Radio Room and sat down, looking in amazement at the buzzing radio equipment. "Welcome. Sit down, Steve, I won't be a minute, I'm taking the weather report and traffic list from New York."

The list was long and repetitive, but there was nothing for the *Cuban Trader*, and I made a note in my log book. "Nothing for us," I said.

"This place is fantastic," observed Steve. "You must be a bloody genius to work all this. I've listened to you hundreds of times blasting through everybody's radio back aft, and wondered how long it would take to learn the Morse code. You go like a machine gun."

"It's about twenty words a minute, that's all, and took me about nine months of practice to reach that speed. How fast can you read?"

"Not as fast as that," answered Steve. "I wish I could."

"You will. Just make up your mind to read something every day." Fortunately, Axel, the previous Radio Officer, had been teaching someone to read English and left all the books on the shelf, so Steve was able to start right away. I opened the book and inwardly groaned, one of the first sentences was THE CAT SAT ON THE MAT in large type. Steve was either half-blind or dis-interested in where the cat chose to sit down, so I put the book back on the shelf. His eye caught sight of a copy of *Country Life,* a colorful British magazine, with photographs of the English countryside.

"How about this one, Sparks?" Steve picked up the old magazine which my mother had sent me.

"Do you like the countryside?" I asked.

"Of course, I lived on my Gramp's farm in Wiltshire when I was kid. Feeding the pigs and chickens, looking for eggs, and I even learned to milk a cow."

"So, why did you leave all that?"

Steve looked sad. "My Grampy didn't own the farm. They said he was too old and we all had to move and then he died." Steve hesitated for a second. "You don't wanna hear all this, Sparks."

"Yes I do, but take your time. Do you like horses?"

"Course, I do," he replied.

"My mom and dad look after old horses and pit ponies, and have a farm in Gloucestershire. If you ever want to get away from this damn hell ship, you would always be welcome there."

Steve looked at me for a few seconds. "Do you really mean that, Sparks?"

"Sure, but it wouldn't be a holiday. You'd have to work."

"I'd love that. I got nowhere to go in England, not since . . ." Steve swallowed, choking back his emotions.

"You haven't got anywhere to go?"

"My mom and dad got divorced. Neither one of them wanted me, and I didn't like them much either," confessed Steve. "So I kinda ran away, but they didn't care. I got a job washing up in a café, until somebody mentioned working on a ship where I could learn a trade. So, I ended up in a ship's galley, cleaning out chickens and peeling spuds. It's supposed to be the best way to see the world, 'ceptin I haven't seen much yet."

"Why not try and a job on one of the new passenger ships, they're always looking for chefs," I suggested.

"Nah! Not after this lot. I'm tired of the sea life. I'd love to go and stay with your Mom and Dad and all the horses. I reckon that would suit me a treat."

"Think about it, Steve. We'll talk about it again tomorrow, and I'll write to them about you."

It was a satisfactory feeling knowing that I was teaching someone to read and write, especially when he was so eager to learn. Steve was the only seaman back aft who spoke English, with the exception of J.J. Anderson, the Australian who was not very sociable after our confrontation in the English classes.

After the first lesson, Steve couldn't wait to come up to the Radio Room most evenings to learn how to spell and talk about horses, and never failed to bring a package of ham or chicken sandwiches, which went down well with a cold beer after my evening watch.

Helmut was waiting for me outside my cabin when I got off watch. I invited him in and asked him to fix us both a rum and Coca-Cola. He sat on my bunk grinning, handing me the drink. "Herr Schparks, you are my friend," he said. He still wanted to leave the ship, and reminded me I had promised to leave with him when we got back to Philadelphia. "When you go back aft, do you still have to sleep with the Bosun?" I asked.

"The Bosun now sleep with Kano," replied Helmut. "I sleep on the floor in the Officer's dining room, he no find me there." Helmut looked at me with his sad blue eyes. "You not leave in Philadelphia this time, Herr Schparks?"

"I have to meet with Berners, the ship's owner, and talk to him first." Immediately the smile left Helmut's face. "It will depend if he can find another Sparks."

Our secret conversation was interrupted by Schmidt, banging on my cabin door. "Herr Schparks, the radar on the bridge is kaput."

"Helmut, that was the Second Mate," I whispered. "He was listening outside the door. Don't let him see you." I reluctantly returned to the Bridge to fix the overheated radar.

"We are at sea, and no radar," yelled Schmidt. "You disobey orders; I enter all in the log."

"Go ahead. The ship's log is full of shit anyway, so who cares what the hell you put in there." I grabbed Schmidt's coat which was again flung over the radar set, "and be sure to enter in the log that the Second Officer's coat was overheating the radar screen and preventing it from operating." I yelled, hanging Schmidt's coat on the hook.

Schmidt snorted and went into the chart-room. I waited for the overheated radar to flicker back to life. "The radar is now working; make sure you put that in the log that I fixed it, because I'm claiming one hour overtime."

When I got back to my cabin, Helmut was sound asleep on my couch. He looked so innocent and peaceful. I couldn't send him back aft to sleep on the deck in the Officer's dining saloon and vowed I would do something to help him when we got to Philadelphia.

"I'm going on watch now," said Richard, looking around the connecting door. "I helped myself to some ice cubes, but I didn't wake up your young friend. Let him stay there." Before I could reply, Richard had closed the door and gone on watch.

Eventually, we sailed into the calmer waters of Delaware Bay and headed upstream toward Publicker's refinery in Philadelphia, where there would be some welcome letters from home, and a lot of awkward questions from Ludwig Berners, when he came on board.

"You spent fifty thousand dollars for this cargo," yelled Ludwig Berners, angrily. "Fifty thousand dollars of my fucking money!"

Captain Krause flinched at the ferocity of Berners' voice. For a wealthy ship owner, Berners was surprisingly scruffy. He was an obese man with a bald head, a round face that often turned various shades of red as he studied Krause's amateurish accounting, frequently mopping his sweating forehead with a large white handkerchief.

Berners had brought with him his usual herd of ass-kissing assistants, all of whom swaggered on board wearing slick navy-blue suits, white shirts, flashy ties and a condescending look of disdain like they had just stepped in a fresh dog shit. Deiter, the Captain's swishy little German steward, sashayed around the Captain's office with a tray of drinks, smiling at Berners' assistants, and making damn sure Berners' glass was never empty. Krause watched nervously as the paperwork from the refinery appeared on the top of the pile.

"You're telling me you paid over fifty thousand fuckin' dollars for this cargo?" snapped Berners, guzzling from his glass of Scotch. "I told you to negotiate a good price."

Krause nodded his head. For this special occasion he was wearing his new uniform with rows of unrecognizable medal ribbons, and looked like the concierge at the Waldorf Astoria. Nevertheless, despite all this outward show of authority he was obviously very nervous.

"Captain Krause, where's the other two signatures I asked you to get?" queried Berners, studying the papers. "Where were the others when you signed this contract and handed over my money?" Berners drummed his stubby fingers on the table impatiently.

The Captain and I briefly exchanged glances. Now it was my turn to give him a supercilious grin. How good it felt to see him squirm in front of the bullying Ludwig Berners.

"Err, there were no other officers," began Krause, nervously. "Herr Schparks and the Third Mate were in jail. Herr Schmidt speaks no English and Herr Bessler was back aft. We had to leave. Castro's men were going to attack us. We were damn lucky to leave with no damage to the ship." Krause gulped his drink. His face was twitching, and he had probably shit his pants.

"You were going to be attacked? Who in the hell was going to attack you?" demanded Berners. "For crissake, weren't you handing them a fuckin' bag full of my dollars?"

"Yes, for the refinery, but it was the revolutionaries who were attacking us," stammered Krause.

"It sounds like a lot of fuckin' hogwash to me, but I'll find out. I don't take crap from nobody," snapped Berners, helping himself to another drink from the steward's tray. "Now tell me about this prison, Sparks. Did you meet any of these bloodthirsty revolutionaries that Krause's been talking about?"

I briefly recounted what had happened to Richard and me, skipping quickly over the sexy evening at Maria's place, and concentrated on our stay in Batista's jail. "For fuck sake, is that right? They lined up ten guys and just shot 'em?" repeated Berners, obviously surprised, "and they was their own men?"

"Actually, they shot thirty, altogether," I added. "We both thought we were going to be next, and the soldiers forced Richard the Third Mate . . ."

". . .Forced me to eat shitty stew," interrupted Richard, glaring at me.

Berners nodded his head. "Well, I'm tellin' y'all right here and now, nobody ain't going ashore next trip, and if any one of them horny young bastards back aft goes ashore and gets their asses thrown into jail, they can fuckin' stay there. Y'all understand?"

"Of course," we all replied.

"Well, you guys, I'm real sorry y'all had such a rough time." Berners then went back to the dreaded refinery paperwork. "Now, Captain Krause, what about this fifty thousand dollars you spent on this trip. Where did it go?" demanded Berners, again drumming his fingers on the desk.

Krause, who was inwardly praying the company would deduct the ransom money from my salary, momentarily forgot where he was and snapped to attention at the mention of his name. "Where did it go?" he repeated, nervously clearing his throat. "That is simple, forty thousand dollars for the molasses, and ten thousand dollars was paid to Batista's soldiers to release the two officers from jail."

"Ten thousand dollars?" screamed Berners, his face now almost purple.

"Ya," continued Krause, trying to control his twitch. "If they are stupid and get arrested, then they get punished. Next time I let them rot in jail."

Berners feverishly mopped his brow. "Krause, are you trying to tell me you paid ten thousand bucks to some fuckin' half-assed Cuban soldier; ten thousand dollars of my money?"

I thought Berners was about to have a heart attack. I wanted to interrupt the argument and tell him the truth, but how could I prove it? It was obvious that Berners didn't believe Krause, so I thought it better to remain silent. "I should leave them in jail," groaned Krause, muttering under his breath.

"Captain Krause, you cannot sail without a Sparks, and you can bet your fuckin' boots I'll have Henri Bloom check out all these figures you got here. He speaks the Cuban language real good, and when he gets there he's gonna find out what you really paid for the cargo, and how much to get these fuckin' idiots outta jail." Berners took a hefty swig of whisky, and glared at us over the rim of his glass. "Now, you better listen. Next time I want three of you to sign the contract, and I wanna see the proper official receipts," he snapped, signaling the steward for more whiskey.

"Do we have to go back to Cuba again?" questioned Krause, unable to disguise his disappointment.

"Of course," snapped Berners. "Captain Krause, this company has no quarrel with either Batista or Castro or

118

their goddamn revolution. Frankly, I don't give a shit if they put a fucking whore in charge of the country. From the mess it's in, that might not be such a bad idea."

"Herr Berners, you don't know what it's like doing business with these refinery men," replied Krause.

"For fuck's sake, Krause, the refinery's got cheap molasses to sell, and we want to buy it. It's business and I've heard that Castro owns a sugar plantation, so he knows he's gotta sell the fuckin' stuff. I don't reckon he'll bother anyone who wants to trade, but if'n you need rest, we've gotta standby officer ready to take over this ship whenever you wanna resign."

Captain Krause stared at me, obviously wishing I wasn't present so he could blast off about me. "Herr Berners, if I sign off, is there another ship for me?"

Berners looked around at his associates, who in turn looked sheepishly at each other. "I ain't sure about that," replied Berners after some thought. "We got more officers than ships right now, but if you're too tired and you wanna rest, I reckon you should take your leave right now and I'll sign up the other captain right away."

"No. No! I'll make another trip," shouted the Old Man, nervously wringing his hands. "I'll make another trip."

Berners allowed himself a brief smile, then glanced across at me. "Okay. What about you, Sparks? You wanna make another trip?"

Berners' question caught me unawares. "Of course," I replied, without even thinking. Inwardly, I was expecting the company to deduct some of the ransom money from my salary, but there was no mention of it. I therefore felt obligated to make at least one more trip.

"Now, what about this here radiogram, Captain Krause. You mean to tell me the refinery wants paying in gold? It sounds fuckin' crazy to me."

"It is true, they tell me they want gold ingots from the bank," repeated the Captain.

"I'd sure like to know the reason why. What the hell's wrong with good old American greenbacks?"

I nodded in agreement. "I know what you mean, Sir, but it's amazing, Castro's mob doesn't like American dollars. They don't like anybody or anything that's American," I replied, glancing at Richard, "except Lucky Strikes cigarettes."

"Well, I did ask around. It's not only American dollars they don't like, all the shipping companies gotta pay in gold," groaned Berners. "So I guess from now on, we'll have to trade in gold bullion, but for crissake, no more than forty thousand bucks for a full cargo of first grade molasses. We figured it out, and it comes to exactly eight ingots of pure gold, and they're all sealed up direct from the bank," he announced, signaling his assistant to open his briefcase.

Everyone watched as Henri Bloom, the pokerfaced assistant opened up an expensive leather case and placed eight cellophane envelopes each containing a small ingot of pure gold on the table. "Ain't that a beautiful sight?" observed Berners. "They're fuckin' beautiful."

He was right, the ingots were a beautiful sight, but I always thought forty thousand dollars in cash looked pretty good as well.

"Now, I want y'all to know my assistant, Henri Bloom will be on board this trip, and we're putting a special safe in your cabin, Captain Krause," announced Berners. "It'll have two locks and two keys. Henri will have one and you're gonna have the other. Cash for the crew and paying out them fuckin' bribes will be kept in your office safe, Sparks, just as before, and Henri will do all the accounting. Nobody will be allowed ashore. If'n any one of them horny bastards back aft sneaks off and gets thrown in jail, they're gonna stay there, y'all make sure they knows this. I don't want no fuck-ups like last time. Now, anybody got any questions?"

The Captain and I exchanged glances. There were a lot of questions I wanted to ask, especially about the crew's accommodation back aft, but not with the Old Man listening to the answers. "Then that's it, you guys. I just wanna introduce my personal assistant, Henri Bloom. He'll be on board for the trip and talking to the guys at the refinery to figure out a good price," explained Berners. "Now, y'all look after Henri for me, he's a nice guy."

Henri Bloom grinned at us for a few seconds, then resumed his conversation with Berners' associates. Quite a cold fish I thought. "Now, y'all have a good trip, don't get into trouble and look after Henri. He's my personal assistant, and a very valuable employee," concluded Berners.

The meeting was over. Krause had gotten away with it. He grinned at me as I left the meeting. I could see he had already cornered Berners and Henri Bloom, and was no doubt telling them how incompetent he thought I was. If Bloom thought he was going to have a pleasant little Caribbean cruise, he had quite a shock in store.

~~~

CHAPTER EIGHT

Bloom on Board - but Not for Long

As soon as we left Philadelphia and sailed out into the open sea, I felt Henri Bloom was going to be trouble. He was Berners' personal assistant and he was on board to find out what had happened in Cuba. He was also to negotiate an on-going deal with the refinery officials. But what else was he supposed to do?

Henri Bloom was about thirty years old. A tall, gangling, sallow looking character with squinting eyes, large horned rimmed glasses, and long, slick black hair combed straight back over his receding forehead. Richard described him as a shifty looking, four-eyed pen pusher who couldn't be trusted, and I agreed with that description.

After my first watch in the Radio Room, I went to my office to start entering the expenses incurred while we were in Philadelphia, but Henri Bloom had already beaten me to it. He ignored the surprised look on my face when I saw him sitting at my desk, and continued going through a stack of old accounts from previous trips. "I'm trying to figure out how you do your accounts," he said, making no attempt to dislodge himself from my chair.

"I can see that," I replied, coldly. "If you'd asked me, I would have shown you." My first thought was to leave him to it, but the company paid me five hundred dollars a month to look after the ship's accounts. If Bloom took over, half my salary would disappear. Although I resented the shifty-looking pen-pusher, he was Ludwig Berners' personal assistant and I would have to cooperate with him. "All those accounts have been verified by the New York office," I said, opening up my cupboard and taking out a bottle of rum. "Would you like a drink?"

He shook his head and continued to read through the old ledger. "No, it's too early. I don't think anyone should drink until after dinner," he said, glaring at me with a look of disapproval as I fixed myself a Bacardi and Coca-Cola.

Normally, I would not have made it so strong, but I wanted to show the interfering bastard that I had no intention of heeding any of his sly hints. "Do you think this will be our last trip to Cuba?" I asked, reluctantly sitting on the office couch.

He continued to stare at the books. "I'm not at liberty to say," he eventually replied. "I notice the crew get paid in American dollars when they go ashore in Cuba."

"Yes, they do." I was in no mood for any inquisition, and got up to leave.

"Why are they paid in dollars?" repeated Bloom, turning around to face me for the first time. We exchanged glances, both of us anxious to establish who was in charge. Bloom was Berners' assistant, I was the officially appointed ship's purser, but with him sitting at my desk, going through my accounting books, without first asking my permission, he had gained the upper hand.

I shrugged my shoulders. "Firstly, they get more value for a dollar than the equivalent in Batista's paper money. Secondly, it would require the ship's agent in Santiago to bring a large sum of Cuban money on board to pay out the crew, and thirdly, I can give the crew their shore spending money the day before we arrive, which saves time once we have docked."

"But the company orders. . ."

"The company orders, if you read the fine print, leave it up to the Captain to make the final decision, and the Captain thought it easier if we paid the crew in American dollars." I stared at Bloom, trying to convey my resentment, but he took no notice.

"I see. I also wanted to question this here, Sir."

"Henri, most of us are very friendly on board, and everybody calls me, Sparks."

"I see. This figure here, it's a long list of grocery items purchased in Santiago. Aren't you supplied with provisions in Philadelphia?"

It was obvious Bloom had the hide of a mule and was going to continue with his stupid questions. I hoped he hadn't been sent on board to check up on every sack of spuds we bought. I topped up my glass with rum and sat down on the couch again. "The basics, flour, tea, coffee, meat, and canned goods, are put on board in Philly," I explained. "In Cuba, we sometimes buy fresh vegetables, fruit and dairy produce as required, and they're much cheaper than those supplied by that thieving bastard in Philly."

"I see." Bloom continued to go over the figures in the book.

"Henri, I came down here to enter up the expenses while we were in Philadelphia," I said with an exasperated sigh. "But I'll come back when you have finished going over my books. If you have any questions, I'll be in my cabin reading, and drinking and generally relaxing, because I've just spent two hours with a pair of earphones glued to my ears in the Radio Room and I'm now off duty. Belated as this may seem, please make yourself at home in my office." I left before he had time to answer.

"You should have told him to get the fuck out of there," Richard said, when I told him about Henri Bloom taking over my office. Richard had just finished his watch and came into my cabin to relax. He helped himself to a drink from my liquor cabinet and made himself comfortable on my couch.

"Apparently, one doesn't tell Bloom anything. He's Berners' personal assistant and he's going to do what the hell he likes. God knows how long he'll be on board, but he refused to say if this was our last trip when I asked him."

"Sparks, you said it yourself. This company will keep trading with Cuba until hell freezes over. Molasses is cheaper in Cuba than in Puerto Rico. Anyway, screw it, I thought you and I agreed this was going to be our last trip?" replied Richard, producing a packet of Planter's peanuts. "Want some?"

I nodded and poured a handful of nuts into the palm of my hand. "Thanks. Okay, we sign off when we get back, and then what?"

"Don't you want to go home for a few weeks? Take in all that beautiful countryside and help out with the horses?"

"I'd love to," I sighed, thinking of home, "but at this moment it's covered with snow, and once I got there, I wouldn't want to leave. Furthermore, I haven't saved up any money yet. Why don't we sign on a passenger ship?"

"Sure, if we can get one, but you don't save money on passenger ships. I know. It all goes on booze and broads. We can always go to my folk's place for a few weeks. We can have a great time there, and it won't cost a dime. Come and have a look at the photos my mother sent me." Richard topped up his drink again before leading the way through our shared bathroom into his cabin. It was obvious why he always choose to relax in my place, because his was always in a mess.

"What the hell have you got all these for?" I groaned, lifting a set of barbells off his couch. "You never lift all these weights."

"What do you mean? I work out every morning, and you ought to do the same. We gotta get in shape for our vacation. Look at this." Richard handed me a letter and some photographs. "My folks have just bought this place in Palm Springs. We can have a ball there. I already called them from Philly and said we'd probably go out there for a few weeks."

I looked at the photographs of the huge, luxurious Spanish-styled hacienda with an enormous swimming pool surrounded with deck chairs under sheltering palm trees. The ultimate in luxury. "Wow! It's fantastic."

"We can stay there for a few weeks and fill the place with broads while we figure out what we'll do next. What do you say, Sparks?"

"I say, let's go!"

"Now you can see why we've gotta work out with these weights. We gotta get in shape." Richard struggled with a set of barbells, puffing and groaning as he struggled to lift them above his head. "You can start with those small ones, Sparks." I settled back on Richard's couch and watched him struggle with the weights. His parents' weekend retreat in Palm Springs looked idyllic. I don't think he realized how lucky he was; he just took it all for granted.

The Radio Room, where I spent eight hours a day was on the top deck next to the Bridge, and in my opinion too damn close to the Captain's quarters. All three places were out of bounds to everyone except those on a specific duty.

I was very curious to know what specific duty Henri Bloom was performing, snooping around on the top deck outside the Bridge. Richard, who was on watch, hadn't yet noticed him and I waited impatiently to hear him ordering Bloom to remove his skinny carcass to the deck below. It was our second morning at sea. The weather was good, the sea was relatively calm and, since we were sailing south, the sun was getting warmer. I was in the Radio Room listening for the traffic list from New York, a list of the ships that had telegrams in New York awaiting collection. As usual there was one for the Cuban Trader. I was expecting the routine "destination confirmed" message, telling us that the orders we were given in Philly were now confirmed.

I switched on the transmitter, tuned in to the New York frequency, and started calling them. So did all the other ships with messages to pick up. Unfortunately, my transmissions were blasting through every radio and television set on board, and nobody appreciated the interference, especially the Captain while he was watching his favorite black birds, "Heckle and Jeckle" cackling away in black and white from some TV station near the coast.

When I did finally contact New York and took down the message, I was surprised to find it was a company-coded telegram addressed to Henri Bloom. I typed up the five groups of letters on the normal radiogram paper, sealed it in an envelope, and intended handing it to Bloom as soon as I got off watch. Whilst I had been busy calling New York with headphones clamped to my ears, I missed the initial confrontation between Richard and Henri Bloom. "The Bridge is out of bounds to everyone not on duty, Mister Bloom," I heard Richard saying loud and clear, but Henri Bloom's reply was inaudible.

"I don't care if you do represent Ludwig Berners. Even he isn't allowed up here when we're at sea unless he's invited." Again, I couldn't hear Henri's reply, but he was obviously putting up an argument.

"I also have my orders," argued Richard. "If you wish to complain, go and see the Old Man." Bloom obviously intended doing just that, and strode off across the deck in search of the Captain. I could have handed him the radiogram as he passed by but since he was not supposed to be on that deck, I thought it best if I took it to his cabin. Richard saw me standing at the Radio Room door grinning and ostentatiously gave Bloom the finger as he disappeared down the slippery steel ladder to the deck below. Seconds later, Richard buzzed me on the phone. "See, Sparks. You have to be firm with the nosey bastard; otherwise he'll crawl all over you."

"That's all right for you to say," I replied. Fortunately he has nothing to do with the navigating of the ship, so he has no reason to go on the Bridge, but he has got Berners' permission to go through my accounts." I hung up the phone and wondered what Bloom would have said if I'd told him to stay out of my office. He spent most of the day reading a book in his cabin, as far as I was concerned, he was welcome to stay there.

Later, during supper in the dining saloon, Richard and I discussed the latest developments concerning our unwelcome company employee. "What was in the telegram for him?" asked Richard.

"I can't tell you."

"Bullshit!"

"I can't tell you because it was in the company code and only Henri Bloom has the codebook."

"So does the Old Man," replied Richard. "That son-of-a-bitch!"

"Sure, he's got one. I must say Bloom seemed very nervous when I handed it to him. He was very embarrassed it was in code, so now I am very curious to know what it said."

128

"So am I," agreed Richard. "We'll have to try and get hold of the company code book."

Steve, the chef, who had lovingly cooked up our late supper, approached with a bottle of vinegar. "It's Sarson's Vinegar," he said, grinning. "I bought it in Philly. You gotta have real English malt vinegar on your chips, Sparks." Steve was right; chips without vinegar were not the same. "That new guy, whatzisname Bloom? He was just in here. He eats like a bloody horse. I told him I was off duty, but he saw me cooking up the egg and chips for you two, and the hungry gutted-sod wanted the same. That's why there weren't many chips left for you."

"Ah!, but he didn't get any of this, Steve," I replied, holding up the bottle of Sarson's Malt Vinegar and liberally dousing my chips from Steve's special bottle.

"Who is he anyway? He's been snooping around back aft, looking into all the cabins and even told Heinz to take down his dirty pictures."

"Bloom is Ludwig Berners' personal assistant. He thinks the sun shines out of his ass at the moment, but he'll get more than a suntan before long," replied Richard, shaking a few drops of vinegar onto his chips.

"Well, I'm glad we can't see it. You know, the sun shining out of his ass," joked Steve, laughing on his way back to the galley. "If you want some more, give me a shout."

"Coded messages for Bloom. Sounds rather sinister doesn't it?" observed Richard, stabbing his knife into a succulent pork chop. "Did you know Bloom has a loaded revolver under his pillow? I think the guy's bad news."

I stared at Richard's appetizing pork chops that Steve had especially grilled for him, and then at my plate of egg and chips, and wished I'd ordered the same as him. Why was I always on a diet?

"First Bloom takes over the desk in your office," continued Richard, "and then just wanders onto the Bridge and starts questioning the helmsman. He's a menace."

Menace or not, I thought to myself, at least he provided a much needed new topic of conversation. "I'm just waiting for the Old Man to have a go at him, especially if he starts digging too deep into his accounting." I caught the steward's eye and signaled for some more beer.

"Krause won't say anything to him, he's too shit-scared, and he'll probably wind up kissing his ass and offering him the dubious delights of Deiter's favors, that goddamn swishy little Kraut steward of his," replied Richard, finishing his pork chop.

My imagination immediately went to work conjuring up a disturbing mental picture of Henri Bloom making out with the Captain's detestable little steward. I wasn't very successful. "Jesus, we're jabbering on like a pair of old women. Bloom's not interested in the Captain's little faggot. And how the hell do you know there's a revolver under his pillow?"

Richard grinned. "Because I saw it," he replied, lowering his voice. "While he was having breakfast, I went into his cabin and snooped around. You know I have to check for leaky portholes."

"Go on."

"That's it. As I kneeled on his bunk to check out the fucking porthole, I moved the pillow and saw the revolver."

"Now you know it's not smart to fool around with him. Next time you go into his cabin uninvited, he might shoot you."

The next few days were like all the rest, just dull routine. Richard and I spent hours dragging Henri Bloom and the Captain over the coals, whilst drinking Bacardi and Coca-Cola in my cabin.

Henri Bloom took it upon himself to go back aft and inspect the crew's quarters. Kimmel, the Bosun immediately complained to Herr Bessler who, as usual, ignored the complaint. Bloom continued his unofficial inspections and apparently was pelted with stinking oil rags when he told some of the engine crew they should clean up their filthy cabins. He wasn't too impressed with the way the galley was run either, lifting the lids on various pots and pans until the Chief Cook accidentally-on-purpose opened up a safety valve, enveloping his unwelcome visitor in a cloud of hot steam and a barrage of threats until he literally ran out of the galley like a scalded cat.

Bloom continued to go over all my account books, frantically working the ancient adding machine and eagerly pointing out any errors. "Sparks, I was checking September's list of vegetables bought in Santiago. What in the Sam-hill is rhubarb?"

I shook my head in disgust. I couldn't believe my ears. "Rhubarb is a long stick of sweet and sour. It's chopped up and boiled, and when applied to an infected scrotum, it cures galloping dog rot."

"Galloping dog rot?" yelled Bloom. "What the hell is that?"

"It's quite common in the Caribbean. It affects the testicles. One of them swells up to the size of a coconut. It's a rather alarming sight, very frightening and I hear it's quite painful."

"My God!" groaned Bloom, looking horrified. "Balls the size of a coconut?"

"Yes, sir, but only one of them." I replied, trying to keep from laughing.

"So, it's a cure for galloping dog rot? Then in that case, Sparks, it should have been listed under medical supplies," replied Bloom. So, that's why these books don't balance." I chuckled to myself at the thought of applying boiled rhubarb to a seaman's balls and watching them squirm. It was too funny for words. Just to show Bloom I didn't give a shit about his bossy attitude, I ostentatiously topped up my glass with more rum and tonic and noisily rattled the ice cubes. He glared at me but never said anything.

Bloom never strayed onto the Bridge during Richard's watch any more, but the groveling Herr Bessler and ass-kissing Schmidt both welcomed the intrusion, and gave Bloom a personal tour. Herr Bessler was particularly charming, perhaps trying to make up for the Nazi persecution of Bloom's fellow Jews, while Schmidt tried to explain the workings of the ancient depth sounder, sending an audible PING to the sea bottom to measure the depth. Unfortunately, Bloom insisted on operating the echo sounder himself and discovered to his horror that the section of the Atlantic we were steaming through was only five feet deep. After further questioning, Schmidt had to admit the depth sounder hadn't been calibrated since the end of the war, and was more useful as a coat hanger and hat rack for the officer on duty. Bloom continued to ask more questions until Schmidt finally admitted that half the electrical gadgets on the ship were either kaput or he didn't know how to use them.

Actually, Henri Bloom was like a fish out of water. I got the impression he was just checking my account books for something to do. In the dining saloon, the Old Man invited him to share his table, and afterwards they often had drinks and watched television in the Old Man's cabin. "Now he's going to kiss his ass," whispered Richard, as the Captain followed Bloom out of the dining saloon.

The English conversational classes were full of Bloomerisms, as Richard called them. Every crewmember had something to say about the unwelcome visitor. Apparently, Bloom's biggest blunder was to order the removal of the erotic nudes pinned up in Heinz's cabin. "Herr Bloom, he look very closely at all the futsa, until his face was sweating. He very shy man," observed Heinz. "How you say, futsa in English?" Everyone knew in a second what part of the female anatomy Heinz was referring to and burst out laughing, followed by a chorus of replies, no two of them alike.

"The Chief Cook soon told him to get lost," confided Steve, "especially when he wanted to check the stores in the cold room. That's where the cook hides all his rum and Coca-Cola. The bastard also snoops around when it's dark, opening doors. Last night he caught Kano and Dombrowski in bed together, bare-assed naked going at like rabbits. Now everybody locks their cabin door. That's if it has one that works."

These intimate revelations during English classes were quite an eye-opener, especially as my infamous 'clap book' revealed Dombrowski had availed himself of more Cuban whores than anyone else on board. Apparently his need for something to screw every night had gotten completely out of hand!!

After the English class was over, I went on deck to see the lights of Port au Prince on the port side sparkling in the distance. It was a pleasant evening. I heard the old man laughing at some Spanish TV program from a local shore station. It was time to go on watch, ten until midnight, the last one for the day. There was not much to do except listen to the unofficial chatter from other radio operators passing on football scores and gossiping like old women.

When the watch was over at midnight, I switched off the equipment, set the Auto-Alarm and was walking back to my cabin when I saw Helmut hiding behind the lifeboat. "Herr Schparks," he whispered. "Can I talk to you?"

"Helmut, my friend," I replied. "Come to my cabin." Just as we were about to walk across the deck, the Old Man opened his cabin door and crossed over to the ship's rail only a few yards from where Helmut was hiding. "Herr Schparks, again you blast through my television."

"Yes, Sir, it was another ship asking about CLN, Santiago de Cuba. He wanted to know if they were still operating."

"You only use transmitter for company business, Herr Schparks. That is an order," yelled the Old Man. My immediate thoughts were for Helmut crouched down behind the lifeboat. I had to detract the Old Man's attention so that Helmut could sneak into my cabin without being seen.

"Sir, the ship wanted to know if the refinery was still open," I explained crossing over the deck. "We all help each other at sea."

"Herr Schparks, company business only for transmitter," repeated the Old Man. "I again log you for insubordination."

"Yes, Sir, that log book of yours is sure going to be full up by the time we get back to Philly." I deliberately argued back and forth with the Old Man while Helmut crept into my cabin.

"That is all, Herr Schparks," snorted the Old Man, staring at me like I was piece of shit.

"Good Night, Sir, I'll try not to use the transmitter while you're watching your favorite educational program 'Heckle and Jeckle', and I sincerely hope those blackbirds have the irresistible compulsion to frequently evacuate their bowels upon your person while you somnambulate during the night." I hurried back to my cabin leaving the Old Man to figure out if he had been insulted.

Helmut was sitting patiently on my couch. "Herr Schparks," he said, smiling. "That was the captain."

"Yes, and the bastard nearly saw you. Would you like a rum and Coca-Cola," without waiting for a reply, I fixed two glasses of my favorite drink and handed one to Helmut. "How are you, my friend?"

Helmut just stared at me for a few seconds. I could see the tears welling in his eyes. "Herr Schparks," he sobbed. "We no leave in Philadelphia?"

"Helmut, I am sorry, but I have to make one more trip. Berners didn't deduct any of the ransom money from my check." I could see Helmut wasn't listening and slowly falling asleep on the couch.

"Herr Schparks," he began. "I have no bunk. No place to sleep. The Bosun now sleeps with Kano and they now lock up the officer's dining room."

"That's monstrous!" I felt so angry I wanted to go straight to the Old Man and demand he do something, but it was past midnight and he was probably drunk. "Helmut tomorrow I will demand that Captain Krause find you a place to sleep." I watched Helmut sipping his drink, he looked so tired and I felt guilty I had broken my promise to leave the ship with him in Philadelphia. He smiled and lay back on the couch.

While Helmut was quietly sipping his drink I re-read my letter from home. Apparently, the only road to our village had been cut-off for a few days due to snowdrifts and there was a list of the various stables that needed repairing. My sister, Christine, had enclosed a note to say we had acquired four more pit ponies from South Wales and she had named them Jamie, Pele, Leon and Davey.

The letter reminded me of their urgent need for money, so, despite my promise to Richard and Helmut, I decided to stay on the Cuban Trader for at least two more trips before accepting the invitation to go to California. I could hear the sounds of hysterical laughter coming from the Old Man's cabin, and wondered whatever he and Henri Bloom could be laughing at, until I realized they were watching a television program from Port au Prince which was just off the port bow. I was going to suggest to Helmut he come out on deck and look at the lights, but he was fast asleep on the couch.

I was too wound up to go to bed, and decided to go for a stroll around the deck. The sea was calm and it was a beautiful night. Walking across the deck, I noticed somebody was in Bloom's cabin. The door was open, so I peeked inside and saw Deiter, the Captain's steward rummaging through Bloom's suitcases, which he had dragged from under the bunk. The little bastard hadn't noticed me and continued searching the bags. What the hell was he after? Where did he get the key to Bloom's cabin? I contemplated whether I should walk into the cabin and catch him red-handed, or confront him later. I decided to leave him to it. When I got back to my cabin, Helmut was now sound asleep on the couch. His cherubic face was smiling. Hopefully, he was having a pleasant dream. He was certainly more comfortable than on the floor in the Officer's dining room.

The next morning, while filing some papers in the Radio Room, I discovered the copy of the radiogram to Henri Bloom was missing. I was sure I had left it in the wire basket to be filed with the rest of the papers. It was fortunate for me that Richard arrived waving a piece of paper. "Sparks, can you send this message off to my folks? It's their wedding anniversary tomorrow." As soon as he entered the Radio Room, he started sniffing. "Has Deiter, the Old Man's steward, just been in here?"

"Not that I know of, why?"

"He must have been in here! Can't you smell that God-awful after-shave he uses?" It was then I realized how unobservant I was. I realized now, who had taken the copy of Bloom's telegram.

~~~

CHAPTER NINE

Bloom's Last Supper

Later that afternoon, I was laying on my bunk reading, when I heard a very faint tapping on my door. It was Henri Bloom, and he looked very nervous. He was wearing a white T-shirt which was far too small and a pair of baggy black shorts that were much too large. He nervously shifted his weight from one white skinny leg to the other, and dragged heavily on his cigarette. He truly looked pathetic. "I gotta see you, Sparks," he whispered, stubbing out his cigarette on the steel deck.

I invited him in, and was surprised he went to the trouble to close and lock the door. Usually outside doors are left open during the day, promoting a cross draught which keeps the cabin cool. He should have known better. "Sorry to bother you when you're off duty, Sparks," he whispered, "but I was hoping you could send this radiogram to New York when you next go on watch." He nervously handed me a sheet of paper.

"Of course I'll send it. I'm going on duty in half an hour." I could see it was in code, addressed to the head office in New York. "No problem, it'll be in New York in thirty-five minutes."

It was obvious Bloom didn't want to leave. He struggled to light up another cigarette, nervously puffing away. Something was really worrying him. Finally he pulled himself together. "Sparks, can I talk to you in confidence?"

he said, lowering his voice, and glancing around the cabin to make sure we were alone.

"Of course. Sit down, please. Can I offer you a drink? Or are you just an after-dinner drinker?"

Bloom smiled and sat down on the couch. He took deep drags on his cigarette. "This is my first trip on one of these ships," he replied. "I now realize the routine at sea is a lot different from a nine to five office job. I'm sorry about that remark I made, you know, about drinking before dinner."

"That's okay. What's worrying you?" I asked, fixing him a Bacardi and Coca-Cola, with a generous helping of my precious ice.

"I really don't know where to start," he began, nervously looking around the cabin. "Are you sure nobody can hear us?"

"I'm sure. Richard is on watch. Nobody is listening, I promise you. What's the problem?"

Despite my assurances that our conversation would be private, Bloom leaned toward me and spoke in whispers. "Well, I suppose I should tell you that I'm not on board to check your accounting books. That was just a front, and I'm sorry I pissed you off. I'm actually checking on Captain Krause. Berners is well-aware that you and Krause are not exactly on good terms. You know, Krause always files a shitty report about you at the end of each trip?"

"Yes, I know." I handed Bloom a tall frosty glass which made him smile. "What does Berners think about Krause's complaints about me? Does he believe all that shit?"

Bloom became a little more relaxed and made himself comfortable on the couch. "Confidentially, Berners thinks Krause is crazy. You should hear all the shit the Old Man tells him when they're alone. Berners is looking for an excuse to dump him."

"Berners needs an excuse to dump him?" I exclaimed. "Surely he has enough just from the last trip. He spent fifty-thousand dollars. And then, there's the Coast Guard always filing reports about him. Isn't that enough?"

"Last trip, he had excuses. You and the Third in jail, and dealing with Castro's mob isn't routine, is it? The Coast Guard thinks he's crazy but they don't think he's doing anything sinister, like spying on Cape Canaveral," whispered Bloom, gratefully sipping his drink.

"But he doesn't even obey the first rule of maritime law, like passing green to green," I explained. "The idiot is a danger to other shipping."

"Berners is aware of his accident record, but he's the only Captain we've got who is willing to go back and forth to Cuba these days. By the way, my cabin's been searched. I don't know what they were looking for except, perhaps, this key. It's the second one to the safe containing the gold bullion." Bloom held up the key. "I thought you might be able find a place to hide it."

"Me? How about the safe in the office? Only Krause and I have a key."

"No. It's the Captain I'm hiding it from. Do you have a copy of the company code book?"

"No. Only the Captain has a copy."

"Is that so?" Bloom looked very surprised. "Then you couldn't de-code the message I got from New York?"

"No, I couldn't."

I wondered whether to tell Bloom that the copy of his radiogram was missing, and that I suspected Krause's steward of stealing it, but I wanted to find out a little more about what was going on in Bloom's head before I gave him cause to lose his temper. "Was the message important?"

"Yes. Berners has set up a meeting for me with Ramon Perez. He's the owner of the Cuban bank in Santiago. He

140

knows what the Old Man really paid for the molasses and how much it cost to get you guys out of jail. Berners also warned me that Fidel Castro's mob has taken over the refinery."

"I rather suspected that, but why the big secret? Surely the Old Man should be the first to know about the refinery."

"I'm sure he knows all this. Sparks, I'll give you the second key to the safe where we have the gold. Hide it someplace safe. I'll ask for it when I need it."

Bloom handed me the key which I put in my pocket. "I'll hide it inside the transmitter. That's safer than any steel safe because I've got it wired up to give anyone a nasty two hundred volt shock if they start getting too nosey."

"That's clever. Are you going on watch now?"

"In about fifteen minutes. I have to stick to the international communication rules. We work to Greenwich Mean Time," I explained. "I'll send your radiogram directly to New York. Are you expecting an answer tonight?"

"I hope so. It's still evening in New York, and there's always somebody in the office to accept ship's messages," replied Bloom, finishing his drink. "Sparks, I'm sorry I stepped on your toes when I first came on board. I mean by taking over your office and going over the old accounts. Berners told me to do that. It was just a cover up for what I was really doing." Bloom smiled and got up to leave. "All that shit you told me about rhubarb and balls as big as coconuts, and I believed you."

I laughed. "Who knows, it might even cure galloping dog-rot."

"Is there such a disease?"

"If there is, you can bet a Cuban whore will have it," I said. "They fuck seamen from all over the world and have their diseases to prove it."

"Yeah, I know. Berners warned me about the drip and blue balls and all the rest," admitted Bloom, getting up from the couch. "Look after this key, Sparks, and I want you to be present when the Captain and I open up the safe."

I accepted the key, but didn't really want the extra responsibility. "I'm glad we've had this little talk, Henri and you're welcome to come back anytime. I get a better picture on my TV than the Old Man."

"Thanks. If I have to watch another "Heckle and Jeckle" episode in the Old Man's cabin I'll go nuts." Bloom slowly opened the cabin door. "Sparks? Thank you. I'll be waiting up for the reply."

After Bloom left, I realized I should have told him the Old Man had a copy of Berners' radiogram and probably decoded it. I refilled the ice trays, and then went up to the Radio Room to start my last watch of the day. If Bloom had problems, so did I. We were literally in the same boat, and Captain Krause, the man in charge, was a cold, calculating bastard who many thought was insane. It wasn't easy for any of us, because when he gave orders, he expected them to be obeyed, and we all knew that Bessler was his executioner if we didn't.

Immediately after I sent Bloom's Radiogram to New York, the Captain appeared at the Radio Room door. "You use too much power for the transmitter," he shouted, banging on the door with his fist. "You blast away my television set with too much power. Was that a radiogram for me?" He held out his hand for the message.

"No, Sir. It was private," I replied, coldly, not even bothering to look up from my log book.

"It was private?"

"Yes, I sent it for a member of the ship's crew."

"Was it Bloom?" shouted Krause, angrily.

"Sir, it was a private radiogram," I replied, finishing up the entry in my log. "Now, if you'll excuse me, I've got to take the weather report." I put on my headphones leaving the Old Man muttering to himself outside on the deck. I felt tempted to slam the door in his face, just as he had once done to me.

"I do not need the weather report, we are now in the Caribbean," he yelled, angry that I was ignoring him. "Did you hear me?"

"Sir, I always take the weather report. It's part of my job." I continued to take down the official marine forecast from Washington whilst Krause bristled with rage.

"You will not use the ship's transmitter again except for ship's official business," he shouted.

"Sir, you cannot forbid the transmission of private messages if they are paid for," I replied, trying to maintain my cool, calm, superior attitude that always drove him to distraction.

"You will listen," he roared. "I now forbid the use of that transmitter! The signal interferes with the ship's radar." Krause glared at me, his face bloated and flushed. "You only use the transmitter for official ship's traffic. I will make the entry in the ship's log." He glared at me with a look of hatred then waddled back to his cabin.

As soon as he had left, I checked the rules and regulations regarding the transmission of private messages. Obviously he had checked them himself and knew he had authority to forbid the use of the transmitter except for official ship's business.

The rest of the watch was routine. I heard one ship's operator surreptitiously tapping out the British football scores, which he must have picked up from a BBC overseas program, and there were several ships trying to contact Cuban shore stations without much success.

Just a few minutes before I went off watch, I picked up a New York Radio station calling me with a radiogram, probably the reply to Bloom's message, which I knew he was anxiously waiting for. I switched on the transmitter and called New York, knowing the Old Man's television picture would be going haywire again as I blasted away through the ether. The message was for Bloom and it was again in code. I typed it up, sealed it in an envelope, and phoned the Bridge for Weicecz, the duty seaman. Seconds later he appeared at the door and I told him to take the radiogram to Bloom's cabin and hand it to him personally.

I stared at the carbon copy I had made; five groups of letters which made up the message. Whatever they meant must have been important, so I decided to hide the copy. I wasn't going to let the Captain's steward find it this time.

A few minutes later, Weicecz was back, banging on the Radio Room door, his face almost frozen in fear. "Sparks," he shouted, "I think Herr Bloom is dead."

I quickly followed Weicecz across the deck. Before we had even reached Bloom's cabin, I could hear the Old Man and Herr Bessler yelling at each other in German. They were already in Bloom's cabin when I got there. I saw Bloom's body lying on the floor near the door. He was wearing a large grey, terry towel robe. His face was contorted like he was in pain, and from his half-open mouth oozed a yellow colored vomit all over the carpet.

"Are you sure he's dead?" I asked, attempting to enter his cabin. The Old Man immediately stepped in front of me. "Herr Bloom is dead. He is dead. That is all," he snapped, using his high toned, clipped voice. "There is nothing that can be done for him."

Krause was not about to let me enter the cabin. He glared at Weicecz, the duty seaman who discovered the body, and screamed at him in German. Immediately the

144

young seaman scurried away across the deck like a scalded cat. Krause continued to block the doorway while he argued with Herr Bessler. Both of them would be required to sign an official report about Bloom's death in the ship's logbook, and send a copy of it to the Head Office in New York. No doubt they were arguing about what they should say. When the Old Man saw me still standing in the corridor, he angrily slammed the door in my face.

Seconds later, Deiter, the Captain's steward came sashaying along the corridor with a bucket and mop. He glared at me with a look of contempt as we both listened outside the cabin door to the argument going on inside. "What are they saying?" I asked.

"You not understand German?" he replied, in his guttural, swishy accent. "Then, is not your business."

I inwardly cursed myself for having spoken to the grinning little swine, and wished I had confronted him when he was searching Bloom's suitcases. Suddenly the cabin door opened and the Captain glared at me. "You, Herr Sparks. Go at once to the Radio Room. I have urgent message for New York." He then spoke to his steward in German, pointing to Bloom's clothes strewn all across the cabin. "Schnell. Schnell," he screamed, when he saw me still outside in the corridor. "I tell you go to the Radio Room." Again, Krause slammed the door in my face. *How much of a hint did I need?*

There was nothing else I could do. Bloom was dead. The fact the Old Man had taken over, forbidding me to enter Bloom's cabin was very worrying. He and Bessler would no doubt work out some deal to their advantage. Since I was still on duty I went back to the Radio Room but Krause's urgent message for New York didn't materialize during the remainder of the watch, *so what was the Old Man up to?* I signed off duty and went back to my cabin. It was hard to believe Bloom was dead.

Richard came straight to my cabin when he got off watch. "What's the latest news, Sparks?"

"You tell me. The Old Man has locked up Bloom's cabin, and hasn't reported his death to New York," I replied, getting the glasses out to fix a drink. "I think Bloom was murdered."

This time it was Richard who took the trouble to close my cabin door. He then sat down on the couch. "Bessler recorded it in the log as death by natural causes," he whispered. "Heat stroke caused by excessive sunbathing."

"Heat stroke? Bullshit! Bloom never went out in the sun," I replied, reaching into my bookshelf for a copy of INTERNATIONAL MARITIME LAW. "I'm looking up about reporting a death at sea. Here it is. DEATH AT SEA. It's a lot of legal jargon, but it says the autopsy will decide the exact cause of death."

"Autopsy? Are you kidding? There won't be any autopsy," replied Richard.

"According to this, the law says an autopsy must be performed by a competent authority as soon as practical."

"Now read the small print, Sparks. I'm already one jump ahead of you. I read it as well. It says if there are not adequate facilities to store the body in a refrigerator, then it's up to the Captain to decide on its disposal," explained Richard. "So, the Old Man has decided to bury him at sea before we even get to Cuba."

"Bury him at sea?" I was shocked. "When did you hear this?"

Richard quickly returned to his cabin to make sure nobody was listening and returned with a bottle of whiskey and two small glasses. "I heard the Old Man ordering the Bosun to sew up the body in canvas."

"You're kidding? He can't do that. There has to be a death certificate signed by a doctor." I continued to read through long chapter about the rules and regulations that must be carried out after a death at sea.

Richard carefully put the glasses on the table and uncorked the bottle. "You can bet the Old Man has looked up the rules, Sparks. He has already signed the entry in the logbook, and if he thinks it's necessary to dispose of the body quickly, then he can order a burial at sea. And that's just what's he's doing." Richard generously poured out two glasses of whiskey "Here, take a swig of this. I was saving it for a special occasion."

"Is this a special occasion?" I replied, sipping appreciatively from the glass. "This is so much better than rum. What is it?"

Richard held up the bottle. "You've had some before. It's Glenlivet Special Malt."

"I must get a case." I held up my glass. "Cheers, it's great stuff." Richard nodded in agreement. "It's hard to believe what's happened," I continued. "Did you know Bloom wanted to confide in me? He came in here a few hours ago asking for my help."

"So, what did he want?"

"The poor bastard was so nervous, I felt sorry for him. He apologized for being so officious and told me he was actually checking up on Krause, not my accounting."

"Go on," replied Richard. "What did he find out, and what was in the messages back and forth to New York?"

"Bloom told me he had to contact Ramon Perez who owns the Cuban-American bank in Santiago and find out what the Old Man paid for the molasses, and how much he really paid to get us out of jail," I replied. "Oh! Dear God! I just realized the duty seaman didn't bring back the radiogram he was supposed to give to Bloom. If the Old Man gets his hands on that he'll have a conniption fit."

"Who was the duty seaman?"

"It was Weicecz, Herr Bessler's little punch bag."

"That poor little bastard, Shit! He's on the Bridge with Bessler! I'll try and find out what he done with it," replied Richard, draining his glass.

"I'll be in the Radio Room and make sure the copies are still in the file." I finished my whiskey and followed Richard to the Boat Deck. I could hear Bessler on the Bridge yelling at somebody in German. Richard and I hid behind a life boat. "Who's he yelling at?" I asked.

"The duty seaman, Weicecz. He's just slapped the poor little bastard across the face." Again and again, Weicecz yelled in pain as Bessler's hard hand whipped across his face. "The son-of-a-bitch is beating up on that kid," whispered Richard, clenching his fists. "Jesus, I wish he'd go ashore in Cuba and give us all a chance to knife him."

"Bessler's too smart for that, and you'll notice he never gets too close to the rail, especially when it's dark. One day somebody will push him overboard," I replied. "I wonder what he's yelling at him about."

"He's probably mad at the kid for going to you first when he found Bloom's body."

"That's crazy, it was me who sent him to Bloom's cabin, naturally he'd come back to tell me."

"Well, obviously Bessler doesn't agree with you. Anyway, he's scared the poor kid half to death, so we won't get much information from him now. I guess he just dropped the radiogram on the carpet when he saw Bloom dead on the floor."

"I'll bet the Old Man deciphered the message about Bloom meeting Ramon Perez," I replied. "That's why he got rid of him."

Richard and I soon got tired of crouching behind the lifeboat and crept back to the Radio Room. Luckily I had the original messages Bloom had sent to the Head Office in New York, and a copy of their reply. Unfortunately, so did the Captain, and thanks to Deiter, his thieving little steward, he also was able to decode it. "If only we could get hold of the code book." I mumbled to myself.

"No problem. I've got the key to Bloom's cabin." Richard held up a set of keys. "Shall we go in and look for it?"

"Go into Bloom's cabin now? Where's the Old Man?"

"Where else? In his cabin watching television," replied Richard, jangling the keys. "Let's go."

Bloom's body was on his bunk, his skinny frame covered with a white sheet. I shuddered inwardly, but the reality of his death had not yet penetrated my befuddled brain. I was shocked to see the cabin had been ransacked. Bloom's suitcases were opened and his clothes were thrown all over the floor. The cupboards were opened; the papers on his desk scattered all over the place, and the cabin smelled of disinfectant. At least the steward had cleaned up the carpet where Bloom had vomited.

"Krause has torn this place apart," whispered Richard. "I wonder what the bastard was looking for."

"The second key to the safe containing the gold bullion I expect."

"That's right! Bloom had the second key. I wonder if they found it?" queried Richard, examining some of the paperwork scattered across the desk.

"No, they didn't. Bloom gave it to me for safe keeping." I replied, realizing I still had to hide it in the transmitter.

"For crissake, Sparks, why didn't you tell me?" exclaimed Richard. "If the Old Man knows you've got it, then you'll be the next one on his list to kick the bucket."

"He doesn't know I've got it. Bloom gave it to me this evening just before I went on watch. Anyway, we're here to find the code book."

"In this mess?" Richard sifted through more papers. "Krause has probably taken it, Jesus what a conniving bastard."

I noticed a small green bottle under the bunk and picked it up. It was half full of liquor. "Hey! Look at this." The cork was missing and some of the syrupy liquid had soaked into the carpet.

"What is it?" asked Richard, now rifling through some drawers.

"It's Maria Brizzard Apricot Brandy. Krause's favorite after-dinner drink." My first thought was that Krause had put poison in the bottle. "Do you think Bloom was poisoned?" I asked, gingerly sniffing the contents of the bottle. When I saw him he was laying face down in a pool of yellow vomit, which Deiter has now cleaned up. "Let's keep this bottle for evidence."

"For crissake, Sparks, quit acting like a detective! Bloom is dead, and the Old Man's dumping the body over the side as soon as he can. If we're not careful we'll be the next ones to go over the side. Remember, we're dealing with an insane lunatic. Let's find the code book and get out of here."

"Okay, but I'd still like to know how Bloom died."

Richard glanced at his watch. "We're pushing our luck, Sparks. In a few minutes, the Old Man's going for a stroll around the deck. And who knows? He might decide to come in here." I needed no second warning and hurried outside, back to the fresh air on deck, leaving Richard to lock the door. Leaning against the deck rail I stared at the black water swirling by just a few feet below, and tried to piece together all that had happened. A few minutes later, armed with two glasses and his special bottle of whisky Richard joined me on the deck. "You're going to need this," he said, pouring out two more glasses of Glenlivet. "I reckon Bloom died a very painful death judging by the look on his face. I also noticed his revolver wasn't under his pillow."

"Now who is playing detective?" I replied, appreciating the warm glow of the special malt whiskey.

"I'm not playing detective. I was just curious that's all, so I lifted the sheet and examined his body."

"My God, better you than me."

"One of us had to do it. We have to know how he died. He could have been shot or stabbed. Somebody had to look and see."

"Well, what's your verdict? Was he shot, stabbed or poisoned?"

"I think he was poisoned. The pupils in his eyes were wide open, and his tongue was all swollen up and purple. He must have choked to death. I'll bet the poison's in that liquor bottle you found under the bunk."

"You mean this one?" I replied, holding up the brandy bottle. "I told you, it's Maria Brizzard Apricot Brandy, Krause's favorite drink. It's still half full. I'll give it to the police as evidence when we get back."

"Maria Brizzard? You're right, the Old Man's liquor cabinet is full of that stuff," replied Richard. "It's simple. He filled the bottle with poison and gave it to Bloom. In other words, Krause slipped him a Mickey."

I chuckled. "A very lethal Mickey. Now, he'll soon start looking for the empty bottle," I replied. "I'm going to call it our Exhibit A and hide it in the transmitter cabinet in the

Radio Room. I have the door wired to give anyone who tries to open it a nasty little shock."

Early the next morning, just as I was going on my first watch, I saw the Captain and First Officer Bessler standing on the Bridge. The sun was about to rise out of a calm sea and already coloring the clouds with an orange glow. It was a beautiful sight until I saw Kimmel, the Bosun and two seamen struggling across the deck with Bloom's corpse, now sewn up in ship's canvas. Without any ceremony, they balanced their gruesome cargo across the deck rail and glanced up at the Captain waiting for his signal. Seconds later, he nodded his head, and Henri Bloom's body was pushed overboard into the Caribbean. It was 0600 hundred hours on October 25th, 1958. He had been on board exactly one week.

Twenty minutes later the Old Man strutted into the Radio Room and handed me a terse message addressed to Ludwig Berners in New York.

REGRET TO INFORM YOU HENRI BLOOM
DIED OF HEAT EXPOSURE. BURIED AT SEA
0600 THIS MORNING.
  SIGNED: CAPTAIN KRAUSE,
     CUBAN TRADER.

~~~

CHAPTER TEN

Santiago Refinery Abandoned

It was close to noon when we entered Santiago Bay, and as usual, it was a hot sweltering day. The crew had been told that nobody would be allowed ashore, but that was a routine order that none of them really took seriously. A few of them gathered on the poop deck and looked across the bay to the refinery. It was not a very attractive view and the stench of the stinking molasses had already reached us.

"Have you contacted the pilot station?" demanded the Captain, striding into the Radio Room. I shook my head in reply to his question, pressing the earphones closer to my ear trying to decipher a rather garbled message from another ship. Suddenly he reached out and pulled the earphones off my head. "You will answer me when I speak to you," he snapped.

My first impulse was to reach for the loaded revolver I kept in a drawer and shoot him. "You bastard," I yelled, restraining my urge to shove him through the door. "Don't you ever do that again. Get the hell out of here."

"You don't speak to me like that. I will enter this insubordination in the ship's log book immediately."

"You ARE crazy! You're completely insane, and what's more everybody at the Head Office knows it. They'll be seeing a lot more in that log book beside my name when we get back to Philadelphia. I'm giving Ludwig Berners a full report of everything I know about Henri Bloom's death, so you can chew on that piece of news. Now get the hell out of here if you want me to contact the pilot station."

"Bloom's death? He was seen drinking in your cabin just before he died, and I have many witnesses," replied the Old Man, looking very worried. "That is what goes in the logbook, and you and Bloom always argue about the ship's account, that also goes in the logbook. And Bloom found many mistakes you make. That also goes in the logbook. I too, make a report when we get back to Philadelphia. Now, Herr Schparks, you will contact the Cuban pilot station and argue with me no more," yelled Krause, striding out of the Radio Room.

An hour later my temper had cooled down a little, but the temperature in the Radio Room was rising. We proceeded into Santiago Bay at three knots, and waited for a pilot to come aboard and steer us to a jetty. It was all routine. The ship could no doubt have found her own way into the refinery loading area as we had done it so many times before. Usually there were the port officials to entertain and bribe with cases of Scotch and wads of twenty dollar bills before they gave permission for us to enter the dock. The Customs launch usually came alongside to buy a few cases of cigarettes from the Old Man. In return, their agents conveniently turned a blind eye when the crew smuggled a few cartons of Lucky Strikes ashore with them.

Where was the pilot launch and all the port officials now? Richard, who had been watching the shore with his binoculars, came into the radio room where I had a refrigerator and some cold drinks. "Any contact?" he asked, nodding at the transmitter.

"Not a sausage. Three other ships have been calling as well, but I haven't heard CLM Santiago on the air for days."

"Maybe none of Castro's men know how to operate a transmitter," replied Richard, popping open a bottle of Coca-Cola.

"That's very true. What's the Old Man going to do?" I asked.

Richard shrugged his shoulders. "He's watching the shoreline like a hawk. We're still heading into the refinery dock at three knots. In less than an hour we'll be alongside."

"Pilot or no pilot?"

"It seems that way, and since we're empty and high out of the water, there's not so much worry about the sandbanks, but when we're fully loaded. . ."

"We'll need a pilot." We both walked out on deck and looked over the side of the ship wondering if at any moment we might run into an underwater mountain of sand. "Have you ever gone aground?"

"Only once, it was on a Vancouver ferry. The Old Man thought he could navigate the ship without a pilot. Twenty minutes later, CRUNCH! It's like slamming your car into a bush. There's a helluva grinding sound and everyone falls on their ass. It's definitely not recommended when you're on a tanker full of hot molasses. We'd all be swimming about in the shit."

"Thanks for the lurid description. I think I'll try calling the pilot station again."

"Sparks, don't worry, it's too late. We're nearly there. It's when we're fully loaded we gotta worry. So where are all the leeches? The Port Captain, the health authorities, and refinery officials? They're usually guzzling booze in the Old Man's cabin by now, holding out their hands for a few hundred bucks."

"Yes, it's very ominous. Just keep me informed of what's happening on the Bridge. I think the Old Man is scared to come in here after our dust-up this morning. He knows I've got a loaded revolver in this drawer and I'll shoot the bastard if he does that to me again."

"Does what?"

"The idiot ripped off my headphones while I was listening to a ship trying to contact a Cuban station."

"Jesus! What a lunatic. I would have kicked him in the balls, but I don't think he's got any." Richard finished his drink, threw the empty Coca-Cola bottle over the side and went back to the Bridge. I tried once more to contact Radio Santiago, tapping out CLM on the Morse key and straining my ears for a reply, but I had a strong feeling I was wasting my time.

At exactly noon, we inched alongside the loading dock of the Santiago Los Canos refinery without the aid of tugs, and immediately the deck hands leapt ashore and secured the ship, fore and aft. Normally the whole docking procedure would have been carried out under the direction of the Cuban docking pilot, but since he didn't show up and there had been no answer to any of our radio or flag signals, the Old Man had decided to dock the ship himself.

We had arrived, but the refinery was deserted. It was an eerie feeling. Nowhere ashore was there any sign of life. The refinery was its usual entanglement of pipes and pumps, all fizzing and farting from every ill-fitting joint and worn-out connection as the hot molasses was pumped around the refinery. Had it been oil, the whole hissing mess would have exploded in flames from the escaping fumes.

As usual, the deck hands went ashore and winched the long flexible pipes on board and connected them to the ship, taking their orders from the nautical version of the famous American Dolly Sisters, Bessler and Schmidt, the two blond, blue eyed First and Second officers, while poor Richard, who was the junior Third, was sent back and forth, up and down the slippery gangplank conveying the messages.

156

The Old Man, safely ensconced on the Bridge, glowered at me when I went out on deck to see what was happening. "We will load up as usual," he shouted at me. I shrugged my shoulders. I didn't think we were there to appreciate the view. Nevertheless, I was glad I didn't have to make the decision. Normally, with the help of the experienced refinery docking crew, the loading pipes would have been connected in less than an hour. It was two and half hours later when the hot molasses started flowing into the *Cuban Trader's* empty belly.

On previous visits, it seemed anyone wearing a uniform felt entitled to come on board and avail themselves of the ship's hospitality. The top brass were first on board by grabbing a ride on the rickety old Customs Launch which came alongside in the middle of the bay. Everyone scrambled onto the deck and headed for the Captain's cabin where Deiter, the detestable little steward, sashayed around with a tray of drinks, hors d'oeuvres and cocktail sandwiches that Steve, the chef, had so painstakingly prepared. When we arrived at the dock, a small mob of minor Cuban officials were waiting to collect their share of the goodies. They usually elbowed each other impatiently waiting for the crew to lower the gangplank before scurrying up the slippery slope like a herd of wildebeest dying of thirst in the desert, but not this time. Where were all the hungry and thieving bastards now?

On my first visit to Cuba, I made the mistake of playing host to the minor officials, handing out booze and cigarettes like it was Christmas, but I soon discovered the thieving bastards were not satisfied with these presents. They stole anything in the office that wasn't nailed down. I quickly realized it was better to ignore them, and take refuge behind the locked door of my cabin.

About two hours after we had docked, I heard the familiar *splash, splash, splash* as Deiter tossed the empty booze bottles into the bay. I wondered how much the Old Man had drunk on his own because there were no Cuban Officials in his cabin this time.

Richard eventually finished his deck watch, and groaned with fatigue when he entered his cabin. There were even louder groans when he discovered he had no ice. "Sparks," he yelled. "Have you got any ice?"

I'd never admit it, but I always felt very guilty lying on my bunk whilst Richard was out on the sweltering deck working his butt off. I had already guessed he would have no ice, and started fixing him a drink as soon as he entered his cabin. "Here you are," I shouted, meeting him half way in the bathroom.

"Thanks, Sparks," he said, "I'll drink it in the shower."

Twenty minutes later, he entered my cabin, peeled off his oversize white bath towel and wallowed in the breeze from the Sears & Roebuck heavy-duty cooling fan that Axel gave me. "Sparks, have you any idea what this feels like?" he asked.

"Breezy?"

"Breezy is right."

"So, you like my electric fan with the fresh wind of reality blowing up your intimate corridors?"

"Sparks, if you mean I like cooling off my balls in front of a fan after a hot shower, then you're right." He then began flapping the huge white towel, twisting and turning to get the full benefit of the cooling breeze.

"Richard, did you know all this will go down in my book?"

"Yeah, Sparks. You already warned me, so tell it like it is. The handsome, well-endowed Third Mate, stood balls-ass naked in front of the fan drinking Bacardi and Coca-Cola, hint, hint, hint." Richard turned and held up his empty glass, grinning. "He stood there balls ass naked drinking Bacardi and Coca-Cola."

"Unfortunately, he stood there too long," I continued, "and eventually his balls shriveled up like two pickled walnuts and he was never able to get an erection again."

"God forbid!" groaned Richard, moving quickly into his own cabin. "If you had taken the hint and fixed me another drink, Sparks, I would have posed for you, balls ass naked, while you took a photograph to illustrate your book. Just think about that, you might have had a best seller."

Eventually, Richard got dressed and came back to my cabin bringing with him two drinks. "Just needs ice, Sparks."

"Thanks," I said, switching off my television set which was filled with unrecognizable mayhem from the bowels of some awful Cuban television station. "So, what happens now, do we just load up and leave?"

"Not JUST load up, we're going to be here longer than usual, there's only one pump working. God knows what will happen while we're here. I can't figure out where everyone is hiding. Didn't you say that Castro's men have taken over the refinery?"

"That's was the information in Bloom's radiogram."

"Then where are they? Is it a Communist holiday or something?"

"A Communist holiday, surely the Cubans haven't been brainwashed already? Maybe they're celebrating a victory. Who knows? What's the Old Man going to do with all those cigarettes he has in the storeroom if the Customs don't buy them?"

"Sparks, you know as much as I do. The only thing I know for sure, is that the Old Man will try to sneak out of dock without paying for any of this shit. That's what he'll try to do. And he'll take his cigarettes and whatever is in the safe back with him to Philly." Richard stood and opened the cabin door. The air was warm and sticky and reeked of hot molasses. "I feel like taking a walk along to the refinery office and see if I can find Maria."

"Not smart. If she was in the refinery, she would have been down to the ship by now, waving her panties in the air."

Richard grinned. "That's true. Maria is certainly a little nympho and I hope she's never cured. Richard gazed at the nearly empty port. "It's really weird out there. The place seems deserted without all the refinery workers, but I can see a few whores creeping up the crew's gangplank, so there's gotta be plenty of action back aft."

There was nothing more enterprising than a Cuban whore. If the johns didn't go to the whorehouse, then they took their goodies to the johns. "Those Cuban whores are on the ball. I'm glad the crew are getting a piece of ass, otherwise they might start a mutiny."

"Yeah, they're getting a piece of ass, but what about us?" moaned Richard.

"We'll survive. I've seen too many blue balls to risk availing myself of those *femme de nuit*."

"Fam de what?"

"Femme de nuit. Ladies of the night, it's French."

Richard stared longingly across the deck to the whorehouse. "Do you reckon they're all poxed up?"

"Up to their ears," I replied

"So? Who cares?" answered Richard. "I'm not interested in their ears."

I rattled the ice in my empty glass, wondering why it melted so quickly but took such a long time to freeze. "Let's hope it stays quiet like this. The sooner we fill up and get out of here, the better."

"You're a dreamer, Sparks. There's the pay-off, remember? This shit has to be paid for. Poor Henri Bloom was supposed to negotiate an on-going deal with these bastards, now he's fish food at the bottom of the Atlantic. Anyway, fuck it! I'm going to lay down for a while." Richard took his drink and disappeared through the connecting bathroom and went back to his cabin.

A few minutes later he was back. "The Old Man just phoned, he wants to see me," he yelled, dragging on his uniform coat. "Jesus! How I hate that bastard."

Apparently the whores back aft were doing a roaring trade selling their wares, but there were not enough of them, and eventually a couple of seamen started fighting. Naturally, Deiter, the Captain's detestable little steward, reported everything to the Old Man, who immediately sent for Richard, and ordered him to get rid of the women.

I watched from my cabin door as the whores reluctantly emerged from the crew's quarters, cursing and moaning as they struggled to get back into their street clothes. Twenty minutes later Richard reported back to the Captain and confirmed he had sent the women ashore. He then noticed Deiter hiding behind a lifeboat. If looks could kill, the Captain's steward would have died on the spot. "It was you who told the Old Man there were women on board, wasn't it?" shouted Richard. "You sniveling, rat faced little Kraut asshole. I hope the crew hang your balls out to dry."

Minutes later, Richard was back in my cabin grinning. "Well your "famda newy" all went ashore as ordered, but what I didn't tell the Old Man was they went down one gang plank and back up the other," chuckled Richard, pouring himself a fresh drink. "Jesus, they're having a wild orgy back aft, screwing in every cabin, including your friend Helmut. All the doors are wide open to let the breeze blow through and they're standing in line."

"Ugh! I can imagine the line up at the surgery for penicillin in a few days' time," I groaned.

Richard gratefully swigged his drink. "Hey! How much rum do we have left?"

"Only two cases of that cheap crap left, how long before the ship is fully loaded?" I asked.

"At this rate, with only one pump working, I'd say another thirty-six hours. Plenty of time for us to sneak ashore, buy some rum and have a quickie."

"Richard, count me out. It's too dangerous. I feel as if we're sitting on a time bomb as it is."

It was now nearly midnight. It had been a long day and I wanted to turn in. Fortunately, I was off duty and could sleep if I wanted to, but Richard was duty officer from midnight, and was checking the temperature of the molasses. The hotter it was, the easier it was to pump. Unfortunately, he had to stay up all night and watch over the loading operation.

Suddenly, I realized the handle on my cabin door was moving. Thank God it was locked. Most seamen would have knocked, and Richard always entered through the interconnecting bathroom. It could be some sneak thief on board, trying all the cabins. I grabbed a heavy flashlight and crept through the bathroom into Richard's cabin just as Maria came in through the door.

"It's me, Sparks," she whispered, throwing her arms around me. "Richard sent me here to wait for him."

"That's fantastic. How are you, and how's Consuela?"

"I am okay, but very nervous." Maria brushed her long black hair from her face. She wasn't wearing any make-up, which was unusual, and she looked tired.

"Sit down. Relax. What can I get you to drink?" I asked. "Where's Consuela?" Maria was obviously distressed by the question, and looked at me for a few seconds wondering what to say. "Consuela? She was too scared to come to the ship. Everywhere there is Guerrilleros. Some of them are bastards, and some are okay. Many friends of mine are now joining the Fidelistas, because they are for the peasants."

"But why is the refinery deserted?"

"My father and all the other workers left when the Guerrilleros came here two days ago," replied Maria. "Can I have some Coca-Cola?"

"Yes, of course." I handed her a bottle from Richard's refrigerator. "But where are Castro's men now? The place is deserted."

"They will be back. Already they have moved into the Manager's house. They are watching you, and will be here tomorrow for the money."

"What about your father?" I asked, "And the refinery workers?"

Maria shrugged. "They all scared. They wait to see what happens, but no ships come here now and they have too much molasses. It is okay to take a shower, yes?"

"Yes, of course. You know where everything is. I'm going to lie down and maybe get some sleep."

"I no get much sleep," whispered Maria, grinning and starting to undress. "I am so glad to see my Ricardo."

"Will I see you in the morning?" I asked, before returning to my cabin.

"No, Sparks. I leave before the Guerrilleros get here. They warn us not to come to the ship, but when I see all those putas from the whorehouse creeping on the ship I come here as well." I pointed to the bag of toiletries Richard had brought for her and watched her face light up. "Thank you, Sparks. You are so kind."

"These are for Consuela, in case I don't see her." Maria began to cry. "Whatever is the matter?" I asked.

"Sparks, I am so sorry she not here."

"It's okay. I wasn't expecting her. You relax, take your shower, I'm going back to my cabin." Maria was still sobbing when I left and I couldn't figure out why. I helped myself to some of Richard's Glenlivet, then lay on my bunk.

So, Castro's men would be paying us a visit in the morning for their payment. Did they expect to be paid in gold bullion? We certainly didn't have enough in cash. This was not the kind of news I wanted to hear before trying to sleep. I finished my drink, appreciating the warm glow all the way down to my innards. It sure hit the spot, and I soon drifted off to sleep.

~~~

CHAPTER ELEVEN

The Fidelistas Plunder the Ship

I didn't sleep well, and was up early the next morning. As usual, when we were in dock, there were no fixed meal times because the officer's dining saloon was packed with gluttonous shore officials eating their heads off. This time, however, I was pleased to see the place was almost empty.

"Good morning, Sparks," yelled Steve from the galley. "Where are all the hungry-gutted officials this morning?"

"The rebels have scared them away, thank God!"

"Too true."

Hans, the steward, brought the menu. "The usual, sir," he asked, trying to hide the scratches on his face.

"Yes, please. What happened to your eye? And all those scratches? You better come and see me later. I'll put some iodine on them."

"Yes Sir, but will you report me to the Old Man?"

"Of course not," I reassured him, but you went ashore last night, didn't you?"

The steward nodded as he poured my coffee. "The whorehouse was full of drunken soldiers."

"And they roughed you up?"

"I thought they would shoot us."

"Well, you can't say you weren't warned. Shore leave is forbidden. How about Helmut, did he get beaten up as well?"

"Ya, he has same as me."

"You both come along to the surgery, and you better tell your mates those soldiers will be coming on board today. They're likely to be a thieving lot, and will just help themselves to whatever they can see, so hide all your cameras, radios and valuables. Otherwise they will just take whatever they fancy, and there's nothing we can do about it."

"The bastards."

"And for crissake, don't start any arguments with them. They're armed, and they'll shoot first, and ask questions later. You'd better warn everybody back aft. I've already put a notice up on the board, but a fat lot of good that will do. Has the Old Man been in for breakfast?"

"No, Sir. He sent his steward for it. Everybody say he's too scared to even go out on deck."

"Hans, there's nothing to be scared about. If the soldiers do come on board, don't fight or argue with them because they will have guns. You and Helmut don't need any reminder what soldiers with guns can do."

"No, Sir. They shoot anybody," relied Hans. "We will hide in my cabin."

I ate my breakfast of ham and eggs, drank some coffee and went back to my cabin. When I got back, the bathroom doors were open and Maria had left, leaving the tantalizing aroma of her perfume lingering in the air. It must have been very strong to overpower the sickening stench of the molasses.

Richard was already back on deck checking the temperatures, so I quickly went around his cabin and collected his typewriter, camera and binoculars and locked them with all my valuables in the emergency battery locker.

Out on deck, I noticed the Old Man was standing in the doorway of his cabin. He glared at me for a few seconds, "Herr Schparks. We have not found Herr Bloom's key, the second key to the safe. The soldiers, they will need payment." I could see Krause was very worried and he had good reason to be, the ship was now more than half full of molasses, but Henri Bloom wasn't around to pay for it.

"Sir, the responsibility for paying for the molasses was entrusted to you and Henri Bloom. Since Henri met with such an inexplicable accident, and you cannot find the second key, you'll have to give the soldiers the safe. If they know it contains some gold ingots, I'm sure they'll be able to open it with a small stick of dynamite." I knew I had touched a raw nerve by mentioning the gold, Krause was hoping to keep that for himself.

"Herr Schparks, we do not tell them about the gold in the safe. That is an order. We pay in cash, how many dollars in the office safe?"

"Only a few thousand dollars, Sir, not enough to pay for the molasses," I replied. "Because you spent too much of his precious money the last time we were here, Ludwig Berners drastically cut down the amount of cash I could keep on board."

"Herr Schparks, you will tell me how many dollars in the office safe, and bring them to my cabin," he snapped.

"Sir, that money is expressly on board to pay the crew's subs and for small expenses. I don't want to disobey Berners' orders. You heard what he said."

"You will not argue with me, Herr Schparks. You will bring me the money, all of it. Schnell! Schnell! That is an order."

Ten minutes later, I counted out five thousand dollars onto the Captain's desk, then handed him a slip of paper. "Please sign this receipt for the five thousand dollars, Sir."

"I sign nothing," snapped Krause, grabbing the wad of dollars. "This is ship's money. When the soldiers come on board, I want all deck officers in my office. You will watch and see nothing is taken or stolen. We will try to pay them with cash."

I must admit, the five thousand dollars in cash did look very tempting, but I doubted if the Cubans would accept that amount as payment. I could see the small safe containing the gold in a closet, partially hidden by a tattered brown curtain just inside the Old Man's bedroom. It didn't appear to be very heavy. If the soldiers found out it contained gold bullion, they would take it. It was obvious the Old Man was thinking the same as me. "Herr Schparks, you will say nothing about the gold. I will tell them five thousand dollars, in cash, was what we pay for the cargo. Now, go. Let me know when they come on board."

I returned to my cabin wondering if the soldiers knew how much a full tank of molasses was worth. "The Old Man's shit-scared isn't he?" observed Richard, popping his lathered-up face around the bathroom door. "He hasn't come out on deck once."

"He wants all deck officers in his cabin when Castro's men arrive," I replied. "We have to watch them all carefully."

"Yeah, he's such a chicken shit. Hey! Thanks for stowing away my valuables, Sparks. Where did the Old Man hide all his stuff, up his steward's ass?" joked Richard returning to the bathroom to continue shaving. "Do you reckon we should lock up any of this toilet gear?"

"I don't think we should leave it on show. My God! I hope they don't come in here. How are we doing? Are we half full yet?"

"More than that," shouted Richard, while he brushed his teeth. "The other shore pump is working now, so we should be able to leave on the mid-day tide tomorrow."

"Thank God for that," I replied. "Let's get the hell out of here."

168

"Maria thinks this will be our last trip for a while. She cried a lot last night. I really felt sorry for her. The soldiers took over the office building where she works, and they've also moved into the Manager's house next to the refinery office. She said one of the officers is going to use it for his headquarters," explained Richard. "Did she tell you about Consuela?"

I wondered how long it took Richard to shave, our conversation was getting ludicrous. "Maria told me Consuela was too scared to come on board."

Richard appeared in the doorway, razor in hand. He stared at me for a few seconds. "Didn't she tell you what happened? Consuela was raped by some soldiers two nights ago, and then thrown into the dock. She hid underneath the pier until it was nearly morning, then went back to the Manager's house. She's hiding in the basement.

"My God!" I flopped back onto my bunk devastated. "They raped her? Fucking bastards! They're all Cubans, it's not like they're a bunch of foreigners. Most of them are peasants. Maria said she knew some of them."

"All drunken soldiers are the same, Sparks, no matter what nationality they are. Sorry my friend, I thought Maria had told you. She said that Consuela was bruised and had some cuts, but she would be okay." I lay on my bunk thinking about Consuela. Why did they rape her when there were so many willing whores around?

"I notice you didn't hide my Scotch, Sparks. Do you want a swig?"

"Yes, please. Do you think I should try and get an emergency first aid kit to Consuela?"

"Maria said she was okay now, I'm sure they'd ask if they needed anything, so don't worry. By the way, Bessler has just informed the Old Man we'll be ready to sail on the noon tide tomorrow."

"Wouldn't that be great, but we haven't got enough cash to pay for the cargo, and the Old Man's shit scared because he can't find the second key to the safe with the gold bullion."

"Tough shit," yelled Richard from his cabin where he went to get his booze. "He shouldn't have knocked off poor Henri Bloom. The Old Man doesn't know you've got the second key does he?" Richard returned and generously filled a glass with his expensive malt Scotch and dropped in an ice cube, which was equally as valuable.

"Of course he doesn't know I've got it, and I'm not about to tell him. He's taken all the cash from the office safe, all five thousand bucks, and hopes the soldiers will accept that in payment."

"Not a chance. Don't they know what the cargo is worth?" asked Richard, holding up his bottle to see how much he had left.

"Maybe not, and the Old Man forbids me to mention the gold bullion." I sipped the special malt gratefully. "Wow! Richard, this Scotch is fantastic. Thanks."

"You're welcome. It sure hits the spot doesn't it?" Richard sat down on the couch and sighed. "Tell me, Sparks. What should I do about Maria? Try and smuggle her back to the States?"

"Smuggle her back to the States? What makes you think she wants to go? My God, Richard, think about it."

"I am thinking about it. I'd get a piece of ass every two or three hours all the way back to Philly."

"What happens when you get there?"

"She'll be on her own."

"On her own? You can't just leave her in Philadelphia! You're morally obligated to look after her! She's crazy in love with you. She wouldn't let you stray out of her sight."

Richard sighed and nodded his head. "Jesus, Sparks, as usual you're right. You're most definitely right, but you know I'm gonna feel like hell leaving her here, I mean look what happened to Consuela."

"You gotta remember this is their home. Maria may not want to pack up and leave. Have you asked her what she wants to do?"

"Not really. I assumed she would want to go back with me."

"You assumed? I think both girls are smart enough to know you and I are not serious. We're all out to have a good time, and they haven't missed out."

Richard nodded his head. "Yeah, you're right."

I sipped the special Scotch, appreciating the warm glow now enveloping my body. "Damn it! I wish this mob would hurry up and get this payment settled. This waiting is driving me crazy."

It was a nerve wracking experience knowing that any time we were going to be invaded by a mob of rebels, and we were constantly being watched. Suddenly Richard came into my office. "The soldiers, they're on their way, Sparks, and they've got rifles!" he yelled. "Is everything battened down? Have you hidden all the goodies?"

"Yes, everything except your Scotch."

"Don't worry, I hid that. Well, I suppose I'd better go out and greet them. What are you going to do Sparks? Hide, like the Old Man?"

"No. I'll come with you." When Richard and I went out on the deck, we saw about twenty or so soldiers dressed in scruffy green uniforms scrambling up the gangplank, each one carrying a rifle. "They look as if they mean business don't they? I just hope none of the crew are stupid enough to argue with them," I said, walking with Richard across the deck. As was expected, Herr Bessler, the Chief Officer, all dolled up in his best uniform, was at the top of the gangplank to welcome them aboard, reaching out his hand to greet the Cuban revolutionary officer leading the parade.

"The Capitan," snapped the Cuban, refusing to shake hands. Herr Bessler glanced warily towards the upper deck, but the Captain was nowhere to be seen.

"The Capitan," repeated the Cuban, pointing to the upper deck. He then ordered ten of his men to go back aft and search the ship. They all grinned and eagerly shuffled across the deck towards the crew's quarters while Herr Bessler reluctantly led the rebel officer to the upper deck, followed by six grinning soldiers. Richard and I nervously followed behind.

The Old Man met us at his cabin door wearing his best uniform and the usual display of medals ostentatiously pinned across his chest. "Look at the old fool," whispered Richard. "Who does he think he's fooling?" The Old Man grinned nervously, inviting everyone to go inside. He too offered to shake hands with the Cuban officer but was ignored. Leading the way into the Old Man's cabin, the Cuban officer was eagerly followed by his six rifle carrying soldiers. Herr Bessler, Richard and I dragged reluctantly behind.

"We have come for the payment," yelled the Cuban.

Deiter, the Captain's steward, all dressed up in his special black uniform, nervously stood in the center of the cabin with a tray of drinks until the Cuban officer glared at him in horror, frightening the young boy back into the corner. "The molasses and the refinery is now belonging to the people of Cuba," he announced. "You now pay us thirty thousand American dollars in cash."

The Old Man gulped down a glass of whisky and glanced at me, but I pretended not to notice. "Thirty

172

thousand dollars is too much. We usually pay only five thousand American dollars." He said handing over the five thousand I had given him from my office safe.

The Cuban officer examined the packet of dollar bills. "It is thirty thousand, and next time you come it will be more, much more."

At thirty thousand dollars, we were getting a bargain, except we didn't have that amount of cash on board, but we did have the gold bullion. I glanced at the Old Man, beads of perspiration breaking out across his forehead, and he was visibly shaking. Obviously he never intended to mention the gold.

"We have some food now," announced the Cuban officer, stuffing the wads of notes into his uniform pockets and grabbing a bottle of whiskey. Two soldiers immediately hustled the Old Man and the Chief Officer out of the cabin, leaving Richard and I staring at the four remaining soldiers who apparently intended to stay.

"Food, comida," I said, pointing to their departing comrades. The soldiers grinned and shook their heads, eagerly looking over the bottles of whiskey and cigarettes which Krause had on display. As soon as their officer had left the cabin, the four remaining soldiers immediately opened up two or three bottles of whiskey and filled their glasses to the brim with straight Scotch. Grinning and chattering to themselves like kids in a toy shop, they began to rummage through the Captain's office.

Suddenly grabbing a bottle of Scotch, one of them stumbled into the Captain's bedroom. "Jesus Christ, Sparks we gotta get them out of here. Hey! You can't go in there," yelled Richard, following him into the bedroom. Suddenly I heard a loud ZONK followed by a scream of pain. "Son-of-a-of-bitch," yelled Richard. "You goddamn son-of-a-bitch."

"What happened?" I yelled, hurrying into the bedroom.

"The thieving bastard slammed me on the head and rammed his rifle butt into my guts," moaned Richard, writhing in agony. The soldier was grinning like a fool, obviously enjoying the sight of Richard doubled up in pain.

"For God's sake, don't annoy him. I'll bet that rifle he's got is loaded. The asshole may go berserk, and there's nothing we can do about it." For the next fifteen minutes we had to watch four ignorant peasants dressed in badly fitting, bottle green uniforms, ransack the Captain's cabin. They opened cupboards, emptied out drawers, scattering the contents all over the floor, and frequently helped themselves to full glasses of whiskey.

Suddenly, one of them tripped on the carpet, crashing headlong into the couch. Richard was tempted to grab his rifle, but luckily thought better of it. The soldier awkwardly dragged himself to his feet and then angrily pushed over the couch, cursing and swearing as he tossed the whisky soaked cushions out onto the deck.

While he staggered across the cabin to refill his glass with Scotch, I noticed a canvas bank bag stuffed with hundred dollar bills lying on the floor. It must have been hidden in the lining of the couch. I quickly pushed the bag under the seat, hoping nobody had seen it.

"We knew they'd be a bunch of thieving bastards, Sparks, but I never figured it would be like this. Look at them, they're ransacking the place," groaned Richard, holding his stomach. "Jesus! I hope they don't go into my cabin."

Dropping his glass, one of them staggered across the bedroom, grabbed the brown curtain concealing the safe and fell to the floor, dragging the curtain with him. There was the safe standing out like a sore thumb. The soldier stared at it for a few seconds then struggled to his feet. *"Abierto."* he yelled, grabbing Richard's arm.

Richard shook his head, pointing to the lock. "Capitan," he yelled.

"*Abierto,*" repeated the soldier, thumping Richard with his rifle.

"*No hay llaves,*" I shouted, trying to remember some Spanish. The soldier obviously believed me and tried to move the safe.

"Oh no, Sparks, for crissake, they're going to haul it away. We can't let them do that. I feel like grabbing a rifle and shooting the bastards!" shouted Richard. "What the hell can we do?"

"I know what I have to do. I've just found a canvas bag full of hundred dollar bills. It's got to be the cash the Old Man stole from the last trip," I whispered. "How the hell can I get it out of here without them seeing it?"

Richard and I watched the four soldiers struggling to drag the safe out of the cabin. None of them was very sober. "Sparks, all that gold!" groaned Richard. "How can we stop them?"

While the soldiers were pushing and shoving the safe towards the cabin door, I watched Richard edging toward a rifle propped up against the couch. "Don't be an asshole, Richard! Screw the money, or they'll shoot us. It's better to come out of this alive with no gold, than wind up a rich dead hero!"

The soldiers took no notice of me when I slipped out of cabin onto the deck and quickly hid the canvas bag in the battery locker, thanking the Lord I was the only one who had a key. Richard and I stood on the deck wondering how we could prevent the soldiers from taking the safe.

A few minutes later, the Cuban officer came striding across the deck, followed by his two henchmen escorting the Captain who looked scared to death. Herr Bessler had disappeared. At the entrance to the Captain's cabin they were greeted by the four drunken soldiers struggling with the safe, anxiously waiting to show off their prize discovery.

Immediately, the Cuban officer turned to the Captain and demanded the key. The Old Man stared at the safe in a state of shock. Because he didn't get a quick response, the Cuban officer yelled at one of his men, who promptly thumped his rifle butt onto the Old Man's foot.

"*Schwienhund!*" screamed Krause, hopping about on his uninjured foot. "It's in my cabin," he groaned, painfully hobbling inside. When he saw the damage that had been done, and all his precious possessions scattered over the floor, he nearly collapsed. There were tears in his eyes as he leaned against the overturned couch, wringing his pudgy pink hands in despair. As much as I disliked the old bastard, I couldn't help feeling sorry for him. Another thump with the rifle butt across his foot produced the desired result. Moaning in agony, the Old Man staggered over to his liquor cabinet and produced a key.

The Cuban officer struggled unsuccessfully to open the safe. Richard glanced at me and I shook my head. When the safe wouldn't open, the Cuban officer screamed and shouted, ordering his men to beat up the Old Man. Slipping out of the cabin, I went to the battery locker to get the money, and returned immediately. Holding up the canvas bag, I signaled to the Cuban officer to come out onto the deck. He caught on pretty quick.

"This is for you!" I said, thumbing through the wads of hundred dollar bills. "It's for you. *Mucho dinero.*"

"How much?" he asked, his face now smiling.

I shrugged my shoulders. "About ten thousand dollars, that's all we have. That safe is just full of papers and our passports, there's no money in it."

"You have more money?" he demanded, grabbing the canvas bag. "You have more?"

I shook my head. "No more, that's all there is." For a few seconds he glanced through the canvas bag, running the hundred dollar bills through his fingers. His face broke out into a smile again, and he seemed satisfied.

When we returned to the cabin, I noticed Krause had passed out, lying in a bloody heap on the floor. "Sparks, I swear to Christ I'll shoot these murdering bastards if I can get my hands on a rifle!"

"You will not shoot anyone. We have been paid and we now leave," replied the Cuban, ordering his men to follow him. I breathed a sigh of relief until I saw the four soldiers dragging the safe out on to the deck.

"Not the safe!" I pleaded, running after them. "There's no money in it, No dinero, only ship's papers and our passports."

"We will open it and see," replied the Cuban, signaling his men to carry on. Slowly they dragged it across the deck and struggled down the gangplank to their waiting truck.

"Jesus Christ, Sparks! They've got the goddamn lot," groaned Richard, slumping down on top of the battery locker. Together we watched the soldiers struggling with a safe containing more gold than they could possibly imagine.

"Yes, they got the goddamn lot," I sighed, "but we're all still alive. We've paid for the molasses and we can go back to Philly tomorrow and get out of this horrible mess."

"We may have survived up here, but I wonder how the crew managed?" questioned Richard, looking back aft.

"Not very well by the look of that loot," I replied, watching the soldiers laughing and shouting, staggering across the deck carrying radios, clothes and bags of food all stolen from the crew. They were even dragging bed sheets and blankets across the filthy deck.

"The thieving bastards stealing from the crew," cried Richard, tears streaming down his face, "those thieving bastards."

After I finished bandaging the Old Man's foot, he lay on his bunk sipping brandy and muttering to his steward in German. From the few words I understood, he was more concerned about the stolen money from his couch and the gold bullion in the safe than his bruised body and feet.

In my opinion, he was in no state to be in charge of the ship, but apart from giving the order to leave port, there were no other major decisions he would have to make. Hopefully, it would all be plain sailing, once we got over the dreaded sandbanks at the entrance of Santiago Bay.

Hans and Helmut were waiting outside the surgery when I got back from the Old Man's cabin. They looked like two naughty schoolboys waiting outside the headmaster's office for some corporal punishment. Both had scratched faces and looked very dejected. "I'm sorry I only have iodine. It stings, but it will disinfect the wounds. Shall I put some on?"

They both nodded their heads. "Herr Schparks, you will not tell the captain?" asked Helmut.

"Of course not, but don't go there again until the soldiers have gone"

"Herr Schparks, we not leave in Philly?" asked Helmut.

Again, I chickened out on giving him a straight answer. "I hope so. I sure hope so." Helmut squirmed as the iodine soaked into the scratches on his face. "I'm sorry it stings, I will get some proper ointment when we get back to Philly." I knew Helmut was disappointed because I didn't give him a positive reply, but he would soon cheer up. He now had place to sleep, sharing a bunk with his friend Hans.

~~~

CHAPTER TWELVE

Go For Gold

The tropical sun had turned the steel decks into a massive hot plate, burning through to the soles of the feet, and scorching any bare flesh that came into contact with it. The rising heat from the deck, plus the overpowering stench of the hot molasses seared the mouth and throat like a well-done steak, relieved only by frequent quantities of ice-cold liquid, usually rum and Coca-Cola. I made sure that both refrigerators were constantly making ice and there was an extra case of Coca-Cola nearby. We all waited impatiently, listening to the ancient refinery pumps transferring the hot molasses from the storage tanks into the hungry belly of the ship.

I lay on my bunk reading a novel when I heard Richard enter his cabin moaning and groaning about the heat. Feeling sorry for him, I fixed him a rum and Coca-Cola and was very generous with the ice. "Here, I made you a drink."

Richard slumped back on his couch exhausted. "Goddamn it, Sparks, one of the refinery pumps has quit working," he groaned. "Now we've missed the afternoon tide. Shit! We're never going to get out of this fucking place."

"Jesus, I'm sorry. So, how much longer are we going to be here?"

"God Knows. I'm so tired of this place. I can't wait to get back to Philly and tell Berners he can stick this fucking ship up his ass as far as it will go." Richard gratefully slurped on his drink.

"Why don't you lay back and take it easy awhile. How's your war wound?"

"You mean where the bastard thumped me in the guts? I have a bruise about the size of my hand and it's sore as hell. I thank God it was no lower down. Can you imagine getting a rifle butt in your balls?"

"It makes me shudder to think about it."

"I wonder if those bastards have opened the safe," questioned Richard. "All they need is a small stick of dynamite, or they can blast the lock off with a few rifle shots." I had also been thinking about the safe and the look on their faces when they see the gold ingots. It just made me sick. "Can you fix me another drink, Sparks? I don't wanna waste these." Richard rattled the ice cubes in his empty glass.

While I was fixing Richard another rum and Coca-Cola, he lay back on his couch. "You're the only one on the ship that's got any sense, Sparks," he continued. "I mean, being a Radio Operator you've got nothing much to do in port."

"Ah! It ain't that easy," I replied, trying to dispel the myth that marine radio operators have it easy. "So, how goes the battle out there?"

"That's a poor choice of words isn't it, Sparks? Especially when we're in enemy territory and likely to be raided at any minute. All those sons-of-bitches who didn't steal anything this morning will get good and drunk, load up their rifles and come back later on for their share of the spoils. The bastards will take anything and everything that takes their fancy. Toilet soap, shaving cream and even razor blades. I feel sorry for those poor bastards back aft, they've all been robbed blind."

"I know, I've heard all their complaints. I advised them all make a list of what was stolen and Berners will have to replace it," I replied, handing him another rum and Coca-Cola.

"That's great, if he'll do it, but I wouldn't bet on it, they're all sex maniacs, remember." Richard lay back on his couch and closed his eyes for a few seconds. "I've been thinking about women."

"Well, that's not unusual." I replied.

"Remember that girl, Kate? I told you she called me when we were in Philly? She's been chasing me for years to get married," continued Richard, who was obviously more drunk than sober. He kicked off his shoes and lay back on his bunk. "Honest to God, you only have to spend a dirty weekend with a broad and she wants to get married. You know they get as much out of a good fucking session as the guy does. A broad can have dozens of screaming orgasms, but they're never satisfied with a fun relationship. They always want to get married, and then, if you're not interested, they pull out their diaphragm and deliberately get themselves knocked up. The next month, you're served with a platernity suit in court."

"What's a diaphragm?"

"Jesus Christ, Sparks, you haven't screwed around much have you? It's a condom for women."

"Oh! That's a good idea," I replied, wondering if they were available in Cuba. "Anyway, it's called a paternity suit not platernity."

"Who gives a shit? It's the same fucking thing. You either pay up for the rest of your life, or get married. You're right, Sparks," he continued. "I figured it all out. If Maria came back with me, I'd be morible oggligated," he slurred.

"Morally obligated. Hey, you've had enough to drink. Is this the second bottle of rum you've had today?" I opened Richard's fridge and tried to count the bottles.

"Save your time, Sparks, I've already started on a second bottle, and there's going to be a third one before I've finished this watch."

"Damn it, Richard, you're already loaded! Isn't the Second on watch now?"

"Herr Fucking Schmidt on watch? That's a joke. He should be, but the asshole went ashore hours ago to buy some rum and he's not come back. The son-of-a-bitch! Did you know he's hornier than me? You didn't know that did you," replied Richard, slipping further and further down onto his bunk. "That German screwball, he's hornier than me."

"For crissake, Richard, you've got to sober up," I replied, taking his glass and throwing the contents down the sink. "I'm going back aft to get you some coffee. As I opened the cabin door, the overwhelming stench of hot molasses and stifling humidity nearly made me choke, and seconds later, the thin rubber soles on my shoes were no protection from the broiling hot deck burning my already sore feet. How lucky I was not to work on the deck all day.

Back aft, I could hear the raucous laughter from the crew, many of whom were already drunk, singing and playing guitars whilst consuming cheap rum obtained from the enterprising peasants who had set up a trading base at the foot of the gangplank. Occasionally there was the sound of female laughter. Obviously a few enterprising whores had risked their necks clambering aboard to sell their wares.

A number of seamen followed me into the galley complaining about Castro's mob stealing their radios, electric shavers and everything else that took their fancy. "They just helped themselves, Sparks," complained Steve.

"They came into the galley and took all my copper pans, my big copper pans for crissake. They're a thieving lot of bastards, and I'm telling ya, they better not go near my cabin."

"Steve, I told everyone to hide all their valuables."

"I hid my stuff, but how do I hide fucking great big copper pans in the galley? That's what I want to know. I never thought they'd wanna pinch them."

"All I can say is, make a list of everything they took, and you know they're gonna be back again tonight," I warned him. "So lock the galley."

"I can't lock the galley, it's always open. The crew on watch are always going back there for coffee, you know that."

"That's what I want, coffee for the Third. He's been working for twenty-four hours." While Steve filled up a small jug from his special pot, I again told the crew members who had followed me into the galley to make a list of what was stolen and promised the company would reimburse them when we got back to Philadelphia.

Walking back across the deck with coffee, I realized that when Castro's mob had come on board earlier that morning, the crew had all been sober and on their guard, but if any Cuban soldier attempted to rob them tonight, when many of them would be drunk, all hell would break loose. There would be a bloodbath.

When I got back to Richard's cabin, he was sprawled across his bunk fast asleep, snoring like a chainsaw. Because Schmidt, the Second Officer, had not returned from his shopping spree, Richard had been forced to cover for him and had been on duty for a solid twenty-four hours.

Where was Schmidt? Shot dead? In jail, or shacked up in the whorehouse? I had no intention of finding out where he was. He was a mean, selfish little Kraut who shunned everybody on board and made sure he was nowhere to be found if there were any problems. Since it was Schmidt who should have been on watch, I decided to let Richard go on sleeping.

The setting sun painted the clouds with a spectacular mixture of orange and gold, hovering above the horizon just long enough to be appreciated by those who like such things before it slowly disappeared into the bay. Richard, who had slept for a couple of hours was now taking a shower, but despite the noise he was making, I could hear someone knocking at his cabin door. When I opened it, I was surprised to see the young Cuban boy now dressed in a cut-down bottle green uniform, a severe crew cut, large brown eyes and he was painfully thin. He looked around him nervously like a frightened young deer, then handed me a note. Just as he was about to run away, I gently grabbed his arm and beckoned him into the cabin.

"You want a Coca-Cola?" I asked, opening up a cold bottle from Richard's fridge. He smiled gratefully, slurping noisily from the bottle while I read the note. It was from Maria to say she and Consuela were at the Manager's house and hoped Richard and I would go and see them. They also wanted us to bring some soap and ointment for Consuela's wounds.

"What shall we do, Sparks?" asked Richard, drying himself off. The young Cuban boy watched while Richard sprayed his feet with antiseptic foot powder and doused himself with deodorant and body talc until his cabin smelt like a New York drugstore.

"The Second is back on board, and on watch, if you want to go," I replied, "Or I can go on my own. I wonder what Consuela's wounds are like?"

"She was raped by some horny soldiers and thrown into the dock," replied Richard. "I guess she's pretty beat up."

"I'll take her a First Aid kit. What about you?" I asked. "Do you have the guts to tell Maria you can't take her back to the States with you?"

Richard sighed, flopping back onto his bunk. "No. I don't, especially if she starts crying. You know something, Sparks? As soon as that heat out there hits me, I'll be drunker than a skunk again, and I'm dog tired."

"Okay, so stay here. I'll take the First Aid kit, and some more toilet crap, then come straight back."

"You've got a lot of guts going on your own, Sparks. I've always heard you Limeys were crazy," groaned Richard, nearly falling asleep.

"Not all the time. While I go and get the bandages and stuff, talk to the kid. Try and find out who else is at the Manager's house?"

"Are you kidding? All I can say in Spanish is 'besame mi coulo'. That means 'kiss my ass'. How far do you reckon I'll get saying that?"

"You never know your luck, Richard. He might just do it," I teased.

Ten minutes later I was walking through the refinery, following the young Cuban boy. It was now quite dark and many of the overhead floodlights had burned out. Fortunately, the boy knew the way through the maze of ugly black pipes. Escaping steam hissed out from thousands of leaky joints and openings. Large, sticky pools of black molasses had collected under the leaking pipes, and the overpowering stench frequently brought vomit to the back of the throat.

The Manager's house, a Spanish colonial mansion built on a hill away from the evil smelling storage tanks had been taken over by Castro's army. A group of dirty army trucks were now parked in the once elegant driveway, and every room in the house was ablaze with lights.

The boy led me around to the back of the house and peered into a kitchen window, tapping on the glass with a coin. Seconds later, an old woman opened the back door and we both went inside. Maria, who was sewing some buttons on a shirt, quickly threw it down and embraced me. "Sparks, thank you," she cried, looking around for Richard. When she saw I was alone, the smile quickly vanished from her face.

I shook my head. "He has to work. He can't get away." I explained, but Maria was still very disappointed. "I've brought this First Aid kit, some ointment and bandages and toilet soap for you and Consuela. Where is she?"

Maria jumped up and led me across a courtyard to the servant's quarters. "My poor Ricardo, I am so sad he not come tonight," she continued, as we entered the small building behind the house. Consuela was lying on a couch in her tiny bedroom. She smiled when I entered the room and tried to sit up. "Sparks," she cried "You come to see me."

I was shocked when I saw how badly she had been beaten up. Her face was bruised, her arm was in a sling, and it was obvious she was in pain whenever she moved.

"My God, whatever did they do to you?"

"I was attacked by soldiers. They were drunk," she explained, "but I feel much better now."

Maria unpacked the First Aid kit and took out some of the bandages and ointment. She fetched a bowl of hot water and poured in some of the antiseptic I had brought. "Sparks, in the kitchen there is some food. Eat, you are welcome. It is not steak, but you will like it," said Maria, already removing the bandages from Consuela's arm. "There is also some cold cerveza."

I wasn't interested in the food, but the beer sounded good. As I retraced my steps back across the courtyard, I couldn't resist taking a look into some of the brightly lit rooms. On previous trips Richard told me he was always invited to the house for dinner with the refinery manager and his wife, who were both Americans. Apparently they did the smart thing and went back to the States when Castro got a little too close. The ebony grand piano in the formal dining room that the manager's wife had played so brilliantly was now covered with dozens of empty glasses and beer cans. Some soldiers were lying around on the couches drinking beer, and the mirrored shelves of the once fully stocked bar were now bare, the empty liquor bottles strewn all over the floor.

When I looked through the window into the next room, which was the library, I immediately drew back into the shadows. Only a few yards away, seated in an old leather chair, was the Cuban officer who had ransacked the Old Man's cabin earlier that morning, and in the middle of the room was the safe, still unopened.

Twenty minutes later I had miraculously found my way back to the ship and retrieved Bloom's safe key from its hiding place inside the transmitter.

"The safe is on the floor in the library. Still unopened," I yelled, waving the key in Richard's face. "And the Cuban officer who came on board this morning is sitting staring at it and I think he's drunk."

"So? What are you going to do?" groaned Richard, trying to open his eyes. "How was Maria, still fuckable? I get a hard-on just thinking about her. Do you think she'd sneak back here for a farewell fuck, Sparks?"

"Damn it, Richard. I'm telling you there's a chance to get our hands on the gold, and all you're interested in is a piece of ass. I'm sorry I woke you. Go back to sleep."

"Tell Maria to come back here if you see her, Sparks. I need her." Richard's voice trailed off and he was asleep again. I forgot he hadn't really slept for over twenty-four hours.

In my mad dash back to the mansion, I nearly slipped and fell headlong into a pool of black sludge, but managed to save myself by clinging to a small bush, but my white shirt was covered with molasses when I finally reached the servant quarters again.

Getting back into Consuela's bedroom was easy. Maria had finished the bandaging and they were looking over the bag of toiletries I gave them. "What happened?" asked Maria, staring at my uniform.

"I slipped and nearly fell."

"Did you go back to the ship?" asked Maria. "Did you see Ricardo?"

"Yes, but he's so tired I couldn't even wake him up. He's been working all day and night."

"My poor Ricardo, he work too much, now I can't see him tonight," cried Maria, tears streaming down her face. "You think maybe I should go to the ship?"

"That's up to you, but he is tired."

"My Ricardo is never too tired to make love to me," replied Maria, blushing.

"He's also Duty Officer," I continued, hoping to dissuade her from going to his cabin. Maria frowned and reluctantly agreed it was better to let him sleep.

"What will happen if the officer in there catches me in the house?" I asked, pointing in the direction of the library.

"He is drunk," explained Maria. "He has asked us to help with all the office work, and wants my father to keep the refinery going."

"He is also a thief," I replied. "He robbed us this morning, and his men beat up the Captain. They also stole cameras, radios and many things from the crew. He is a son-of-a-bitch. How does he treat you?"

Maria glanced at Consuela and I could see they didn't want to answer the question. I guessed that Maria was not just working in the office, she was probably forced to share the officer's bed. It was not surprising that she wanted to get away. I quickly changed the subject. "All those books in the library, I'd sure like one or two for myself."

"You are welcome," replied Maria. "Tell me what you want and I will go and get it for you." Maria glanced through the window across to the house. The lights had been switched off in the library and we heard the officer calling Maria's name.

"He's calling you," I said.

Maria looked at me. "Ricardo not come here tonight?"

I shook my head. "He's too tired to move. To make love would be impossible."

"The officer he make me go with him. You will not tell Ricardo, you promise?"

"I promise." At that moment I would have promised anything I was so eager to get my hands on the safe.

"Then, I will go with him and you can get your book from the library, but hurry! There are many soldiers who go in there for the cervesa and the magazines."

"Sparks, don't go," advised Consuela. "I will go to the library and get you a book."

"I'm not going for a book. I want to try and open the safe," I replied. "It's full of passports and important papers."

"I don't know about the safe. I no want them to catch you." Consuela groaned in pain as she tried to get up from

190

the couch. "Please, Sparks I will go." It was obvious to both of us Consuela was not going to go anywhere for a while. The ointment and painkillers I had brought from the ship would certainly help her, but right now it was best if she stayed on the couch.

A few minutes later, I couldn't believe my luck as I scrambled through the open library window. The lights were out and the room was in semi-darkness. It was perfect. Surely retrieving the gold bullion wasn't going to be this easy? I assumed the officer had already used the Captain's key and unlocked the first bolt of the safe.

I knelt beside the safe and fumbled in the semi-darkness for the second keyhole. Bloom's key fit perfectly. Seconds later I pulled open the door and could hardly believe my good fortune, the blue velvet bag containing the gold ingots was still there.

I reached inside and grabbed the bag. I was surprised by the weight. I never thought eight golden ingots would be so heavy. *So far, so good.* I quickly re-locked the safe door and crawled toward the window. Suddenly, the huge room was ablaze with lights. Immediately, I ducked down and slid into the kneehole of a large wooden desk. My heart was pounding so hard I thought it would break through my rib cage. Heavy footsteps clattered across the bare, wooden floor and stopped just in front of me. Thoughts of being caught and spending a lifetime in a Cuban jail swept through my mind.

As I crouched down, pressing myself against the back of the desk, I realized I was on top of a metal grill, some sort of air duct. I couldn't tell. It rattled back and forth when I moved. The shoes in front of my eyes were reasonably clean, and their owner was using the phone right above my head. It was a short conversation in Spanish, something about a party. He hung up and I heard the tinkle of ice in a glass.

He poured himself a drink and sat down in a nearby armchair.

My legs were scrunched up under my chin and screamed in agony, and my back was twisted up like a question mark. The seconds ticked away like hours. I could see the officer had wriggled deeper into the leather chair. The smell of a freshly lit cigar wafted down into my hiding place and I heard the tinkle of ice as he sipped on his drink. The pain in my legs was now almost unbearable. I would have to crawl out and give myself up, still clinging to the blue velvet bag of gold ingots.

The incessant beat of a rumba band poured forth from a radio in the adjacent room, covering the noise I made when I lifted the metal grill. I felt around inside the hole. The duct was loose, and I was able to push it slightly aside and drop the bag of ingots. The velvet bag deadened the rattle as they fell down into the duct. I carefully slid the metal grill back into place. Seconds later, whoever was in the chair, got up and left the room, switching off the light.

Painfully, I crawled out from under the desk and gratefully stretched my legs, but there was no time to waste, any second someone might walk into the room and catch me. I slithered back under the desk and quietly lifted metal grill. As I lay outstretched on the floor, my arm reached into the void, frantically groping around. It was much deeper than I thought and I couldn't find the velvet bag. I was completely shattered. What could I do? Any second I would be discovered. *What rotten luck! If only I had held on to it for a few seconds more!*

I replaced the grill and slid from under the desk. *Why did I have such rotten luck? A few minutes ago I had the gold ingots in my hand, and now they were at the bottom of some ancient heating duct!* I clambered out of the open window and crept back to Maria's place, but she had gone with the officer. Consuela was asleep on the couch. I had no choice but to go back to the ship empty handed. At least I had hidden the gold ingots. No one was likely to look into the duct, so they were relatively safe. Until I could return and get them.

~~~

CHAPTER THIRTEEN

The Jail Revisited

It was after nine when I awoke the next morning. My first thought was of the eight gold bars hidden in the heating duct at the Manager's house and we were leaving on the high tide at noon. I had less than three hours to get them. It seemed like an impossible task, but I was going to try.

As soon as I had showered and dressed, I went out on deck to find Richard. He was sitting on the capstan going over a page full of figures, adding up the amount of molasses pumped on board. "You missed all the excitement last night while you were asleep, Sparks," he began, eager to tell me what happened. I sat down beside him and prepared myself for the bad news.

"Did the soldiers come back?"

"About ten of them, all drunk and carrying rifles, and they couldn't wait to start robbing the crew."

"My God, I knew it. Were there any fights?"

"A few. Five of the crew, including Steve, the Limey second cook, objected to having their personal belongings taken and put up a fight, until one of the soldiers threatened to shoot. Then they all got beaten up, their hands tied behind them and dragged onto the deck while their cabins were ransacked. When the soldiers finally left they dragged the five guys with them. There was nothing I could do. Bessler and Schmidt hid in their cabins and locked the door."

"Jesus Christ! I warned them the soldiers would come back. I suppose all the crew were all drunk."

"Of course, they'd been drinking all night. It's a miracle they weren't shot. Now the five of them are in jail, so we both know what they're going through."

"We most certainly do," I agreed.

"How about you? I'm sorry, I was too tired last night to figure out what you said, something about finding the safe, and I'm almost scared to ask, but how did Maria take the news?"

"What news?"

"About not being able to go back to the States with me?"

"She cried and kept on and on about how much she loved you."

"Jesus, don't make me feel any worse that I already do!" Richard looked across to the Manager's house. "What can I do? You said yourself I'd be responsible for her if I took her to Philly."

"Morally obligated are the words you couldn't say last night."

"I'd also be financially responsible. I just don't want to get married, but she does," groaned Richard, doodling with his pencil on the deck log book. "How was Consuela?"

Immediately, I remembered her lying on the couch, her arm in a sling, her faced bruised. "I was shocked when I saw her, battered and bruised, but she's cheerful and recovering okay." I thought it a good idea to change the subject, and described how I opened up the safe, got the gold bullion and was forced to drop it into the heating duct.

"Jesus, Sparks, what can I say?"

"Usually it's 'tough shit' but this time I'd prefer a little more sympathy and understanding from you."

"Christ, Sparks, you know I'm sorry, I mean having the gold in your hands, then having to hide it."

"I know, but being realistic, it's far safer hidden in a heating duct than in the safe which they will eventually open. At least nobody will think of looking down there. Now what about our five seamen in jail? What's the Old Man going to do?"

"He'll leave them to rot in jail. Isn't that one of Ludwig Berners' orders?"

"That's what the bastard said."

"Then you know the Old Man will leave them there. So it's up to us. We have to go to the jail and try to bribe them out," replied Richard, putting away his paperwork. I stared out across the dock. My mind was filled with thoughts of the gold bullion just sitting in that heating duct just waiting to be picked up. Eight gold ingots would buy a lot of land, and take care of a lot of old horses.

"What do you say, Sparks? Shall we try and get them out?"

"It's crazy, but do we have a choice? Anyway, what do we use for a bribe?"

"I've been thinking about it, we'll have to steal the Old Man's cigarettes. He won't miss them until we get back to Philly."

"Are you kidding? He's always going to his storage room."

"Yes, but he's been in bed since yesterday moaning and groaning, sending his steward back and forth to the galley for his food. He's in no shape to go back to his storage room and there's no way he will help. We have to do something, otherwise those guys will be used for target practice. Remember?"

Of course I remembered. "Do you realize I would have been shot last night if they had caught me? I had the eight

196

gold bars in my hand. I just opened the safe with Bloom's key and took them out."

"Jesus, what a lousy break, I mean having to re-hide them."

"I was hoping to go over there this morning and try and get them back."

"In daylight, are you crazy? The place is crawling with soldiers," continued Richard. "Didn't you tell me it was better to be alive and broke, than a dead, rich hero? That's what you yelled at me when I wanted to try and rescue the safe from those goddamn thieving bastards."

"I remember very well what I said, but even as they were carting it away, I promised myself I'd make an effort to get the gold back, and I nearly succeeded." I stared across the dock to the Manager's house, my own personal Fort Knox perched on the side of a hill. Inside was a fortune in gold, and only I knew where it was. If I tried, would I stand an earthly chance of getting into the library and reaching down into the heating duct, grabbing the velvet bag, and escaping with the gold? It didn't seem likely.

"Sparks, what are you going to do?" questioned Richard. "Chase after that gold, or try and get the rest of our crew out of jail?"

We both looked at each other, and knew we didn't have any choice.

Ten minutes later, Deiter, the Captain's steward, caught us red-handed trying to break the lock on the Old Man's storage room. He was so scared he couldn't move. "You have the key don't you?" I yelled. "Give it to me." The young steward stared at me for a few seconds then fumbled in his pocket and handed me a key. "We are taking cigarettes to the jail. You understand?" I said.

"Yes, sir," he replied, nervously.

"We are going to get the seamen who were arrested," explained Richard, while I unlocked the storage room. "You will not tell the Captain."

"No, Sir. I will not tell the Captain," repeated Deiter, like a programmed robot. He followed us into the large room filled with cases of Lucky Strikes cigarettes. There were also numerous pieces of antique furniture which the Old Man had collected from his various trips. The top half of a crystal chandelier stuck out of a wooden crate. Cardboard boxes filled with porcelain dishes and crystal vases, all wrapped up in tattered newspapers were gathering dust in a dark corner. Lashed against one bulkhead were about two dozen cases of Cutty Sark Scotch Whiskey, and beside them a few cases of the now infamous Maria Brizzard Apricot Brandy. It might have been the Old Man's favorite after-dinner drink, but it sure as hell didn't give poor Henri Bloom much pleasure.

Deiter watched us fill two suitcases with a hundred cartons of Lucky Strikes cigarettes. I wondered if we could trust him, or would he go racing to the Old Man before we could even get off the ship. I stared at the young, fifteen year-old teenager. He looked so innocent standing under the naked light bulb, his blond hair, as always neatly combed. I knew he had very few friends back aft because nobody trusted him, and he never attended the English classes. "You will not tell the Captain," I repeated, giving him a stern look. "We are going to rescue your friends from the jail."

"Go outside and tell us if the coast is clear," ordered Richard.

The young steward looked puzzled, but went out on deck to look around. Seconds later he was back. "Herr Bessler just go back aft to see the Bosun," he whispered, "Captain Krause, he is in bed."

Minutes later, Richard and I were hurrying down the gangplank, struggling with the two heavy cases, leaving Deiter to relock the storage room door. "I don't trust him, Sparks."

"Neither do I, but we had no choice. Anyway, we have at least got away with the cigarettes." The taxi driver told us the five seamen were in the central jail, where Richard and I had spent three unforgettable days and nights. He also told us it had now been taken over by Castro's soldiers, and their most important prisoner was the Chief of Police who had arrested us.

"Jesus, how I'd like to give him a swift kick in the balls," observed Richard. We promised the taxi driver he would be well rewarded if he helped us. He grinned but gave us no positive answer. Perhaps we should not have confided in him, we both knew how dangerous it was to trust taxi drivers. For all we knew, he could have driven us to some damaged building, shot us and just helped himself to the cigarettes which were as valuable to him as the gold bars would have been to me. Evidence of the street fighting was everywhere. Many buildings were still smoldering and it wasn't easy maneuvering through the streets littered with rubble, burned out cars and trucks.

After fifteen minutes, I began to get worried. Richard looked at me and it was obvious we were on the same wavelength. "The jail, is it much farther?" I asked, trying not to appear nervous.

The taxi driver grinned. "It is over there, but there is much damage in the streets." Two minutes later we pulled up in a cloud of dust outside the jail. It was about the only building in the area that was completely intact. On our previous visit, we had been dragged into the building unable to see where we were going. This time we could see the large sandstone entrance with its huge ancient wooden doors hanging precariously on rusty hinges. About a dozen soldiers, dressed in the now familiar dirty bottle green uniforms, were sitting on the steps fanning out from the entrance and watched us pull up outside.

"Sparks, I vote we quit. Let's go back. We're putting our heads in a noose," advised Richard, reluctant to get out of the taxi.

"Are you sure the seamen are in here?" I asked the taxi driver, who was now smoking a cigarette. He nodded his head, and continued to grin.

"We can't quit now, Richard. You stay here and hang on to the cigarettes. I'll go in and bargain."

"If you're not back in ten minutes I'm supposed to go back to the ship? Goddamn it, Sparks. This was all my idea. We're both crazy."

"Yes, we're both crazy, but if I hadn't come here, I would have been risking my neck searching for you-know-what, you-know-where."

As I scrambled out of the taxi and walked up to the entrance, I was carefully watched by the soldiers sprawled all over the stone steps. Some grinned, others fingered their rifles, and one stuck out his foot attempting to trip me. I tried to ignore them as I walked up the stairs. Inside the entrance was a courtyard. The original red and green mosaic floor was now broken up and covered by inches of dirt and gravel, and the battered antique desk where we had been dragged only a few weeks previously, was now in the middle of the huge entrance hall. Scores of shabbily dressed soldiers watched me walk toward the officer standing by the desk, grinning at me like an idiot. "Buenos Dias." I began, trying to smile.

"Who are you?" he asked.

"I'm from the ship. I would like to bail out the five seamen you arrested last night."

"Ugh!" he scoffed. "You are too late. They have already been shot."

For a few seconds my mind went blank as I stared at his ugly, grinning face. "You've shot them?"

"They all bad. They fight with my men. Kick my men, they all bad guys."

"I can't believe you shot them," I groaned, trying to keep my balance.

"They were shot. They all bad guys." The officer looked at me and grinned, revealing the usual mouthful of gold fillings. I stood there unable to move. What a fool I must have looked, humiliated and crying like a lovesick woman. Pictures of the various seamen flashed across my brain. Steve the chef, fixing my breakfast, Weicecz the duty seaman who had discovered Bloom's body, Hans, the young steward who waited on us in the dining room and Dombrowski, all shot to death in some godforsaken Cuban jail.

"You killed them?" I sobbed, choking on my words.

"When the sun comes up, all prisoners are shot, it is duty."

"But they were just young seamen," I cried, tears running down my face. "They were only protecting their things from you thieving bastards."

The officer continued to grin at me. "Ah! How you say in America? I kid you," he said. "They not shot. We shoot them now."

I tried to control myself. "They're still okay?"

"They still okay. You bring money, Americano dollars?"

I gulped and swallowed half my next sentence. "No tengo dinero. We have no money, just cigarettes."

The officer laughed out loud like it was a funny joke. I looked around uneasily. Except for the noise of an occasional car going past outside, it was quiet. Everyone was standing around, watching and waiting to see what would happen next. "So, you have cigarettes. How many cigarettes you have?"

"How many cigarettes?" I asked in a trembling voice. "We have a hundred cartons to bail them out. The prisoners are my friends, and the Capitan is going to sail without them. He will let you shoot them, but they are my friends, my amigos." The words coming out of my mouth were brittle and harsh. Tears again poured down my cheeks. I was shit-scared and everyone knew it. "We have one-hundred cartons of cigarettes in the taxi."

The officer shook his head. "You come back next time from America and bring many cigarettes and American dollars, and then you take the seamen. We look after them for you," he replied. He then said something in Spanish and started to laugh. It must have been a funny joke because his cronies all started to laugh with him.

"We will not be back here again. Next time the ship goes to Puerto Rico for molasses"

The officer shrugged his shoulders "How many cigarettes you got on the ship?" Immediately I remembered all the cases in Krause' storage room. "How many cigarettes you have on the ship?" he repeated.

"I can find another hundred cartons."

"Okay, it's a deal," he replied, laughing.

"It's a deal?" I tried hard to regain my composure. "Where are the seamen?"

The officer shouted something in Spanish and five or six soldiers walked out to the courtyard, rattling their keys. I ran back to the taxi and frantically signaled Richard to bring in the suitcases.

"Did you get all five, Sparks?"

"Yes, I hope so. Just play it cool."

Richard and I carried in the cases, and put them by the desk.

"*Abierto!*" yelled the officer.

"Take your time, Sparks," whispered Richard, "We're not even sure he's got these guys."

While Richard and I struggled to open the old leather cases, the five seamen came shuffling into the room. All of them looked battered and bruised and covered with dried blood. Just to see their faces light up when they saw us was worth all the cigarettes on the ship.

The cases finally opened, spilling cartons of Lucky Strikes all over the dusty floor. To all the soldiers watching, it was quite a sight. I remembered my thoughts when I saw the gold ingots for the first time.

"Okay, you guys, let's get the hell out of here," ordered Richard, starting for the door. While the officer examined the various cartons, our shipmates eagerly followed us out of the door and down the steps. The taxi driver shook his head, until Richard produced a wad of dollar bills. I had never really appreciated the strength of an old Chevy before, but somehow that taxi managed to transport all seven of us back to the ship, closely followed by some soldiers in a battered army truck to collect the rest of the cigarettes.

A crowd of seamen, including Helmut, all cheered and waved when we piled out onto the dock. I thanked the taxi driver, and asked him if he wanted any cigarettes. He shook his head and showed me the wad of dollars Richard had given him. I recognized at least four twenties. "Thanks," he said. "I like Americanos, you all nice guys. Your men very lucky, they shoot them tomorrow. You tell them, they very lucky."

The five seamen were all given a hero's welcome as they struggled back onto the deck. They must have felt the same as Richard and I when we were welcomed back on board. The Dolly Sisters, Herr Bessler and Schmidt watched the whole arrival scene from the boat deck and with them was the Cuban pilot. We had actually done them a big favor. It wouldn't have been easy running the ship with five men short. I wondered if they would report the whole thing to the Old Man.

Twenty minutes later the soldiers drove away with another hundred cartons of Lucky Strikes, all donated by the crew, and we were ready to leave. I was glad Richard had persuaded me to help rescue the seamen. I watched them join with all the others to secure the gangplank and stow the cables that had kept us tied up to the refinery dock. We had finally severed our physical ties with Cuba.

As we headed out of the harbor, I looked at the refinery manager's house through my binoculars. It looked different now with the army trucks all around it, and the revolutionary flag flying from the flag pole. I thought of Maria having to shack up with that bastard who beat up the Old Man. I thought of Consuela recovering from her ordeal, and I thought of those eight golden ingots, hidden away in the heating duct. Would I ever return to claim them?

Ten minutes later, we kept our fingers crossed as we approached the notorious sandbanks. Thank God we had a pilot on board to guide us safely through, and then it was full steam ahead for the good old USA.

~~~

CHAPTER FOURTEEN

Ludwig Berners Pays Up

We all had a lot to talk about during the ten day trip back to Philadelphia. The crew recounted their battles with the soldiers and made up exaggerated lists of stolen property. Many of the crew, suffering from cuts and bruises after fighting with the soldiers, lined up at the early morning surgery with my regular patients, the sex maniacs. "So, what did the soldiers steal from you?" I asked Artymuik, a swarthy Polish deckhand, who, judging by his facial bruises, didn't hand over his precious possessions without a struggle.

"They take my television set, a radio, a camera, and lots of clothes. My new suit and shirts, too "

"It sounds as if you were one of the most unfortunate guys on board," I replied. "Well, make a list and give it to me. I'm sorry I only have iodine to put on your cuts, it's going to sting like hell."

"Yes, sir, everybody tell me." I daubed some iodine and ointment on his cuts and bruises and told him to come back tomorrow.

Dubinsky, Hans, Gunter, Kruger and Krusciewicz all received treatment for lacerations and bruises, groaning and moaning as I applied the iodine. Then they all made claims for a television set, camera, clothes and shoes stolen by the invading army. I wondered what Ludwig Berners would say when he saw the crew's list of stolen goods.

"So, what did they take from you, Heinz?" I asked, recognizing his bronzed ass sticking out for an injection of penicillin.

"They take my magazines. All my pictures of naked women," he replied. "How is Berners going to pay me for them?"

"I don't know. List them as reading matter, books and educational material," I replied, jabbing Heinz's left buttock with a hypodermic syringe. "Didn't they take your television set, camera and clothes as well?"

"I have no television set, Schparks," he admitted. "Only two seamen have TV back aft."

"I'm glad you obeyed orders and didn't go ashore, Heinz."

He grinned, "The whores came to see me," he replied. "They all good clean women, you want to see my balls now, Schparks? Today they not so blue." The ship's number one sex maniac quickly turned around, lifted up his semi-erection and showed me his bulging scrotum.

"Excellent specimens, Heinz, you could get a job as a prize stud bull on a breeding farm. Now, put them away. I don't think you'll need any more injections."

"No more injections? You think my balls are okay now?" he asked, examining his crotch.

"Like I said, they're fine specimens and you're hung like a bull."

"Thank you, Schparks," replied Heinz, proudly. "The whores all tell me how beautiful I am." Reluctantly he covered up his family jewels, pulled up his jeans, and left the surgery a very happy young man.

Steve, the second cook was last in line. Because he put up a fight when the soldiers arrested him, he was badly beaten up in jail. He now had two black eyes, his body was covered in bruises and he had a nasty gash on his head. He had managed to wash off all the dried blood, but still looked a very pitiful sight seated patiently outside the surgery.

"Good morning, Sparks," he said, trying to smile. I wished him a good morning and warned him I only had iodine antiseptic that stung like hell. He needed no warning, having already experienced the contents of my antiquated medicine chest.

For the next ten minutes, Steve clenched his fists in agony as the iodine soaked into the wounds. Tears streamed down his face, mingling with the evil smelling antiseptic, but he never complained. "I'm sorry it's so painful, Steve."

"You did warn us not to argue with them, Sparks," he cried, "but I just couldn't let the bastards help themselves to my gear. They even took my projector and all my colored slides, and the only pictures I had of my Mom and Dad." Steve was too upset to go on, choking back his real feelings. "Sparks, I couldn't let those bastards take my pictures without putting a fight."

"I don't suppose anybody could," I replied, wondering what to put on the open gash along the top of his head.

"Were you in the same jail, Sparks?" he asked, grinding his teeth in pain.

"Same place, different guards. Batista's mob threw us in there. Now they're the ones behind bars."

"They should all be behind bars," Steve replied angrily. "One of them smashed his rifle butt over my head and knocked me senseless. Kruger was thumped in the guts, and Weicecz was kicked in the balls, if you and the Third hadn't got us out of there, they would have shot us. God knows how we can ever pay you back."

"We knew what you were going through, so there was no way we could leave you in there. Anyway, I don't think it will happen again. You'll have to go ashore when we get to Philadelphia and spend a few days in hospital." I didn't want to worry him, but in my opinion he needed expert medical attention immediately. "I'm going to pour iodine on this gash," I warned him. "I'm sorry, but it's the only thing I've got." As the first few drops of the dreaded antiseptic soaked into his head wound, I don't know how he endured the pain. It was as much as he could do to stop from screaming. "Keep thinking about staying with my folks and helping out with horses," I said. "All those green fields and the peace and quiet of the country thousands of miles away from all this insanity."

After treating Steve, I went to the Captain's cabin and knocked on his door. Deiter, his steward, who had just brought him some coffee, glowered at me when he opened the door. I wondered if he had mentioned anything about the cigarettes we had taken, I would soon find out.

"It is the Schparks!" he yelled, allowing me to enter. "The Captain's foot is damn bad," he said. "That medicine is no good."

I felt like kicking the little bastard in the rear·end as he led the way into the bedroom where the Old Man was laying on his bunk resting his foot on a pillow. "Herr Schparks. My foot is much worse," moaned the Old Man. "What are you going to do?"

I knew as much about treating bruised feet as I did about flying, which was nothing, but I was a good actor and bent over to look at the Old Man's wounds. His right foot was various shades of black, blue and purple and there was an open gash which had dried into a scab. My first thought was to douse the foot with iodine, but I knew the Old Man would probably shoot me if I did. "You will give me different medicine today."

"Sir, I have nothing except iodine."

"Iodine no good," interrupted the Old Man. "Everybody say iodine no good."

"It is the only antiseptic I have on board. You refused to okay my order for extra medical supplies, including penicillin," I reminded him, "Now I don't have enough to go around."

"Not enough?" he replied. "You give the crew penicillin this morning?"

"Every morning I have surgery, the crew. . ."

"They are all sex maniacs back aft. No more penicillin for sex maniacs." Deiter propped the Old Man up in bed with an extra pillow. "Look at my foot. The Cuban soldiers did that. What will Herr Berners say when he see my foot?" continued the Old Man, now sitting up in bed trying to see his wounds.

"The Cubans wanted payment for their molasses, and you didn't want to pay them, so they beat you up," I replied. "It's that simple."

"That is a lie," he shouted. "You not say that. You tell Herr Berners they take my money. The soldiers take my money, they take everything in my cabin."

"I shall tell Berners the truth about everything, including Henri Bloom's death."

"Bloom's death?" screamed the Old Man, waving his arms about. "You schwienhund, you will say nothing about Herr Bloom. Nothing."

"I shall give Berners a written report on all the events leading up to Bloom's mysterious death."

"You schwienhund," screamed the Old Man, now purple in the face. "Get out! Get out!" I needed no second bidding, quickly grabbed my First Aid kit, and hurried from his cabin.

Twenty minutes later, Richard came to visit me in the Radio Room with the news that Captain Krause had logged me for refusing to obey orders. "He even wrote it up in red ink so it stands out."

"He went onto the Bridge to write that in the log book?" I asked, very surprised.

"Hobbled in there," replied Richard. "Is he really hurt bad?"

"He has a badly swollen foot. It's his own fault for trying to cheat the Cubans, and that's what I'll tell Berners."

"Then I'll back you up," replied Richard. "You know, this is going to be a bitch of a trip back: we didn't get any rum."

Later, Richard and I were given two cases of rum from grateful crew members, and we helped ourselves to six packs of Coca-Cola from the Old Man's private stock. These libations were greatly appreciated as we both meticulously wrote down the events leading up to Henri Bloom's death in preparation for our meeting with Ludwig Berners, but Krause intended to be first with the news.

"You will send this to Berners now," shouted Herr Bessler, handing me a long hand written note. "It is from Captain Krause."

I looked at the note trying to decipher Krause's spidery handwriting. "It's a lot of bullshit," I said. "We were not attacked by Castro's army, and there were only five seamen thrown in jail. It's all bullshit. It's oxensheisse."

"You send it now," screamed Bessler.

"If I send all this, it will cost a fortune and I'll be fired. It's all bullshit anyway." Bessler bristled with rage, his hand on his revolver. "So you refuse to obey the Captain's orders." His tone of voice sent chills up my back and I was scared he was crazy enough to shoot me. "Captain Krause orders you to send to Berners now."

I again looked over the Old Man's spidery writing. "I will send it," I replied. "Then I will note in my log book it was sent under threat. And I don't want you watching me." Bessler stood outside the Radio Room while I supposedly sent Krause's long winded message to Berners, which claimed our ship was attacked by Cubans, five seamen were sent to jail, he had been beaten up by the Cuban soldiers for arguing about the price of the molasses and he would need hospital treatment when we docked.

After I switched off the transmitter, Bessler stomped into the Radio Room and grabbed Krause's hand-written note. "I need to file that," I yelled, but Bessler was already striding back to Krause's cabin. If he had known what I really sent, he would undoubtedly have shot me.

During the next ten days, I continued to administer iodine and penicillin in the surgery, and my efforts were rewarded when the wounded seamen gradually healed up. Steve's head wound didn't get any worse, and the Old Man's foot, which he now looked after himself, healed up sufficiently to allow him to resume his normal routine. This meant making a nuisance of himself on the Bridge, and complaining bitterly about the food in the officer's dining saloon. Our standing feud continued and we never spoke to each other face to face. All messages for me were conveyed by one of the Dolly Sisters. Herr Schmidt in particular seemed to enjoy telling me what to do.

"The Captain orders you to listen for messages from New York," he snapped, suddenly appearing at the Radio Room door.

"Is he crazy? That's my job. I don't need him to tell me what my duties are."

"Then, you refuse?" replied Herr Schmidt.

"I refuse to listen to any more of this stupid claptrap."

"I will tell the Captain." Herr Schmidt straightened up and marched out of the Radio Room like a well-trained German officer. Minutes later, my phone rang. It was Herr Bessler, the Chief Officer, ordering me to the Bridge.

"Sir, I am on duty, I cannot leave the Radio Room for another hour." Suddenly the phone went dead. Seconds later, Herr Bessler stomped across the deck and thumped on the Radio Room door. "Again the Captain log you for insubordination," he screamed. "You refused to obey an order."

I was flabbergasted. My first thought was the Old Man had really flipped his lid this time. "The Captain ordered me to listen to New York for any messages. I do it all the time, every time I go on watch. He doesn't have to order me to do my job."

"So you again refuse to obey the Captain's orders," snapped Bessler.

I went to the receiver and turned up the volume filling the room with the sound of a dozens of ships and shore stations chattering back and forth in Morse code. "That's New York," I shouted. "I was listening to their traffic list until you interrupted me. Now they've finished. It's over, and I'll have to wait until next watch before they transmit it again. Herr Bessler, I'm warning you, the Old Man has flipped his lid, you better watch him."

Bessler stared at me for a few seconds not knowing what to say. Suddenly he snapped his heels together. "I will report this to the Captain immediately," he said, again clicking his heels. I burst out laughing. It was like a scene from some old Marx Brother's movie as Bessler strutted across the deck back to the Bridge to tell the Old Man he had flipped his lid. He was crazy, and Bessler, Schmidt, and the two Dolly Sisters weren't far behind.

A few days later we picked up the river pilot and steamed up the Delaware River, eventually docking at Publicker's wharf in Philadelphia about four o'clock in the afternoon. The deck crew and stevedores soon connected the ship to the on-shore storage tanks and the unloading began.

While the Custom officials and I went over the routine paperwork in the office, Ludwig Berners arrived with his usual entourage of cronies, all dressed in their slick suits, white shirts and colorful ties and headed for the Old Man's office where Deiter was waiting with the drinks.

The Old Man was propped up on his bed playing a scene that would earn any movie actor a well-deserved Oscar. Wearing his best uniform and the usual display of medals, he rested on his bunk like a deceased South American dictator in an open coffin on display in the cathedral awaiting the arrival of his adoring public to pay their homage.

The Dolly Sisters, Bessler and Schmidt were wearing their best uniforms and stood nervously waiting on the deck outside the Old Man's office for their employer, Ludwig Berners, then dutifully followed after him as he hurried into the office. Richard and I crept in behind them.

Berners immediately went into the Old Man's bedroom and closed the door. Seconds later we could hear them arguing. Deiter, the steward, reluctantly brought round the tray of drinks, glaring at Richard and me in horror when we took one. As the shouting increased next door, I was very glad it wasn't me on the receiving end of Berners' filthy temper. When he finally emerged and gave permission for the ambulance men to collect the Old Man, they placed him on a stretcher and carried him across the deck and down the gangplank. Reluctantly he had agreed to allow Steve, Kruger and Hans, our dining room steward, who also required hospital treatment, to accompany him in the ambulance.

"Now you guys, we gotta lot to talk about," growled Berners. "There's a lot of questions to be answered, starting with my friend Henri Bloom, God rest his soul."

The dreaded inquisition had begun. Bessler and Schmidt handed Berners their hand-written statements which he agreed to read later. I also handed in the statements that Richard and I had written which he promised to read later. Bessler handed him the cargo figures and Schmidt a brief summary of the trip. It was all routine paperwork, but so far no mention of the gold.

"Okay you guys, I'll see you both again tomorrow," he said, dismissing Bessler and Schmidt. For a few seconds they were in a state of shock, until one of the assistants opened up the office door and gestured for them to leave. When they were gone, Berners gave his assistants their orders and waited for them to leave before he sat down in the Old Man's office chair. "Now you two," he said. "You talk a language I understand. Is Krause really in bad shape?" gesturing for us both to sit down.

"He's got a bruised foot, but it was healing up okay the last time I saw it," I replied.

"He's been hobbling about on the Bridge for the last few days," added Richard.

"He told me he was beaten up real bad by the Cuban soldiers, and they took all his money, but I read your message, Sparks, that he only offered them five thousand bucks. Jesus Christ, he's crazy, now I know why they beat him up."

Richard and I then told Berners all that took place when the Cuban soldiers came on board for the payment, including the money that spilled out from the back of the Old Man's couch, enabling us to pay for the molasses. "So

214

the old bastard hid it in the couch. How much do you reckon?"

"Wads of hundred dollar bills, but I never had time to count it," I replied.

"It was probably about twenty grand. Now, what about the gold?" Berners glared at us, drumming his short stubby fingers on the Old Man's desk. "Krause tells me they took the safe as well. Is that right?"

"That's correct. The Cuban soldiers took away the safe," replied Richard.

"Unopened?" questioned Berners.

"Krause handed over his key, but the second key couldn't be found." I felt Richard's foot pressing against mine, and realized we were both on the same wavelength.

"So where is the second key?"

"You gave it to Bloom," I replied.

"It says here in this statement of yours, which I ain't properly read yet, that Krause's steward was searching Bloom's cabin, is that right?"

"Yes, I saw him. And after Bloom's death, the cabin was ransacked."

"Who did it?"

"The Old Man and his steward were the only ones who went in there, but Richard and I did sneak in and examine the body."

"We've explained all that in the statements," continued Richard. Berners reached across to the tray where Deiter had left the bottle of whiskey. Refilling his glass, he sipped his drink while re-reading the statement we had submitted, shaking his bald head like he didn't believe a word.

"How long do you think it will take the police to investigate this?" I asked.

"Investigate what?" snapped Berners, angrily.

"Bloom's murder," replied Richard and I together.

"There ain't going to be no police investigation," replied Berners. He glared at us for a few seconds. "We ain't going to have the cops snooping around the ship wasting our time for a few days. Krause wrote it up that Henri died of heat stroke."

"But that's bullshit," interrupted Richard. "Bloom never went out in the sun. Krause poisoned him. The Sparks and I have got it all figured out."

"Well, you can figure it out again," ordered Berners. "It's official. Bloom died of a heat stroke and was buried at sea, that's what's in the official report. You remember that. I'm sending somebody to pick up his clothes and stuff later today, that's it, and I'm very sorry."

"You're sorry?" replied Richard, stunned by Berners' uncaring attitude. "I thought he was your friend, your personal assistant."

"He was my friend, and I'll miss him a heck of a lot, but he's dead and buried at sea, and no goddamn police investigation will bring him back." Berners began tearing up our typewritten statements. "I'm gonna tear these up and y'all better forget what happened."

"But Krause murdered him!" I argued. "He poisoned him."

"Poisoned him? Can you prove it?" Berners momentarily stopped tearing up the paperwork.

"I have the bottle of apricot brandy that Krause gave Bloom, I'll bet it contains the poison."

"Well, y'all can do me a favor and toss it overboard when you're back at sea," replied Berners, resuming his task of ripping the statement into small pieces.

"But it's the only evidence we've got."

"I said toss it overboard and forget it!" repeated Berners.

"Just like that, forget it? So Krause not only steals you blind, he also gets away with murder. He poisons your personal assistant and gets away with it," yelled Richard.

"Krause ain't getting away with nothing. What you guys don't know is that I have a spy down there who tells me everything that's going on." Berners refilled his glass amused that Richard and I looked so shocked. "Y'all think I'm stupid? I know all about the young assholes who were thrown in jail. Didn't I tell them no shore leave? For crissake, how long do you reckon I'd be in business if I had to rely on Krause's lousy book-keeping and these fuckin' stupid statements you give me at the end of each trip?"

Richard and I were literally speechless and stared at Berners like he had just dropped in from another planet. "For crissake, I knew all about the money that German bastard stole from me, but shit, what can I do? It's gone, and right now, Krause is the only son-of-a-bitch willing to take this fuckin' ship alongside the refinery without a pilot, and that's what counts more than anything else."

"Jesus Christ, you're a cold-blooded, uncaring bastard," said Richard.

"Yeah? Well, son, I gotta be. I am cold-blooded bastard," agreed Berners, "but there ain't nothin' I can do to bring Henri back. If there was, I'd be real happy to do it. I really did like the guy, and I'm sorry he's dead, but shit, it don't make no sense delaying the next trip with a fuckin' police investigation, now does it? That German bastard is more useful to us navigating the ship into the refinery than rotting in jail. I know what he's been up to and what he really paid to get you guys out of jail, but the asshole won't get away with it again. You gotta understand we have a signed contract to supply cheap molasses to this distillery, and there's plenty of it just waiting to be picked up in Cuba, and if'n we don't deliver on time, the bastards will sue me for millions of dollars. Understand?" Berners glared at us across the desk. "Its money. High finance. Business. That's the name of the fuckin' game." Richard and I leaned back in our seats not knowing what to say. We were shocked, disappointed, angered and speechless. "Now, are you willing to make another trip?"

"No way," replied Richard, without hesitation. "I don't like working for such a cold hearted bastard who treats the crew like shit and only thinks of money."

"Okay, suit yourself. So I gotta get another Third Mate," replied Berners, taking out his notebook. "How about you Sparks?"

"Can you give me a few minutes to talk privately to Richard?"

"Sure, take your time. I need to take a piss anyway." Berners got up and left the room.

"No! I'm not making another trip. It's not worth it," said Richard, getting up to leave. "What about the vacation at my folks' place in Palm Springs?"

"What about Consuela and Maria?"

"You bastard!" snapped Richard. "Why did you mention her?"

"I don't know. One more trip, Richard."

"I can't. I won't be able to say NO to her the next time. She'll beg me to bring her back and I'll be stuck with her."

"Okay, it's your decision, but I'm making one more trip, and I'm sure you know why."

"You're an asshole, Sparks. A stupid, fucking asshole if you think you're gonna get that gold. You told me there was no sense in winding up a rich, dead hero. You said that, and it's true."

For a few seconds my mind reeled through the events of the past few weeks. The machine gun bullets rattling around our heels as we ran for our lives. Pietro's burned·out restaurant, the jail cell and the open sewer, the firing squad and the mangled bodies of our fellow prisoners. I remembered Consuela lying in bed covered with bruises, and Maria's face when I gave her the First Aid kit, and then there was the gold. The feel of that blue velvet bag full of ingots. It was enough gold to buy all the land we needed, enough feed for a hundred horses and perhaps a college education for my sister. Eight golden ingots and I was the only one who knew where they were hidden. I had no choice. I had to make one more trip. "I've gotta make another trip, Richard. I *have* to." How could I convince Richard that I desperately I needed the money? "I know where the gold is hidden and I know the risks. Maria and Consuela will help me."

"Jesus Christ, Sparks, how the hell can I say no when you're determined to go back," groaned Richard. "But just one more trip, promise?"

Minutes later, Berners reappeared and sat in Krause's chair. "Okay have you guys made up your mind?" he said. "I know y'all been through hell down there and y'all went ashore after you was all warned about the consequences."

"Sir, the crew are all horny young men and Cuba is the only place they can go ashore and relax. They're all working every day on the ship, they need to go ashore and get drunk once in a while."

"Good speech, Sparks, but Cuba's not the same as it was. There's a fucking war going on down there, and it makes no sense the crew poking their noses where they're likely to get the son-of-a-bitch shot off," explained Berners. "So I'm giving y'all a hundred dollar bonus and fifty bucks each for all them fucking television sets the soldiers stole, that's if'n y'all sign on again. Next trip, I'll look into sending you down to Puerto Rico where there ain't no fucking war going on, leastways not yet anyway."

Richard and I looked at each other and nodded. "Okay, one more trip," agreed Richard, "and that's because you took care of the crew."

"How about you Sparks?" asked Berners, grinning.

"Yes, Sir, one more trip. I'm glad you know Krause is crazy as a dingbat and don't take any notice of his complaints about me seriously."

"They're all fucking crazy," agreed Berners. "What do you call them, the fucking Dolly Sisters? Well, they're even worse."

~~~

CHAPTER FIFTEEN

Drunk and Disorderly in Philadelphia

Ludwig Berners was not only a cold-blooded bastard, he was also a clever psychologist. By generously reimbursing the crew with a hundred and fifty dollar bonus, and not questioning their long lists of stolen property, he got everyone to sign on for another trip, thus saving his company a great deal of time and expense in finding a new crew. After the meeting, Berners went out onto the deck with his entourage of slick-suited young assistants. "Look at those ass-kissing young assholes," sneered Richard. "What the hell do they do, except kiss Berners' ass all day."

"I expect that's a full time job, but you've got to give him credit, Richard, he's a good company man," I said, watching Berners walking down the gangplank to his company car.

"He's a cold-blooded bastard."

"A very smart, unscrupulous, cold-blooded bastard. Who else could have got this crew to sign back on again after what they've been through?"

"A hundred and fifty bucks each? Big deal. So he paid through the nose for all those television sets the crew supposedly had back there."

"More television sets than crew members," I joked. "Yet, very few of them have even got their own bunk to sleep in."

"Well, he can afford it. We both know he gets this stinking, black shit for peanuts in Cuba, and sells it at a fantastic profit. So the bastard can afford to be generous. I still hate his guts. Anyway, I'm spending most of my bonus on some Glenlivet Single Malt, how about you?"

"Good idea. I'm getting tired of rum and Coca-Cola."

Later in the afternoon, Richard and I leaned over the deck rail and watched the seamen climbing up the gangplank loaded with shopping bags full of toiletries, records, beer and an assortment of girlie magazines, they all seemed very pleased with the way Berners had settled their grievances, and spent their money in the dockside market like drunken sailors.

"Those poor guys," observed Richard. "They could have got that shit at half the price if they'd been allowed to go ashore and do their shopping in Philly."

"I agree, but they don't have passports, so they won't let them through the dock gate, poor buggers." Another group of seamen, laden with shopping bags, looked up and grinned at us as they came on board. I noticed Helmut standing on the deck watching them struggling up the gangplank with their bags of goodies. He too had collected his hundred and fifty dollar bonus from Berners but didn't look very happy. He looked up at me and smiled.

"There's your little buddy down there," observed Richard. "Has he been up to see you lately?"

"Not lately. He was sharing a bunk with Hans, but they just took him ashore in the ambulance. He has a nasty gash on his head that needs stitches. A few nights ago Helmut was hiding behind the lifeboat waiting for me to get off watch, but the Old Man came out on deck."

"What happened?"

"Nothing. I just kept the Old Man talking while Helmut crept back aft. I promised him I would leave after the first trip and take him with me, and now I've just signed on

222

again. I know he's disappointed with me and he's got no family, poor little bugger."

"Sparks, you'd be morally obligated to look after him," replied Richard. "That's what you told me about Maria."

"Yeah, I know, but he's all on his own, and very vulnerable. I'll have to help him after the next trip."

"I expect he'll probably get beaten up and killed by those bastards in Cuba if he's not careful," moaned Richard, angrily. "Jesus, Sparks, I'm really pissed off! We could have been on our way to Palm Springs by now, and spent the next month lazing around the pool, with plenty of booze and broads."

"We'll go there after this next trip, Richard."

"If we get back alive, and what about Maria? She'll be waiting for me, expecting me to bring her back here, and then what? She'll get pregnant and expect me to marry her and then I'm trapped." Richard angrily kicked the deck rail with his foot. "Fuck it, Sparks! I'm going into Philly, and I might never come back." Without another word, Richard hurried across the deck, ran down the gangplank, and climbed into a waiting taxi. Seconds later it bumped across the railroad tracks and disappeared through the dock gate into the afternoon traffic. Earlier that morning he had reluctantly signed on again for another trip, but only after Berners had given him a bonus and agreed to his demands for new charts and other navigational equipment that the Old Man was too scared to order.

I went back to my cabin to answer a few letters the agent brought for me. Christine had written to say her favorite horse, Mister Lee, had died of old age. I searched for the right words to comfort her. I also sent glowing reports to my folks, telling them what a wonderful time I was having, if they only knew the truth. After addressing the envelopes, I went on deck looking for Mike Bradshaw, the ship's agent, who mailed all the crew's letters. He had come on board at noon with the Customs agent to deliver the liquor and cigarettes ordered from the bonded warehouse. Richard and I replaced the cigarettes we had taken from the Old Man's storage room and both ordered a few cases of Glenlivet.

"Someone has good taste," observed Mike, watching the Customs man unload the booze that Richard and I had ordered. "Four cases of Glenlivet Single Malt, Sparks. That's the best. Know what I mean?"

"Sure. Richard ordered it," I replied, signing the paperwork. "We're both tired of rum and Coca-Cola."

"Rum and Coca-Cola is all right, Sparks, but I prefer a good Scotch and soda. Know what I mean?"

"Would you like to try it, I've got some in the cabin." Without needing any further invitation, Mike Bradshaw followed me across the deck to my cabin. "So you like Scotch and soda. I think it's a good, clean drink." It was always a good idea to be friendly to the ship's agent, because they knew all the gossip from Head Office and nobody liked to gossip more than Mike Bradshaw. He watched me pour out a generous measure of Glenlivet into a glass and helped himself to some soda. After a quick peek through my porthole to make sure the Custom's guy had left, he made himself comfortable on my couch. "You know Sparks, we were all shocked to hear about poor Henri Bloom. He was a nice guy and I got along with him okay, know what I mean."

"Yeah, he was okay after you got to know him, but did you know he was put on board to check up on Krause and find out where all the money was going." I explained, surprised at how quickly the ship's agent finished his glass of Scotch.

"Berners told everyone he died of heatstroke. I always thought he was a bit pale, and I suppose that hot Cuban sun was just too much for the poor bastard," surmised Mike. "Know what I mean?"

"Actually, he died before we even got to Cuba. What did Berners have to say about it?"

"He just said he died of heat stroke," replied Mike finishing his drink. "Then you buried him at sea. What did you guys do, just dump his body overboard? I reckon they should have brought him back home, know what I mean?"

"We couldn't, there was nowhere to keep him in the fridge. Wasn't anyone at head office suspicious?" I asked.

Mike drained the last drop from his glass, ignoring my question. "It gives me the creeps thinking about it. Did he float, or sink right to the bottom after they chucked him overboard? You don't mind me asking questions do you? My wife is very interested in all this stuff, know what I mean?" Mike slid his empty glass across the table. "This is good stuff, Sparks. I wish I could buy a bottle, but it's too expensive ashore. You guys are so lucky, you can buy booze cheap out of bond and then go sailing off to Cuba to have a good time." Mike nudged me with his elbow and grinned. "Know what I mean?"

I poured a little more Glenlivet into Mike's glass and topped it up with some soda and wondered how I could get rid of him. I needed a ride into Philadelphia to do some shopping, but there was no way I'd spend an hour riding with him. "Have you heard any rumors that we might be going to Puerto Rico for molasses?"

"I also like vodka martinis," continued Mike, again ignoring my question. "Yeah, I like vodka martinis, especially when the wife and I go out to dinner."

"Vodka martinis, me too," I replied, wondering when I last had one.

"My wife reckons after two of those I'm the best lover in town. I can keep it up for hours. But if I have one too many,

I'm out like a light. Out like a goddamn light, Sparks. Know what I mean?"

"Yeah, I know what you mean."

Mike raised his glass. "Thanks for the drink, it's good stuff." He took a quick sip then looked around to make sure we were alone. "Hey, Sparks, I don't know whether you've noticed, but Berners has been acting very suspiciously lately. Something is worrying him. Know what I mean?"

"Yeah, I wonder what it is."

Mike laughed, "Perhaps he can't keep it up. He needs a vodka martini, Sparks."

"Yeah, I know what you mean."

Mike finished off his drink in one gulp and stood up. "Well, that's it for today," he said, closing his briefcase. "I've got about a hundred letters from the crew to mail, mostly to Germany and Poland, if they ever get there." Mike gingerly stood up and headed for the door. "You wanna ride into Philly, Sparks?"

I hastily declined Mike's offer of a ride into town. The thought of riding with him for an hour made me shudder. "Okay, Sparks," he slurped, shaking my hand. "Have a nice trip and I'll see you in about three weeks. Why don't you go out tonight and have a couple of martinis." He again dug me in the ribs with his elbow. "Know what I mean?"

The portable onboard phone was ringing, giving me a perfect excuse to get away from Mike Bradshaw, still chuckling to himself as he walked down the gangplank. Thank God I only saw once every three weeks. It was a call from California, a female by the name of Kate, wanting to speak to Richard. When I told her he was ashore in Philadelphia there was a long silence. "Did he get my letters?" she asked.

I told her I didn't know, but the mail was delivered to his cabin as soon as we docked. When I mentioned that

226

Richard had signed on for one more trip, there was another long pause. "One more trip?" she repeated, obviously disappointed.

"But it's definitely the last one. As far as I know, we'll both be flying back to California in about three weeks' time." I promised to tell Richard she had called, and hung up. So that was the infamous Kate who was chasing him. I wondered what she would do if she found out about Maria?

The crew, who had all signed on for another trip and collected their bonus money earlier that morning, were now celebrating their windfall. Some of them had never had so much money in their lives before. Everyone had bought something from the dockside market, new clothes, magazines and especially crates of cold beer. It was certainly a pleasant change to hear the sounds of laughter coming from the crew's quarters. They hadn't had much to laugh about during the past few weeks.

With Steve and Hans in hospital, the food in the Officer's dining saloon wasn't worth eating, so I decided to go into town and treat myself to a perfect Martini and a steak and lobster dinner at Bookbinders.

The taxi ride into Philly took nearly half an hour. As we sped along the Camden Turnpike I opened the window, enjoying a welcome change of air. It was exactly four o'clock when we stopped outside my favorite restaurant. The cocktail hour was in full swing. I made a reservation for dinner, then managed to find a seat at the crowded bar. The vodka martini I'd longed for was perfect, and so was the second one.

"You sipped that like it was nectar," she said. "They're good, aren't they?" I nodded and eyed the sleek, blonde woman perched on the stool next to me. "Are you waiting for a table?" she asked, giving me the once over with her heavily made up eyes as she fluttered her long lashes to deflect the smoke from her cigarette.

"Of course. I hear they serve the best lobster in town." We stared at our reflections in the mirror at the back of the bar. I would have guessed she was about forty. She held her glass in the air, her fingers covered with rings, and a variety of bracelets jangling on her wrist. With a plunging neckline on a yellow satin dress and a blonde hairdo copied from the latest Lana Turner movie, she fitted the description of the typical barfly I had heard so much about from Richard who was an expert on the subject.

"Are you just visiting here?" she asked, managing to move a little closer without getting off her stool.

"That's right, I'm just visiting."

"You're English, aren't you?" Again she fanned me with her long eyelashes, puffing away on a long thin, perfumed cigarette.

"That's right. I'm English." I was wondering what she was after, maybe a free drink or perhaps she just was lonely and wanted to chat.

"How about that, my mother came from London," she said, taking a long drag on her cigarette and blowing the smoke up to the ceiling. "She lived near the Queen's place."

"The Queen lives in Buckingham Palace," I replied. "Southwest London."

"Yeah, well some place near there."

"Well, well. Small world isn't it." I was getting very bored with the stupid conversation and looking forward to my lobster dinner.

"Yeah, small world isn't it," she agreed. "Are you going to have another one? Mine's Dubonnet over ice." The bartender grinned when I signaled for two more drinks. I wondered when she was going to get to the point. Any minute my table would be ready and I could eat. I was starving, and the martinis were making me even hungrier. The drinks soon appeared and the bartender scooped up some money from my change on the counter.

"So, you're far from home," she continued, again fluttering her eye lashes.

"Yes, about a few thousand miles."

"So, I expect you're lonely?" She picked up my glass and sipped it. "You're right, they do make good martinis." She replaced my glass on the counter, pushing it closer to me with her manicured, jewel encrusted hand. "Let's drink a toast to the English," she purred. "I think they invented Martinis."

Bullshit was the word I wanted to say, but I settled for "Cheers!" as we clinked glasses.

"It's terrible to be lonely, isn't it?" she purred. "When did you last, you know?"

"Eat dinner?" I replied, hoping she would take the hint.

"No, enjoy female company?"

"Last week, I think."

"So, I'll bet you're real horny by now." I jumped when her probing hand slid up my thigh and began fondling my crotch. She certainly had a delicate touch. I swallowed my martini in one gulp, and didn't flinch when she stroked the bulge in my pants. "I live just around the corner, Honey," she said, expertly massaging my balls. "You wanna good fuck, or just a quickie?"

What was she saying? I may not have known what she said, but I sure knew what she was doing, grabbing my genitals and dragging me off the stool. My head began to spin. How many martinis did I have? I remembered the famous saying about a stiff prick having no conscience. Well, I had one now, and absolutely no conscience, so the saying was right. I found myself being pulled out of the bar by my schwanz. Suddenly, I was in the crowded street, blinded by the glare of the setting sun. "This way, Honey," whispered my prospective lover, pulling on my manhood. "I gotta place just around the corner."

Thoughts of my steak and lobster dinner intermingled with female breasts and squirming asses certainly confused me, but her warm hand massaging my erection certainly wasn't unwelcome. I followed her closely inside a doorway. I had no choice. With glazed eyes, wobbly legs, and a penis being pulled out by the roots, I followed like a rampant lamb to the slaughter but where were we, an alleyway, a shop door or the entrance to the subway?

Everything was blurred. The whole world was reeling, and the pain in my head zapped through the whole of my body, until everything went black.

I can't remember what happened, everything was a blur. I did remember lying on my back looking up at the fluffy clouds in the sky. Huge, white cumulonimbus thunderclouds, too dangerous to fly through. Then I recognized the smell of shit, dog shit. After a few minutes I finally came back to reality, there was a cold wind blowing up my ass. I tried to sit up, but my head was spinning around like a top. Gradually my eyes became accustomed to the early evening light and I realized I was in a back street lying on a pile of stinking garbage. Squinting to focus my eyes a little more, I was able to see my bare legs and feet. I had no shoes, socks or trousers on. Where the hell was I? What had happened? I remembered having a drink at the bar, a dry martini, and there was a blonde woman sitting next to me and her mother lived in London near the Queen. Slowly the cloud around my brain melted and I came to the conclusion I had been robbed; stripped half naked and dumped in a deserted street in the middle of Philadelphia. Should I laugh or cry? A passing truck slowed down, and the driver wound down the window. "Are you okay," he yelled. "What happened?"

"I can't remember. I was with some blonde and I've been robbed."

"I'll bet she slipped you a Mickey," he shouted, grinning. "I'll bet you didn't even get laid. It happens all the time in these back streets. You must have been in a cheap bar."

"So what should I do? I'm half-naked and I can't even stand up."

"You'll be okay. Just stay there, the cops will be along in a minute," replied the truck driver, chuckling to himself as he drove away. The humor of the situation escaped me as I lay back on the stinking garbage still trying to remember what had happened.

The truck driver was right. A police car did come along. The cops were very polite, obviously guessed what had happened, and helped me to my feet.

A few minutes later I was in the back of their car being taken to the Central Police Station for interrogation and something to cover up my naked extremities. Yes, I am the Sparks on the Cuban Trader now docked at the refinery. No, I couldn't remember her name, but she was a middle-aged blonde with a very firm grip and her mother came from London. She picked me up at Bookbinder's Restaurant where I had a reservation for dinner.

The cops were mildly amused. "Perhaps because her mother came from London she felt sorry for you, you know a comrade down on his luck. So that's why she was kind enough to put your empty wallet back into your coat pocket before stripping off your pants and tossing them over the fence," explained the cop, much to the amusement of his fellow officers who had gathered around to discuss the case. "At least that was something you should be thankful for."

"Thankful for what, being drugged, robbed and left half naked in a back street of Philadelphia?" I groaned when I heard them contacting Berners' office and asking them to send someone to pick me up.

It was the ship's agent, Mike Bradshaw who came to the Police Station to rescue me. He brought some old jeans, a pair of shoes, a big shit eating grin, and for the next hour I sat beside him driving back to the ship discussing the dubious delights of sexy barflies and lethal martinis, know what I mean?

It was well after midnight. I was watching television and feeling very hungry and wondering if I should go to the galley and make a sandwich, when Richard staggered into his cabin drunk as a Lord. Seconds later he stumbled through the interconnecting bathroom grinning from ear to ear. "I've just been fucking my head off, Sparks. A tall, middle-aged blond with legs up to her ass, then they got cheeky," he slurped, almost falling on his face. "Honestly, she fucked like a wild mink, Sparks, three times."

"By the sound of it, you've had a good time," I replied, moving a stack of papers off my couch to let the drunken bum sit down.

"I had a very good time. We've been fucking all night, but she wasn't as good as Maria." Richard kicked off his shoes and put his feet up. "Where did you go, Sparks?"

"Me? Nowhere much," I replied, wondering if anyone on board had heard about my misadventure.

"You didn't go ashore, Sparks?" continued Richard. "I thought you liked to eat at, at. . .what the fuck is that place called? It sounds like a library? Anyway, they serve lobsters, the best lobsters in town you told me." Richard was now struggling to take off his belt while trying hard not to laugh.

"It's called Bookbinders."

"You should have gone there first and had a lobster, then got laid, Sparks," continued my drunken friend. "There's plenty of ass in Philly, if you know the right places to go." From the way Richard looked at me, I had a strong feeling he knew what had happened. "Plenty of women wanting to get laid in Philly, if you know what I mean, but you're such an old stick-in-the-mud, Sparks." Richard continued to grin at me. "You should have got laid, Sparks. Fucking is such a great way to spend a few hours. Know what I mean?"

"Richard, did you come back in a taxi?"

"Course not. I had a ride in a car," he sniggered. "All the way from Philly on the Camden Turnpike in a car."

"Whose car was it?"

"Whose car?" teased Richard. "Jesus Christ, Sparks, she was a blonde, a middle-aged blonde barfly called Mickey, and fucked like a rabbit with no pants on, a naked fucking rabbit with no pants or shoes on." Richard roared with laughter trying to get up from the couch. "And she loved martinis with steak and lobster. Know what I mean?" Richard crawled back into his cabin roaring with laughter. The son-of-a-bitch had obviously bummed a ride back to the ship with Mike Bradshaw and he had told Richard everything.

The Old Man returned from the hospital in a taxi at ten o'clock the next morning, hobbling up the gangplank. He was followed by Steve and Kruger all bandaged up. Steve smiled and waved when he saw me watching him from the boat deck, but where was Hans? Surely they hadn't kept him in the hospital, he wasn't as badly injured as Steve or Kruger. Herr Bessler was supervising the loading of two wooden crates onto the deck when the Old Man came on board. For a few seconds Krause glared at the huge boxes, then hurriedly crossed the deck and disappeared into his cabin. There was always a stack of routine paperwork waiting for his signature, a chore he always left to the last minute. Richard checked over the navigational charts he had ordered, winking whenever he saw me. I was sure the bugger knew what had happened to me in Philly, because he was acting very strangely and always seemed to be on the point of bursting with laughter.

It was always a strange feeling severing the physical links with the shore. The hoses, filling the ship's tanks with drinking water were the first to be disconnected. Then the portable telephone was taken ashore. The Delaware River pilot arrived and directed the crew as they unhooked the heavy ropes securing the ship to the jetty, and lastly the gangplank was taken up and stowed on deck. The ship was now at the mercy of the tugs, pushing and pulling her into the middle of the river until she could maneuver under her own steam. All this was completed by 1300 hours and we were chugging down the Delaware River on our way back to Cuba. Hopefully it would be our last trip. I was after the gold and Richard was dreading a tearful re·union with Maria. We would have plenty to talk about, there was no doubt about that, especially the way Richard kept on grinning at me. "Okay, Sparks, what happened?" he finally asked. "I was told you got a great a piece of ass in Philly?"

"That's true. I was seduced by a barfly. Her mother lived in London next to Queen. She drank Dubonnet and smoked like a chimney." Richard tried hard not to laugh. "She was a big titted blonde barfly, who certainly knew what she was looking for, then when she found it, dragged me outside by my schwanz and we did it three times in a shop doorway next to Bookbinders and I woke up on a pile of garbage with no socks, shoes or pants on and staring at my bare feet, do you know what I mean?"

"Sorry I laughed, Sparks, but it is funny, do you know what I mean?"

~~~

CHAPTER SIXTEEN

Just One More Trip

After all the problems we had in Philadelphia, the *Cuban Trader* was finally on its way back to Cuba. Richard stopped by the Radio Room on his way to Bridge. "Last trip, Sparks. Okay?" He glared at me expecting a positive reply.

"Okay, last trip. Let's hope I get what I want."

"And I will be locking myself in the cabin while we're there. You can tell Maria I signed off in Philadelphia. Okay?" He again glared at me expecting a positive reply.

"Okay, I'll make sure you are well supplied with Rum, Coca-Cola and lots of ice."

"Just remember that, Sparks. Did I tell you, Kate sent me a photo of herself in a swimsuit, her boobs were enormous and her legs went right up to her ass."

"And then they got a little cheeky," I replied. "Yes, Richard, I've heard that one before."

"So every time I get horny I'll think of Kate," concluded Richard. "Now, I've gotta go and sort out the new navigation charts and get this fucking half-assed show on the road." He gave me one stern look and went onto the Bridge. I switched on the transmitter and sent an ETA (*Estimated Time of Arrival*) to the Pilot Station at Cape May so they knew when to pick up their river pilot.

An hour later, as we left the narrow river and entered Delaware Bay, the ship slowed down and the launch came alongside to take off the pilot, which was all routine, except, this time as the pilot got off, a shifty looking character dressed in military uniform climbed on board and quickly disappeared into the Old Man's cabin.

"Who is he?" questioned Richard, entering the Radio Room.

"I was wondering the same thing. Very suspicious isn't it, sneaking on board like that."

"No kidding, and what's in those wooden crates stowed on deck?" continued Richard. "They're not listed as cargo."

"Maybe extra supplies of cigarettes for the Old Man. Perhaps he has plans to buy the refinery this time." My little joke didn't sit well with Richard who shrugged his shoulders and went back to the Bridge, while I watched the pilot launch chugging back to Cape May, filling the clean salty air with acrid fumes from its powerful engine. I wondered whether our passenger had missed the ship in Philadelphia, or had come on board via the pilot launch to avoid being seen. It was all very mysterious and certainly would give us something new to talk about during the next ten days. I dreaded the thought of being teased about the damned barfly for the rest of the trip.

At lunchtime, the Old Man escorted his guest to the dining saloon, but never introduced him to anyone. "Jesus, how I detest the Old Man's superior attitude," moaned Richard. "He's treating us like we're all ignorant sheep."

"From the way he and his Spanish speaking guest are conversing, I don't think we're missing very much," I replied, digging into my sea pie. For some unknown reason it seemed an unwritten law in the galley that the first day at sea, *thou shalt be served sea pie,* a concoction of ground meat, chopped onions, various scraps left over in the fridge and heavily laced with a thickened bouillon. It always reminded me of English school lunches served up during the war by big bosomed, middle-aged, grey-haired ladies from the WVS, all ladling out mashed potatoes, stewed cabbage and Irish stew. Then there was our Sunday school teacher, Miss Philips with a perpetual dewdrop on the end of her red nose; and all us kids were petrified it would drop into our plate of stew.

I stared at our new visitor picking away at his food. "I wonder what he thinks of the Chef's daily special."

"He's eating it. He looks Cuban to me, probably some half-assed refinery official going back to smooth out future deals," surmised Richard, pushing his lunch plate aside. "Which means this ship will be going back and forth to that stinking refinery until hell freezes over."

"Who cares? You and I will be living it up in Palm Springs." I knew Richard was very disappointed I had signed on for another trip. "Did you tell your folks we'd be there in three weeks?"

"Yeah, I told them. I hope we make it, but I have a gut feeling we're in for a lot of nasty surprises this trip."

Settling down to shipboard routine again always annoyed me. It made me realize how useless it was chugging back and forth between Cuba and the States with a cargo of stinking, blackstrap molasses to be made into rum, an alcoholic drink that served no utilitarian purpose whatsoever. The fact that my earnings contributed to the well-being of my family and the upkeep of the horse sanctuary certainly made me feel better, but I would have preferred to be doing something more practical than helping to make booze.

I had just finished taking down the weather forecast when Richard came rushing back into the Radio Room. "Bad news, Sparks. I just read in the Captain's log book that your buddy Helmut Schickel fell overboard and was drowned while working on the deck. That's all there was in the log."

"Helmut? Fell overboard and was drowned? That's impossible," I groaned. "We saw him on the dock. He smiled at us. When is this supposed to have happened?"

"Sparks there was nothing else in the log, but it may not be true. He may have jumped ship and found a way through the dock gates into Philadelphia."

"Then why did the Old Man enter in the log that he had drowned?"

"It's less paperwork, and the son-of-a-bitch didn't enter it until we left this morning. He's left all the shitty paperwork for Mike Bradshaw, the agent. Now he'll have to deal with the Immigration and the cops." Richard poured me out a glass of rum. "Sorry, Sparks, I mean he was a nice kid."

"Did anyone actually see him in the water?"

"Sparks, I don't know anything, just what I read in the log. It's an easy way out for the Old Man to say the kid drowned and hand over all the responsibility to the ship's agent."

"Well, I won't believe it until I hear that somebody saw him in the water."

"I'll ask around Sparks, I gotta go back up the Bridge. We got the new charts and I have to mark them up." Richard hurried back to the Bridge, leaving me still in a state of shock.

As soon as I finished typing up the weather report I took it to the Old Man's office. He was sitting at his desk, almost falling asleep. "Sir, here is the weather forecast for Cape Canaveral." Krause sat up in chair and blinked. "Visibility good with light Easterly winds. Sir, I hear that you wrote in the ship's log that Helmut Schickel, the steward, fell overboard and was drowned. Is that true?"

"How you hear that?" snapped Krause, suddenly waking up.

"You wrote it in the ship's log book on the Bridge."

"You no read ship's log book. That is an order."

"I want to know about my friend Helmut Schickel. Did he fall overboard? Or did he jump ship in Philadelphia?"

"I write in log he fell overboard. He drown, you ask no more questions. Now get out. That is an order."

It was pointless talking to the old fool. I went back aft to get some coffee from the galley and talk to my friend Steve who was struggling with heavy pots and pans cooking dinner. "Sparks, I've just made some fresh coffee. Didja hear about Hans? He ran away from the hospital. As soon as they bandaged him up, he just disappeared. There was a hell of a fuss. The Immigration guys asked me about him. Do you know if they caught him?"

"I don't know. I hope he got away," I replied. "I want to know about Helmut, the steward. The old man says he fell overboard and drowned." I poured myself some coffee and tried to stay calm. "He's written it up on the ship's log."

"Helmut fell overboard? When? I haven't heard anything, but I haven't seen him since we left," replied Steve, handing me a jug of milk from the huge refrigerator. "Here Sparks, this is fresh."

"Helmut and I came on board together. I showed him around Philly while we were waiting for the ship."

"Yeah, the poor little bugger told everybody about it and the big steak you bought him in Philly."

"So, now you know why I'm so concerned. If you hear anything, Steve will you let me know. I'm taking my coffee with me." I left Steve struggling with his huge pots and pans and went back to my cabin and lay on my bunk still in a state of shock.

Afternoons on cargo ships are usually quiet, giving the crew members who have to work the midnight watch a chance to sleep. Normally the Chief Officer works out a schedule with the Bosun for the deck crew to do some painting, but Herr Bessler, the Chief Officer on the *Cuban Trader* was different. He didn't give a damn about his crew.

"Listen to that racket out there," moaned Richard, entering my cabin through the bathroom. "Bessler has decided this is the time to chip the deck."

I glanced through my porthole and saw about a dozen or more deckhands on their knees, hammering away at the clumps of rust on the main deck. "Bessler's an asshole, what can you expect."

"Asshole or not, I've got a hang-over and I'm entitled to some sleep in the afternoon. I go on watch at midnight, remember?" Richard had brought with him a bottle of rum and waved it in front of me. "Let's save the Glenlivet for special occasions," he suggested, opening my fridge to find some ice. "I've given our steward ten dollars this time and told him to defrost our fridges and make plenty of ice this trip."

"Thanks. I was just thinking how useless we both are, transporting molasses thousands of miles to make this stuff," holding up my glass for another shot of rum. Richard refilled my glass and made himself comfortable on my couch. "Have you talked to Dubinsky yet?"

"No, what about?"

"He's supposed to have seen Helmut jump overboard, but he won't talk to anyone about it," replied Richard. "He said he saw him jump into the wake and got sucked under by the propeller just as we were leaving."

"I don't believe it. I want to talk to him."

"The Old Man's ordered him not to talk to anyone. He's shit scared of the Old Man just like everybody else back aft, so you won't get a peep out Dubinsky."

"Nevertheless, I am going to talk to him, maybe later when the Old Man has gone to bed. Steve tells me our dining room steward, Hans ran away from the hospital after they bandaged him up."

"Good for him. I hope they don't catch him. Now I've got some news," announced Richard. "Herr Schmidt told me our passenger's name is Rafael Caballero, and he's going to the refinery to sort out the problems, but nothing has been entered in the logbook. No mention of him boarding from the pilot launch, and that's illegal."

"That all makes sense. Bradshaw told me there was something fishy going on."

"Mike Bradshaw? That guy is a damned old gossip. Know what I mean?" Richard started to grin.

"Richard, for crissake do me a favor, don't you ever repeat what happened to me."

Mike had obviously had a ball telling Richard about me and the barfly.

"So, our passenger's name is Caballero. It sounds like a dance doesn't it?" suggested Richard.

"That's a bolero. I think a Caballero is a Mexican cowboy."

"A Mexican cowboy? That's all we needed on this ship to complete the cast. A crazy Kraut for Captain; the nautical Dolly Sisters, an ugly American for Third Mate, a deck crew of poxed up Poles, and the drunken, naked Limey Sparks, rescued from the back streets of Philadelphia," laughed Richard, falling over himself to get out of my cabin. "Jesus, what a motley crew! Know what I mean."

The next morning the only person attending my early morning surgery was Steve. "I shall go out of business," I joked. "Where are all the sex maniacs this morning?"

"You cured them, Sparks. Only Heinz got a piece of ass in Philly," replied Steve.

"That doesn't surprise me. Who was the recipient of his largess?"

"His what?"

"Who did he screw?"

"Oh! She was the cashier at the dockside market. Old enough to be his mother," joked Steve. "Everybody's teasing him back aft."

"Well, you know what they say, there's many a good tune . . ."

". . . played on an old fiddle." Steve finished the sentence for me. "From what I've heard she was more like a full size double bass, but they must have made sweet music together because she paid for all his magazines, and bought him a crate of beer," continued Steve, "So I expect she got her money's worth."

"That's for sure. I hope she didn't give him a reason to pay me a visit, like a dose of clap or galloping dog rot."

"Or blue balls," added Steve. "Heinz told everybody back aft that you really admired his balls."

"Admired them? I just said he was hung like a stud bull, that's all."

"He *is* a stud bull," agreed Steve, sitting patiently while I carefully checked out the wounds on his back which were healing up very well. "By the way, Steve, have you heard any more about Helmut?"

"You mean the poor little bugger who drowned?" replied Steve. "He was always miserable. I felt sorry for him."

"Dubinsky told the Old Man he saw him jump over the stern into the propeller, a sure way of drowning himself."

"Dubinsky and Hans were the only real friends Helmut had back aft," replied Steve, wincing, when I pulled too hard on the plaster. "He used to sleep in their bunks. The poor little bugger never had one of his own."

"What do the rest of the crew think? I mean about Helmut supposedly drowning himself?"

"They ain't much bothered," replied Steve. "The poor kid never talked to anybody 'ceptin' Dubinsky. You ought to talk to him about it."

"I will, when the Old Man's in bed. He's ordered him not to talk about it," I explained. "I think Dubinsky is shit-scared of the Old Man."

"I don't blame him. I'm shit-scared of the Old Man as well, just like everybody else back aft," replied Steve, putting on his shirt."

"How are you coming along with the book I gave you to read?"

"I'm on chapter seven. You were right, once you get started, it's hard to put down."

"Good for you. Now let's have a look at your head wound. Did you say the bandage should come off?" I asked, admiring Steve's professionally bandaged head.

"That's what the Doc said, and I've got this ointment to put on." I was grateful Steve supplied his own ointment. I really didn't have anything suitable despite my new supply of pills and potions which were delivered before we left, but I now had enough penicillin to cure an army of blue balls. My brief conversation with Dubinsky in the crew's galley was a waste of time. He still insisted he had seen Helmut jump into the churning wake of the propeller and drown. "Schparks, I gotta go, Bessler's following me," he said, quickly hurrying back to his cabin, well aware that Deiter was also hanging around and that little bastard told Captain Krause everything that happened back aft.

Despite all the warnings from the Coast Guard, Krause still went off course, hugging the coastline in order to watch television. It was smooth sailing, and gradually getting warmer. Groups of seamen sunned themselves on the poop deck, finished off their crates of beer, and planned various tactics to protect their newly acquired possessions when we arrived in Cuba.

The English conversation classes deteriorated from the recommended textbook phraseology, to the usual open discussion about sex and unusual sexual practices. It was all very interesting, but of little use to anybody ordering a steak and kidney pie at a London restaurant, or trying to find their way around Hoboken in New Jersey.

Heinz, as usual, was the acknowledged expert, and willingly gave us all the intimate details about his night with the dockside market cashier. Apparently they carried on like two sexual acrobats in a three ring pornographic circus. It was therefore not surprising she paid for his beer. If everything he said was true, he deserved a truckload of beer, and some shares in the brewery.

"Older women are zee best," repeated Heinz. "They know what to do and they do it many times." I wanted to interrupt and correct Heinz's grammar, but feared the rest of the class would shout me down for spoiling his interesting lecture. While everyone listened to Heinz's graphic description of his paramour's bedroom habits, I wondered how he would have handled my blonde barfly. I'm sure she wouldn't have robbed him, at least not until he had finished what she had started!

Rumors about Senor Caballero spread around the ship like wildfire. Steve told me all the crew back aft were convinced there was a woman in his cabin, and that he was in his bunk all day screwing her.

According to Richard, he was seen taking food back to his cabin, and nobody had been allowed in there. If the rumors were true, when did she board the ship? "Let's just go into his cabin when he's in the dining saloon and look for ourselves," suggested Richard. "I can always say I'm checking the porthole for leaks, you know that's part of my job."

"Yes, I know. But who cares about Caballero's women?"

"I do for one. If he can bring a woman on board, why can't I?" Richard stared at me for a few seconds then nodded. "Okay, Sparks, don't say it, I might have to bring a woman on board, Maria."

"That's up to you, but if there is a woman in Caballero's cabin, why the secrecy? Surely the Old Man must know, and if he knows, why doesn't she eat in the dining room. Maybe she's his wife."

"Maybe she's not his wife. Maybe she's a puta. Cuban's are hot as mustard. They've got to have a piece of ass every day. Didja know that, Sparks?" Richard drained the last few drops of rum into his glass and pushed the empty bottle thru the open porthole. "Those Latino's have got to have a piece of ass every day."

"So what happens if they don't?"

"I guess they fuck the dog."

We were watching a TV program from Key West, the last chance to see American television until the return trip. "Fucking the dog would be better than watching this crap," I said, switching off the set. "What a load of rubbish."

"It sure is. I guess I'll turn in for awhile," groaned Richard. "See you in the morning." He finished his drink and ambled back into his cabin. I undressed and crawled into my bunk and had no problems going to sleep.

Like all experienced seamen, I automatically woke up when the engine revolutions changed. Normally this happens only when entering or leaving dock, or when slowing down to rendezvous with the pilot launch.

"Sparks, wake up. There's a boat coming alongside," announced Richard, entering my cabin. "Come out on deck and see."

I slipped on my robe and went out onto the deck. The bright moonlight illuminated the whole eerie scene as a powerful tugboat, with no navigational lights, chugged alongside us. Herr Bessler was on deck directing two or three crew members to lower the scrambling net over the side. Minutes later about twenty uniformed soldiers silently climbed on board and were welcomed by Caballero, while Herr Bessler escorted them back aft. "What's going on?" whispered Richard. "Are we being invaded?"

"If we are, it's too damn late now, they're already on board, and that's Senor Caballero on the deck welcoming them."

We watched as the last of the midnight invaders silently disappear into the crew's quarters. The noisy tugboat turned around and headed back into the misty night. "I'll bet it's from Key West," said Richard. "Of course, it all adds up! They're fucking mercenaries sent to guard the refinery!"

"Maybe Berners is paying them to guard the ship."

"Jesus Christ! They'll be fighting with Castro's mob, maybe on the deck and we'll be right in the middle of it," groaned Richard. "We'll be in a goddamn war zone."

"Calm down, Richard, nothing has happened yet. When do you go on duty?" I asked, looking at my watch.

"In half an hour, I was just getting ready when I heard the engine revs go down. Look, the Old Man's on the Bridge, the son-of-a-bitch. He knows what's going on."

"I'm glad somebody does 'ceptin' he's crazy as a loon."

"I gotta finish dressing," replied Richard, hurrying back to his cabin, while I watched the dark shape of the tugboat heading back to Key West. I wondered what the crew back aft thought about the midnight intruders. Where would they sleep? There were no empty cabins and certainly no spare bunks they could use. My curiosity wasn't aroused to the point of going back aft to check what was going on, but I didn't get much sleep, and thought it damned unreasonable of Ludwig Berners not to let Richard and I know about his plans.

Richard and I were the first ones in the officer's dining saloon for our usual early morning breakfast. Piled up in the corner were some brown blankets, a stack of army knapsacks, and judging by the yelling and shouting going on, their owners were eating in the crew's dining saloon. According to Richard there was no entry in the ship's log book about the midnight boarding party, and the Old Man refused to say anything about it.

"It's illegal, all cloak and dagger stuff, as you Limey's would say. I'll bet the U.S Government and the CIA are involved," continued Richard, buttering his toast. "I'm pissed off nobody told us about it. Don't you reckon we have a right to know what's going on, Sparks?"

"Yes we do, but who's going to tell us? Certainly not the Old Man, and I'll bet you won't get much out of Caballero either."

Steve, the second cook, came to our table with two sizzling plates of Canadian bacon and eggs. "Good Morning. Did you know this mob was coming on board?" he asked, placing our favorite breakfast on the table. "I thought something funny was going on when they sent a lot of extra food on board just before we left, but the bastards are eating their heads off and coming back for more, there's not enough for the crew. It's a bloody imposition, that's what it is, and nobody knows why they're on board."

"We're as surprised as you, Steve. Maybe they're on board to guard the ship, who knows. Don't let it worry you." I felt sorry for my overworked friend, it was bad enough cooking for a hungry crew and he certainly didn't need twenty more hungry guys lining up with their empty plates.

For the next two days, the soldiers remained cooped up in the Officer's dining saloon during the day, and exercised on the main deck after it was dark. Waving their arms about and jumping up and down they all followed their leader, Senor Caballero. Many of the crew came out and watched them. They must have been a well-disciplined lot or getting well paid because they all obeyed Caballero's orders. Since they all had beards, shaving wasn't a problem, but the crew sure complained to Bessler about the crowded overflowing toilets.

We arrived in Santiago Bay about noon after the usual ten day trip. It was a bright sunny day and very humid. Everything looked peaceful. The hills and mountains were still shrouded in early morning mist. Yet we knew they were alive with soldiers training for the upcoming civil war. The Old Man was on the Bridge with his powerful binoculars looking for the pilot launch but there was nothing on the horizon except a shimmering mist obscuring the shoreline.

My radio transmissions to CLN, the shore station, went unanswered, which didn't surprise me. Most radio stations operated by the Batista regime were not transmitting. There was no pilot boat to meet us when we entered the bay, so apparently nothing had changed from the previous visit. Slowing down to about three knots we glided effortlessly across the calm water and headed for the Los Canos refinery as usual. Since the ship was empty and high out of the water there was little chance we would bump into a sand bar. I went out on deck with my binoculars to take a look at my private Fort Knox, the old refinery Manager's house, it was still there, flying the Cuban flag and unfortunately swarming with soldiers.

Krause was able to steer the ship alongside the jetty without the aid of a pilot or the assistance of tugs. This navigational procedure was the only reason he was still employed. It required a lot of maneuvering, but the Old Man finally got the ship close enough to the berth to throw two heavy ropes to the dock workers who hooked them over the bollards fore and aft, thus enabling the ship's winch to pull us slowly alongside. About two hours after entering the bay, we were safely tied up at the refinery loading dock.

"Here we go again, Sparks," sighed Richard, dragging on his clean white overalls. "The only thing that keeps me sane is the fact it will be our last trip."

We looked out across the filthy, black loading bay, but there were no refinery workers on hand to connect the huge pipes to the ship. "I guess it's a case of do-it-yourself," moaned Richard, starting down the gangplank. "I hope I can remember which pipe goes where."

Somebody must have been keeping the refinery ticking because there was plenty of steam hissing from hundreds of badly fitting joints, and presumably the molasses was hot enough to circulate through the pipes. Richard operated the crane, taking directions from the Dolly Sisters, Schmidt and Bessler, who as always, remained safely on the boat deck. The well-worn black pipe was hauled up and over the deck, while the crew dragged it to the coupling above the ship's tanks. It was two o'clock in the afternoon and the hottest part of the day. The sun beat down unmercifully onto the steel deck. Everything was hot and covered with black sticky molasses and thousands of swarming flies. The connecting pipe had dripped all over the deck crew, covering them from head to foot with the sickly smelling black treacle.

Cursing and swearing in many languages, the crew eventually connected the pipe, tightened the bolts, and waited in the sweltering heat for Herr Schmidt to inspect them, but as always, he shunned that procedure, and yelled at Richard to open the control valve and allow the hot molasses to flow into the ship's empty tanks. The whole connecting procedure had taken just over two hours.

Afterwards, using the salt water deck hoses, the crew stripped their clothes off and took turns in hosing each other down. The heavy jet of warm sea water soon got rid of the sticky mess, and they all ran about naked to dry off in the afternoon sun. Richard preferred to take a shower and cool off in front of my electric fan in his cabin.

A few putas and some enterprising tradesmen soon arrived on the dock. The girls openly flaunted their well-worn charms, jiggling their naked breasts, and baring their rear ends inviting the crew to sample their wares. The naked crew members lining the deck rail responded accordingly, waving their sexual equipment and making dates with the girls.

Unfortunately everyone was forbidden to go ashore, and Caballero soon posted an armed guard at the top of the gangplank to prevent any women coming on board. But for how long could he keep his soldiers imprisoned below decks on a sweltering, hot afternoon, or a group of naked, horny seamen away from dozens of teasing whores displaying their charms just a few yards away on the dock?

"It's hell back aft," announced Richard, entering my office to fix himself a rum and Coca-Cola. "The soldiers have been ordered to wait until it's dark before they can go ashore, and Caballero is threatening to shoot any one of them who goes on deck."

"And all those whores out on the dock teasing them." I went out on the boat deck and watched a half-naked puta with long red hair and enormous breasts lifting up her skimpy dress and wriggling her bare ass at the crowd of cheering seamen lining the deck rail. "Look at her! She'll cause a mutiny very soon. My God, Richard, we're sitting on a damned time bomb!"

"No kidding!" he replied, following me out on the deck. "Caballero's got a loaded pistol, and his soldiers are locked in the Officer's dining saloon. They've got nothing to drink except warm water. No booze or broads are allowed up the gangplank, Caballero's orders and that bastard means business," warned Richard. "I told you, he has a loaded pistol."

"And I suppose Castro's mob is watching us, just like last time, and they'll come on board demanding payment just when we're getting ready to leave."

Richard nervously rattled the ice cubes in his glass. "Just one more trip, you said Sparks. One more fucking trip! Goddamn it, we'll be lucky to get out of this hellhole alive." Richard finished his drink, then angrily tossed his glass through the porthole into the bay.

"I'm sorry, Richard. I had no idea all this would happen," I said, trying to apologize. "I thought it would be another routine trip."

"Routine trip?" he snapped. "The last two trips we were lucky to escape with our lives. That's routine?"

"But I've nearly got my hands on a fortune in gold bullion."

"And you'll wind up either very rich or very dead."

"And what about Maria?"

"What about her? I don't want to see her this time. I'll take one of those dockside putas to my cabin."

"Most of them are poxed up to their ears."

252

"So? You've got plenty of penicillin." Richard reached for his drink, and then cursed when he realized he had tossed the glass into the bay. "So? What are you going to do about the gold?"

"I'll have to play it by ear, but it's the only reason I came back," I replied, reaching to get Richard a clean glass.

"I know, you keep telling me. If you do sneak across to the Manager's house, you might see the girls, right?"

"If they're still there," I replied, pouring out a shot of rum for Richard and being very generous with the ice.

"So tell Maria I signed off in Philly."

"Is that what you really want me to say?"

"Yes, and I wish I had signed off in Philly," growled Richard, hurrying back to his cabin, taking his fresh drink with him.

My phone rang. It was the Old Man wanting to see me in his cabin. I assumed it was about payment for the molasses. Berners had hastily changed the subject when I questioned him. Krause's cabin door was opened by Deiter, his sniveling little steward who glared at me with contempt. "It's Herr Schparks," he announced, before beckoning me into the study.

As usual, the Old Man ignored me for few minutes, and continued cleaning out his booze cabinet. No doubt he intended restocking it with some cheap Cuban liquor before we sailed. Deiter resumed his job of dusting the shelves and wiping off the remaining bottles of Maria Brizzard liqueur, the Old Man's favorite tipple. I noticed one of the bottles that Deiter was dusting was identical to the one I found under Henri Bloom's bunk, which was now Exhibit A and stored on top of the transmitter in the Radio Room. I fully intended to have it chemically analyzed to determine for myself if Bloom was poisoned. I had no intention of following Berners' orders and tossing it overboard.

"Did you want to see me, Sir? I have got a lot to do."

"Herr Schparks. This time will be different, we leave everything to Senor Caballero," explained the Old Man. "He is one of Castro's men and has the payment for the molasses."

"Sir, if Caballero is one of Castro's men, why are all his soldiers waiting until it's dark before they go ashore?"

"They are on guard. They protect us. You do not ask questions, Herr Schparks."

"But don't you think it strange? If Caballero is one of Castro's men, and Castro's soldiers have now taken over the refinery, why haven't Caballero and his men gone ashore?"

"Herr Schparks," repeated the Old Man, raising his voice. "You will not ask these questions. Herr Berners arrange everything. Now go." The Old Man waved his hand at me. "Go! Go!"

"Does Caballero have the cash to pay for this cargo?" I asked.

"Herr Schparks," shouted the Old Man, going red in the face. "Herr Berners give Caballero the money to pay. You don't ask me no more questions. Now go. Schnell! Schnell!"

I was glad to get out of the old fool's cabin, but I had a strong suspicion that Caballero was taking Berners and all of us to the cleaners.

~~~

CHAPTER SEVENTEEN

Caballero's Mercenaries go AWOL

It was late that afternoon when I heard the pistol shot, and immediately went on deck to find out what had happened. From the commotion back aft I assumed it must have been Caballero. Richard had mentioned he had a loaded gun. Someone must have phoned Herr Bessler who emerged from his cabin wearing his ex-army leather belt and an awesome looking German Luger in the holster. He glared at me for a few seconds, and then strutted across the deck to the crew's quarters. Since we rarely spoke to each other, I was quite used to being ignored, and went back into the office. Seconds later the phone rang. It was Bessler ordering me to take the First Aid kit to the crew's quarters where a Cuban soldier had been shot.

The stinking heat and humidity in the crew's accommodation nearly knocked me backward. In the Officer's dining saloon, where the soldiers were housed, a young, bearded Cuban lay on the floor, blood gushing from his leg. There was a large gash just below his knee, and the bullet was lodged in the carpet. A group of angry Cuban soldiers were kept at bay by Caballero who was waving a pistol. He was obviously very scared, and had reason to be, judging by the angry mood of the soldiers.

Bessler and I worked together applying a tourniquet, wrapping the long bandage around the young soldier's thigh, twisting tighter and tighter until the flow of blood stopped. I hesitated before pouring iodine into the wound knowing how painful it was going to be, but the young soldier had passed out and wouldn't feel it.

After dousing the torn flesh with the dreaded antiseptic, Bessler and I bandaged the wound as best we could, but it was obvious the victim needed immediate professional treatment. When I had finished I was soaked in sweat, the heat and humidity was almost unbearable, little wonder everyone was on edge.

During the whole time that Bessler and I were bandaging the soldier, we were watched by a score of bearded young men dressed only in their underwear, all mumbling angrily in Spanish.

"He try to go on deck," explained Caballero, keeping everyone covered with his pistol.

"My God, I don't blame him, it's unbearable down here. He needs to see a doctor right away," I said. "A doctor."

Caballero shook his head. "He okay now. Later, he go see a doctor." From the mood of the soldiers, I feared for Caballero's life, but more importantly I feared for mine. Bessler also sensed the dangerous situation.

"That is all, Schparks. We shall go." Since I could do nothing else for the young soldier I was glad to get out of the stinking hole. I packed up the First Aid Kit and followed Bessler back to the deck leaving Caballero to sort out the mess. The guard he had stationed at the head of the gangplank was no longer there, and neither were the deckhands who had been flaunting their ever-ready sexual equipment to the delight of the screaming putas on the dock. Obviously the girls had convinced the horny seamen that self-abuse was a waste of time. Everyone unanimously agreed, then raced each other to the whorehouse. Herr Bessler looked around the empty deck, realizing his deck crew had disobeyed orders and gone ashore. He snorted with contempt and angrily strode back to his cabin. If he didn't care, neither did I. Richard, who had remained out of sight on the boat deck waited until Bessler had gone inside, then came over to my office.

"What happened?" he asked.

"Just as you figured, Caballero shot some guy in the leg for trying to go on deck."

"Ugh! I doubt if he'll be the only victim. How is the poor bastard?" Richard reached into the office fridge and took out a Coca-Cola. "You want half?"

I shook my head. "Bessler and I bandaged him up, stopped the bleeding, but he'll have to see a doctor. Were you trying to avoid Bessler?"

"Of course, he was going to ask me why I didn't stop the sex maniacs going ashore. It was like a stampede. As soon as the pistol went off and the guard ran away, all the horny sex maniacs ran down the gangplank and chased the girls back to the whorehouse."

"Just as I thought. Boys will be boys," I joked, walking out on deck which was now deserted. A few members of the crew were on the dock trading cigarettes for rum. "They'll all be good and drunk very soon. I hope we don't get invaded by any of Castro's mob again."

"Don't worry, my friend, we've now got our own army to defend us. Like I said, this deck will be a fuckin' battlefield. Jesus, what the hell have we let ourselves in for?" Richard finished his drink and tossed the empty bottle into the bay. "I'm going to check the temperatures, as if I haven't got anything better to do."

While Richard trudged back and forth across the deck, checking the temperature and flow of molasses, I checked the emergency batteries for water and put them on trickle charge. I then remembered the Old Man had complained the radar scanner was making a noise. It was a very ancient contraption and was in constant use on the Bridge. To check the revolving scanner I had climbed onto the roof of the Old Man's cabin where the radar equipment was located.

"What you doing up there?" he demanded, coming out on deck.

"I'm greasing the motor, Sir. Remember you complained it was making a noise."

"I want you should leave it. We get proper man in Philadelphia."

"Sir, it only needs some grease."

"Get off my cabin roof," shouted Krause. "Schnell! Schnell!"

"With pleasure, Sir," I replied. "I hope you will make a note of this in the ship's logbook: Radio Officer refused permission to grease radar scanner." I immediately returned to my cabin, grabbed a carton of Lucky Strikes and scurried down the gangplank to swap them for a case of Bacardi rum. When I got back, Richard was in his cabin fixing himself a drink.

"I heard the Old Man telling you to get off his cabin roof. What was wrong?"

"I wanted to grease the radar scanner, it squeaks."

"Of course it squeaks," agreed Richard. "It's revolving 24 hours a day, seven days a week while we're at sea. The old fool never turns it off. Anyway, you tried, Sparks."

"I sure did." I poured myself a shot of rum and topped it up with the remainder of a bottle of Coca-Cola. "I hope he enters it in the ship's logbook, because I'm certainly going to enter it in mine."

"You know he won't log that, there's not even an entry in the logbook about those poor Cuban soldiers back aft," continued Richard, refilling his glass. "Krause has broken all the rules."

"Well, he seems to get away with it every time."

"It won't be long before they'll overpower Caballero and strangle the son-of-a-bitch, and we'll have a full scale mutiny on board," growled Richard. "Isn't that something to look forward to?"

After dusk, some of the soldiers came on deck and began removing the covers from the wooden crates which were still stowed on the deck.

Richard ran quietly up to me. "Quick, Sparks, they're opening those wooden crates." I grabbed my binoculars and joined Richard on the boat deck. About six or seven Cuban soldiers were tearing at the wooden boxes with their bare hands, ripping the flimsy wooden slats from the cover.

"It's full of rifles," announced Richard, looking through my binoculars. "Scores of them, and some machine guns, take a look."

I stared through the binoculars. I didn't know much about guns, but they looked new to me. "Now they're opening the other crate."

"It's full of ammunition, maybe some hand grenades. Jesus! I told you, Sparks. I fuckin' told you, there'll be fighting here on the ship. Now I know why Berners never mentioned anything about all this, he knew we would have refused to make another trip."

"If we'd known."

"Goddamn it, I'm going to see the Old Man and find out what's happening. Are you coming with me, Sparks?"

Minutes later, Richard and I burst into the Old Man's cabin. He was dressed in his tattered red robe, slouched in front of the television set. "I've just seen what was in the deck cargo," yelled Richard. "Goddamn it, we've been shipping rifles, machine guns and ammunition for this stupid revolution. Didja know that?"

"You will not shout at me," replied the Old Man.

"Do you realize if the other side finds out what you've done, they can shoot the lot of us? Blow up this ship?" continued Richard. "Did you know what was in those wooden crates?"

"You will not ask questions!" Krause developed his usual nervous tick, and became very red in the face. "It is company business."

"Goddamn it! Ludwig Berners is the company and he's sleeping safely in Philadelphia. He doesn't give a shit about us. We could get shot for all he cares. I'm asking you, did you know what was in those crates?"

"Herr Bessler look after deck cargo," snarled Krause.

"Bullshit!" shouted Richard, "He had to secure it to the deck, but you knew what was in those two wooden crates."

The Old Man looked scared and reached for his phone. "I call Herr Bessler. You will not come in here."

"Herr Bessler, that asshole. You both knew Caballero and all those goddamn soldiers were coming on board didn't you? It was Bessler out there waiting for them with the scrambling net, and no entry in the log book about all this. Nothing was written in the log."

Suddenly, Bessler strode into the cabin. He'd obviously dressed in a great hurry, but still had time to strap on his belt with his German Luger all ready to use in the holster. He stared in horror at Richard and me, and then yakked to the Old Man in German.

"I can guess what you're saying, and I don't give a shit. You both knew what was in the crate and all about the illegal boarding party," yelled Richard.

Bessler pointed to the door. "Get out," he yelled. "You never come in here again."

"There's no entry in the logbook about them sneaking on board, or that son-of-a-bitch Caballero. Why isn't it all in the logbook, and what the fuck are they doing here?"

260

"Get out," ordered Bessler, his hand hovering near the Luger.

"Richard, it's no use, we won't get anywhere talking to them. Let's go."

"When we get back to Philly, if we get back, I'll nail you and Berners' asses to the cross," shouted Richard, storming out of the cabin. "I'll sue the company," continued Richard. "If there was an airport near here, I'd fly back right now and drop you all in the shit."

I gladly followed Richard out of the Old Man's cabin. "Richard, didn't you see Bessler reaching for his Luger? We have to play it safe. That bastard could easily have shot us."

"I know. I know. He's as crazy as the Old Man, and so are we for making this trip."

When we got back on deck, the soldiers and crates were gone.

"Where are they?" snapped Richard. "The bastards can't have just disappeared."

We went back aft and found the crew's quarters almost deserted. The only things left belonging to the soldiers was a pile of stinking army blankets and boxes of garbage piled up in the Officer dining saloon.

"They've gone and taken the rifles with them", Richard observed.

"...and left all their shit behind."

"No kidding. I'll tell the crew to toss this fucking lot onto the dock and let the Cubans clear it up!" Richard yelled.

I was appalled at the stacks of dirty plates and broken glasses scattered all over the saloon. "Look at this mess in here, it's like a pigsty. It needs to be fumigated," I replied. "Thank goodness they've gone."

"And so are all the crew," replied Richard. "They're all in the whorehouse fucking their heads off. It's only assholes like you and me who are still on board."

"What about Herr Schmidt? I haven't seen him lately."

"Sparks, I've told you, he's even hornier than me. He's had a bitch in his cabin ever since we've docked. Screw it! I've finished my watch," announced Richard. "I'm signing off, taking a shower, and I'm going to get myself a piece of ass."

Richard was on the Bridge filling in the log book. There was a knock on my cabin door. It was the young Cuban boy who delivered Maria's first message. He nervously handed me a note. '*Ricardo, please come to see me at the house. (signed) Maria.* I opened the fridge and held up a bottle of Coca-Cola. The young boy grinned, and gratefully accepted the cold drink and a bar of chocolate, but since he spoke no English I couldn't ask him any questions about who was staying at the Manager's house. However, if Maria had invited Richard around to see her, it must have been reasonably safe.

"It's from Maria," I said, showing Richard the note as soon as he came in. "She's at the Manager's house."

"I wish she was here right now, we could take a shower together. Jesus, I'm horny!" he replied, stripping off his clothes and turning on the shower. "What shall I do, Sparks?"

"Oh no, you don't involve me any more in your personal life."

"Why don't you fix a drink of Scotch?" he suggested, "a clean, cold drink with some fresh soda water and lots of ice. Did you give the kid anything?"

"Yes, a Coca-Cola and some chocolate." While Richard wallowed in the shower, I poured out two shots of Glenlivet, and filled the glasses with ice-cold Canada Dry soda water from the fridge. Minutes later, dripping wet and wrapped in a large white towel, Richard gratefully accepted the frosty glass.

"Cheers," I said.

"Cheers," repeated Richard, as we clinked glasses. "We sure deserve this." The exquisite taste of the famous single malt seemed to have a calming effect on both of us. It was what we both needed and well deserved.

"Are there many Fidelistas at the house?" asked Richard, talking to the boy. He immediately grinned, then shrugged his shoulders. "Sparks, if I go back to the house, is there any place where Maria and I can fuck?"

"I should think so. She'll soon find a bedroom, you can bet on that."

"Why didn't she come on board? She did last time," continued Richard, spraying himself with deodorant, and dusting his crotch, toes and back with talc before starting to get dressed. "I'd much rather fuck her in my own cabin."

Twenty minutes later, Richard and I were following the young Cuban boy through the deserted refinery carrying the usual bundle of toiletries for the girls. The young lad avoided the main road and led us behind the buildings. It was nearly dark and difficult to see the pools of black sludge churned up by the army vehicles. As we approached the Manager's house where Maria and Consuela were now living, we saw at least a dozen battered old army trucks parked outside.

"Jesus, Sparks! The place is swarming with soldiers."

"Batistianos or Fidelistas?" I said, pointing to the soldiers.

The young Cuban boy grinned. "Batistianos."

"Batistianos is right," moaned Richard. "Now what do we do?"

"Maria wouldn't have asked us to come if it wasn't safe. Let's follow him." Holding on to my sleeve, the young boy pulled me in the direction of the house.

Dodging behind more buildings, Richard finally arrived at the Manager's house, which was now quite familiar to me. "The bullion is hidden in that room," I whispered to Richard, as we darted around the back to the servant's quarters. The boy pushed open a door, and Maria leaped from her chair and threw her arms around Richard. "Ricardo! Ricardo!" she shouted, smothering him with kisses. "You come back to see me."

I grabbed the young boy's hand and led him outside, closing the door behind me. "*Donde esta Senorita Consuela?*" I asked.

"*Si, Senorita Consuela,*" he repeated, and led me to a room close by.

"Sparks!" shouted Consuela, suddenly appearing from the back of the room, hugging me like a returning hero. I was so pleased to see that her wounds had healed and she looked her usual beautiful self and smelled like a rose garden. There was a bottle of rum, some beer and sandwiches on the table but at that moment I wasn't hungry. My thoughts were of the gold bullion, but Consuela wanted to talk. "I never thought I would see you again," she whispered. "Everything here now so mixed up, and we are all so scared."

"Are the Batistianos still here at the refinery?"

"It is crazy. There are Batistianos and Fidelistas. All they want is money from the ships," replied Consuela, pouring me out a beer.

"Are there many ships that come here for molasses?"

"Three or four, and last week only two ships from Europe. The soldiers take the money, but they don't do any work." Consuela eagerly opened the package I brought for her. "Sparks, you are so kind," she said, sniffing the various packages of soap and talcum powder. "Ricardo, he bring something for Maria?"

"Yes, he brought her the same."

Consuela looked at me for a few seconds then began to cry. "He take her back to Philadelphia this time?"

"I don't think so. . ."

Tears rolled down her face. "Maria, she is pregnant," she sobbed. "Two months, but she won't tell Ricardo."

Immediately after Consuela mentioned the word pregnant, I knew why Richard was so worried. He must have known it would happen sooner or later. Very few Cuban women wore a diaphragm, and Richard never used condoms. "I am so sorry. You no tell Ricardo," whispered Consuela. "Maria, she wants Ricardo's baby, she. . ."

Suddenly there was knock on the door, and I recognized the nervous voice of the young boy. "The Batistianos are coming back," whispered Consuela, immediately hiding the toiletries under the pillow. "You have to go, Sparks. It is not safe."

"I need to get into the library," I replied, thinking about the gold and wishing I had made that my first priority.

"No. Not now, library full of soldiers. You and Ricardo come back later, you must go," insisted Consuela. I quickly finished my beer and followed the young boy outside where it was now quite dark. Richard was already dressed and waiting for me. Maria hugged him, tears streaming down her face. "Ricardo. I love you," she cried, "You come back later?"

"I'll come back," promised Richard, extricating himself from Maria's passionate embrace, then hurrying to catch up with the young boy who was weaving around the various huts trying to find a safe way back to the ship. "Jesus, Sparks we're both crazy, do you know that?" he concluded.

"I mean risking our lives for a piece of ass. But shit-damn, Maria sure knows how to fuck!"

The young boy led us through the back of the refinery and onto a hill overlooking the dock. We had never been this way before. From the top of a slight incline we could see the ship bathed in an eerie blue floodlight. It looked deserted. "Okay?" shouted the boy, pointing to the ship.

"Okay," I repeated, giving him a five dollar bill. Seconds later he had vanished.

"Where are we?" asked Richard. "I can see the ship over there, but how do we know what's in between? We might be walking into a platoon of soldiers."

Some emaciated donkeys, tethered to a nearby pole, moved nervously about as we crept passed them. I wanted to untie their ropes and let them go free, but feared they might make a lot of noise. Richard cautiously led the way down the hill and through some bushes toward a country road that was occasionally lit up by the headlights from passing army trucks. "If we keep heading toward the ship, we should be okay."

"That's if we don't walk into a campsite. These hills are crawling with soldiers," I replied. An occasional break in the clouds allowed some welcome moonlight to show us the way down the hillside. The tall bushes scraped our faces, and we often stumbled on loose rocks. Ahead was a clump of trees. Our footpath wound itself through the middle.

"What's that god-awful smell?" whispered Richard. "We must be near a slaughterhouse." As we got closer to the trees, the clouds parted and we could see the moon, a bright ball of yellow light shining through the branches. Suddenly Richard yelled out a blood curdling scream that sent a steel cold shiver like an arrow straight through my body. We had walked into about ten naked corpses swinging by their necks from the branches of some trees.

266

"Jesus!" screamed Richard. "They're all young boys and they've been ripped open. Oh! My God, they're all young kids."

I disentangled myself from a rotting corpse and ran headlong down the hill, falling over Richard, who had stumbled and was throwing up. I helped him to his feet and we ran across the path between some peasant huts. Dogs started barking, chasing after us as we leapt over fences, crashing through backyards full of squawking chickens. Nothing could stop our desperate headlong dash toward the refinery and up the gangplank onto the ship.

Once inside the comparative safety of my cabin, my hands were shaking so badly, it was all I could to pour out two glasses of Scotch. I handed one to Richard. He was sobbing as he buried his face in a towel. My shirt smelled of rotting flesh and was covered with blood from the corpse. I stripped off and threw my clothes out of the porthole and took a shower. The hot soapy water felt good, but nothing would ever wash away the stench of death still locked in my head.

"They were just young kids," wailed Richard, when I got out of the shower. "Just young boys, hanging there, ripped open. Jesus Christ!" He continued to sob, covering his face with a towel.

I dried off and sat on my bunk sipping my drink, neat Scotch, no ice. Richard threw his clothes out of the porthole and took a shower. I could hear him in there, still sobbing. "They were just young boys," he sobbed, "just young boys."

I then realized how lucky we were to be alive. If the Cubans could do that to young boys, and shoot the hands and feet off prisoners in jail, what would they do to me if they caught me stealing the gold? Richard was right, no amount of gold was worth the risk. When he came out of the shower, he grabbed the bottle of Scotch and went into his

267

cabin, muttering to himself about the young boys until he passed out, curled up on his couch.

I lay on my bunk trying to make sense out of everything that had happened. Why was I risking everything for some gold ingots, it would be suicidal to try and get them. They were well hidden and might be there for years. Maybe, when the revolution was over. . .I could take a trip to Cuba and –

The sound of Richard rolling off his couch and hitting the floor brought me back to reality. I went into his cabin. He was on the carpet passed out, the empty bottle beside him. I put a pillow under his head, picked up the bottle, went out onto the boat deck and tossed it overboard. It was an eerie feeling. A bright moonlit night, the constant chug, chug, chug of the shore pumps filling the tanks with hot molasses, and the raucous sounds of music from the busy whorehouse filled with drunken seamen, laughing, drinking and fucking like rabbits made me feel uneasy and disconnected with reality. And just a few hundred yards on top of the hill were those young boys.

I tried to push the thoughts from my head, and went to my cabin and opened a bottle of Glenlivet. I needed something to obliterate the memory of all those mutilated young boys hanging from the trees.

~~~

CHAPTER EIGHTEEN

Heinz is Shot

I woke up the next morning and lay in my bunk staring at the bulkhead. No longer did Hans bring a pot of coffee every morning, that little luxury ended when he went into the hospital. I wondered where he was now, still hiding from the Immigration or had he found a safe place to stay? I crawled out of my bunk, dragged on my robe and headed for the bathroom.

"Hi, Sparks, how about some coffee?" suggested Richard. "I also got some cookies." Richard's cabin was always a mess, but there was room to sit down and have a drink.

"How do you feel? You sure tied one on last night. You finished up the bottle of Glenlivet," I reminded him.

"Sparks? Don't remind me. I'll never forget those kids. Jesus! How in God's name could anyone do that to a kid? And why?"

"Richard, we have to talk about something else."

"Something else? How about this for starters? Caballero's disappeared! Gone! Fucked off and took the money Berners gave him to pay for the molasses." Richard poured me a cup of coffee from his special pot. "Now what do we do?"

"What about his army?"

"They all crept out in the middle of the night, took all their rifles and ammunition with them. I guess some seamen went and told Bessler they were leaving, but he's not giving out any information," replied Richard, "because it was he and Old Man who allowed them on board."

I sipped my coffee and wondered if things could get any worse. Richard was still on his early morning watch. He checked the temperature of the molasses. "What about the Old Man? What's he going to do about it? We have no money to pay for all this black crap that's being pumped on board."

"Sparks? I don't give a shit any more. As soon as I am off watch, I am going to find Maria and fuck my head off."

"Well, that will certainly make her happy." I knew Richard would get a very warm welcome when he showed up at her place. I topped up my cup with coffee then went back to my cabin. "How long before we're fully loaded?"

"Later this evening, if all the pumps keep going, but that's Schmidt's worry, it's his watch," replied Richard, following me into my cabin. "Do you mind if I take a few bottles of Coca-Cola. I'm going to see Maria and fuck like a rabbit."

"Good for you." I sipped my coffee, which was hot and strong, but I wished I could find a way to brew tea in the morning. "So, when's the next high tide?"

"Six o'clock tomorrow morning, but we'll need a Pilot because we're fully loaded and deep in the water, and I don't wanna slam into the fucking sandbar," explained Richard. "But first, we have to pay for all this shit."

"Paying for the molasses and finding a Pilot is the Old Man's responsibility," I reminded him.

Richard sprayed himself all over with the rest of my aftershave and ran a comb through his hair. "I gotta be all slicked up for Maria."

"She'll love you just the same, but we might be here forever if we can't pay for the molasses," I replied, wishing I had hidden my aftershave.

270

"The Old Man and Ludwig Berners should never have trusted Caballero. What a pair of assholes they are. Now we're the ones dropped in the shit. Anyway I'm gonna see Maria for a farewell fuck." Richard helped himself to three bottles of Coca-Cola and put them in a paper bag. "What are you going to do, Sparks?"

"I'm still tired. I'll lie on my bunk awhile and think about England," I replied. "Oh! If you get a chance to grab the gold."

"Sparks, I'll try, but the first thing I'm gonna grab is Maria."

Later that afternoon I was dozing off in the radio room when I was suddenly aroused by a loud knocking on the door and was very surprised to see Deiter, the Captain's steward, standing outside on the deck sobbing and shaking like a leaf.

"Herr Schparks, Heinz has been shot," he wailed. "Please, Herr Schparks, you come quick!"

"Heinz has been shot?"

"Ya, he is bleeding very much," continued the steward. "You come quick." I grabbed the First Aid kit and followed the sniveling little Kraut across the deck. He was half-crying, babbling on and on about a drunken Cuban soldier who had gone berserk in the whorehouse and shot Heinz in the stomach. Unable to get a doctor, Kimmel the Bosun, Artymuik and Weicecz brought Heinz back to his cabin, then went to Herr Bessler for help. Apparently, they wasted their time as Bessler angrily reminded them of the Captain's orders, and then slammed his cabin door in their faces.

I nearly stumbled on the slippery steel steps leading down into the crew's quarters. The humidity was almost suffocating even though it was a lot less crowded than my previous visit. It still stank of sweat and overflowing toilets.

Heinz's little cabin was much tidier than the rest. His famous collection of photographs of naked girls adorned the bulkheads. I was shocked to see his muscular, bronzed body covered in blood, now spurting from a hole in his skin just below the ribcage. It looked grotesque with flaps of dark bloody flesh literally hanging off his chest. His face was drained of all color, and he looked more dead than alive. If he had been shot, where was the bullet, still inside the wound?

Deiter, the little sniveling steward, immediately knelt down at the bedside sobbing uncontrollably. "Please, Herr Schparks, help him."

"He needs a doctor, a blood transfusion, I can't do that," I yelled. "We must get a doctor." One of the seamen standing by the cabin door tried to explain how the Madam at the whorehouse had sent for a doctor but they were all at the army hospital.

"Please do something," pleaded Deiter, staring at me with tears streaming down his face. It was obvious Heinz was in great pain, drifting in an out of consciousness, moaning, opening and closing his eyes. I knew there was some morphine in Krause's study.

"Go and ask the Captain for some morphine," I yelled at Deiter. "It's in the drug cabinet and Krause has the keys. Hurry."

"Herr Schparks, please help him," begged Deiter, hardly aware of what I had said.

"Okay. Okay, but go and get some morphine from the Captain, and tell Herr Bessler we've got to get a doctor. Quick! Schnell!"

For a few seconds the Captain's steward stared in horror at the blood soaked bunk where his friend lay writhing in pain. "Mein Gott!" he screamed, racing out of the cabin. Unfortunately, Heinz had been shot in the stomach at close range, shattering his skin. Somebody handed me a clean white towel which I pressed against the black hole only inches below his heart, and held it there while I mopped the sweat from my own forehead on a filthy towel hanging near the washbasin.

Why me? I thought. I knew no more than the average person about treating such wounds, yet a dozen seamen stood around the bed expecting me to work a miracle. Heinz needed immediate surgery to remove the bullet and stitch up the hole, but I had absolutely no knowledge of how that could be done, and in any case, I had no surgical equipment.

Steve, the second cook came into the cabin. "Oh, my God!" he yelled. "They brought him here. I heard he'd been shot."

"Yes, damn it!" I cried. "They brought him here. I've got no proper equipment. We've got to get him into a hospital, or at least taken to a doctor."

"No chance, Sparks. They tried at the whorehouse to get him to a doctor, but they're all working for the army."

"But I can't sew him up, that's what it needs. It's an open wound, torn flesh. Go and get some clean sheets and a bowl of hot water and I'll have to use this iodine." Heinz face was ashen and he felt cold, even though the cabin was very hot and humid. He hadn't moved for a while and I was scared he was dead. I took his wrist to feel for a pulse. Suddenly he groaned, staring right at me with his big blue eyes as if pleading for help. Seconds later he was unconscious again. His pulse was strong and racing. There was still a chance.

Steve soon returned with a large stainless steel basin filled with hot water and some Listerine antiseptic he had bought in Philadelphia. "The Bosun is bringing clean sheets," he said, kneeling beside the bunk. "My God, Sparks, the poor bugger is in agony."

"I know! I've sent Deiter to get some morphine from the drug cabinet in the Old Man's cabin."

"Deiter, the poor little sod, he worships Heinz, worships the ground he walks on. He'll do anything for him," added Steve.

"Good, Heinz is going to need all the help he can get."

The Bosun arrived with some clean sheets and began tearing them into strips. Steve soaked them in the antiseptic and handed them to me. I washed away the blood from the gaping hole, and we all groaned when we saw the extent of the wound.

"Is the bullet still in there?" asked Steve.

"I don't know, but I sure as hell can't get it out. I have no instruments and I don't know how! He needs a blood transfusion. We've got to get him into a hospital."

Deiter rushed into the cabin, his face white with rage. "Herr Schparks, the Captain say no."

"What?" I screamed.

"He say no. Please Herr Schparks, the Captain he is drunk."

"Where is Herr Bessler?"

"I don't know."

"Keep cleaning up the wound, Steve. I'll be back as quick as I can." As I raced across the deck, the Captain's steward ran alongside me, sobbing and crying and making no sense. I burst into the Old Man's cabin and went straight to his study where the drug cabinet was fixed to the bulkhead. Krause was sitting watching television.

"Captain Krause, it's an emergency," I yelled. "I need the morphine"

"Ugh!" he sneered, "for the sex maniac who disobeys orders and went to the whorehouse?"

"I want the key to the drug cabinet!"

"Herr Schparks, it's in the desk," confided Deiter.

"Ludwig Berners' orders! No shore leave," continued the Old Man. "If they shot or in the jail, is their fault. On Ludwig Berners' orders."

While the Old Man and his steward were shouting at each other in German, I went through his desk drawer and found the key to the drug cabinet. Fortunately it had recently been restocked, and there were now disposable units of morphine.

Leaving Deiter to argue with the Old Man I raced back aft where a crowd of worried seamen had gathered outside Heinz's cabin. "Anybody know what happened?" I asked nervously. "I need to know if the bullet is still in there." I slowly realized I was wasting my time, because very few of the crew spoke English.

"It was a Cuban soldier. He shot him," answered the Bosun.

"Yes, I know that, but where is the bullet, that's what I want to know?"

Steve had done a good job of cleaning up the gore and blood was no longer oozing from the hole in Heinz's side. I quickly gave him a shot of morphine in the arm and within a few seconds his whole body relaxed. "Sparks, he looks as if he's dead."

"He's not dead, but close." Steve and I wrapped the wound as best we could, while some of the others took away the bloody sheets. Another seaman plugged in an electric fan, which I greatly appreciated.

For a few brief seconds we all stared at Heinz lying motionless on the bed, each one silently praying he would survive. He was the most popular guy on the ship, everybody liked him. I looked around at the crowd of anxious faces. "Please, we have to get him to a hospital! The bullet has to be removed, and he needs a blood transfusion."

Deiter was sobbing, kneeling beside the bunk, nervously dabbing the perspiration from Heinz's forehead. He looked up at me, tears pouring down his anxious face. "Herr Schparks, will he be okay?"

"I don't know, Deiter. He must go to a hospital. The bullet has to be removed. It's a major operation. I can't do that."

"But Herr Schparks, what do we do?" he sobbed.

"I can't do any more now. He's no longer in pain. Nobody will look after him better than you, Deiter. I promise I'll try and get him into a hospital in Santiago. If not, I'll call the Coast Guard and make sure he's sent ashore in Key West. We should be there in two days."

"In two days?" repeated Deiter, continuing to wipe the sweat from Heinz's forehead.

"Did you find Bessler?" I asked.

"Herr Bessler? Ya, he do nothing for sex maniacs," cried the young steward.

"Deiter, I promise I'll do all I can. He'll sleep for a while now, the blood has stopped. He's no longer in pain. I'm going ashore to try and find a doctor. You look after him."

"Danke, Herr Schparks," sobbed Deiter, looking up at me through tear-filled eyes. "Herr Schparks. I am sorry. You are good man and I have been a little bastard and call you names. I am sorry, Herr Schparks."

"That's okay, Deiter, you look after Heinz." I left him sobbing uncontrollably beside Heinz's bunk, dutifully cooling his compatriot's forehead with a cold bandage. Steve followed me out onto the deck where we both breathed in the cooler air. "What do you reckon, Sparks?"

"I'm surprised he's not dead. I don't think he stands a chance unless he gets immediate surgery."

"But where, Sparks?" questioned Steve.

"I don't know, but I'm going ashore to see what I can do." I hurried back to my cabin hoping nobody had seen the tears streaming down my face.

Ten minutes later I bribed the guard at the foot of the gangplank with a packet of Lucky Strikes. He nodded gratefully, and allowed me to head off in the direction of the Manager's house. My main concern was getting Heinz into hospital, or at least some professional treatment and a blood transfusion. The second biggest worry was finding some way of paying for it. I remembered the Old Man had a massive store of cigarettes locked away and Deiter had the key to his storage room.

A couple of soldiers glared at me as I hurried toward the Manager's house, but I ignored them and carried on walking. I was a bag of nerves. The same collection of battered army trucks was parked in the driveway. Groups of soldiers were drinking beer sitting on the steps leading up to the once magnificent front entrance, tossing their empty bottles into the bushes. I dodged behind a building, breathing a sigh of relief when I eventually walked past the library and knocked on Maria's door. *"Donde esta Ricardo?"* I yelled. *"Ha habido un accidente"*

Maria immediately opened the door, she was wearing her robe, and I assumed she had been in bed. "Sparks," she said, "Come in. What has happened?"

Richard was asleep on the bed, but woke up when he heard the sound of my voice. "What's the matter, Sparks?" he said, reaching for his clothes.

"Heinz has been shot in the stomach by a drunken Cuban soldier. He needs to get into a hospital."

Maria immediately started crying. "Sparks, the hospital is full of soldiers."

"How about a doctor, he also needs a blood transfusion."

"Where is he?" asked Richard, tying up his shoes.

"In his cabin, I've been in there for an hour trying to stop the bleeding." I tried hard to control my feelings. I couldn't believe that Heinz might die.

Richard poured me a shot of rum. "Drink this, Sparks. You look as if you need it."

"He has a gaping hole in the side of his stomach," I continued, trying to pull myself together. "I don't know what to do." I sipped the rum. I did need it, and appreciated the warm glow. "Maria, don't you know where we can get a doctor?" I asked. "We can only pay with cigarettes."

"No doctors," she replied, her brown eyes welling with tears.

Consuela hurried into the room and gave me a hug. "Sparks, Maria's father is in jail. She has just come back from there. We need a lot of cigarettes to get him out."

"The Old Man has a storeroom full of them and Deiter has got the key," I replied. "He'll help us."

I looked at Maria sitting on the edge of the bed. "How many cigarettes do you need to get your father out of jail?"

"I don't know," she replied, looking at Richard for some help.

"Probably a hundred cartons, the same as the seamen, I expect," answered Richard, now fully dressed. "But we could try the guards with fifty."

"You will help get my father out of jail, Sparks?" cried Maria, her face suddenly smiling.

"Of course, if we can get the cigarettes. Can you help to get a doctor for Heinz?"

"I will try," she said, hurriedly getting dressed.

"Maria, get a taxi and wait for us at the bottom of the gangplank. We'll get the cigarettes." Richard hugged her for a few minutes and then we headed back to the ship.

The guard at the foot of the gangplank stared at us, but said nothing. We immediately went back aft. "I feel sorry for these poor bastards back here trying to stay cool in all this heat," moaned Richard. "Where's Heinz?"

"In his cabin, poor bugger, and it's a hell hole."

"Jesus Christ, this place is disgusting. Ludwig Berners should come back aft once in a while and take a look at the way his crew has to live, the cheap bastard."

Deiter was sitting beside Heinz, holding his hand. He smiled when we entered the cabin. "Herr Schparks. You get a doctor?"

"We're trying. How is he?"

"He still sleep, but very cold," replied Deiter. "I cover him with a blanket." I reached for Heinz wrist and felt his pulse. It was weak but regular.

"How's his pulse, Sparks?" enquired Richard.

"It's still ticking, but we have to get a doctor."

Richard stared at the young steward kneeling beside the bed. "Deiter, we need your help to get cigarettes from the Old Man's storage room," he whispered, "to pay the doctor."

"Captain Krause has many cartons of cigarettes in there," replied Deiter, hopefully. "I give you the key."

"Come and help," suggested Richard. "I'll get a suitcase." Richard and Deiter went to get the cigarettes. I sat beside Heinz and checked his pulse. The morphine injection had mercifully knocked him out and he was in no pain. He had lost a lot of blood, and looked more dead than alive. Even if we found a doctor, could he get a supply of blood, and all the equipment needed? I stared at the almost lifeless body. Fortunately, Heinz was still breathing gently, his face no longer contorted with pain. That, at least was a blessing, but inwardly I didn't think he would survive.

Luckily, the Old Man was asleep when Richard and Deiter robbed him of two hundred cartons of Lucky Strikes cigarettes and stashed them into an old suitcase. They had already bribed the guard at the foot of the gangplank where Maria was waiting. She quickly put the suitcase in the taxi, gave Richard a hug and seconds later the taxi was bumping its way out of the refinery.

"Maria's got fifty cartons, I hope that will be enough," explained Richard, following me back to Heinz's cabin. "The rest are in your office."

"The lady, she is gone for a doctor?" enquired Deiter, resuming his place at the side of Heinz's bed.

"She is going to try and get one," I replied, truthfully.

"Heinz will be okay now?" questioned Deiter. The Old Man's steward looked at me almost pleading for a positive answer. When I first met him, Deiter was flouncing about in the Old Man's cabin and I disliked him right away. He was the Captain's little spy telling him everything that went on back aft. Consequently I always tried to ignore him, treating him with the contempt I thought he deserved. Now, kneeling at the side of Heinz's bed, he looked like a young German schoolboy with tousled blond hair. His normally blue eyes were now red and puffy, and a worried look creased his cheeky little face. He didn't look old enough to be away from home, yet I knew he had stowed away on a Polish freighter to escape from East Germany on his fourteenth birthday. So far he hadn't got much out of life, and now he was about to lose his idol. For the first time I felt very sorry for him, and wished to God I could give him more hope.

"Deiter, we're doing all we can. Maria is trying to get a doctor. All you can do is to watch over him, and keep him warm."

"*Vielen Dank, Herr Schparks.*"

"Let me know when he wakes up," I replied, sadly as I left Heinz's cabin and returned to my radio room.

Richard was already packing cartons of Lucky Strikes cigarettes into an old leather suitcase when I got there. "I hate to say it, but I don't think Heinz stands a chance, Sparks. He needs a blood transfusion."

"And all the rest, poor bugger. I've given him a shot of morphine, but that only deadens the pain." I poured out two stiff drinks, and gave one to Richard. "Do you think we can pay for the cargo with the cigarettes the Old Man has stashed away? How many are left?" I asked, searching for some ice.

"I saw a lot of cases stashed against the bulkhead, and Deiter says there are thousands more, but I'll have to count them. We can suggest trading cigarettes for molasses, but we both know the bastards like cash and plenty of it," replied Richard, stuffing more cartons of Lucky Strikes into the suitcase.

Richard was right. The Cubans would expect to be paid in cash for the molasses. "I suspect Caballero has long gone, don't you?" It was a very silly question, because we both knew the answer.

"Maria asked some of the soldiers about him. They said he was not one of Castro's men, he was a mercenary just like all the others," replied Richard, "And he had taken off with the money he got from Berners to pay for the molasses."

"I always thought Ludwig Berners was a smart businessman. I mean fancy trusting someone like Caballero with all that money." I topped up our glasses with the rest of the Coca-Cola. "What else did Maria find out?"

"It's what her father has found out. That's why he's in jail. The guys who have taken over this refinery are a bunch of crooks. They're neither Fidelistas nor Batistianos, and that so-called Cuban Officer we've been dealing with is a fucking crook," replied Richard.

"It seems we're all crooks," I sighed. "We've just stolen two hundred cartons of Lucky Strikes from the Old Man's storage room."

"It's all for a good cause. Deiter also gave me a slew of papers and stuff taken from Bloom's cabin. Krause ordered him to toss them overboard, but because the Old Man refused to help Heinz, Deiter gave Bloom's papers to me," replied Richard.

"Reading Bloom's paperwork will be very interesting," I replied. "It will answer a lot of questions and we'll find out what he was up to."

"I'll say. Now what about the gold? Are you still seriously thinking about it?"

"Naturally, I'm always thinking about it. All those ingots will solve a lot of problems and buy some land for the sanctuary. That's what I want it for."

"Well, that's a good cause, Sparks. We can come back to Cuba and get it next year when all this fighting is over."

"Well, it's certainly well hidden, but I'm surprised to hear you suggest that, especially considering your current relationship with Maria. You know she worships you."

"Yes, I know," he replied, "and I wish she didn't." Obviously Richard wasn't very keen to become a father. I wondered if Richard ever thought about her getting pregnant.

"I wish Maria would hurry back, what can we do if she can't get a doctor?"

I wondered how they closed up a gaping black hole in the stomach, what did they use and how did it work?

"Sparks, we're doing all we can"

"Are we?" I slumped back into the old leather chair. "I'm too chicken to sit with him in case he dies right in front of me. Poor Deiter has to face that possibility. My God! I feel sorry for that poor little bugger. He worships the ground that Heinz walks on."

Richard went to the Old Man's storage room to count the cigarettes while I packed up what we had into the suitcase. Five minutes later he returned looking very disappointed. "There are only about two hundred cartons in there," he announced mournfully. "That's not enough. The huge boxes at the back are almost empty."

"So it's no good thinking of trading cigarettes for the cargo?"

"Are you kidding, forty thousand dollars' worth of top black strap molasses in exchange for a few thousand cigarettes, no way." Richard glanced at his watch. "I hope Maria has been able to get her father out of jail."

"I hope she finds a doctor, but how will you know?"

"She promised to stop at the end of the gangplank and I gave the guards a few packs of Lucky Strikes to let her on board."

"And then what do we give the doctor?" I hated to face the reality that our chances of getting one were very slim.

"Sparks, we've got a hundred and fifty cartons here, but you know it won't happen. Maria will try, but she won't be able to find a doctor"

"Damn it, Richard!" I replied, angrily banging the office desk. "Don't be so bloody complacent. There's a guy bleeding to death back aft, and we've got to try and save him. If the doctor doesn't get here, we'll have to take him ashore to the hospital. We've got to do something," I yelled, choking back my tears.

"Sparks, calm down. I know you're upset about Heinz. We all are, but be practical. What can we do?"

"I don't know, but we can't just sit around and let him die." Richard stared at me for few seconds, waiting for me to calm down, but I was a bag of nerves. I just couldn't take the heavy responsibility of trying to save a man's life, watching Heinz laying there, occasionally opening his eyes, like he was silently asking me to save him.

"Sparks, we can call the Coast Guard and send him ashore in Key West. So our first priority is to get the hell out of here, but where do we get the money to do that? There are only a few thousand cigarettes left, hardly enough to pay for a doctor, if we can get one."

"Then we have to get our hands on the gold. We have to do it as soon as we can," I shouted. "There's enough gold there to pay for this cargo and bribe a doctor to patch up Heinz. It's the only way out. We have to do it."

"Sparks, calm down. Why don't you go out on deck and I'll bring you a Scotch," suggested Richard. "We both need one." I was shaking and very nervous as I walked out into the cool evening air on deck. It was so quiet and peaceful. I knew I had to pull myself together.

Richard came out with a glass of Glenlivet. "Try this, Sparks," he said. "Look at those Cuban gunships anchored in the bay. With our luck they'll fire on us, sink this goddamn hell ship and we'll drown in our own molasses."

~~~

CHAPTER NINETEEN

Illegal Midnight Sailing

Ten minutes later, a taxi drew up alongside the gangplank. Maria and a young man got out and hurried up the gangplank. "We have my father in the taxi," she said. "I am so pleased. He is okay, but they take all the cigarettes."

I stared at the young man she brought with her. He was wearing a hospital white smock and carried a small case. Was he the doctor we had been praying for? "This is Juan Carlos, he is from the hospital," continued Maria.

I automatically grabbed Juan Carlos and gave him a hug. "We are so pleased to see you," I gushed. "I will take you down to Heinz right away." Leaving Maria and Richard to talk, I led the way down into the crew's quarters. "Heinz has been shot in the stomach by a Cuban soldier. I have given him some morphine."

Deiter, who was sitting beside his idol, jumped up when we entered Heinz's cabin, "Herr Schparks you find a doctor," he said, smiling for the first time in days.

Juan Carlos was obviously disgusted with the state of the cabin. "This is a very bad place to bring an injured man," he said. He then pulled back the sheet and groaned when he saw the extent of the wound. "Is the bullet still in there?" he asked.

"I'm sorry, but I don't know."

"Without an X-ray I can't tell. They'll have to take out the bullet at the hospital. And he needs surgery right away. It's serious. All I can do is pack the wound with gauze to stop the bleeding and make him comfortable. Our hospitals are all full of soldiers."

Juan Carlos repeated what I already knew. He put on a pair of rubber gloves and swabbed the open wound with some antiseptic, then opened packets of surgical gauze he had brought with him. Deiter watched him almost in a trance, tears running down his face. I felt so sorry for him, he had never left Heinz's bedside except to get the morphine.

"I am hoping we can send him ashore in Key West in two days," I replied. "I can radio the Coast Guard."

"He needs a blood transfusion," advised Juan Carlos, as he took more sterile packs of gauze from his case. "The Cuban soldier, he was drunk. Yes?"

"Yes, they were in the whorehouse."

"The hospital is full of young soldiers and we have not enough medicine for them," replied Juan Carlos. "Senor Castro tells us to hate the Americanos, but it is from them we get all the medicine." He pushed his gloved hand into the open wound and started packing it with gauze like he was stuffing a chicken.

I didn't want to watch and needed to talk to Maria before she left. "I'll go on deck and arrange for you to have some cigarettes, but we have very little cash."

"I do not need anything. Your friend was shot by a Cuban soldier. I am ashamed of my Cuban comrades. I will do all I can," replied Juan Carlos. "He seems to be a very strong young man, but the wound in the chest is very serious."

Deiter stared transfixed as Juan Carlos lifted up the bloody flesh around the wound. I didn't want to watch, I had already seen far too much blood and gore.

When I got back on deck, Maria was just leaving in the taxi. "She's taken her father to her place to look after him," explained Richard. "How's Heinz?"

"The doctor is packing the wound with gauze. All he can do is to stop the bleeding and make him comfortable," I replied. "I'll radio the Coast Guard to pick him up in Key West."

"Great, if we ever get out of this fucking place." Richard kicked the gangplank in anger. "Now we gotta find some cigarettes to pay this goddamn doctor."

"He doesn't want any payment. He said he is ashamed that Heinz was shot by a Cuban soldier. Richard, we have to get our hands on that gold, it's the only way to get out of here."

The bright moonlight helped us avoid the pools of black sludge as we retraced our steps back to Maria's place later that evening. We were very wary of the soldiers laughing and drinking beer while sprawled all over the steps to the entrance to the Manager's home. "They're already drunk," whispered Richard. "God knows what they will be like after they find out we can't pay them for the molasses."

"Richard, I know where the gold is, we just have to get them out of the library."

"Is that all, Sparks? You're daydreaming."

"Damn it, Richard. It's our only chance." We arrived at Maria's tiny apartment. Richard tapped at the door which was immediately opened by Maria. She smiled. "I have been worried, how is the wounded seaman?"

"Your doctor friend is patching him up and he doesn't want any cigarettes," I replied. "He is a good man."

Maria's father was propped up in her bed. He looked in a very sad shape, but smiled when we came in. "Gracias," he mumbled, "for the cigarettes and all your help."

Maria brought in two beers and we told them all our problems. How Caballero had stolen the money to pay for the molasses, and we now couldn't pay for the cargo. Then, I mentioned about the gold ingots hidden in the library and how they got there.

"In the library?" repeated Maria. "That's the officer's bar. It's their room now."

"If only they can be distracted for ten minutes, I can get in through the window, reach into the heating duct and grab the velvet bag with the gold ingots." I explained. "When we have the ingots we can pay for the molasses and leave."

"I will go and look in the library," offered Maria, wrapping a bright green shawl around her. She smiled at Richard and went outside.

"The soldiers, they get drunk at night," whispered Consuela. "They shoot their guns at the cats and dogs. They are very cruel. You have to be very careful."

"Ten minutes in the empty library, that's all need." I tried to be casual like it was the easiest thing in the world, but I could see Consuela was still very skeptical.

"I'll be helping him," confirmed Richard.

Maria's father groaned and got out of bed. "I do not like staying in bed," he explained, reaching for his clothes. "I will help you."

A few minutes later Maria returned. "The library is empty. The soldiers say the Fidelistas are attacking the jail. In a few minutes they will all be gone."

We could hear the sound of the army trucks revving up and driving away, then waited another minute while Maria went outside to check. "It is okay, they are gone," she said, then started yelling at her father for getting out of bed.

The library window was already open and it was so easy climbing inside. The room was dark, reeking of beer

288

and cigarillos and there were empty bottles and beer cans strewn across the floor. I had mentally rehearsed this scene so many times I could have done it blindfolded. Now I couldn't believe my luck as I groped my way across to the desk. Seconds later I was flat on the floor, pushing back the heavy metal grille, reaching down and down into the heating duct. Dear God, surely the velvet bag was still there. I anxiously groped around the dusty old pipes until I felt the top of the velvet bag. Forcing my arm even deeper into the duct, I managed to get hold of the bag between two fingers and gently ease it from between the pipes until I had it in my hand. It was an incredible moment, my heart raced and I wanted to shout out, instead I quietly slid the heating duct grille back into place and climbed out of the window where Richard was waiting for me. "I've got it," I whispered. "I've got it. I've got it."

"Sparks, you're a fucking genius! A lifesaver." Richard patted me on the back as we hurried back to Maria's little room.

Consuela, Maria or her father had never seen a gold ingot before and stared in wonder at the eight shiny gold ingots on the table. "They are beautiful," observed Consuela, "too beautiful for the bastardos who steal the molasses from us."

"They are not Fidelistas," explained Maria's father. "They are just renegades who take the money belonging to the refinery."

"My father and the other workers make the molasses and do not get any money," explained Maria.

"Then some of this is yours," I said, handing Maria, Consuela and the father each a shiny ingot. "That is for helping us." Richard looked at me and grinned, nodding in agreement.

All three of them looked at me in awe. "For us?" yelled Maria, excitedly. "Gold ingots? Sparks, you are wonderful."

"It's from both of us, Ricardo here helped me." It was a joy to see the look on their faces; but all three of them deserved a lot more.

Suddenly, there was a knock at the door. It was the young boy Maria used to send messages to the ship. He rattled away in Spanish. "Quick," yelled Maria. "He say the ship is leaving." Richard and I rushed outside and saw the ugly silhouette of the *Cuban Trader* slowly moving away from the dock.

"Damn! They're leaving without us," I yelled. "How did they pay for the cargo?"

"I'll bet Krause is crazy enough to try and get away without paying for it, but it's not high tide for another eight hours. We've got a full cargo," yelled Richard. "They'll get stuck on a sandbank."

Maria yelled at her father in Spanish as he continued to get dressed. "Ricardo, my father wants to know what is happening."

"The Captain is a crazy drunk. He probably saw the soldier's leaving the dock and decided to cast off and leave."

"But he can't leave without me, the Sparks." I quickly stuffed the remaining five ingots into the velvet bag. "Krause is insane, International Law states no ship can sail without a Radio Officer on board."

"Krause is only worried about getting away," yelled Richard. "Do you think he cares about you and me, or the goddamn International Law?"

Maria's father hobbled outside to watch the *Cuban Trader* slowly leaving the dock, then yelled something to Maria in Spanish.

"My father says we chase after the ship in the refinery launch. He use it many times," replied Maria, still admonishing him for getting out of bed.

"It is the company launch. I use it to take harbor Pilot's to the ships," explained Maria's father, dragging on his shoes. "Come, follow me."

Running, hobbling and sliding thru the oily mud, Maria's father led the way around the huts to the back of the dock where the launch was tied up. We were soon joined by a dock worker who immediately helped to untie all the ropes while yakking away to Maria's father in Spanish.

"My father's friend tells him that just before the ship sailed, a rich Cuban businessman got out of a taxi and went onto the ship, then the ship leave. He say he tried to tell them they needed a Pilot, but they no listen."

Maria's father helped his daughter and Consuela into the company launch while Richard and I clambered in beside them. The motor roared into life, pushing us slowly away from the company jetty.

An eerie mist hung just above the water, obscuring our view. Fortunately Maria's father had operated the launch many times before and soon we were moving at quite a pace following in the wake of the escaping ship. "She's going about three knots," explained Richard, "but what about the sandbank? It's not high tide until early tomorrow morning." We all hoped the ship would wait for the high tide before attempting to sail over the dreaded sandbank, thus giving us a chance to clamber aboard.

Maria and Richard were cuddled together. He was trying to persuade her to go with him to America, but she wouldn't leave her father. "Maria still not tell him about the baby," whispered Consuela, "She hope Richard come back again. She will not leave her father."

"The gold ingots I gave you will sell for mucho pesetas. You will have lots of money," I replied. "Richard and I will come back." Whether Consuela believed me I couldn't tell, but she clung to me shaking with fear. "Gracias for the gold, Sparks," she sobbed.

"There's the son of a bitch," yelled Richard, pointing to the ugly shape now half way across the bay. "It's not slowing down, so they're not going to wait for the high tide."

"Jesus Christ! What about the sandbank?" I groaned.

"Sparks, Krause is insane. He's going to try and plough over it." The launch speeded up and headed for the *Cuban Trader*. We could hear voices echoing across the calm water. It was the crew on deck cheering us on. They had dropped a scrambling net down the side of the ship which was fully loaded and low in the water. Slowly, Maria's father expertly steered the launch closer and closer to the rusty old hulk and the argument between Richard and Maria got louder until she was crying hysterically.

The gap between the ship and the launch closed a little but we were still not close enough the grab the scrambling net. Consuela hugged me as I reached out for the slippery net trailing along in the oily black water. The crew on deck were yelling and shouting, urging me on, but I knew one slip and I'd be in the water, sucked into the churning wake from the racing propeller and drown.

Finally, Maria's father inched the launch close enough for me to grab onto the slippery ropes and drag myself across the treacherous gap onto the net, my legs and feet still trailing in the oily water. Hand over hand on the slippery ropes I painfully climbed up the net. At the top, about a dozen pair of hands reached out to drag me on board. "Welcome aboard Sparks," yelled Steve. "Jesus we're so pleased you made it. Bessler and the old man are crazy. They're trying to leave without paying for all this shit."

I looked over the side at the launch struggling to stay alongside the ship and Richard and Maria were still arguing. For a moment I thought perhaps he decided to stay with her. Maybe she told him she was pregnant.

After a few agonizing minutes, Richard reached out, grabbed the scrambling net and hauled himself across the ever-widening gap. For a few brief seconds his feet and legs were under the water. Consuela screamed, which must have given him the impetus he needed to start climbing. Again a dozen pair of hands reached out and dragged him soaking wet on board. When he got to his feet, we looked over the side but the launch had disappeared into the mist.

"Jesus, Sparks, we made it. We made it, Buddy." Richard and I were surrounded by seamen overjoyed to see us back on board. "Hey! You guys, I gotta go onto the Bridge and find out what these mad bastards are doing," yelled Richard, shuffling across the slippery deck.

"I'm going back aft to check on Heinz." All the crew were now on the deck and very worried. They knew about the sandbanks and there was no pilot on board and that it wasn't high tide until dawn.

"Schparks, Krause not wait for the tide, and there is the sandbanks," yelled Dubinsky, following me to Heinz's cabin. "Bessler is a crazy. He yells at Igor in the engine room to go faster."

Bessler was indeed a crazy SOB. Even worse than the Old Man. When Deiter saw me enter the cabin the tears rolled down his face. "Herr Schparks," he said. "We all scared for you, the ship go and you not on board."

"Richard and I came out on a launch. How is Heinz?" I could see he was sleeping and certainly looked more comfortable than the last time I saw him. I felt his pulse which was still weak but regular. "Has the bleeding stopped?" Deiter pulled back the sheet to show me the wound, which was now clean and professionally bandaged. "Yes, I can see the bleeding has stopped. We have to get him ashore at Key West and into a hospital."

"You can do that, Herr Schparks?" Deiter looked up at me, almost pleading for it to happen.

"I can try, Deiter. I will try. You look after him and let me know when he wakes up. Do you know how the Captain is?"

"I hate him," replied Deiter. "He is drunk. Herr Bessler now tell everyone what to do."

"Did you see this Cuban who came on board just as the ship was leaving?"

"Herr Bessler take him to Herr Bloom's cabin and tell Kruger to take him some coffee."

"Will you ask Kruger to try and find out who he is? Find out his name."

"Ya, I do that, Herr Schparks, and tell you when Heinz wakes up." Deiter looked at me getting ready to leave. "Herr Schparks, what about the fucking big sandbank?"

For a brief second or two I smiled to myself. Deiter assumed that '*fucking big sandbank*' was the proper name for the mountain of sand waiting for us at the entrance to the bay. I didn't want to correct him because at that moment it was a very appropriate description. "You look after your friend, Heinz," I replied, "and don't worry about the fuckin' big sandbank."

"Vielen Dank, Herr Schparks, you are good man."

When I got back on deck, it seemed all the crew were on the deck nervously waiting for the sandbank. They all knew that Igor Petrovich, the Chief Engineer and Bessler had been yelling at each other. I went up to the Radio Room and listened to Richard arguing with Bessler who was now on the Bridge and just telegraphed the engine room to go FULL SPEED AHEAD.

With the increase in engine revs, the crew immediately knew that Bessler was hoping to plough over the top of the sandbank. Some of them were wearing life jackets, others were silently praying. It was an eerie scene, the moon reflected off the calm waters of the oil-slicked harbor while the *Cuban Trader* raced at full speed, hoping to skim over the treacherous mountain of sand blocking the entrance to Santiago Bay.

"The bastard threatened me with his German Lugar if I didn't get off the Bridge," explained Richard, entering the Radio Room. "Bessler is mad and Krause is drunk in his cabin. We've left without paying for the molasses and we're surrounded by Cuban gun boats, and if that isn't bad enough, we're heading full speed into a pile of sand a mile high. You know what? I'm climbing into my life jacket and going out on the boat deck and have a large glass of Glenlivet, and wait for the crash."

"Good idea, fix me one as well." It felt strange, after all we had been through, we were now patiently sitting on the vibrating deck waiting for the ship to smash into a sandbank and perhaps drown in the hot molasses we had just stolen, how ironic. "Do you see any Cuban gunboats?" I asked. "I know they are about somewhere."

Richard looked through his binoculars. "There are about a dozen at anchor in the military dock near the entrance to the bay, but so far no activity." Richard handed me the glasses. "You wanna look?"

He was right. I could see their ominous shapes in the bright moonlight across the bay. "What happens if they decide to chase after us?"

"Are you kidding, an armed gunboat? We're a sitting duck. They would have a ball using us for target practice," scoffed Richard. "Just one or two shells and that would be it."

Suddenly there was tremendous shudder. Everything that wasn't nailed down crashed to the deck. A dozen or more seamen waiting for the catastrophe were sent sprawling across deck as a massive wave of water swept over them. Richard and I hung on to the ship's rail as the *Cuban Trader* ploughed into the sandbank. We heard Bessler screaming in German on the Bridge. "Why don't we shoot the bastard," suggested Richard, still managing to finish his drink.

The engine revs were still going full blast, slowly and painfully pushing the ship off the sandbank. Everything rattled, shuddered and creaked. Bessler's hysterical screaming orders to the engine room could be heard all over the ship and I envisaged the old rust bucket breaking up into a thousand pieces, slowly sinking into a swirling mass of hot, stolen molasses.

After several agonizing minutes, there was a tremendous surge forward as the ship slid off the sandbank and into the open sea. Immediately a tremendous cheer went up from the bedraggled crew on deck, now praying that the worst was over. We had escaped from Santiago Bay into the open sea, but was there any underwater damage? Could we still stay afloat if there was?

We had got away without paying for the cargo and were now in the open sea. "Well, the crazy bastard made it, Sparks. Let's just hope the gun boats don't chase after us and there's no underwater damage," said Richard. "I'm going back aft to see."

It would be another ten days before we got back to Philly, if we were lucky.

I went up to the Radio Room and switched on the transmitter expecting a visit from either Krause or Bessler with the usual routine E.T.A message for Head Office, our *Estimated Time of Arrival in Philadelphia*. Listening to the radio traffic everything seemed normal until Richard entered the Radio Room. "The Chief Engineer says the boiler is damaged and we're only going at just over half speed. That means it will be about fourteen days!"

"Fourteen days?"

"That's if the fucking boiler holds up. The Old Man is drunk in his cabin and Bessler has taken over," explained Richard. "He and Schmidt are trying to work out an E.T.A in Philly and yelled at me to get off the Bridge."

"Two weeks to get to Philly? Dear God, this is insane."

"Insane? I'm the one that's insane for making another trip," groaned Richard. "We could have been in Palm Springs now having a good time instead of risking our lives on this goddamn deathtrap. I'm going to my cabin and let the fucking Dolly Sisters take over."

After Richard left, I thought about all the things that had happened. The street fighting and then the jail; my episode with the barfly at Bookbinders in Philly and Richard's impending fatherhood; Caballero's taking off with the money for the molasses; Heinz being shot in the stomach; and the incredible feeling of joy when I finally retrieved the gold ingots from inside the heating duct. *The gold ingots? Where were they?* I then realized in my desperate haste to clamber back on board our fucking, goddamn, rat infested stinking fucking hell ship, I had left the gold ingots in the launch!

~~~

CHAPTER TWENTY

Bessler Takes Command

The next morning Richard didn't show up for breakfast. "Did he come in early," I asked the steward.

"No, Sir, he has not been in yet." That was unusual. I had never known Richard to miss breakfast. I then remembered he was in a miserable mood the previous evening.

He had just found out the boiler had been damaged and we were only going at half speed. What else could go wrong? He was right. We were both insane to sign on for another trip. It was almost like committing suicide to sail on the *Cuban Trader* at any time, but even more so in the present circumstances. I stared at the remainder of my breakfast, but no longer was interested.

Bessler, who never missed a meal, scraped some butter onto his last piece of bread and mopped up the rest of the egg on his plate. He glared at me for a few seconds, gulped down his coffee and hurried out of the dining room. When I got back to the cabin Richard was in the shower. I wondered if I should apologize for this disastrous trip, but it wasn't my fault. To make matters worse, it turned out to be a waste of time. I had experienced the joy of holding the gold ingots in my hand again, and then left them behind in the launch. I hoped Maria or Consuela would find them, but there was no chance in hell of me going back again to get them. Why did I have such rotten luck?

After his shower, Richard came into my cabin to dry off in front of the Sears & Roebuck electric fan that Axel had left behind for me. ""Good Morning," I said. "We all missed you at breakfast."

"Yeah, I didn't get much sleep last night and since Bessler ordered me off the Bridge yesterday, I obeyed his orders and didn't go on watch."

"He was in for breakfast, scoffing down eggs and bacon as usual."

"I'm surprised the bastard is still alive, the Ruskies in the engine room are sure after him for ordering the ship to go full speed over the sandbank," explained Richard. "Apart from the possibility of underwater damage to the hull, they reckon the main boiler won't make it back to Philly."

"What a pleasant thought we won't have to see Ludwig Berners again and listen to a torrent of verbal diarrhea."

"Verbal diarrhea?" repeated Richard, laughing "Is that the Limey way of saying a load of bullshit?"

"Yes, a load of excrement from the bowels of frustrated bull," I explained, grinning.

"Sparks, thank God for your sense of humor. You always seem in a good mood. I was very pissed off last night," admitted Richard, slapping himself all over with talcum, filling the cabin with the scent of pine trees. "We should have quit while we were ahead and gone to Palm Springs. It now looks as if we won't even make it to Philly." Richard poured himself a cup of coffee from his special pot and offered me one. "No thanks, I had two cups at breakfast."

"Igor, the Chief Engineer asked me to make sure it's in the log book that he warned Bessler not to risk going at full speed," continued Richard. "Igor also told Herr Schmidt to make sure it's in the log book that the boiler was nearly shaken to pieces and there were steam pipes leaking all over the place."

"So, did Schmidt enter that in the log book?" I asked, knowing that he wouldn't do anything without Bessler's permission.

"He told Bessler, then they ignored it, but that's typical." Richard sipped his coffee looking very glum. I felt sorry for the poor bugger. He had to work with Bessler who never went anywhere without his dreaded Lugar.

"What about the leaking steam pipes?"

"You know the cargo of molasses is kept hot by steam pipes because it's easier to pump ashore," explained Richard. "That's what causes this god-awful stench. But now the old boiler is fucked up and can hardly make enough steam to get us back to Philly."

"And we're fifty miles from the nearest land and probably heading into a gale," I replied. "That's comforting news first thing in the morning. Bessler must be very optimistic, he ordered me to send an ETA to Head Office arriving in ten days."

"He's dreaming," concluded Richard. "I told you, Igor reckons it will be fourteen days, if we're lucky."

"So all we can do is bitch and moan and hope this hell ship stays afloat," I replied, wondering if there was any other bad news. "Was there any underwater damage?"

"We can't tell until we go into dry dock, but you and I will be in Palm Springs, eating, drinking and screwing our heads off, right Sparks?" Richard looked at me straight in the eyes. "You are coming back with me to Palm Springs, right, Sparks?"

"Yes, I'd love to, but. . ."

"But what?" snapped Richard. "Jesus Christ, Sparks, do I have to drag you there by your balls like the fucking barfly?" Richard finished his coffee and began brushing his teeth.

I wanted to mention my desperate need for money, but decided not to mention the gold. We had both been through hell trying to retrieve it and I didn't want another lecture about a rich, dead hero.

I went back to my cabin and made sure my porthole was firmly screwed down. The weather forecast had mentioned the possibility of gales. "Are you going onto the Bridge and face up to Bessler?" I asked worried sick at what might happen if Bessler lost his temper.

"I don't have much choice, Sparks. I wanna make sure we're on course for Philly, but I'm scared the fucking Dolly Sisters might commandeer this fucking wreck and take us back to Germany to start another war."

Back in the Radio Room, I made a lot of entries in my log book, including Igor Petrovich's statement about the boiler. It was strange listening to the radio chatter. Everything seemed so normal. I wondered how many more hell ships were at sea. I had often picked up a *T T T Man Overboard* emergency signal being sent out, but I had never heard a radio operator sending out a *T T T* about a worn out boiler or a drunken captain and two insane deck officers. The weather forecast wasn't very encouraging, especially when they repeated the warning of imminent gales in the North Atlantic.

Before going off watch, I checked to make sure the Auto Alarm was working. At least that would send out an emergency SOS if I wasn't able to do so. I also looked at the lifeboats outside the Radio Room. They were not gleaming white like the ones on the Swedish tank ship at the Camden refinery, but at least some smart deckhand had greased the davits.

Later in the morning, I was pleased to see Richard had shown up for lunch.

"It's the usual sea pie," I groaned. "One of these days I'm going to ask Steve why it's always served the first day at sea."

"They have no imagination, that's why," replied Richard. "It tastes like chicken not fish."

"Was everything okay?" asked Steve, the second chef.

"It was okay, but why do you serve sea pie the first day at sea?" I asked.

"And what's in it?" questioned Richard.

Steve grinned. "The chef makes up the menu, I just help him cook it, and today it's made of chicken."

"Left over from yesterday," added Richard. "I thought it tasted familiar."

"So, who's in Bloom's old cabin?" questioned Steve. "Bessler ordered a special breakfast of ham and eggs, served on the best china plates, the silver plated coffee pot, linen napkins, and he even checked Kruger's fingernails to make sure they were clean before he took it in there," announced Steve. "So who is it? Bessler's bit of crumpet?"

"Why don't you ask Kruger to check?"

"We did, he said whoever was in there was still in the bunk and he couldn't see who it was."

"Next time, tell him to lift up the bed sheet. Meanwhile, thanks Steve, for the special breakfast."

"Come on, Sparks. Who's on board that rates the best china and a silver plated coffee pot?" repeated Steve. "It's somebody posh, I'll bet."

"Let me know when you find out," I said, leaving the dining salon before Steve could worry me again. Out on deck, the crew, who had just hosed off the remains of the molasses, were now splashing about in the warm sea water and running around naked, drying off in the warmth of the noonday sun. No land was in sight and no Cuban gunboats chasing after us, so we were free. It felt so good to be away from what was virtually enemy territory, but as Richard again reminded me, the ship's boiler was damaged and we were only going at half speed. Since he had resumed his watch on the Bridge, Richard had obviously made a truce with Bessler, although I knew both hated each other's guts.

Heinz was sleeping when I went to his cabin after breakfast. Deiter, who rarely left his bedside, smiled when I entered the cabin. "He is sleeping, Herr Schparks," he said. "Kruger tell me it is Senor Ramon Perez in Herr Bloom's cabin."

"Senor Ramon Perez? Thank you, Deiter. Let me know when Heinz wakes up, I will give him a shot of morphine." So, it was Ramon Perez that Bessler smuggled aboard. I repeated the name over and over on the way back to the Radio Room. Berners had asked Ramon Perez to work with Henri Bloom negotiating a deal for the molasses. He owned the Cuban-American Bank and was a director at the refinery in Philadelphia. And he was now conveniently a passenger in Bloom's old cabin.

Bessler was waiting impatiently outside the Radio Room when I got there, and handed me a radiogram. "Send this immediately," he said, glaring at me like I was a piece of dirt. I glanced at the handwritten message which was addressed to the Coast Guard station in Key West requesting they rendezvous with us to pick up an American agent.

"Is the Coast Guard going to pick up Heinz as well? You know he needs to go ashore for a blood transfusion."

"Heinz is sex maniac. He not worry me," snapped Bessler.

"You should be worried. He's a member of your crew who needs urgent medical attention," I replied, entering the

Radio Room and switching on the equipment. While I was listening to the traffic list from New York, Bessler angrily paced up and down on the deck outside. "Heinz disobey orders and went ashore," he yelled, re-entering the Radio Room. "Herr Berners forbid that and won't pay Heinz expenses for hospital."

"Okay. Then make it part of your cozy little deal with Ramon Perez that he pays Heinz's hospital bill in Key West. Perez owns the Cuban-American Bank for crissake, he can afford it."

Bessler glared at me from the doorway. "You no talk about Ramon Perez."

"You mean the passenger in Bloom's old cabin? The guy who paid you to sneak him on board?"

"You are a bastard, Herr Schparks," screamed Bessler. "So you refuse to send this message to the Coast Guard?"

"I'll send it if Heinz can go ashore as well," I replied, otherwise you'll have to get Krause to authorize it, if you can sober him up."

"You are a bastard, Herr Schparks! I will log you for refusing to obey an order." Bessler grabbed the radiogram and stomped off across the deck to the Bridge. After making sure there were no messages for us from New York, I switched off the receiver and hurried to my cabin. Richard, who had just taken a shower, quickly dried himself off. "Deiter just told me it's Ramon Perez in Bloom's old cabin," he yelled, filling the cabins with the smell of pine scented talcum.

"Yes, I know. Ramon Perez owns the Cuban-American Bank. He was supposed to meet Henri Bloom."

"Now he's a passenger in his cabin." I then told Richard about my confrontation with Bessler in the Radio Room.

"So you refused to send the message?" asked Richard, hastily getting dressed.

"No, I agreed to send the message if Heinz could go ashore as well, otherwise he would have to get the Old Man's permission to send it."

"Clever move, Sparks, especially as the Old Man was out like a light when I peeked in there earlier. You've got Bessler by the balls."

"I do? But even if the Coast Guard agrees to take Heinz ashore, Berners won't pay Heinz's hospital bill."

"But Ramon Perez might," suggested Richard.

An hour later, Richard and I followed Kruger, the new cabin steward, who was taking a tray of coffee and sandwiches into Senor Perez's cabin. He was both surprised and pleased to see us and invited us to sit down. He was a very smart and articulate businessman who spoke excellent English. We told him about our time in jail and how we had sheltered in the doorway of his bank. He apologized for his countrymen, and then listened sympathetically when we explained that Heinz had been shot by a Cuban soldier and should be taken ashore in Key West for urgent medical attention.

"Is it possible to see him?" enquired Perez, genuinely concerned. Richard and I were both flabbergasted at the request, but willingly agreed to take Perez to see the patient. Fortunately, Bessler was taking his afternoon nap and didn't see us escorting his famous passenger across the deck. Clattering down the slippery metal stairs, Perez was obviously shocked at the cramped and stuffy crew's quarters back aft. "This is disgraceful," he muttered, walking along the dark and narrow corridors to Heinz's cabin. He was even more shocked when he saw Heinz's almost lifeless body lying on the bunk in his squalid little room. The porthole was open, allowing some fresh air to circulate, but it was still uncomfortably hot and humid.

Deiter, who was sitting at the edge of the bed, immediately stood up when we entered. "Herr Schparks, Heinz is asleep now," he said.

"This is disgraceful," whispered Perez. "Berners makes a huge profit from the molasses, there's no reason the crew should have to live in such filthy conditions, and this seaman is seriously ill. Why hasn't Krause made his own arrangements to transfer him ashore in Key West?"

"Because it's cheaper to let him die and bury him at sea, like he did with Henri Bloom," replied Richard.

"Yes, I heard all about my friend Henri Bloom. It was sad."

"You don't know the half of it," replied Richard.

I glanced at my watch, it was nearly four o'clock. "I have to back to go on duty, Senor Perez. Richard will tell you everything."

"Thank you, don't worry. I will make arrangements with Bessler for your friend to go ashore with me in Key West."

I left Richard to escort Ramon Perez around the dilapidated crew's quarters and went back to the Radio Room. I didn't care whether he was sleeping or not, I phoned Bessler in his cabin and told him I could now send his radiogram to the Coast Guard, but not until he had revised the agreement he had with Senor Perez, his number one passenger.

Ten minutes before the end of my late afternoon watch, Bessler stomped into the Radio Room. He glowered at me, holding out his hand with the radiogram. "You will send this immediately," he said. "It is for Senor Perez."

I glanced at the hastily written note, the same one he had given me that morning. It was addressed to the Coast Guard station in Key West, requesting they rendezvous with us at 0900 hours off Key West the next morning to take off an American agent. It was supposedly signed by Krause.

"The Old Man didn't sign this," I said.

"You will send it now," demanded Bessler, his face bloated with anger.

"Is Heinz being transferred ashore with Senor Perez?"

"You will send the radiogram now," screamed Bessler, his hand hovering near his now infamous German Lugar. "You will send it now, Herr Schparks." With Bessler's hand on his gun and his face contorted with rage he stood over me while I switched on the transmitter and sent the radiogram.

I had never entertained a Bank President in my cabin before. Surprisingly he didn't drink alcohol and was quite content with the black coffee that Kruger delivered to my cabin. "I have a son about the same age as Heinz," explained Senor Perez. "He is studying law at Harvard University. I am so proud of him. I'll make sure Heinz is well taken care of when we get him ashore in Key West, and what about his friend who was with him?"

"That's Deiter, the Captain's steward." I was surprised that Ramon Perez would even care about him. "He worships Heinz. He's been watching over him ever since they brought him back from the whorehouse."

"Then he should go with Heinz to the hospital. I will tell Bessler," replied Senor Perez.

"That's a great idea, Deiter, the poor little bastard hasn't had much of a life so far," added Richard.

"He ran away from home in East Berlin when he about fourteen," I explained. "Then, he stowed away on a Polish freighter. Most of the crew are from behind the Iron Curtain and risked their lives escaping to the West."

"Then he comes all the way here to work for Ludwig Berner," responded Perez, shaking his head in wonder. "I shall have to tell him what I think about the crew's quarters on his ship." I was pleased to hear about Deiter going with Heinz, but didn't think Berners would take much notice of what Senor Perez said about the crew's quarters.

"It's very sad," continued Senor Perez. "We have tried to keep producing molasses. Nearly everybody in Santiago relies on the refinery for work." He poured himself more coffee and politely declined my offer of a shot of rum. "It is now a sad time for my country," he continued. "We don't know who to trust. Even Bacardi has had to remove the secret yeast cultures for the Rum and send to Puerto Rico, where it it will be safe from Castro's hands. And the Batistianos, they rob and torture everyone, even young boys who they think are helping the Fidelistas. Everybody is afraid."

Richard and I glanced at each other, vividly remembering the dangling corpses strung up on the branches of a tree outside the refinery. "Did you ever find out what happened to Caballero?" asked Richard.

"Caballero is a crook. Ludwig Berners hired him to recruit some mercenaries in Miami to protect the refinery and pay for the molasses, but when he reached Santiago, he disappeared with the money."

"Yes, we know all about that. So what happens now?" I asked.

"Castro has grabbed the refinery, so I go to Miami to talk to the American government. Then make our plans."

Twelve hours later, we rendezvoused with the Coast Guard launch off Key West. Ramon Perez eagerly jumped on board and nervously watched as the crew transferred

Heinz across to the launch on a stretcher. It seemed everyone wanted to lend a hand to make sure the ship's famous sex maniac got safely aboard the powerful Coast Guard cutter. Deiter, who had been nervously trying to help, quickly followed his friend.

"Don't worry, Sparks, they will both be well taken care of," shouted Perez, waving goodbye.

"Zank you, Herr Schparks," yelled Deiter. "Danke Schoen." We all watched the powerful launch churning up the sea as it sped across to Key West, carrying my favorite patient to hospital and hopefully an easier life in the United States. How I wished I could have done the same for my friend Helmut.

As soon as the Coast Guard craft disappeared into the early morning mist, we decided it was now time to find out what had happened to Captain Krause, who had conveniently remained in his cabin for the past two days.

The Old Man's cabin was open when Bessler and I went in. Deiter, the Captain's steward, being a typical German, had carried out orders without question. He had cleaned up the Old Man's cabin, washed the dirty glasses, thrown away the empty bottles, and dutifully provided his Captain with his favorite nightcap, a drink of Maria Brizzard Apricot Brandy.

We found Captain Krause lying curled up on the well-worn carpet, his face in a pool of yellow vomit. Nearby was a wine glass and the half empty bottle of Apricot Brandy, which Krause had laced with poison and given to Henri Bloom as a special tonic for nosey executives. It was my Exhibit A which I had kept on top of the transmitter.

It wasn't a lie; Captain Krause had died from alcoholic poisoning. We all signed the logbook, and the crew stood silently on the deck as Chief Officer Bessler eagerly took command of the *Cuban Trader* and wasted no time pushing

Krause's canvas wrapped body over the side at 11.00, December 6th 1958. Five minutes later, I gladly obeyed Ludwig Berners' orders and tossed what remained of my 'Exhibit A' over the side.

After the burial I lay on my bunk, and for the first time in days I thought about my own problems. How could I have been so forgetful to leave the gold ingots under the seat in the company launch? Why was I such a fool, so engrossed in everyone else's problems that I never looked out for myself?

"A drink, Sparks?" enquired Richard, entering my cabin.

"That's a good idea."

"No more Scotch, I'm sorry to say. It's rum and Coca-Cola again." Richard generously poured out the rum and helped himself to Coca-Cola and ice from my fridge.

"Thanks," I said, accepting a frosty glass of my favorite thirst quencher.

"Isn't it ironic how it's all ending," mused Richard. "That was a brilliant idea of yours to keep the bottle of Apricot Brandy on display in the Radio Room, and allow Deiter to find it. He must have known what was in it."

"Yes, he knew it was on top of the transmitter," I replied.

"Now justice has been done, Krause was his own executioner, and serves the bastard right."

"We have to thank Deiter for handing it to the Old Man on a tray," I replied. "That lad will go far. Now he's on his way to Miami with Heinz and I'm sure Senor Perez will look out for them. I wish I could have done the same for Helmut."

"Sparks, I'm sure he didn't drown. Even Dubinsky admits he never really saw him in the water. It was easier for the Old Man to say he drowned, saving him all that legal paperwork when a foreign seaman jumps ship in the

States," explained Richard. "I'll bet your little friend ran off, squeezed through the dock gates and is now with some German family in Philly and being well looked after."

"I hope so."

"I'll bet there's a letter from him when we get back, and about a dozen for me from Kate," replied Richard. "If my Dad wasn't a Hollywood producer she wouldn't be hanging around."

"But there are plenty of others hanging around who like you." I thought about Maria who worshipped Richard. "So you don't have to look very far."

"I know. I know." Richard topped up our glasses with more rum and tonic and was generous with the ice. "You're a great guy, Sparks, I mean, look at the way you took care of Heinz. You saved his life for crissake."

"We all did. You, Maria and especially Deiter," I replied. "I hope they are okay. Now we have to worry about us. What kind of reception will we get in Philly, that's if we ever get there?"

"You mean from Ludwig Berners? He'll scream and shout as usual and secretly welcome the news that we dumped Krause over the side," replied Richard, finishing his drink.

"What about Caballeros running off with all the money for the cargo? He'll have forty fits hearing about that."

"I expect he knows about that already. Remember he has a spy in Cuba telling him everything. All we do is confirm it all."

"I wonder who it is, Berners' spy." Richard glanced at his watch. "I gotta go on watch. Herr Schmidt, the lamebrain, logs me if I am even a minute late."

"He's a crafty sod. A shyster, hiding when there is any trouble," I replied. "I wonder what he does all day locked up in his cabin."

"He sleeps, types up some shit, reads sex books and jerks off. Fuck him. Fuck all of them. I'll be glad to get to Palm Springs." Richard finished his drink. "I'm going on watch. I'll let you know what's going on Sparks. Like I just said, Schmidt enters nearly everything in the log book, except when he takes a crap."

Ten minutes after Richard left, I remembered it was time I filled in my official log book and went up to the Radio Room. Igor Petrovich, the Chief Engineer was outside the Radio Room door. He was a heavy set, short man with a shock of grey hair and a very weather beaten face. His squinty little eyes, partially hidden by his bushy black eyebrows, looked nervously around the Radio Room. Dressed in a filthy uniform, he brought with him the stench of hot burning oil. It was the first time we had met face to face. "Mister Sparks," he said, taking a seat in the Radio Room. "I wish to talk, but I wait until you not work."

Apart from listening to the traffic from New York, which I did automatically, I could give Comrade Igor my full attention. "Go ahead and talk," I said. "I am listening."

For the next ten minutes I tried hard to understand Comrade Igor's broken English, which was about the state of the main boiler. He went to great trouble to explain over and over again, it was Bessler's fault for deciding to go full speed to get over the sandbank. "No do. Boiler no work. "

"Kaput, burned out," I replied.

"That is it. The boiler is, how you say, burned out and the engine is going slow," explained Igor. "I want you to enter in the log book what happened going over the sandbank. I want you should write down what Bessler do to my boiler."

I assured Comrade Igor that it was already in my official log book, all the details. I then asked him how long he thought it would take to get to Philly.

He shrugged his huge shoulders. "My engine is slow. She is like a tired old lady," he sobbed. Was it possible that Comrade Igor was actually crying? "But she get us back to Philadelphia okay." Comrade Igor patted me on the back and we shook hands. "Everybody like you, Mister Sparks," he said. "We will get to Philadelphia okay."

"I'm sure we will," I replied, opening the Radio Room door. I watched him clinging on to the safety ropes stretched across the deck as he made his way back aft. I would have liked to have talked to him a lot more and find out why he and his three sons remained in their tiny cabins above the engine room and never mingled with the other crew, but he seemed eager to get back to the relative safety of his engine room.

After he left, I sat down and checked my logbook and made sure I had entered everything Comrade Igor had said. For the first time I realized the Chief Engineer and his three sons were real and, not just shadowy figures in the officer's dining room. They did a great job keeping the old, tired and worn out engine working and living most of their life in the stinking hot and noisy engine room doing a job I wouldn't have done for a million dollars.

Ten minutes later, Bessler stomped into the Radio Room. "The Russian from the engine room was here, he is sending a message?"

I shrugged my shoulders. "No message."

"No message. He talk about the engine?" snapped Bessler.

"No, he asked me for the weather forecast and if there would be snow in Philadelphia for Christmas, but in any case, it's none of your business," I replied, noticing Bessler's infamous Lugar.

"Everything on this ship is my business. You send no message for him. That is an order." Bessler then turned and stomped out of the Radio Room.

"You're an asshole. You're acting like a punch-drunk dictator, just like your leader Adolf Hitler," I yelled, "and you'll get what's coming to you sooner or later, just like he did!"

~~~

CHAPTER TWENTY-ONE

Stormy Weather

The next morning, when I woke up, the ship was rolling about like a drunken sailor. Richard entered my cabin with a cup of coffee from his special pot. "Good morning, Sparks. Hey! They sure got the weather forecast from Washington right for a change," he said. "I think we're heading into a fucking gale."

"Thanks for the coffee. I'll go up and check the local weather from a Florida station," I said, "just as soon as I get dressed."

"Be careful, Sparks. Bessler's on the Bridge screaming at the helmsman and bitching and moaning about the weather. I think his illegal promotion to Captain has gone to his head. He's insane, really crazy, and we got to remember he's always got a gun. That German Lugar's always loaded. And from what I hear, he's a trigger happy son-of-a-bitch." Richard slumped into the chair and sipped his coffee. "Do you realize, if we were going a few knots faster, we wouldn't be rolling about like a son-of-a-bitch."

I continued to get dressed and tried to drink my coffee at the same time, it wasn't easy with everything sliding back and forth across the cabin floor. "Did I tell you Comrade Igor came to see me in the Radio Room?"

"Comrade Igor? The Chief Engineer?" replied Richard, surprised by the news. "Did you ask him if they got a woman down in their cabins? If they have, the poor bitch is getting screwed from asshole to breakfast time."

"No, I didn't ask him that, and I very much doubt it's true. He wanted to make sure I put down everything in my logbook about Bessler ordering him to go full speed over the sandbank despite being warned there was a risk to the boiler."

"Yeah, Comrade Igor's got to cover his ass, that's for sure," replied Richard. "I guess he's only running the engine at half speed, hoping the old bitch will keep going until we dock in Philly. I just hope we're not running into a fucking gale."

"As soon as I can get dressed, I'll go up and check the local forecast from Florida, but where the hell are we?"

"God knows. According to Bessler's dead reckoning, about fifty miles off Key West, right where all the shitty weather is, and we're only doing about eight knots that's all," growled Richard. "I'll tell the Bosun to check the lifeboats, that'll scare the shit out of them all back aft."

"For crissake Richard, you're in a bad mood this morning," I replied. "What's the matter?"

"Only peanut butter sandwiches for breakfast, that's what's the matter."

"It's because of the weather. You know they can't mess about with hot pans fixing eggs and bacon when the ship's rolling like this." I took everything that was about to fall onto the deck and stuffed it into the drawer, then checked my porthole to make sure it was closed tight.

"Yeah, Sparks, make sure that shiny porthole of yours is closed," advised Richard. "Those poor bastards back aft better make sure their portholes are closed as well, because their cabins are underwater half the time."

"I'd hate that, trying to sleep knowing my cabin was below sea level." I dragged on some clothes and finished my coffee. "I'm going to get a local forecast from Key West. I hope it's good news."

"And I'm turning in. I've been on the Bridge since four o'clock, watching the weather getting worse. Wake me up if we're about to sink." Richard went back to his cabin and collapsed onto his bunk without bothering to get undressed.

As I entered the Radio Room, Bessler phoned me immediately. He yelled and screamed, "The radar is not working," he yelled. "You will make it work, now."

"I was just going to get a local weather forecast from Key West," I replied.

"NOW," screamed Bessler, and slammed down the phone. Remembering Richard's warning that Bessler was insane and also carried a loaded gun, I went onto the Bridge as ordered.

"The radar is kaput," he yelled. "We are at sea with no radar."

"It's the rotor. Remember I wanted to grease it when we were in Cuba, but the Captain told me to leave it until we got to Philadelphia?"

"Ah! So you refuse to make it work?" yelled Bessler, now standing over me. I glanced at Weicecz who was the helmsman. He looked petrified with fear. I wondered what hell Bessler was putting him through and what was in store for me. I switched on the radar and fiddled about with some of the controls, but I knew what was wrong before I started. "I'm telling you the trouble, Herr Bessler. The rotor on the mast is kaput. It is not rotating. Krause should have let me grease it while we were in Cuba."

"I will log you for refusing to obey an order," screamed Bessler.

"I obeyed your order. I came up here right away and told you what was wrong with the radar. If Captain Krause had let me fix it while we were Cuba, it would now be working," I replied. "So why don't you enter Captain Krause in the log book. He was the cause of all the problems we've had on this goddamn ship."

"Get off my Bridge," screamed Bessler. "I will log you not fixing the radar."

"And I will enter in my log the reason why. Captain Krause ordered me not to touch it, so my ass is covered," I replied.

"Get off the Bridge. Get off the Bridge. You are being logged for not obeying an order. Go now." I needed no second bidding and hurried back to the Radio Room and locked the door. I switched on the receiver and took down the latest weather forecast from Key West.

GALE FORCE SEVEN BACKING TO GALE FORCE THREE DURING THE NEXT TWENTY-FOUR HOURS.

That was all I needed to hear. It was bad enough, but the weather wasn't going to get any worse. I typed up the forecast and took it to the Bridge where Bessler was in the chart room on the phone, yelling at the Chief Engineer. Weicecz was still struggling to keep the ship on course. He looked at me, too scared to say anything.

"Good news, Weicecz, the weather is getting better," I said. "Hopefully, we shall soon be in Philly."

"Herr Schparks, I now enter in the log book the radar is still kaput." yelled Bessler.

"Yes, Sir, I have entered in my log book the rotor needs fixing, but Captain Krause ordered me to leave it alone. Here is the latest forecast from Key West," I replied, handing Bessler the typed weather report. "There will be another in one hour." I then made a hasty retreat to the comparative safety of the Radio Room and again locked the door.

At least the weather wasn't going to get any worse. Nevertheless, the old ship was still struggling up the side of mountainous waves, balancing on the crest until the propeller came out of the water then speeding up until the ship rattled like a thousand empty cans before crashing down into the black watery abyss. It had been like this for nearly two days. There was no cooked food, only hastily prepared sandwiches. The chef had managed to heat some coffee, but all the heavy pots and pans in the galley were safely stowed away.

It was both frightening and painful trying to keep one's balance, clinging on to anything that was firmly attached to the ship and trying to avoid the treacherous waves crashing across the deck, sweeping everything that wasn't firmly battened down over the side. With weather like this it was not surprising that seamen always made the most of their time ashore with plenty of wine, women and song. Unfortunately, this trip hadn't given the crew much to sing about.

The next few days were the same boring routine: sandwiches for breakfast, no cooked meals and constantly reaching for something solid to cling on to as the ship rolled from side to side. Consequently, everyone was in a bad mood, tired, cold and hungry and made even worse with Herr Bessler screaming and threatening everyone around him.

Fortunately, the weather slowly got better, but we were still only going at half speed. "Another two more days of this," groaned Richard, stumbling into the Radio Room. "Bessler's noon reckoning now puts us just off Cape Canaveral. The asshole doesn't even know where we are."

"And he's logging me because I can't fix the radar. It's the rotor. It needs greasing but Krause wouldn't let me do it in Cuba," I explained.

"Cover your ass and make sure you enter that in your log," advised Richard. "Anyway, Bessler's now worried that because the leaking steam pipes have been shut down, the molasses will be too cold to pump ashore."

"That's tough shit. He should send a radiogram and warn them at the refinery."

"And drop himself in the shit," replied Richard. "He won't do that. He'll blame everything on Krause and Herr Schmidt."

"Herr Schmidt? I haven't seen him for days."

"He shows up for his watch like a zombie," explained Richard. "He never talks to anyone, takes his sandwiches back to his cabin. He's so spaced out, he makes his reports in the log book in German. I don't give a shit any more. As soon as we get to Philly, I'm signing off this fucking hell ship and going to Palm Springs. I hope you'll be coming with me." Richard zipped up his heavy waterproof jacket. "Now, I gotta go on watch for another four hours."

"Wait a minute." I clamped on the earphones to listen to a garbled message being sent out to all ships. "Some Liberian tanker has just sent out a T.T.T. Man Overboard off Cape May. They're requesting all ships in the vicinity to watch out for him."

"Man overboard in this weather? The poor bastard doesn't stand a chance. Jesus, what a fucking way to go, drowned in the middle of the icy cold Atlantic." Richard opened the Radio Room door to leave. "Ah! Sparks, you've got a visitor, Kimmel the Bosun, with the crew's overtime. Make sure the poor bastards get every cent that's coming to them, and then some. I'll phone if there's any news."

The Bosun took off his waterproof cape and nervously entered the Radio Room, clutching his ragged overtime notebook. I was still listening to the T.T.T. message being sent out the Liberian tanker and taking down the exact position.

"Herr Schparks. You have time to see me?" I nodded and pointed to the chair just vacated by Richard. Kimmel gratefully sat down.

"That was a tanker off Cape May sending out a T.T.T. That's a safety message," I explained, taking off my ear phones. "One of their crew has been swept overboard and they're asking all ships in the vicinity to watch out for him."

Kimmel groaned. "Man overboard in this weather? That is bad, Herr Schparks. I order my crew to stay below and not go on deck."

"That's all they can do in this weather," I replied, "but the forecast is getting better." Kimmel and I briefly exchanged glances. He knew I didn't like him, especially the way he had treated my friend Helmut, but it was his job to keep track of the crew's overtime, get it okayed and signed by the Captain, then bring it to me to include in the crew's monthly wages which I had to send to Head Office before we docked in Philly.

"Herr Schparks," he began. "I have done the crew's overtime."

"Good, they certainly deserve it. Did Bessler sign it?"

"Herr Bessler no sign," Kimmel shrugged his shoulders. "What can I do?"

"Didn't you always wait until Captain Krause was drunk before showing him the overtime?" I reminded him, looking at the mess of names and figures scrawled in black pencil in the cheap writing book.

"Ya, Ya," replied Kimmel smiling. "I wait until he was drunk, but Bessler, he no drink and he no sign."

"The bastard, what did he say when you showed him the book?"

"*No ovies*, he yelled, and he throw the book on deck." Kimmel looked at me in despair. "Herr Bessler is crazy, everybody hate him."

I looked again at the bedraggled notebook, a list of names of all the crew members back aft. Half way down there was HELMUT SCHICKEL crossed out. "What do you think happened to Helmut," I asked. "Did he drown or did he jump ship?"

"He no drown. He take all his things and he leave in Philly. He is okay, Herr Schparks." Kimmel smiled. For a few seconds I stared at Kimmel the muscle man, the cruel son of a bitch who terrorized all the crew back aft. He also ravaged and sodomized Helmut every night for the first few weeks he was on board. "Ya. Ya, Herr Schparks, he is okay in Philly."

My thoughts of Helmut wandering the streets of Philadelphia were interrupted when Bessler burst into the Radio Room almost white with rage, yelling at Kimmel in German. For the next few minutes they were screaming at each other like insane lunatics.

"Herr Schparks, no ovies for the sex maniacs! That is an order! I do not sign Herr Kimmel's book and you do not pay them overtime," screamed Bessler, grabbing the book off my desk.

"You can't refuse them their overtime. For crissake, it's only a few hundred dollars. They earned every cent." I thought Krause was a bastard cheating the crew out of their overtime, but Bessler was worse. "The crew work hard for every cent they make."

"They do nothing. They sleep in their cabins," he yelled.

"What choice do they have? It's suicide to go out on deck! They'll be washed overboard by the first wave," I shouted. Bessler wasn't listening to me, he was too busy ripping up the overtime book like he was strangling his worst enemy. There was no doubt he was insane and he still had his infamous Lugar strapped around his waist

"Again you refuse to obey an order, Herr Schparks. No overtime, that is an order." He then grabbed Kimmel's waterproof cape and threw it at him, ordering him out of the Radio Room.

"Bessler, I think you are stark raving mad," I yelled.

"No ovies for sex maniacs," repeated Bessler, continuing to destroy Kimmel's overtime book. "No overtime for sex maniacs."

I watched as Bessler angrily tore up the book into shreds. "You may have destroyed the crew's overtime book, Herr Bessler, but they will get paid," I replied. "I'll make damn sure of that."

"And you, Herr Schparks, will be logged for disobeying an order. And the radar is not working." Bessler threw what was left of the note book across my desk, stormed out of the Radio Room, just in time to be caught in the downpour of a huge wave crashing over the boat deck. I hoped he would have been washed overboard, but unfortunately he was still there clinging to a lifeboat, drenched to the skin when the wave subsided.

Ten minutes later, I had finished my afternoon watch and climbed into my waterproof jacket. Maybe I was crazy for risking my life to go back aft. Crossing the deck in such terrible weather was almost an act of suicide. Hanging on to the safety rope, I cautiously slithered across the deck. The crew were all shocked to see me venturing into their stinking quarters, and they were all very anxious to know the latest weather forecast. I told them the weather was expected to get better, then knocked on the door of the Bosun's cabin. "Herr Schparks," he said, jumping up from his chair.

"I just wanted to let you know, you did the right thing leaving when you did. Bessler's insane, he might have shot you."

"Ya, Herr Schparks, he might have shoot me. All the crew scared of him. They hate him for not signing their overtime."

"Well, you can tell the crew I will send their overtime to the Head Office and I'll make sure they get paid. Can you make me out another list?"

Kimmel nodded his head and fumbled through a stack of greasy papers on his desk. "Ya, I make a list." I looked around his filthy cabin. His double bunk was piled high with sex magazines and his whole cabin reeked of sweat and sex. He had the choice of any young seaman to fill his bed. Many of them were only too pleased to sleep with him. He not only paid them extra overtime but allowed them to stay in his bunk all day, ready and waiting to satisfy all his sexual urges.

Kimmel watched me looking around his cabin and probably guessed what I was thinking. I could see he was embarrassed fumbling for the right words. "Herr Schparks," he began, lowering his voice. "I know you think about Helmut. I tell you he is okay. He tell me he going to leave the ship in Philly, but I not report him to Krause, but Helmut, he is okay."

"Why didn't you tell me that before? Krause entered it in the logbook that he fell overboard. I thought my friend had drowned." Kimmel looked embarrassed and didn't know what to say. "I wish I had known he was okay."

"Captain Krause tell me to say Helmut fell overboard."

"That's because he didn't want the trouble of filling in the legal forms for the Americans," I explained. "Captain Krause was a bastard, now we have Bessler and he's worse."

"Ya ,Ya, Herr Bessler is a schwienhund." As I was leaving Kimmel's filthy office, a dozen or more seamen were waiting for me full of questions. What was the weather forecast? Was Heinz was getting better, and the most important question of all, was Bessler going to sign their ovies?

"Bessler won't sign, but you will get your overtime," I promised them. "I'll make sure of that." They all cheered when I assured them their overtime would be included in their wages. It felt good to give them some good news. "And hopefully the chef will be fixing some real food tomorrow when the weather gets better." Again they cheered, "The latest news on Heinz is that he's much better and ready to start fucking all the nurses in the hospital." That piece of news got the biggest cheer of all.

Back in the safety of the Radio Room, I felt good that I had gone back aft and gave the crew some good news, most of whom were young Germans. I wondered how Bessler could be such a bastard to his own countrymen, but then I remembered he was an ex-Gestapo officer who apparently had no compassion for anyone who stood in his way.

But I had lied to the crew about Heinz, the truth was I hadn't heard anything from Senor Perez, and unfortunately I had no way of contacting him. Then, by a stroke of luck, the next traffic list from New York contained a message addressed to me from Senor Perez. Heinz was making a rapid recovery in the Key West hospital. He and Deiter will be rejoining the ship in Philadelphia. It was signed; Ramon Perez.

"Hey, I'm glad to know that Heinz is going to be okay, that's thanks to you, Sparks," observed Richard, reading the radiogram later in my cabin. "Heinz is a good guy and we all have to thank Deiter for getting rid of the Old Man."

"Now, we've got Bessler, and he's worse," I replied, "but that's not Deiter's fault. So I'll add Heinz and Deiter to the list of wages and overtime if they're rejoining the ship in Philly."

"No chance. I doubt if anyone will be re-joining this fucking hell ship. She's ready for the scrapheap."

"Scrapheap?" I didn't believe it. "I don't think Ludwig Berners will scrap her, not while she is still able to make him a good profit sending her back and forth to Cuba with a cargo of molasses."

Richard topped up my glass with rum. "I still got about ten bottles of this left, we might as well use it up," he said. "And Ludwig Berners won't have any choice. Scraping over the top of that fucking sandbank back in Santiago didn't do us any good. According to one of the Ruskies in the engine room we're shipping water through propeller shaft," confided Richard, "but for crissake don't say anything to anyone, otherwise the crew will be sleeping in the lifeboats."

"Can it be repaired?" I asked innocently.

"Repaired? It's cheaper to buy another ship and sell this for scrap," replied Richard. "All the old Liberty Tankers are for sale. Berners will probably get one of them. Anyway, who cares? We'll be in Palm Springs."

Richard was so determined we both go to Palm Springs, but his family were rich, mine were just struggling to keep the horse sanctuary going. I had nothing but a miserable pay-off check from Ludwig Berners. How could I tell Richard I would not be able to go back to Palm Springs with him, I just couldn't afford it. My fortune was left in the bottom of the launch with Maria and Consuela, six small gold ingots. Six shiny gold ingots were enough to buy all the land I needed in Gloucestershire, and treat my parents to a well-deserved holiday. Retrieving them was the only reason I had gone back to Cuba. But it was all in vain.

~~~

CHAPTER TWENTY-TWO

Welcome back to Philly

It seemed we were all destined to spend the rest of our lives being tossed around in the stormy North Atlantic like the ill-fated *Maria Celeste* which was reportedly found abandoned floating around in the middle of the ocean.

The long days turned into even longer nights. There was no sun, no moon, no stars, and just black clouds overhead shedding their cargo of rain onto a ship that certainly didn't need any more water.

All the crew were physically tired trying to keep their balance, holding on to anything that was permanently attached to the ship. Sandwiches for every meal didn't help the morale and the fact we didn't even know where we were was the biggest nightmare. Without the sun or stars and a clear horizon, the sextants were useless and of course there was no radar. I now realized I should have disobeyed Krause's orders and gone ahead and greased the rotor while we were in Cuba. The radar would have helped, but only if we were within fifty miles of a coastline.

Bessler kept up his hysterical tirade against anyone unfortunate to be within screaming distance. Unfortunately, Seaman Weicecz always seemed to be the helmsman while Bessler was on duty and consequently was a nervous wreck, staring ahead at the horizon like a zombie. I made sure I locked the Radio Room which was normally left open while I was on watch, but not anymore. Not with a trigger happy madman on the loose. It was only when

Richard phoned down from the Bridge offering to pick up the latest weather forecast did I get up and unlock the door. "Where's Bessler?" I asked, handing Richard the latest weather report from Cape Canaveral.

"He's down in the engine room right now yelling at them to fix the leaking steam pipes to heat the molasses before we get back, but the Ruskies will soon kick him out." Richard went back to finish his watch on the Bridge. I reached out and felt the radiator in the Radio Room which was also heated by steam. It was ice cold and the molasses would be the same. I had no problem guessing Ludwig Berners' outrage when he found out his precious cargo of molasses was too cold to pump ashore. Bessler would need more than his infamous Lugar to defend himself then.

The weather forecast from Cape Canaveral was slightly encouraging and the gale force winds had abated slightly, but the sea was still too rough for my liking. Suddenly I heard a seaman shouting on deck and the sound of a shot. Richard obviously heard it as well and was yelling at me when I ran out onto the boat deck and shouted at me. "Sparks! They just phoned from the engine room. The Chief Engineer's been scalded by a burst steam pipe!" I ran back into the Radio Room and grabbed the emergency First Aid kit, then struggled down the treacherous metal stairs to the deck which was almost underwater. I clutched onto the safety ropes which the Bosun had slung across the deck from stem to stern and slithered through the icy-cold water to the entrance of the Engine Room. The water tight door was not only unlocked, but half open, allowing the seawater to cascade down into the bowels of the ship.

"It's the Chief," yelled an unrecognizable seaman covered in grease. "He and Bessler have been arguing." One of the main pipes had burst sending thick clouds of stinking hot steam everywhere. It was almost impossible to see my way down the greasy metal stairs, now wet from the ice-cold sea water pouring in through the open water tight door.

The Chief Engineer was laying on the oily deck, writhing in agony. His three sons, trying to make him comfortable, watched in horror as their father's scalded back and chest developed into a mass of bloody ulcers. I wanted to give him a shot of morphine, but where? He was covered in grease and howling in pain. His eldest son looked at me and held up his father's bare arm. I plunged the needle. It seemed just a few seconds elapsed before the Chief relaxed, unconscious but out of pain.

Bessler was somewhere in the clouds of steam, fighting against the sea water cascading down into the Engine Room, and yelling and cursing in German as he tried to climb up the metal steps to the deck.

"Bessler, you bastard," yelled the Chief's eldest son, cradling his father's head. "Now we kill you." He then shouted something in Russian. Immediately the other two sons chased after their intended victim who had managed to crawl onto the deck.

The Chief Engineer's eldest looked at me, tears in his eyes and said something in Russian. It was obvious his father was dead. Comrade Igor, his face no longer twisted up in pain lay back in his son's arms. There was nothing else I could do, except break down and cry.

The two pistol shots on deck brought me back to the horrors of reality. Scrambling up the metal stairs onto the deck, I saw a crowd of seamen gleefully watching Comrade Igor's two sons wrestling with Bessler who was trying to escape up the metal ladder to the boat deck. Despite a nasty gash across his arm, one of the sons wrestled the Lugar from Bessler's hand and kicked it across the deck into the sea.

The scream of agony sent shivers down my back when Igor's son wrenched Bessler's arm out of its socket and pushed him writhing in pain onto the deck. Three or four crew members emerged from the crowd and gleefully kicked at Bessler's mangled body, urged on by the rest of the blood thirsty crew, now screaming like wild coyotes ready for the kill.

Everybody wanted to get their revenge. Bessler had brutalized them from the day they signed on the ship, forcing them to march back and forth across the deck in the hot sun even when they were in port. He had completely ignored the very basic rules for sanitation back aft. He had refused to help Heinz after he had been shot by the Cuban soldier and worst of all, refused to sign their overtime. One by one each seaman got his revenge, kicking Bessler's lifeless body until it was no more than a mass of bloody pulp.

Richard, who was on the boat deck watching the slaughter, signaled me to join him. "Jesus, they kicked the son-of-a-bitch to death," he groaned. "What a way to die, but the bastard deserved it. Didja see they all took turns to stomp on the son-of-a-bitch."

"Revenge is sweet. I would have put the boot in as well."

"Sparks, we need a drink. And then we have to figure out what to put in the log book." I looked down at Bessler's lifeless body washing back and forth across the bloody deck, until it was conveniently washed over the side into the icy cold waves of the Atlantic. The crowd of seamen silently went back aft. Revenge was sweet, but the consequences were likely to be very serious.

Richard followed me to the Radio Room, both of us in a state of shock at what we had witnessed. "Dear God,

Richard, I can't believe what I just saw, he was kicked to death. They all got their revenge."

"He deserved everything he got," replied Richard. "Now we have to decide what to write in the logbook and tell the crew to corroborate the story. How about Bessler and Igor were fighting and both washed overboard?"

"Igor was scalded and died in the engine room. His sons won't agree with that story, because Igor wasn't fighting with Bessler."

"Okay, do they want us to report they kicked Bessler into a bloody pulp?" argued Richard. "If that's the case, they'll all be charged with murder."

"We'll have to talk to them and get everyone to agree to the same story, but what about Schmidt? Did he see what happened?"

"He was on the Bridge, scared shitless, probably thinking he would be next," replied Richard. "Don't you have any rum here? I need a drink." I pointed to the cupboard where there was just one half empty bottle. "So what do you reckon, Sparks. What message do we send to Head Office? That there was a fucking mutiny because that asshole Bessler wouldn't sign the overtime book?"

"Well, that is the truth." Richard poured out two glasses of rum and topped it up with some Coca-Cola. "You know all hell will break loose if we report that." We both sipped our much appreciated shot of rum. "When do you reckon we'll be close enough to Cape May to request a port pilot?" I asked, tossing the empty rum bottle into the trash can.

"If the goddamn radar was working, we could probably see it," snapped Richard. "Sorry, Sparks, but that's the truth. Jesus Christ, just send this message to the Head Office.

FIRST OFFICER BESSLER WASHED OVERBOARD IN ROUGH SEA. THE SECOND AND THIRD OFFICERS NOW ON TWELVE HOUR WATCH. OUR NOON POSITION SOMEWHERE OFF CAPE MAY - REQUEST INSTRUCTIONS

"That is the truth, but we'll have to get the crew to all agree that Bessler was accidentally washed overboard," I replied. "If Schmidt disagrees, then warn him he'll be next."

"Actually, he hated Bessler as much as we all did, so I think he'll agree," replied Richard, finishing his drink. "But I doubt if he'll sign anything."

Later that day, the sea was calm enough for the whole crew to stand reverently on deck while Igor Petrovich's three sons carried their father's body, now wrapped in a canvas sheet, onto the deck. After a few minutes of silent prayer, they slid his body into the stormed tossed Atlantic Ocean, the graveyard of so many sailors.

As soon as I was on watch, I sent the message to Head office that Richard had dictated. Within thirty minutes they replied. I eagerly took down the message and went to see Richard who was on the Bridge.

"The Cape May radar station has positioned the *Cuban Trader* to be at the entrance of Delaware Bay. They suggest the ship maintains present course and speed, and expect to rendezvous with the Cape May Pilot Boat at 14.00 hours."

"Great! Cape May radar station can see us and their Pilot Boat will rendezvous with us in an hour," repeated Richard. "That's great news." He went into the chart room and marked our position on the well-worn map. "Not bad reckoning, Sparks, considering we haven't been able to take a noon fix for nearly three days. Let's hope it gets a little calmer so the Pilot can come aboard."

Just over an hour later, we had entered the bay where the sea was much calmer. All the crew stood on deck and cheered when the port pilot climbed up the scrambling net and came on board. He was certainly a sight for sore eyes and a much needed boost to the morale of the ship. Hopefully we would be docking in Philadelphia in a less than two hours and then have to face the music; hysterical outbursts from Ludwig Berners, especially when he found out we had arrived with a cargo of molasses too cold to pump ashore.

"Y'all telling me it's too fucking cold to pump ashore?" he screamed, completely ignoring the news that we had buried the Captain, the First Mate and the Chief Engineer at sea. "Jesus Christ, what's the fucking good of a cargo of ice-cold molasses? Don't you assholes know it will take two or three days to warm it up? Two or three days tied up to this fucking dock, costing me over a thousand bucks a day."

Richard and I glanced at each other, not knowing whether to burst out laughing or try to keep a straight face. It was a comedy, a black comedy.

"Sir, I suggest you read the rest of the report," I said, standing up. "Captain Krause, Chief Officer Bessler and the Chief Engineer were all buried at sea. The U.S. Port Authorities will have to be informed. Then there is possible underwater damage to the hull."

"Two or three days to warm up this goddamn cargo," continued Berners. "Two or three days tied up to this fucking dock at a thousand bucks a day."

"Sparks, let's go," suggested Richard. "Listening to this madman is ruining my day."

Richard and I both stood up and attempted to leave Captain Krause's cabin where Berners was holding the meeting. "You two, sit down," yelled Berners. "I haven't finished." This time there was no Captain Krause to bully or Deiter, his steward, to hand around drinks. Just Richard and I were there to answer all of Berners' questions. The rest of his staff, stood around the office looking very glum. I wondered how they could possibly work for such a demented idiot.

"You, Sparks," yelled Berners, pointing at me. "What's all this shit that Ramon Perez was telling me about you arranging for two crew members to be taken off by the Coast Guard in Key West?"

"Ramon Perez agreed with me that Heinz needed urgent medical attention after being shot by a Cuban soldier. He suggested Heinz accompany him on the Coast Guard launch back to a hospital Key West."

"Even though I told Krause no shore leave in Cuba for any of his goddamn sex maniacs," screamed Berners. "I wanna know why Krause agreed to all this?"

"Captain Krause was already dead, he unwittingly drank the same poison he had given to your friend Henri Bloom," I replied. "He was his own executioner and literally got his just desserts."

"What's Bloom got to do with all this shit?" snapped berners.

"Remember, *you* hushed it up last time. You didn't even read the report that Richard and I gave you describing how Krause murdered your friend Henri Bloom by spiking a bottle of Maria Brizzard with poison and giving him some to drink. When Richard and I told you this, you ordered us to throw the bottle away, but I didn't."

"Tell him Sparks," whispered Richard. "Drop the bastard in the shit."

"And Deiter, not knowing the bottle of Apricot Brandy was laced with poison, unwittingly gave it to Krause who was found dead, lying in a pool of yellow vomit, the same fate he meted out to your friend Henri Bloom. So, I repeat, Krause was his own executioner and justice had been done."

Berners was obviously shaken when I mentioned Henri Bloom and wished he had never asked about Krause. "Sparks, as always you talk a load of fucking bullshit."

"Bullshit? Is it bullshit that Captain Krause is dead? Bessler and the Chief Engineer also died and were buried at sea. It's not bullshit and the American Port Authorities will want to know about it."

Berners finally glanced at the report I had given him. "So? What happened to the Chief Engineer, did he drink himself to death like Krause?"

"If you read the goddamn report," yelled Richard, standing up. "You'll see he was scalded to death when a steam pipe burst in the Engine Room, that's why the molasses is cold. You are goddamn lucky we managed to bring the fucking shit back here."

Ludwig Berners glared at Richard like he was a piece of shit. "Burst steam pipes in the Engine Room are the Chief's responsibility. I paid him good money to keep that engine running and the molasses warm enough to pump ashore."

"And the poor bastard died trying to do that," argued Richard. "And did you pay Bessler to risk everybody's life by ordering the Engine Room to go full speed over the sandbank?" yelled Richard, angrily. "That's what caused the burst pipes. The Chief Engineer warned Bessler it would be too much strain on the old boiler, but Bessler was insane. No responsible Deck Officer risks his ship by ploughing full speed over a sandbank. He should have waited for high tide. The asshole deserved everything he got."

I was scared that Richard would explode with rage and tell Berners exactly what had happened, thus jeopardizing Schmidt and the crew who all agreed that Bessler accidentally fell overboard. "So all three of them were buried at sea, and it's entered in the log book, so that's it," snapped Berners. "Now I have to worry about a cargo of molasses too fucking cold to pump ashore."

It was obvious Ludwig Berners never gave a damn about anything except his cargo of molasses. I hoped he wouldn't give a damn about the crew's overtime which Bessler refused to okay. I had sent a copy of the crew's overtime to Berners' accountant at the Head Office as soon as I heard back from Cape May, plenty of time for them to have figured it all out, especially as it was only chicken feed compared to the profit Berners made on the cargo.

Some of Berners' associates, tired of standing, were now looking for chairs to sit on, preparing themselves for a long and very lively session. Richard and I were the only ones from the ship. Herr Schmidt claimed he was sick and remained in his cabin, while the crew were all on the deck anxiously waiting to get paid and find out what would happen to them.

Before Richard and Berners got into another argument, I decided to start my argument with Berners' accountant over the crew's wages, but just as I stood up, Berners yelled at me. "We haven't finished yet, Sparks."

"I'm well aware of that. I want to go over the crew's wages with your accountant. They're waiting to get paid."

"Well, they can wait a little longer," replied Berners.

"In that case, they should get another two hour's overtime. And may I remind you; none of us have had any decent food or sleep for five days." I then stood up and walked out of the office, into the comparative fresh air outside, giving Richard the opportunity to argue with Berners, something he had wanted to do for a long time.

"Was all that true about Henri," questioned the accountant, following me out of the meeting.

"Every word. Krause poisoned him. Richard and I made a detailed report and gave it to Berners. He completely ignored it," I replied. "Krause found out Bloom was on board to check up on his accounting, so he poisoned him and buried him at sea, just as we described it."

"Bloom was my Supervisor, a really nice guy," confided the accountant. "Do you still have a copy of the report?"

"Sure, there's one in my office. I'll get it for you. What will you do with it?"

"I'll make sure Berners is aware that I have a copy. Any time the bastard gets too cheap, I'll wave it in front of his face," replied the accountant. "I'll use it as a kind of blackmail."

"Well, you can start with the crew's overtime. I want to make sure they all get every cent Berners owes them, okay?" I looked across the deck. Most of the crew were already waiting outside my office. Many were all cleaned up and had packed up their meager belongings hoping to go back to Germany.

"They'll get every cent due to them and they're all going back to Germany. Ramon Perez gave Berners a hard time about the filthy conditions on his ship and as a kind of extra pay off, they're all going back on the *S.S. Hawaii.* She's a converted passenger ship taking American serviceman's wives over to Germany to visit their husbands who are still over there."

"Hey, that's great news. Ramon Perez is a good guy."

"He owns a big share of the distiller, so Berners dare not mess about with him."

"That's nice to know Berners doesn't get it all his own way," I replied, wondering what Richard was telling him at the meeting.

"I've brought enough dollars to pay them all off. I just didn't show the overtime list to Berners," confided the accountant. "As soon as he found out he was stuck with a cargo of cold molasses, well, the shit hit the fan and that's all he cared about."

The crew all cheered when I told them we were about to pay them off and assured them they were getting all their overtime, but the biggest cheer was for Heinz and Deiter who walked up the gangplank, looking fit and well. They were immediately welcomed by the crew bombarding them with questions.

"Did you see Heinz and Deiter walking on board?" asked Richard. "They both looked like they had been well looked after."

"Thanks to Ramon Perez," I replied. "Now, I've got to go to the office to make sure they are paid."

"And I'm going to call my folks in Palm Springs and tell them we'll be there in a few days. We can get the train from New York. Five days to relax watching all America going past the window."

One by one, the crew came up to the table to collect their wages and overtime in cash. It wasn't much, but more than they expected because the Bosun and I really boosted their overtime. The American dollar was probably worth a fortune in Germany. I gave Steve, the second cook, my folk's address in Gloucestershire and told him to go and see them. "Thanks, Sparks," he said. "But aren't you coming over with us?"

"I don't think so, but I've already written to home telling them to expect you soon." I could see Steve was disappointed I wasn't going with him, but he wouldn't be disappointed with the warm welcome from my folks when he got there.

Heinz and Deiter were the last in line. "Are these the two who were taken off by the Coast Guard in Key West?" asked the accountant. "Since they were injured in the course of their duty I've paid them up until today."

"Good for you, but Berners will have a conniption fit." I replied.

"Not as bad as the conniption fit he'll have if I tell him I have your report about Henri Bloom." We both laughed.

Later in my cabin, while packing up my things, Heinz and Deiter came in to thank me for all I had done. They both looked very handsome and were looking forward to going back to Germany on the SS *Hawaii* sailing direct to Bremen.

"The lucky bastards," observed Richard. "Two or three weeks at sea with all those frustrated servicemen's wives who haven't had any for two years. I expect the sex-starved women will chase Heinz all over the ship."

When Richard left to telephone his folks in Palm Springs, I sat down in my cabin and stared at my overflowing suitcase. It seemed only a few months had passed since I was staring at Axel's suitcase overflowing onto the same bunk. I was almost packed and ready to go, but go where? I had been paid off with ten one hundred dollar bills, a thousand dollars which was a lot of money if exchanged in Europe. I was also entitled to a free trip back home with the rest of the crew on the *SS Hawaii*, but Richard was convinced I was going back to Palm Springs with him. He never failed to tell me what a good time we would have, but I only had a thousand dollars. I needed the money for my folks to buy more land for the horse sanctuary. Palm Springs was a luxury I could not afford, but how could I tell him?

I was still packing and repacking my suitcase while waiting for Richard, when there was a knock on the cabin door and the ship's agent, Mike Bradshaw came in. "I just had to see you, Sparks. Glad you're all back okay."

"Yes, Mike, we're all glad. It's been a very rough trip."

"No kidding. Berners gave me your report to read." Mike sat down on the chair. "Bessler, Krause and the Chief Engineer all buried at sea and two guys taken off by the Coast Guard," continued Mike. "And there was another Kraut seaman on the run from the hospital. That was a lot of extra fucking paperwork."

"Yeah, his name was Hans, he was the steward. Did they catch him?"

"Not yet, but it happens all the time Sparks. You can't blame the poor bastards, but it's just so much extra paperwork."

"How about Helmut Schickel, the young steward that signed on with me?"

"Krause's report says he jumped overboard. Lost at sea," replied Mike. "Too bad, he was only a young kid."

I hesitated to ask more questions in case Helmut had jumped ship in Philadelphia. "Yes, he was only a young kid. All this carnage for a cargo of cold molasses," I added. "Was it worth it?"

"Berners' going crazy. He's ordered me to get the fucking shit pumped ashore ASAP. Cold molasses, it will take days. Know what I mean?" Mike looked around the cabin. "I can see you're all packed. I'll bet you'll be glad to get off this goddamn ship. It will probably be scrapped, but that bastard will soon get another just like it, know what I mean."

I opened the cupboard and handed Mike a bottle of Glenlivet. "I was saving this for you. It's a thank you for the old pair of jeans and bringing me back from Philly after my wild night with the sexy bar fly."

"Wild night? I thought you said you didn't get a piece of ass, Sparks."

"Oh, I did, two or three times."

Mike grinned, lasciviously. "Was she was hotter than a Cuban puta. Know what I mean?"

"Yeah, Mike, she was hotter than hell. Why don't you take a trip down to Cuba on one of Berners' ships and find out for yourself?"

"Me, sail on one of these fucking death traps, Sparks? No way. Not for all the whores in Cuba. Know what I mean?"

As soon as Mike had left, hiding the bottle of Scotch in his jacket, Richard came bursting in. "Sparks! Grab your case and let's go."

How was I going to tell him I had decided to go back to Europe with the rest of crew? Palm Springs sounded great, but I couldn't afford it. I looked around the cabin, the brass porthole wasn't as shiny, the TV didn't work anymore and I wasn't in the least sorry to leave. The gangplank was still just as slippery as when I first climbed on board with Helmut. I turned and waved to some of the crew on deck, then turned around and stared at a new red and white convertible with a grinning Richard the Third at the wheel.

"A Buick Convertible," he yelled, tooting the horn. "The dealer just delivered it to the dock. It's a welcome home present from my Dad. Isn't it great?" Richard eagerly got out of the car to show me how the shiny white canvas roof was neatly stowed away. "So now we can drive back to Palm Springs and take our sweet time." Richard unlocked the trunk and put my heavy suitcase alongside his. "Jump in Sparks and let's go."

I had never seen such a big and luxurious car before. It was red, white and beautiful. "Wow! Richard, this is the very lap of luxury. You are so lucky to get a present like this."

"And I've got something for you," he said, handing me the blue velvet bag containing the gold ingots. My hand was shaking as I took five of them out of the bag, still in their cellophane wrapping. I was overwhelmed, unable to speak. "Consuela handed them to me as I climbed up the scrambling net, that's why I took so long to climbing up the fucking scrambling net."

"Richard, I am flabbergasted. I don't know what to say" I turned over the gold ingots in my hand. It was unbelievable. I was too choked up to say anything.

"I never mentioned I had them because... Well, I was pissed off because you kept coming up with excuses not to come back with me, so I waited until now to hand them over."

"I don't know what to say, except we have to split, two and a half each."

"No, you keep them all and buy the land for the horses. I've never been short of money and you can see my father isn't either. You come to Palm Springs and I'll come over to your place. You can teach me to ride a horse." Richard started up the car and revved the engine. "Isn't she a beauty? And my folks are looking forward to seeing us very soon."

I lay back on the seat not knowing what to say. I could buy the land in Gloucestershire. I could now do everything I had planned. It was all so unbelievable, and we were now going to drive across America to California and have a wild time.

"And I found out who did all the spying for Berners. It was Herr Fucking Schmidt! The bastard typed up a full report every night in his cabin."

"So that's what he was typing up. What a creep."

"I got all the mail for us. One from Kate, who is probably waiting for me in bed, and this is for you," said Richard, handing me a letter. I recognized the spidery writing and quickly opened the envelope. "It's from Helmut," I yelled. "He's okay and living with Harry and his wife, Bella, at the Seaman's Hotel in Camden where we first stayed. Kimmel told me he jumped ship in Philly. I should have guessed he went there."

"You know, Sparks, that kid really loves you," replied Richard. "That night you left him to sleep on your couch. I went in and talked to him. Poor kid, he's had a rough life so far. So let's stay in town tonight and we can go see him tomorrow."

"Fantastic. I want to see him again and give him some money, and I can pay Harry back the fifty bucks I owe him."

Richard expertly maneuvered the new car across the railroad tracks and headed out of the dockyard. I took one last look at the *Cuban Trader* tied up pathetically to the dock. She was still an ugly black tanker and still loaded with molasses waiting to be pumped into the storage tanks, but this time Helmut and I were safely ashore and well rewarded for the few miserable months we spent on board. I was glad she was destined for the scrap yard and no other seamen would have to suffer on that hell ship. It had been a very hectic few months, but all the suffering and frustration were worth it.

"Hey Sparks, What do you say we go to that restaurant in a book shop and find that barfly who slipped you a Mickey. This time I'll slip her something she won't forget. What was the place called in Philly?"

"Bookbinders, it's on Walnut and Second Street in the Old Town."

"Great! We can have a Martini, crack a lobster and then get laid, and tomorrow we'll go and see Helmut and then off to California. Is it a deal?"

"It's a deal." I never thought I'd be saying it, but California here we come.

###

Author Roger Asquith

Roger Asquith first operated a radio in the Royal Air Force. He later trained as a Marine Radio Officer in London and then set sail around the world on British, Australian, Swedish vessels and finally the hell ship known as the **CUBAN TRADER**. After a year as a trainee TV cameraman for the CBC in Canada, Roger went to Hollywood. Unable to get a job in television, he started writing for magazines and founded the Hollywood News Service, interviewing famous celebrities including Elvis Presley, Elizabeth Taylor and Marilyn Monroe. Roger later opened a bar on the **Costa de Sol** in Spain, which inspired another story, a wild adventure romp *chasing a thief in drag from Palm Springs to Spain and finally a Sultan's Sex Palace in exotic Tangiers*. **SELBY** will soon follow the Cuban Trader hell ship to a book shelf or Kindle near you. Roger now lives a much quieter life somewhere in the English Cotswolds.

Other Books by Roger Asquith

Selby

www.PrestburyBooks.com